1

Destiny

An Historical Romance

Destiny

by

Barbara McCauley Cardona

Alba Books

INTRODUCTION

The main events in the life of Saint Radegund, a sixth century Thuringian princess, are the inspiration behind *Destiny*. When she was about age six, Radegund's uncle, Hermanfred (Gunther in the novel), killed her parents and took her and her younger brother to be raised as his own. Then, when Radegund was about eleven, her uncle and aunt were killed by King Clotaire, possibly in revenge for the killing of her parents. Clotaire took Radegund and her brother to Athies, a royal villa in Clotaire's kingdom, where he left her to be educated. When she was about eighteen, he returned to claim her as his wife. By then, Radegund was well-educated and, having fully embraced Chritianity, extremely devout. She resisted Clotaire's proposal and attempted escape, but was brought back and, against her will, taken to Clotaire's castle in Soissons where they were married.

Clotaire was one of four sons of King Clovis I. It was Clovis who managed to unite all the Frankish tribes in one kingdom under his rule. Clovis had also, as a result of his wife Clotilde's influence, renounced his Germanic pagan gods for the Catholic faith. Upon his death, his sons inherited both his kingdom and his religion. And while they were almost constantly involved in warring campaigns, either against other tribes or among themselves, with their royal influence, the young church gained many converts.

Clotaire is described in one source from that time as lustful and licentious. Indeed he had several wives and concubines besides Radegund. But he is also said to have been generous, kind and glorious. About his marriage to Radegund he once said that he felt he was married more to a nun than to a queen. In fact, Radegund often used excuses to leave the marriage bed at night. Then she would don a hair shirt and prostrate herself on the icy ground to pray until morning. She also continued over the years to inflict truly gruesome punishments on herself, often in secret, as the church did not approve of such measures. And she was apparently the only female saint at this time who did such things.

After some years of marriage, Clotaire killed Radegund's brother for betraying him in some way. At that point, Radegund escaped to Noyons where she persuaded the bishop Médard to consecrate her a deaconess as a way to protect her from Clotaire's marital claims. Clotaire tried to gain his wife back over the years, but various bishops intervened on her behalf. When, later, Radegund had become a nun and wanted to build a convent in Poitiers, it was King Clotaire who provided the funds. And late in his life, he begged her forgiveness for his misdeeds and unkindnesses. Radegund lived out the rest of her life in a cell in her convent, although she feasted with high church officials and other aristocrats and her dear friend, Fortunatus, a poet, troubador and monk.

Radegund was a deeply spiritual and passionate woman. That she continued to brutalize her body throughout her life suggests she may have been quite sensual as well, and used these means to suppress those impulses. In the novel, Radegund becomes Deirdre, a woman who lives out the sensuality that Radegund denied. Deirdre is both attracted to and repelled by King Clotaire. While she shares the events of Radegund's life, she takes a quite different path.

Radegund lies in state in Poitiers, France; Deirdre lives her life here in the pages of this book.Barbara McCauley Cardona

CHAPTER 1

"Why can't I go out riding?" Deirdre demanded, leaning her elbows on the balcony ledge.

"Why don't you ask your aunt or uncle that?" Nurse retorted with less than patience. "I have already told you why a thousand times."

Deirdre sighed and rolled her eyes without turning to look at her nurse.

"Well, I don't believe you! If it's so dangerous, why do the serfs' daughters go out in the fields? I only want to ride out there. I get so tired riding within the walls."

Nurse smiled to herself over her embroidery. Even at so young an age, the girl showed signs of becoming a beautiful woman. With her small waist cinched in even smaller by the dark blue girdle, and the small breasts that were already asserting themselves through the thin fabric of her gown, Deirdre looked thirteen, almost the marrying age. In fact, she was only eleven.

"I have told you it is dangerous. The young vassals, whom you so admire, have to go out to the fields and they go with their brothers and fathers to protect them. You don't see one of them out there alone. Not ever."

"Oh, but they are free! And I...I am a prisoner here. I hate it!"

Nurse looked up again at the sharp, angry eyes that were filling now with tears of self-pity.

"And would you then change places with one of them?"

Deirdre remained silent. This was Nurse's favorite counterattack.

"Would you like working from sunup to sundown washing at the river, scouring the lord's pantry, or planting in the fields with the sun burning your skin to brown?"

Deirdre turned away to look out at the deep forest across the

9

meadows.

"And would you marry one of those rough men who would beat you when you failed to satisfy him in some small way? I ask you, my dear girl, if you would live the life of one of those?

Deirdre heard Nurse's voice as if from far away. Already she had fallen into her favorite reverie about the man who would one day come here from afar and take her away. He would be handsome and strong, but gentle, and would love her so much he would take her with him on all his journeys, even to battle. Oh, then she would be free!

Nurse was wise enough to play on the girl's romantic nature by suggesting the subject of marriage, and smiled now to herself, pleased to have apparently calmed her charge's temper. Deirdre was spirited and restless -- a lot to handle for old Nurse with her ponderous ways -- but, in spite of the girl's temper and not-so-occasional mischief, Nurse was deeply fond of her. She even preferred the fiery Dierdre to Lothar, Deirdre's younger brother, who should have had, to Nurse's way of thinking, Deirdre's strength of character. Many times, the old woman had worried about the two. It was as if each had been born into the wrong sex. As a woman, Deirdre's spirit would be stifled and frustrated; as a man, Lothar would be pushed into a corner, or even, in these rough times, brought to an early end. To make matters worse, the children's uncle, Gunther, paid little heed to the boy and instead seemed to enjoy encouraging his niece's daring nature. Although required to sit side-saddle, Deirdre otherwise rode like a man, handling the most difficult and spirited horses with a man's touch. All of Lady Sigrid's protests that the girl would be ruined as a future wife seemed to fall on deaf ears. Gunther would simply laugh and say he would find a fiery husband for the girl. Perhaps if she were his true daughter and Lothar his....

Nurse's musings were interrupted by Deirdre's cry.

"Nurse! Nurse! Come! I believe someone is approaching."

Nurse dropped her handwork and joined Deirdre at the

balcony's ledge.

"Look! Out there. Isn't that a cloud of dust along the edge of the forest?"

The forest road had once been a real road of broad, flat stones, constructed by the Romans three hundred years before to connect this inland region of Thuringia to the rest of the far-reaching empire. Roman legions had once traversed its length bringing with them the riches of Rome's culture. When the Romans withdrew, their kingdom crumbling, the road fell into disrepair. Now, in this year, A.D. 532, it was simply a narrow winding path, its history overgrown like the stones with the tall meadow grasses that grew between Gunther's manor and the looming forest. The road could not be seen beyond the copses of poplars and chestnut trees that stretched out in front of Gunther's thick-walled castle. But Deirdre knew of this road. She had accompanied her uncle there once with a band of men in order to hunt down a wounded hind they had been unable to fell the night before. The road was poor, bare, uncared for, but it was there, stretching in both directions as an invitation to her adventurous dreams of freedom. She had never forgotten it nor the intuition she had had that day that the road would someday take her away to another life. Now a small cloud of dust rose up along the edge of the plain where the road would be. It hung in the middle horizon between the wide meadows and the dark, brooding trees of the forest. This would be a band then, and she guessed by the amount of dust that they were on horseback. Deirdre felt a thrill of anticipation.

Nurse gazed at the cloud and frowned. Visitors were scarce, especially in these times when the roads were unguarded and bands of thieves and marauders roamed freely. It had been well over two years since even merchants had traveled this way.

"Oh, let me put on my new garment and my slippers!" Dierdre cried and turned to enter her chamber. Nurse reached out to catch her.

11

"No, child. They may not stop here."

"And where would they stop then? The manor can easily be seen even from that distance, and night will be upon us in a few more hours."

"They may not be good men. There are enough of the other kind around," Nurse answered hastily. It was always difficult to convince Dierdre of anything once her mind was made up.

"But of course they're good. Why wouldn't they be? They're probably a band of warriors off to do battle somewhere."

"Even better they don't stop here," Nurse said with a frown. "Come, let us stand by here to see if they approach."

"Then I won't be ready," Deirdre complained, pulling away.

"As if you were to meet them at the front gate, a young maid such as you. If they come for hospitality, it will be your uncle and aunt who proffer it. It would be hours before your aunt sent for you to appear."

Just then a cry was heard from below. Deirdre leaned over the balustrade. The sentry in the far tower had given the alarm to those below in the courtyard, and was now sounding the horn to warn the vassals out in the fields. The horn gave off a deep bellow that was caught by the trees and passed along in ever-diminishing echoes into the peaceful sunshine of the afternoon. The tiny, bent figures of the men, women, and children in the fields straightened up and began moving toward the castle walls. The cloud of dust in the distance was approaching Gunther's manor, but the field vassals would have time to collect their few valuables -- a goose or hen or chair -- and reach the safety of the walls before the strangers were even in sight.

Below where Deirdre and her nurse stood watching, the courtyard was transformed. The lazy, warm day, one of so many like it before, had been suddenly turned into a frenzy of activity. Craftsmen, whose small wooden workshops leaned against the thick stone walls, were hastily throwing up night boards and, helped by their women, were donning their master's colors and armor. The guards, who usually spent their days lazily drowsing outside the gates by the moat, playing lots, or chasing after the serving maids, were gathering and distributing arms and jerkins. Men mounted the crude ladders thrown up against the walls while the women doused the cooking fires and drove the fowl into the now-crowded pens. Children ran and screamed and jumped and tagged after the skirts of their frightened mothers.

Suddenly, Gunther himself appeared amid the activity. Within moments, order seemed to make itself felt. The women, with sidelong glances that revealed no feelings, hushed the children; the men, without looking at Gunther at all, took to their posts. He stood in the center of the courtyard, legs spread, arms across his chest. Though short in stature, he gave the appearance of great physical strength and a power beyond the merely physical. His lips were thick and pulled downward, set in a permanent snarl. At his deep-voiced command, the great wooden doors to the castle behind him were shut with a great groaning and creaking from the uncared-for hinges. The heavy bolt inside, a log full one foot around, was shot closed with a deep bang. The children were finally silenced and gathered in a circle among the women next to the front wall. As far as Deirdre could see, the walls bristled with axes and spears as the men stood, silent, and ready now for defense.

"Why are there guards on the walls?" Deirdre asked, feeling a surge of alarm.

"I expect it's not merchants we're expecting," Nurse answered.

"They...they won't do us harm, will they?" The shred of an old memory crept up in Deirdre's consciousness, almost bobbing to the surface, and sent a shiver of real apprehension through her. She quickly suppressed it. It was the memory of a woman falling backward on a bed, her hair like dark waves engulfing her as she fell. It always happened in slow motion as if the woman would never actually reach the cushions that awaited her; most often it occurred as a nightmare that would bring Deirdre bolt upright in bed, screaming until Nurse arrived to soothe her. Deirdre could never consciously remember details of the dream, but, once in a while, the vision would half appear to her in the midst of some game or activity and she would stop whatever she was doing, puzzled at the apprehension she felt. Then, determined, she would push it out of her mind. The child could not recall any real events surrounding this fragment of dream or memory, but it was precisely these events, lost in the not-so-distant past that ruled her life and set her personality in the mold of an independent and self-sufficient child, quite out of tune with her times.

"Look!" Deirdre cried. "You can just see their flags! Can you make out what they might be, Nurse?"

The cloud of dust had moved close enough now so that the girl and her nurse could make out the figures of a group of men on horseback. Behind them was a larger group of footmen, several of whom carried the banners belonging to the various mounted men.

"I can't make out the banners, child. But those men on horse would be noblemen, I am sure. Perhaps your uncle sent messengers out in search of a proper husband for you," Nurse teased, relieved that they would be spared mere mischief by thieves or a marauding band.

But Deirdre was not listening. The courtyard was once again a bustle of activity as the field vassals herded their children and animals within the walls.

Armor and weapons were distributed to the men and orders given to all to take their places. When the last of them was within the safety of the walls, the chief guard ordered the drawbridge pulled up into place. With a great bang, it closed across the arched opening, cutting off the bright rays of the afternoon sun, which had fallen into the court in a shaft of warm light.

The steward had by now mounted the walls and sent up the flag with Gunther's colors. At his signal, the two trumpeters in

14

either tower at the ends of the gate wall sounded their horns. Both actions were meant to convey Gunther's preparedness in case of an attack, or, depending on the approaching band's response, an invitation to share the hospitality of the house. A curious silence hung over the crowd, broken only by the cackling and clucking and barking of the various fowl and dogs. Those inside awaited the response to Gunther's signal. Deirdre felt herself also tense with waiting until the horns of the band were heard, distant but clear. A great cry of welcome and relief rose up from the throats of all those assembled in the castle court.

"Oh, do let me change, please!" Deirdre pleaded.

"And would you miss the welcome? They're but a short way off now and will be at the gates in moments. You see how they're coming faster now."

Deirdre pressed against the thick stone ledge to admire the riders and their horses as they drew closer.

"Look! That first one, on the black horse, do you see?"

The nurse did not answer, and Deirdre tugged at her sleeve impatiently, pointing with her other arm to the lead horseman.

"Yes, I see," said Nurse in such a voice that Deirdre turned to glance at her.

Nurse's expression changed in moments as if a mask had been pulled over it, but not before Deirdre had seen a look of such intense concentration, a look so mixed with anger and triumph that the girl stared.

"Nurse, why do you look so strange?"

"Nothing, my child. It's just we haven't seen visitors here in so long, I feel anxious."

"Do you know who these men are?"

"How should I know anyone outside of these walls?" Nurse answered with a look of real questioning in her eyes.

"But you came from my mother's house," Deirdre said, and was as immediately amazed by her words as was Nurse. They looked at one another in shock. Since the day Deirdre and Lothar, together with their nurse, had been brought to her uncle's house, Deirdre had not once spoken a word that referred back to that time. It was as if she had forgotten everything that had happened to her prior to living here. And no one else had even mentioned her former life with her true parents further north of these wide meadows and forests.

"Yes, that's true," Nurse answered slowly with a tight knot between her brows. Then suddenly she grabbed Deirdre roughly in her arms, pressing the girl against her ample bosom. "You must never speak of that time," she whispered passionately in Deirdre's ear. "Not here in this house." Nurse looked around nervously as if in fear of being overheard.

Deirdre was so surprised by this action, which was unlike the placid nurse, that she was shocked into silence. A sadness dwelled somewhere inside her; some unknown, unplumbed recess of her being held her in its sway momentarily, and she was not surprised to see tears appear in the woman's eyes.

But the sudden call of a single horn just beyond the gates pulled her attention from her inner concerns to the bright spectacle in front of her uncle's gates. And once again her eyes were drawn to the horseman on the black steed.

"Nurse," she exclaimed, "that man has long hair. Do you see him? It's all the way to his shoulders." Deirdre laughed gaily. "How strange to see such hair on a man."

"He comes from the west," Nurse answered slowly. "I once heard of the custom."

"Do all the men wear their hair that way in the west?"

"No," Nurse answered. "I have heard that only he who is king of the Franks does so. It is a sign of his noble birth."

"Then is he out yonder the king of the Franks?" Deirdre asked, astonished. "And who are the Franks?"

"I can only guess he is indeed the king, since he wears the

16

sign. The Franks are a people with a kingdom that stretches far to the north and west. I know little of them, but...."

Deirdre only half waited for the nurse's answer. She was too involved in the goings-on below her.

"A king," she breathed. "He is very handsome even with his strange hair. He looks very manly, very proud."

Nurse put her hand on Deirdre's shoulder from behind. "He shall be your husband," she said, this time with no teasing in her voice.

"My husband...?" Deirdre felt her dream rise up within her. "I...shouldn't mind that."

Nurse took Deirdre by the shoulders and turned her around gently. "Child," she said with intensity, "whatever happens, you must stay with me and do what I say, do you understand?"

Deirdre pulled back to gaze into Nurse's eyes. "What do you mean, Nurse? You act so strangely. What's going to happen?" Each question rose in pitch as a kind of terror took hold of the girl. She sensed something in her nurse's strange look. The old woman's eyes were almost black, and again there was the hint of something that boded ill; her usually smooth, placid face was tight with an emotion that Deirdre could not decipher. But there was no time for Nurse to answer, nor for Deirdre to hear it. A shock wave of horror was heard from below. Deirdre threw herself forward onto the ledge just in time to see the long-haired king of the Franks let fall his ax with a brutal ferocity into the crown of her uncle's head. In a moment frozen into silence, the sound of bone being crushed and broken filled the whole world in which Deirdre felt herself suddenly flung.

That sound....

CHAPTER 2

She stood transfixed, the sun on her face, feeling its fire as if from far away.

What is that light? It hurts. Until she wakens, pulls the covers over her head. Then suddenly...the realization: it is over! Spring is here. The signal is this harsh light that comes only when the heavy furs have been removed from the window. She leaps from the bed to the newly exposed window, looks out at the snowless landscape. Later, she will recall this momentary scene, how it changed her day for her with its wet bleakness.

That sound. Her mind circled as an animal does before it lies down to its rest.

Yes, winter is done, but it is that between time before spring when only the sun holds the promise. She closes her eyes and lets its thin warmth caress her skin. The air is chill, damp. The smoky torches in her sleeping chamber have been removed. She will have no more of their stench in the daytime until the cold descends again in late autumn. Even now, she smells their odor.

Her eyes took in nothing of what was below her in full view. She moved mechanically with Nurse, Nurse guiding her, pulling her out into the hall.

It is not the torches. She sees the smoke in the hall twisting like a caterpillar in a silence that is all the more pristine above the confusion of noises that have overtaken the whole castle. She remembers the smoke, how she clung to its quiet, hearing its acrid language in her nostrils without understanding its words. Later, when she looks back from atop the hill, her head leaned way out around her uncle's broad chest, peeking under his arm, almost falling from the horse, she recalls the seashell she had once seen. That picture stays with her. The gutted building behind her cannot be her home. It is a seashell whose inhabitants have deserted.

The smoke loses it hold on her. The fullness of the thunder

18

below rises to surround her as the thunder of her own blood rises to drown out all other noises. She runs, her small hands pushed hard over her ears.

She is just inside the door, the door with its one long vertical crack, the one she always peeks through on early mornings when the cold awakens her and she runs, dragging the furs from her own bed to lie with her mother. Nurse would be angry later, would scold her.

The door is open. Three people are inside, one, tall and broad, is flowing with blood. Their backs are to her. They do a strange dance together, it is not good what they are doing. She is frozen. What is this place? She wants her mother's room. She wants to wake up. Her being senses its own boundaries, how easy it might be for the walls of her skin to break away, leaving her with nothing. She wills herself to hold together, to not shatter. As now, the large man falls, broken like a huge oak tree. She hears no sound, notices only how his heaviness hits the floor, rises slightly against its own impact, then settles to be still. She is curious, caught far away from herself in a fold of her mind that has never suspected endings before, never sensed dying. The large man has ended. She sees the face that looks familiar, but no insight comes as to who he might be. Later she will realize her father is lost, simply disappeared. She will recall this man's ending, but never connect him to her father.

Her eyes record. They simply bring in what surrounds her. She feels nothing other than that she exists there within the boundaries of the body she inhabits.

The woman is struggling, her long dark hair fallen free, soft over the shoulders and bodice of her gown. Her mouth and whole face move as though she were speaking, but Deirdre hears nothing. She is in another realm of neither sensation nor fear, only a world of blood still pumping inside her, of water that engulfs her body ready to wash her away.

The woman falls onto the bed. Her hair comes forward as

19

she falls, then flies back forming a soft pillow around her head, the eyes for the first time catching Deirdre's own. In that instant, the sound of her own name comes through the silence. The woman raises one thin arm to ward off the blow of the man. It waves like a small pennant, falls then, as when the breeze fails, the banners on the castle suddenly sag. She collapses into the dark hair, into the pool of blood that spreads out over the coverlet with thin fingers that reach out as if for solace. It is then. That sound as the man lets fall his ax. Bone. A deep echo that will resound forever within the shadows and caves of Deirdre's flesh. And now, at this moment, Deirdre knows her. Just now, as she feels herself picked up, feels her body bouncing against a man's bony chest as he races with her down the stairs. Dimly, it comes through her many layers for just an instant. The woman is her mother.

Deirdre woke from herself, the screams and cries of the present breaking through the wave from the past. Nurse was pulling at her, talking: "He has avenged you! Be not afraid! Oh, your dear mother! Deirdre! Deirdre! Listen to me." Nurse bent over Deirdre, shaking her to the present. But her words made no sense and Deirdre was a single muscle flexed toward one goal. She would survive. Twisting free of Nurse's grip, she raced down the cool stone corridor. She had to find Lothar. He too would survive. Her feet found the way for her blindly. Taking her brother's small hand, she dragged him toward whatever safety she could find.

CHAPTER 3

Felice leaned against the wall a little to the side of the huddled group of women. Her dark green eyes flicked from one of the men to another, taking each one's measure. She had known each and every one of them, had lain with them all in her time. Not one was worth lying with again had it been within her freedom to choose. Life did not offer her choices of that nature, however. She was a woman alone without a family to protect the few privileges she might have had. But Felice had no regrets. From what she observed of the married women, they were, in many ways, worse off than she. Their men treated them as their personal slaves, giving nothing in return. They suffered through childbirth over and over, most of them dying after their third or fourth from one infection or another. By Felice's age, those who survived looked like hags, their faces grey with fatigue, their bodies formless and misshapen. Felice was beautiful, her dark hair wild and long, her mouth sensual and ready for laughter. Even the rags she wore accentuated her beauty, as she knew how to use the least scrap of fabric to show off her best features. As for the men, at least she had their occasional lust, which habit and boredom denied their wives. She smiled to herself. Within her station of life, she had as much freedom as was possible. The other women might alternately pity and despise her. It did not matter.

The tense silence in the courtyard was finally broken by the sound of the horns of the approaching band. All and sundry let out cries and cheers of relief. Had Gunther not been present, the atmosphere would have relaxed into one that resembled the rare holidays celebrated on his estate. But as long as he remained, the serfs shifted uneasily the way horses will when a cruel master approaches.

Felice shrugged to herself and sauntered over to the washing trough. The visitors' intentions mattered little to her. Had they attacked, she would have been taken prisoner, led no better and no worse a life than now. She almost would have preferred that to the boredom of working day after day in the fields. The castle's serving women were massing around the still-closed doors to the castle awaiting entrance. For once, Felice regretted her biting tongue. She would have worked within the castle walls, could have been part of the excitement of the visitors' stay, the holiday atmosphere. But she would manage. She was sure of her powers, sure the men would notice her, would seek her out. She would collect the necessary herbs to make sure of that.

Gunther was issuing orders in his thick voice. Banners were being hung and armor and arms thrown aside to be collected by old men and put again into storage. Felice glanced at Gunther. She despised him. He ruled his vassals with an iron hand. Twice, she had been beaten on his orders, and both times he had ordered her to his chamber afterward. She preferred the men of her own station. Their lust was healthy, real. Gunther was a madman.

Felice had lived under Gunther's dominion since she was twelve. At that time Gunther and his band had sacked and pillaged a whole series of estates from the north country southward. Her own family had been killed defending her former lord's life and property, and it was only through her wits and physical charm that Felice had managed to escape with her life. Had her will and desire to live not been so strong as it was, she would often have had occasion to regret her survival. A young vassal maid, ripe for marriage but lacking the small dowry and a father to protect her, had little chance of gaining a decent place in the social structure of the new community to which she was brought. From the beginning, Felice was used and abused by the men of the estate, both of high and low station. She learned to turn the situation to her advantage as much as possible, but that took time and a growing awareness of her real plight and how she might survive within it.

Initially, she received pity from the women and, occasionally, even from a man, but, as she learned the ropes of her new life, learned to attract a man's lust for her own purposes, all pity turned to contempt and derision. Felice was proud. Regardless of what she might have to undergo, she preferred derision to pity, preferred the vassals' contempt to the occasional scrap of compassion that came her way. She was a realist and recognized that the lot of any of these people -- her people by caste only -- was such that it left little room for the niceties of human emotion. It was enough to have a sod roof over one's head, more than enough to have earned one solid meal. There was no room for more. Gunther saw to that.

Now, eighteen, Felice had learned her lessons well. She was tall for a woman and strong after years of field labor. She could fend for herself against a man's abuse, and the men were well aware of this and thus paid for her services with small rewards. But her strength did not hide her obvious feminine attractions. She had a woman's body, full breasted and round hipped, her teeth were intact, and her hair a halo of thick black waves that set off her large eyes and sensuous mouth. Her only flaw was her sun-darkened skin. Had she been a noblewoman and fair, she would have been courted by the rich and powerful from far and wide.

Beyond her physical powers, Felice had learned the arts of herbs and potions and used them to her advantage for herself and, for a small trade, on behalf of others. This was the one area in which she had the community's respect, a respect based on fear and awe of magical powers.

The huge drawbridge was lowered and the sunlight once again flowed through the wide arch onto the hard-packed earth of the courtyard. The children rushed out in their exuberance to line the pathway that led to the castle walls. The girls picked the small white daisies that grew along the edges of the fields, preparing to throw them in welcome at the guests. The atmosphere all around was festive and gay as the shops' night boards were removed and the rough worktables pulled out to hold the ale and delicacies that would be showered upon the guests within hours. The castle doors were flung open and Gunther's colors displayed everywhere. The serving maids bustled in and out, giggling in anticipation.

After washing up, Felice stood aside, careful to keep out of both Gunther's and the chief steward's view. As a field worker, she was not required to take part in the preparations, but Felice knew that Gunther would set her to work if he saw her. She moved back into a recess in the wall behind the washing trough. Her hands went to her hair and patted its wildness into a semblance of order. As she did so, she glanced upward. High above her, Felice saw the young maid Deirdre leaning out upon the wide ledge, her long silken blond hair flowing forward over the parapet. The girl was obviously excited, her fair cheeks pink with her emotion. Beside her was the old nurse with her stiff white headpiece framing her broad and pale face. Felice snorted to herself. She despised the nobility on principle. But for a change of parents, she too could have had the fineness in which the girl Deirdre lived. But Felice particularly hated the blond girl because everything about her was in direct opposition to Felice herself. Where Felice was dark, Deirdre was fair; where Felice was despised, Deirdre was beloved. All the serfs loved and pitied Deirdre: loved, for her beauty and happy spirit; pitied, for the dark past to which Gunther was whispered to be connected. Felice hated both their love and pity; she was as worthy of both for precisely the same reasons.

As the visitors entered, Felice's attention was attracted to the dark young man who rode a black horse. Here was a man to her liking. As he dismounted, she moved forward toward him, letting her presence move out ahead of her, her womaness like an air surrounding her. She would have him, nobleman though he was. A fine prize he would be.

Felice was close enough to hear Gunther's voice pronounce his welcome and speak his name. The young man rose abruptly from his kneeling position, the position required by courtesy. He leaped toward his steed and, before anyone had time to gasp, loosed his ax and raised it high above Gunther's head. But Felice heard his words.

"To Gunther, from Clovis's son, the king of the Franks."

Felice felt the blow in her arms as though she were partaking in its delivery. The crack of the blade against Gunther's skull and the sound of bone splintering held her transfixed, while releasing a tight knot of hatred that had long lived within her. As she watched the transformation of Gunther's eyes from the glittering light of cruelty and power to the slow dulling as his life seeped out of him, Felice felt as though a small bird fluttered within the cage of her body. Then, as Gunther's knees gave way and he fell heavily forward onto the earth, the bird flew out, soared away into the open sky. A gasp of pleasure escaped her lips. This young man had killed him.

Her gasp was lost among the exclamations of the others. For one moment, the courtyard was held immovable, as though time, like a river, had run into a barrier that held it momentarily in check. Even the visitors seemed caught in it. Clovis's son had broken the most sacred of traditions; he had broken the law of hospitality, the one strong fiber that ran through this land of scattered lords and their fiefdoms, the one law that all could depend upon.

But the moment passed, the river found its way through or around the snag, and chaos suddenly broke out. Clovis's son let out a throaty yell and his men responded with the withdrawal of metal against metal. The sound awakened everyone. The old men on their way to the storage rooms with the armor and weapons were knocked aside as Gunther's vassals rushed for them. Their master was dead. They only thought of themselves now. But their speed was checked by the visitors, whose axes and arrows cut down one after another in a rush of bodies and steel. Women and children ran in a frenzy in every direction trying to seek shelter from the sudden storm of death.

Felice pushed her way through the milling throng. She

25

called on both her gods -- the one of the forest and the one of night -- and commanded them to protect her; then she moved with sureness and speed to the sheltered recess behind the ironsmith's shop. The space was narrow and uncomfortably damp, but she was concealed. Felice crouched there, her heart pounding, as war cries and curses filled the air.

Gradually, the sounds in the courtyard changed, and the noises of a late summer afternoon mixed with soft moans and murmurings among Gunther's vassals. There were voices of pain, of soothing and comfort, and new voices of the triumphant visitor giving sharp orders. The brunt of the battle had moved into the castle, following those who had fled inside. Felice relaxed. The danger for her was past. Women were killed only in the heat of battle, never in the cool aftermath. She had now only to await her fate. With a quick prayer of thanks to her gods, she leaned back heavily against the wall.

The back wall of the shop in front of her suddenly thumped as someone threw himself up onto the inner shelf and let out a deep sigh.

"See to them yourself," she heard a voice foreign to her say. "I will have no more of it."

"You will pay then," another man's voice replied. "The king will have your neck."

"It is not right. We have invoked the gods' wrath."

"Clotaire has but one god now. He pays no heed to ours."

"And what is this god that permits the breaking of courtesy?"

"I know not. Nor why he did so."

"It is sacrilege. I fear for us. It takes my strength away."

"It is done. What comes, comes. You have but to obey your master. It is he who broke courtesy. It is he who must pay."

The other man sighed. "Ah, but it is we who have the gods to reckon with. His god permits his will."

26

"Then we shall make all necessary sacrifices. We do only a soldier's duty."

"Ai, but let me guard only. I will do no more killing today."

"Go then. Out now, Thetan, before the captain sees us slacking."

Again, the flimsy wooden shell shook as the soldier lowered himself with a grunt.

Even Felice, a vassal and among the lowest of the low in this society with its clearly defined pecking order, understood the seriousness of what Clovis's son, this king of the Franks, had brought upon himself and his men. The gods would indeed be wrathful. But in her heart Felice was grateful to the dark young man. And she was sure that her two gods would celebrate Gunther's end with her. She would offer this Clotaire their protection if his own god would accept their presence. Clotaire would need them, for they were truly awesome in their rage.

She closed her eyes then, wishing only that some small amount of warmth from the sun would find her in these damp shadows. She would remain where she was however cold she might get. Tonight would be the worst night for the women, and Felice wanted nothing of men just yet. She would need time to develop the basis with the new band in order to gain favors. She began to rock gently and murmured a chant that would bring sleep and comfort.

"Up wench!"

Felice's heart jumped within her. The command was accompanied with a sharp nudge from the blunt end of a spear. She found herself looking at the leg wrappings of a powerfully built man. Quickly, with instincts that were second nature to her, she concealed the look of fear and shock in her eyes, and let her gaze travel sensuously up the man's body to his face. By the time she reached his eyes, they had already softened toward her.

"Ah, a whoring wench. And a pretty sight once the dirt's washed off. Up, slut."

But the man's eyes twinkled with appreciation, and Felice noticed how he took all of her in as she slowly rose from her squatting position. Felice smiled the smile of the overwhelmed woman, watched desire rise in the man's eyes. She decided against speaking.

"Out with you. The king would have a woman. You look as though you might do him well."

He grabbed her close with one arm, held her head back with the other to look her full in the face.

"Yes," he said, " and after he's done with you, my pretty, you will come to warm my night. A soldier needs to calm his blood after such a day."

"Ah, sire," she breathed, "after the king then. Don't tell me. I will find you."

He laughed and released her. "A true slut. We will bring a good harvest together, you and me."

He pushed her in front of him out into the courtyard. The conquered vassals of Gunther stood or lay or slumped against the walls of the courtyard. Their anxiety could be felt in the air. Felice felt contempt rise in her blood. Now they too would discover the fruits of war, of being made prisoner. They too would now share in the destiny that had been thrust upon her. She threw her head back, and, ignoring their looks of scorn, walked toward the castle doors. She would present herself to a king. She wanted them all to know that. She, Felice the whore, was requested by a king!

CHAPTER 4

Felice could scarcely contain the many feelings and impressions that raced through her. Her moment of triumph in the courtyard was heightened by seeing the serfs of the household, who, by long tradition, scarcely condescended to look at a field serf, stare in open envy and disbelief at her as she passed. They knew immediately where she was going and for what purpose, and they knew further that Felice was therefore the first to be counted among those who would survive, unless she in some way failed to please the new master. But one look at her disheveled beauty convinced them she would not fail. About themselves, they could not be so sure, and their anxiety was evident. Felice's triumph was tinged with pity. These inside were not her enemies, except as a class and at a distance. It was the field serfs who had condemned her to her lonely, hard life. Thus, as she caught one or another's eye in the quick passage through the reception hall, she recognized the fear she had hidden all her years here. A shiver of anxiety ran through her.

She had not been inside the manor in more than a year. It held its own memories; two beatings and Gunther's vicious lust. She felt its walls close in upon her, felt herself fighting against its heaviness. But awe rose up too, as it had before when she had been able to see the richness of the tapestries and rugs and linens, gold and silver serving pieces, the household serfs in their pale-colored serving clothes, their small, neat caps covering their heads. Her own hair, wild and flowing, filled her with both pride and shame. Outside these walls, it expressed her precisely with its willful freedom; inside it was out of place. She was glad for her bare feet, which allowed her to move silently behind the soldier Villem, who held her wrist tightly. Out in the fields, Felice felt her power. Here, within these dark confines, her energy waned and she had to concentrate hard, her eyes fierce on Villem's back, to keep her sense of self from escaping. Thus, she was not prepared, as she turned the corner into the small stairway that led through the back of the castle to the upstairs quarters, to find herself swung up tight against Villem's large heaving chest.

"I'll have you first," he growled low in his throat. With one arm around her waist, he began pulling at her skirts.

"Ai, sire," she gasped. She saw he would be rough.

His mouth was upon her. She tried to calm herself. It was no use to struggle; he would have her. She leaned against him, ran one exploratory hand along his side, inside to the clasp on his trousers. It was now his turn to gasp. He leaned his head back and a deep moan escaped him. Felice would have liked to dig her strong hands into the flesh she was now caressing, but she knew it would be no use. She carried a deep scar on her shoulder from the one time she had done such a thing, the first time a man had used her and her instincts had arisen to defend herself. She gritted her teeth. It was coming to her now, the power of her own desire. She could not help it. When she saw a man lose himself this way, when she felt his member hard in her hand, saw the weakness caused by his desire, her body betrayed her with its own passion.

"Ai, sire," she cooed. "Not like that. Here." She tried to guide him into her own body, but he was already on the edge of his desire and spilled over into it. She barely managed to avoid his lust all over her skirts and shook with anger and disgust at his grunting spasms. Her own body burned with unanswered passion.

He leaned back gasping, then looked down at her. She hid the anger quickly. His look was one of triumph. Then he pulled her more gently against him and held her there as he laughed quietly to himself. Felice sighed. He could be worse.

After a few moments, he led her upstairs to a door she recognized as the one to Gunther's quarters. Felice trembled at the memory of Gunther. But she could also not help the feeling that rose in her that a long-awaited destiny had arrived, that she stood not only at a door into a room where a king awaited her, but also at a door into a dream. She had always sensed a fate for herself different from her present one of hardship and whoring.

This door, which Villem now threw open, was perhaps the entrance into that destiny. She hesitated on the threshold; then Villem pushed her in, taking a last-minute grab at her skirts.

The room was dark, the heavy curtains pulled across the windows. Felice stood quite still.

She felt a presence to her left, slightly behind her, where she remembered there was an alcove. She did not move. Her own mixed feelings, her still-aroused lust, and the confusion of the day's events left her with few protections. She would wait. She silently willed her gods to come to her. This was the man who had let fall his ax into Gunther's skull only hours before.

The room was silent; more so due to the occasional shout or clash of metal that entered the chamber dimly from below. The silence should have calmed her, but every nerve and muscle was waiting. For once, she did not know what to do. This was a king, a lord, a master. He could be the same as any other, except a hope had been born in her when she watched him kill Gunther. She felt oddly tied to this man through that act.

He was moving toward her. The faintest rustle of his cloak gave his movement away. She felt her body go rigid. Then a breath, warm and light, left a moist, tickling path on her cheek and down her neck. The gentlest sensation of one hand slipping around her waist made the hair on her arms rise in fear. What sort of man was this? He would derange her.

"And who is this fair maid?"

She heard the words and did not believe them. It was the accent perhaps, different from her own dialect, that made her think she had misheard. She froze into silence. Yes, surely he would kill her. He was a madman.

Now he moved in front of her. She saw the fine clasp of his cloak. It was a gold pendant, shaped like a crossbow. He was only slightly taller than she, so she had only to raise her lowered lids to look directly into his eyes. Felice felt a shock rush through her. Never before had she seen such a soft, gentle look in any human's eyes. He smiled.

Felice began to tremble. And the greater fear of having her fear seen made her tremble more. She could not hold his eyes.

"Ai, sire, I am but a field woman come to please you. Ai, forgive me. I know not why I tremble so."

She was afraid to look at him, afraid of what she felt rising in her throat, a cry that she had never uttered, one she had never known existed until now after seeing such gentle eyes, such warmth in his voice that spoke of tenderness, not of lust. It rose like a knot deep in her throat, locked there under her sheer will to keep it from pushing its way out through her lips.

"Aiiii," he murmured. "No whore are you, but a woman badly used."

Her cry escaped in a gasp. Another followed. And another. She felt herself led to the bed, which she saw dimly through her tears. But long years of beds and men quenched the sadness as suddenly as it had arisen. A rush of anger pushed all aside, thrusting through her quickly and sharply the way a thorn rises abruptly on the stem of a rose. So he would use her this way. Like Gunther, his tastes would be odd. She should have known. The noble folk were neither simple in their clothes nor in their lust.

She lay down on the bed, closed her eyes tightly. A great weight pushed on her chest. She breathed in deeply, but it would not leave. She breathed in again, this time opening her eyes. To her amazement, the king stood above her, his eyes gentle, a slight smile on his lips. The weight was inside.

She waited, wary of what was next, afraid to show her surprise at the emptiness of the bed around her. Clotaire leaned over. Again, she felt an unbearable weight, a tightness pressing on her lungs. Something soft touched her arms and a lighter weight lay upon her whole body. She waited, felt the air stir. A door closed softly. An incredible stillness filled her ears. She opened her eyes. The king was gone.

Felice lay as though dead. The pressure gradually lifted as

other sensations filled her. A chill ran down her spine and over her arms. She dared to move a little and saw now that she was covered with a light fur wrap. She raised her head and quickly scanned the room. Indeed, he was gone. The odd, handsome king was gone. She sat up abruptly.

"Sire," she called out quietly. Nothing moved or answered from the shadows.

Her mind raced. She was a fool. What had made tears come to her eyes? What was it that had broken like a long-trapped bubble of air from under water to make her behave so foolishly? He would kill her now. She, Felice, the proud Felice, was undone. How she hated him with those gentle eyes. That was what had released her cry. Those dark, kind eyes had penetrated into her and made her feel what no angry word or taunt from among the peasants all these six years had touched. She could not even name what that was, but in thinking of it now, her eyes filled with bitterness and her throat burned.

"A curse on you!" she called out aloud. If die she must, she would open her heart to empty itself of its load of bitterness. "A dark curse from my gods!"

On the opposite side of the room, a door opened quickly.

Felice leaped up, throwing aside the fur wrap. She sat poised on the edge of the bed, one leg under her, one on the floor, ready for defense or flight.

It was one of Gunther's housemaids who entered. Felice lurched forward. Her hair and eyes were wild. She saw her own fear mirrored in the quick, nervous movements of this timid, skinny serving girl.

"You...you called?" the girl croaked out. She glanced sideways at the open door behind her. She looked down then, her face reddening.

"My lady..." she said, biting her lip.

Felice glared fiercely at her. Her own face grew warm with

the insult of being so addressed.

The girl squirmed. Without moving, except to lean slightly forward, she seemed physically closer as she looked with pleading at Felice.

"I mean no offense," she whispered, then jumped erect at a sound behind her. "If my lady is ready, the bath is prepared."

Felice felt the words as a single blow and as a revelation. At last she understood. The king would have her washed. Then he would use her. She threw back her head and sat erectly. The only puzzle now was why he would have her addressed as a lady. She stood, pulled her dress to rights.

"My lady is ready," she said acidly, and moved toward the door.

"This way, if you please," the young maid said with obvious distress.

"The troughs are below," Felice said now with real puzzlement. The girl only insisted with her hand. Felice strode warily toward the brightness of the inner room. It was lit with torches and lamps, and soft perfumes like flowers filled the warm air. A large tub stood in the center of the smooth stone floor. Two other serving maids stood at attention at either end. Felice looked warily from one to another. None met her eyes.

Steam rose from the water in the tub, and small lavender blooms and the leaves and roots from herbs floated in lazy circles on the water's surface. The tub was fashioned of iron with delicate blue and yellow flowers painted in a garland around the rounded lip at the top. On a low platform that ran along two sides of the room, small silver bowls with glistening oils stood ready. Their odors and the odors from boughs cut from sweet-smelling shrubs and trees and strewn in green profusion in the corners and along the borders of the room made Felice feel almost giddy. A robe of the finest and softest linen lay across a stool. It was a pale yellow with small white flowers embroidered into the delicate lace that formed its collar and cuffs. Unconscious of her own

34

gaping, Felice looked around from one thing to another, taking in every detail, until her eyes rested on the face of the tall serving woman. The slightest derisive curl of that one's upper lip closed Felice's open mouth. Her nature was open enough to have wanted to share this moment of amazement and joy and the utter humor of the whole situation with these three women who waited only to attend her. But when Felice threw back her head and laughed, her mouth open wide and the laughter like a fire inside that burned through her, not one of the women moved a muscle, other than the tall one whose expression rearranged itself to show nothing. Felice was never comfortable with these women at Gunther's estate, but never before did she feel quite so outcast. The field women would have at least shown what they felt in their eyes. They would also have laughed, if only in envy or in contempt. These women seemed like corpses, waxen and cold. The small, skinny one stepped forward to assist the now-quiet Felice out of her garments.

"Away with you!"

Felice would not have such a corpse touch her. It would be a bad omen. But the laughter still danced in her eyes. She could not be angry. If she were to die at the hands of this king, then she would enjoy these last, gilded moments.

The bath lasted perhaps a half hour, but for Felice it was over too soon. She tingled and glowed with the attentions of warmth and comfort, and sensual as she was, she would have liked to continue it for hours longer.

The maids rubbed her with fine linen towels, drying the water from her skin. Only her face and arms and calves were dark from the sun. The rest of her body glowed with its own tawny light. They rubbed sweet oils onto her, and the small one wrapped her in the pale yellow robe, dried her thick, wet hair with a rough towel, and then sat her down to fit her feet into the yellow slippers. But her feet were too full, too long, and too strong for such delicate things. Felice laughed with delight and kicked them aside. The tall woman pulled away a screen from in front of a large looking glass, and Felice saw herself for the first time from head to foot. Rather, Felice saw a tall, dark-haired woman, dressed in yellow, seated on a stool looking at her. She did not know this woman was herself until she saw her face. She jumped involuntarily, as if she had seen an apparition. She had only ever seen her face in the washing trough, or in the fast-running stream. She was pleased with this reflection, pleased to realize she had thought, with envy, how beautiful this woman was when she first saw her. She walked close to the glass, curious about its essence and her own. So engrossed was she in inspecting every part of her face and dress and figure that she did not notice when the three women left. And so captivated by her own beauty, so assured at this appearance of fineness was she that it seemed perfectly natural to see, standing behind this reflection, the king, his eyes also laughing, like hers, with delight.

"Indeed, a fair maid," he said, and it was only then that Felice realized this was not a dream. She turned. Yes, he was there, so close she could smell the cool herbs that had recently bathed him, so close she was caught in the aura of his body's warmth.

Her reflection lost its sureness. Felice felt confusion return and, with it, an anger for having been made fun of. He would use her now like any other, but more cruelly for having made her taste a sweetness such as she had never known.

"Come," he said, touching her hair lightly.

She moved as if in a trance. His gentleness dissipated the anger like a snowflake in the palm of her hand. And when he led her to the bed, she felt only awe.

Sliding over to make room for him, she held his eyes, seeing in them an answer that matched the question of her own life. She lay back waiting. He drew her into his arms and pulled her body up against him. Then his lips were on her cheek, over her forehead, a butterfly that circled her face until, soft and full, they landed on her own lips, which by then were ready and wanting his. There was no trick to this. He kissed her as no man had ever kissed her. His hands awakened her body as she had never dared to dream possible. And her own arms and hands moved over him without calculation, simply moving in ways she had known before only as a mechanical skill, ways she now felt as new and spontaneous and guided by a yearning in every muscle and nerve. There was no hurt, no roughness, even as their heat for each other mounted. He loved her gently, thoroughly, bringing her to peaks of ecstasy, one after another, until his own matched hers and they rose together in one held moment, then fell back to lie quietly, holding one another, letting their bodies' warmth gradually subside. Felice fell asleep that way, curled in his arms, after they had both tasted the tears that streamed silently from her eyes. They were tears of such sweetness that Clotaire smiled as he kissed them away.

In her sleep, Felice dreamed of a shaft of light that came from her own eyes like a beam, lighting up whatever it touched, and she understood in the dream how the world was made by the many lights in everyone's eyes. She awoke to Clotaire's mouth playing over her breast, the feeling of his body against hers, firm and urgent, his hands holding her waist. Her arms circled him with a softness and yearning that she had never known in the arms of another. In this man's body, in his caresses and those eyes that understood all of her without words, Felice, the whore, disappeared. She saw that part of herself melt away, felt only the rightness of her body's passion that met and answered his. Her voice became soft as now she whispered to him things she would never have dreamed possible and heard him whisper back. It was not words she heard. It was the song of her own being and of his that they whispered back and forth to one another. Each voice called out and was answered, as each body greeted the other and was answered, this man, Clotaire, and this woman, Felice.

CHAPTER 5

Deirdre felt the knife burn through her shoulder.

"Aiii!" She opened her eyes into the pitch black of the closet. Lothar stirred against her and whimpered. Deirdre released her breath in a gasp.

"Hush," she chided and gently shook him until she could tell by his breathing that he too was awake. She did not know if her own cry had been part of the dream or whether she had called out loud. She shifted. The knife was the weight of her own body, which had leaned for hours against the back of the closet. She rubbed the tops of her shoulders as best she could.

It was quiet now. There were none of the shouts and cries and clashings she had heard earlier; nothing of the long moments when the foreign soldiers had entered this very room where she and Lothar were hidden and had torn through the many chests that stored the tunics and robes of Gunther's household. She and Lothar had scarcely breathed, expecting at any moment for the doors to the wood closet to be thrust open, themselves revealed and killed or carried off. It was some miracle of the household gods that the soldiers became so wild with their discovery of riches in the chests that they neglected the closet. When they had left, sheer exhaustion from the terror combined with the soothing darkness inside the closet to lull both of them off into sleep. Deirdre guessed it might be nighttime from the silence. Lothar tugged on one strand of her hair. She bent over toward him.

"I am hungry," he said.

She whispered back. "Yes, I as well."

"What shall we do?" His voice rose in a whine.

"I will find something," she said.

"And what if they find you?"

"I will be safe. We cannot just stay here without food or water."

Deirdre needed action even when it meant danger. The most difficult thing for her was to be still, to have to wait for something. She leaned forward now and very carefully pushed on the door. It creaked. Lothar recoiled. She kept her breath even and soft and promised herself she would remain calm, whatever happened. By pushing on the door smoothly, it creaked only very softly. Opening it just enough to peer out, she sat up on her knees. Lothar squeezed her arm and she touched his hand, putting one finger to her lips to signal silence. There were no sounds. There was no one in sight.

"I will be back. Stay here no matter what happens."

He grabbed her arm. "No. I want to come with you."

"You will stay here."

"I want to come. I will not stay alone here."

Suddenly Deirdre understood the look on her uncle's face when Lothar reluctantly had learned to ride or shoot with the crossbow; also the way Nurse had of avoiding the boy's eyes directly. Deirdre felt a deep regret as she realized that her brother was a coward.

She pushed him back. "Do not cross me, sire," she snapped.

Deirdre had her own secret way down to the food stores and cooking rooms. But she had never sneaked down at night in the darkness -- the challenge had always been to steal food right from under the serving girls' noses without getting caught -- and though she knew she could do it now, Lothar would only be in the way and slow her down. Without thinking, everything suddenly fell into place. She knew exactly how she would do everything and what to do if someone stopped her. Lothar was breathing with a familiar catch in his throat. She almost changed her mind. She knew how fear could collapse one inside. She touched him gently.

"We will be together no matter what. Fear not, dear brother. I will return safely." She rose stiffly to her feet. Her legs felt locked. She rubbed one, then the other.

Every part of her body became a sensor, alert and aware as Deirdre stepped from the closet. She knew this room. It was a small storage room for clothing, filled with trunks, with narrow walkways between them. The one large standing closet where she and Lothar had hidden held the winter's wood for the bedchambers on either side. The chests were gaping now, with a few leftover shreds of mantles and tunics draped in disarray over the sides. Deirdre felt a chill, recognizing one of her own chemises, torn and discarded, near the trunk that had stored it. All the chests stood with their tops flung open like mouths emitting for Deirdre the scream she felt inside. They bespoke the emptiness of now this home too and the loss of her second parents. She stood and tried to gain control of the cries that seemed stored in every cell of her body, the cries that trembled through her, looking for release. She stepped to the door. She would neither cry nor scream, but get food for herself and Lothar. She would survive.

The hall was empty as far as she could see. The torches sputtered softly in their sconces and created leaping shadows beyond the circles of their dim light. Deirdre took a deep breath and started along the hall. Here on this second story, the floors were constructed of wood planks and had places that suddenly creaked when stepped upon. Deirdre had long ago learned that they were stable near the edges where the wooden dowels held them secure. She walked quickly along this edge. The door to the first room was closed, so she was able to proceed without pause other than to take a delicate leap over the front of its threshold. But the second door, the last she would have to pass before reaching the narrow serving staircase, was open. She slowed and listened intently. She could hear, from within the room, the snoring of someone deep in sleep. She stopped at the edge. This was normally an unoccupied room, kept for guests, long dusty and unkempt with odd, broken pieces of furniture. She made the leap and ran a few steps further before she dared to listen again. The snoring was softer, further away, unbroken. She ran lightly now, sure of safety at least until she got to the bottom of the stairs.

These were of stone, no danger of creaking unexpectedly. She went quickly down to the narrow, low door that opened into the rear of the huge dining hall. A long passage ran behind the dining hall to the cooking and storage rooms. Lined with kegs of mead and ale, it was where, in happier times, Deirdre had hidden whenever she heard one of the serving women coming down the passage to serve at the table. What had been practiced as a game, Deirdre now put to more earnest use. Not all was silent and sleeping in the huge hall. Even through the closed door, Deirdre could hear raucous celebration mixed with an occasional outcry from the lips of one of the women. Deirdre shivered, from both the dampness of the passage and the sudden terror that caught her. And so she ran, stopping at each doorway to the grain rooms that lined the hall, flattening suddenly against the wall, feeling its coolness like an icy hand against her back, ducking suddenly behind one of the mead barrels for no reason other than the sound of her own heartbeat. She panted; she was soaked through with a fear that oozed out of her pores. She paused momentarily to catch her breath and to listen to whatever could be heard above her beating blood. She could scarcely imagine having felt hunger before, let alone wanting to satisfy it now. But she would accomplish her task.

She ducked inside the main pantry and felt suddenly giddy from the many odors that rose up around her. There were barrels filled with sundried apples and pears, baskets of hard pasties stuffed with dried grapes, honey and nuts, a sweet Deirdre could never get enough of. There were covered bins of salted fish, smoked strips of pork and duck and chicken, deep bowls of eggs, both raw and cooked. And bins of onions, garlic, carrots and green vegetables fresh from the summer gardens. Deirdre forgot all in the hunger that now assailed her. She picked up one of the the deep baskets and began filling it as she took ravenous bites of a pasty. She filled the basket to the brim, then dumped it all into the sack her tunic made when held up by the hem. She poked her

41

head out into the passage. Footsteps were approaching. She slipped back into the pantry and crouched down into the space between the apple barrels. Her heart beat furiously. The steps paused, and the room suddenly opened up large from the light of a torch. Deirdre closed her eyes tight. There was a sigh. It was a woman mumbling to herself. She began rummaging around the room, banging metal bowls together.

"Meat, wench!" A man's voice, raucous, imperative, came from down the passage.

"Here, sire! Here! Coming in haste now," the woman cried out, back to him, the alarm clear in the pitch and break of her voice. She rushed from the room, murmuring, "May the gods protect me." As the words trailed off, Deirdre repeated the fervent prayer, for now she had to make the precarious trip back and the door to the dining hall was ajar. She knew this by the sounds of loud shouts and laughing that made their way down the passage.

Deirdre arose, gathering up the hem of her tunic carefully so nothing would spill out. She tiptoed to the door, then moved out into the passage. Her arms and legs were like water. The passage seemed to have elongated itself, stretched into three times its length. She moved as though in a dream, hesitated briefly at the edge of the dining hall door. Then something in her awakened. She leaped past the open doorway and raced headlong up the dark stairway. She kept her wits only enough to race along the edge, to leap across the two thresholds. She did not stop or look behind her until she was back inside the closet, the door pulled to, back into the darkness again.

Her breath came bursting forth in painful gasps. Lothar said not a word. He too was having difficulty with his breathing. When Deirdre burst into the closet, he had fully expected to be rammed through with a spear. Now his sister's fear compounded his own. They sat quietly, not moving for a long time. All hunger had vanished.

After an hour of complete quiet had assured them, their

bodies reawakened. They ate until they were filled, sucking the fruits until their thirst was quenched. It was still silent all around them.

"What shall we do now?" Lothar asked. Deirdre had been thinking of the wide fields, of the forest road, of how, just this morning, she had begged Nurse to let her ride out there.

"We shall escape," she replied. "We shall take our horses and ride off."

Lothar was silent.

"There is a road along the edge of the forest," she continued. "I know not where it leads, but we shall follow it." Deirdre was filled now with the adventure. "You will take with you your crossbow. We will eat the birds and animals you shoot. We shall learn to fish in the rivers."

They whispered back and forth, became lost in the pictures of their adventures, forgetting completely the seriousness of their situation until the whole closet shook with the force of the door pulled suddenly wide open.

"Out with you!" The face that loomed in front of them, the mouth wide and red, the eyes dark and darker still from the wide eyebrows and thick lashes, was like the sudden appearance of one of the forest gods. Both pulled back against the wall of the closet.

"I say out with you, wench," Fabian snarled. He grabbed Deirdre by the hair and pulled her upright. The pain quickly brought her back to this world.

"Let me go!" she screamed.

His hand upon her was an offense. His few teeth, yellowed and worn, were displayed in what pretended to be a smile; his breath was a stench like that which rose from the far side of the moat in summertime. Never had Deirdre come close to such a man. He was less than the least of the house servants. Only the lowest of the field serfs resembled this man. She spit on his filthy tunic and flailed her arms against him. Her revulsion was such she felt bile rise into her throat.

Fabian, for his part, was amazed and dropped her as he would a hornet's nest. Deirdre scrambled back away from him into the closet. Her hand was clamped tight over her mouth; her shoulders heaved. The boy stood white, stricken silent.

Fabian understood immediately that these two were those the king was searching for. These were Gunther's children. Though they were prisoners, without rights, for all practical purposes under his power, Favian felt the awkwardness that came from a life of servitude. An enormous shame descended over his former high spirits. Struck dumb, he watched the girl recover herself. She turned to him with a look that withered him further. He bowed without being aware of doing so.

"My lady," he stammered, "Clotaire, your master, the king, awaits upon your service." Such words were new to him and he blushed for their reach toward a refinement that he had only witnessed before from great distances.

"*My* service! *My* master!" Dierdre pressed her advantage, concealing her terror and revulsion behind a facade, feeling it as an echo only in the quickness of her heartbeat and breath. "Such a swine could never be my master. Out with you!"

Fabian actually turned, with again a perceptible bow, when the slightest look of amazement reddened Deirdre's cheeks bringing to him the reality of his position. He stopped and faced the girl squarely. "Ai, the king, *your* master."

But he dared not touch her, nor the boy. His threat was in his stance a yard in front of her. "Come along now."

Deirdre's mind raced. However much this man sickened her, the mere mention of the king brought up a hatred and fear that made her feel a weakness close to fainting. She threw herself on her knees.

"Oh, sire, I beg you in your kindness, do not deliver myself nor my brother unto that foul murderer. Gunther was our uncle, our second father, now murdered like our first by this godless monster. Take pity on us. I would die simply to be in his presence. Or he would sink his ax into my head also. Of what benefit to the gods is that?"

Deirdre could scarcely believe the content of her words. In play, she and Lothar had acted out such intensity before, inventing pity and compassion or cruelty -- she the cold princess or gentle queen, he the officer of the guard or king, one or the other taking the role of pleading. And here she knelt really at the feet of a monster and it was no playacting; it would be of consequence this eloquence of hers.

"I can embroider fine lace," she lied. "I can ride a horse like a man. I can string bows, shoot...." She listed what she believed to be her achievements or those that such a man would wish to hear.

Fabian listened with his mouth hanging wide. She was beautiful, her eyes moist with tears, her hair golden like the maple in autumn, her fair skin pink with her passion to survive. What a prize. Fabian saw all this without words, even within his own mind. He would possess this maid. He would hide her and make her his own, display her for exchange in the small villages and towns. A lust to possess her rose up to him. With it, he regained the shrewdness that was native to him.

"Cover your hair," he ordered, taking over. He stooped forward, grabbing Deirdre's fine tunic by its hem. He had ripped it upward taking out a section before she had time to realize the sound that accompanied the action was not her flesh being torn to bits. He rubbed the dirt of his hands onto her cheeks, stepped back, threw the rag he had torn out of her tunic, and grimaced as she bound her head with it, hiding her hair.

"Keep your eyes downward," he ordered. She obeyed. "Now, out with you."

He grabbed Lothar by the the back of the neck, threw a piece of torn fabric from the floor over his head and shoulders. "And you stop your sniveling."

Lothar trotted out on the heels of his sister. He too looked downward, hiding his telltale northern blue eyes. Deirdre reached out for his hand and they held one another tightly. Neither could tell which of them was the one who was trembling.

Fabian led them outside into the cool morning. It was still dark with only a hint of light on the edge of the horizon. Small fires burned here and there in the courtyard casting a glow over the numerous sleeping figures that lay about on the ground. They had to pick their way carefully among the sleeping humans, fowl and animals. All was helter-skelter, the foreigners having left off any organization until after they had taken their pleasures. Now most of them also lay snoring drunkenly while a handful sat morosely around the fires keeping a careless guard. Fabian guided Deirdre and Lothar silently with a push against Deirdre's back with one hand. He took them to the small, low-ceilinged shed where the ducks were kept. It was empty now of them except for the flutter of down feathers that rose up with every step. The little yard was muddy and their feet sank in over the soles of their flat-bottomed sandals, but there was a wooden floor to the roosting shed. Fabian indicated they were to crawl into this and hide far back in a dark corner.

"Make no noise, nor call any attention to yourselves. I will be nearby. If you try to escape, I will turn you over to Clotaire." Fabian grinned toothlessly, then left. Deirdre and Lothar sat silently together as, all over the courtyard, one rooster after another began the morning greeting to the sun. They could see little straight out through the wide cracks in the shed walls, but the stirrings and stretchings of the now-awakening people and animals told them that this day would be only a little kinder to them than the last. There were soft cries and moans from the wounded; children whined as they clung hungrily to their mothers' skirts; orders barked out from the soldiers.

Fabian stood a casual guard near the shed. Now he watched as the fowl and animals were rounded up and put in their pens out of the way as the women bustled about fetching wood and water in preparation for the morning meal. He walked over to the pen gate, opening it for the ducks that were herded by a young boy. The boy nodded his head at Fabian.

"Thank you, sire," he said and rushed off to round up the remaining ducks. It did not take long. All the animals were hungry, having missed their last evening's feeding. The boy returned with a pail of grain and an armful of greens. Fabian stopped him.

"Leave those here," Fabian ordered.

The boy looked puzzled. Another soldier had given him orders to feed the ducks. "I would only feed them, sire," he protested.

Fabian's blow to the side of the boy's head sent him flying. He lay stunned momentarily, then scrambled up and dashed out of sight. Deirdre and Lothar watched from within; they felt the blow as if it had been given to themselves.

Fabian dumped the grain out in a wide arc scattering it over the yard. The ducks, raising a loud ruckus, made a dash for it. The boy appeared again with another pail, this one of water, which he left a few yards from the edge of the yard. Fabian used this opportunity, as he stooped to fill the water trough, to warn Deirdre and Lothar.

"When I come back and stand here by the gate, you slip out to stand beside me." He glared at Deirdre.

"Yea, sire," she answered. She was no longer glad to have eaten. The stench from the duck pen made her nauseous. Lothar also looked unwell. Fabian noticed it and laughed shortly, then left. They saw him take a position near the castle walls, talking and laughing with two other soldiers. Occasionally, he would glance in their direction.

Perhaps an hour passed. Deirdre and Lothar said not a word, simply became receptacles for the noises that came to them, the ducks' quacking nearest and the more distant scrapings and voices that accompanied a simple meal around the fires. The ducks would not come inside the shed at all. After the initial alarm they had raised upon discovering the children inside the shed, they had settled quietly along the edges of the pen as far from these intruders as possible.

A horn blew and the yard became silent.

"Gather for the lottery," a voice called out over and over. "Gather for the lottery."

Fabian was at the gate. Having seen him first, Lothar signaled to Deirdre. They crawled on their knees to the low door. The ducks set up another hue and cry, and a storm of feathers. Lothar and Deirdre had to slap at the few males who came at them, wings stretched out low to the ground, beaks thrust forward snapping at them with a low, angry sound in their throats. Fabian grabbed Lothar and Deirdre by the collars of their tunics and spoke low to them.

"Eyes down, speak to no one."

No one had noticed the children's emergence from the duck pen, nor its accompanying uproar, nor now their entrance into the group of women and children huddled together in the center of the courtyard. There was too much activity and noise. Children howled in fright, mothers scolded, the soldiers shouted. Some of the soldiers stood about looking over the group. Others heaped more of Gunther's possessions onto the already large pile of goods. The sun was higher in the sky now and reflections from the many silver and gold pieces danced all around the yard. The goods were the first things to be distributed. The sun had climbed directly overhead before the distribution was completed. Each man had to present to the presiding soldier his claims for certain goods. What was not claimed by the end was thrown into the fires. The flames leaped up and smoke rose black and heavy for a long time.

Fabian was among the first soldiers to present their claims when attention finally turned to the captives. He wanted the two children out of sight while there was still such confusion and chaos. He laid claim to two of the field women, having stopped them from escaping, he said, and to Deirdre and Lothar whom he passed off as the offspring of one of the women. His claim was not disputed by any of the others and he was able to lead off his prisoners with no difficulty. Scarcely anyone noticed at all, except the two women, and they only exchanged a look. At first they did not know who these children were; then a strand of Deirdre's golden hair slipped loose from under the rag and snaked down her back like an accusing finger. Both women saw it and dared look at no one, not even each other. Each pretended she had not seen. Fabian's secret would be safe with them.

CHAPTER 6

Nurse heaved herself heavily up from the chair and walked out through the narrow door onto the parapet. The pile in the courtyard below had considerably dwindled. The field serfs stood or squatted quietly in the shade of the walls or under the large chestnut tree that grew within the walls. They were lost in simply watching, spellbound by the ritual of the lottery in which, one by one, the foot soldiers presented themselves to the captain for payment for their service: goblets, plates, yards of lace and finely woven linen, silver and gold pieces, feathers, tapestries, and rugs. These soldiers were rough men who had scarcely seen such things as now were given them out of Clotaire's generosity.

Nurse sighed. A drop of sweat that had slowly accumulated at the rim of her stiff headpiece now gathered into fullness and swelled beyond its edges to travel in a tickling path down the side of her face. She wiped it away with the wide hem of her sleeve and sighed again. How she longed to sleep. Never had a day been so empty for her. Yesterday and its night had been a long waiting, but, at least yesterday she had hope. She had remained fully dressed, seated erect in her chamber all night long, expecting at any moment the knock on her door to announce that the children had been found. The night had been endless, unbroken, except by the irregular chirping of a cricket somewhere in a corner. The young king had told her in the audience she had had with him this morning that he would leave on the morrow with or without the boy and girl. He was angry with Nurse for having lost her charges, and the old woman had left unsaid her reasons for having never told the two children the truth of their past. She had said only: "They do not know how you are connected to them." He had dismissed her, and Nurse understood that she would be punished, though the king had said no word about that. Something in his sternness toward her had given form to what remained unspoken. It did not matter. Nurse felt the emptiness that dread brings, dread being a prelude to a grief one knows is coming and cannot be turned aside. What she felt was a mother's grief, though she herself had no name for it. She was long in the service of Deirdre's parents, already ten years before Deirdre was born. Gudrun, Deirdre's mother, had not even begun to menstruate when she had married. And there had been one early child, a boy who was defective with a large, swollen head. The infant had been mercifully killed, but Gudrun had refused after that to bear children, in fear of the gods' wrath for the killing. She feared that they would give her an even more monstrous child. Eight years passed again before she discovered she was again with child. Nurse and Gudrun tried potions three different times with no success, and so they went to the old woman out in the woods who made Gudrun a ritual of blessing that this would be a healthy child. Thus Deirdre had been born and, two years later, Lothar. Gudrun loved them both, but feared to be with them much in case the gods would again turn upon her. Nurse held them, comforted them, and raised them all these years, particularly after being brought to Gunther's. Lady Sigrid was oddly aloof toward them, perhaps because the children clung to Nurse as to a mother. So now Nurse sat again in her chair, her own body weight like a stone that pulled her down. Her own body's barrenness, which she had never felt since the children had come to her, now opened up inside her like a void -- the barrenness of loss, of death for a life she had taken for granted to be hers until she died. It did not matter that she had not borne these children out of her own body. They had filled that emptiness in her.

She leaned her head against the hard chair back and closed her eyes. A swirl of color and pinpoints of tiny, starlike lights swam in front of her closed eyes. Her whole body was rigid, resisting what she sensed was coming. Until now, she had given no words to it, no pictures even. But perhaps Deirdre and Lothar were dead, killed in that early frenzy. Perhaps their bodies had been hidden by whoever had committed the act, after the word had gone out that Clotaire wanted the two blond children brought to him. That was the most likely possibility, though Nurse knew

Deirdre was capable of hiding for a long time. She recalled afternoons when she had searched for both of them and Deirdre had eluded her without difficulty and had laughed mischievously when Nurse scolded her later.

You walked right past us a thousand times, she would laugh. Deirdre could disappear like that infernal cricket whose chirping began again, grating on Nurse's nerves. But why had she and Lothar not come to her in the night? The only other small possibility was that they had escaped the castle walls. Nurse sat erect. The idea was welcome to her, though in her heart she knew it was an impossible act. But it directed her, gave her something, however futile, to do. She rose and straightened her skirts. Deirdre was not the only one with skill in sneaking. Nurse would get outside to the stable. If the chestnut mare, which was Lothar's, and the black mare, which was Deirdre's, were gone, then the two had indeed escaped. Nurse had already wandered all the halls and peeked through as many rooms as she could this morning. She had called out, whispering the children's name, only to have the names hit the stone walls and slip down to the floor like the beads of moisture that now dropped down her face. That calling was what had made the dread grow, had made her feel her own emptiness. She could not be blamed then for this one act of foolishness, for the hope that bloomed a sudden flower inside her.

She was in no danger of disobeying orders, since no order had been given her. But as a household servant she understood that it was foolish to go into the courtyard at this time. The inside servants automatically belonged to Clotaire and the few noblemen who accompanied him. They need not suffer the indignities of the lottery. To go outside before the field serfs had been distributed was to risk losing her preferred status. Nurse was too distraught to consider such things. She simply wanted to slip out and get to the stables. If she discovered the children had escaped, she could report this to Clotaire. Perhaps they could be found before they traveled too far. For all Deirdre's cleverness, Nurse could not imagine her and Lothar surviving long alone in the world.

She hurried along the halls to the servants' stairs, passing, as she did, the storage chamber where Deirdre and Lothar had hidden.

You walked right past us a thousand times.

She ignored the voice that taunted her, as so often she had ignored small signals that came to her from corners and doors telling her over and over, if she had only dared to pay attention, that here was where the girl was hiding. Nurse's nature was one of doing and adhering rigidly to the laws of reality as she had been taught them. Thus, she always missed the moments when other worlds reached out for her attention.

Downstairs, she hurried along the passage outside the food storage rooms.

A thousand times. A thousand times.

Nurse went into the cooking area, through which she had to pass to get to the stables behind. The cooks in their skirts and tunics moved about, sweating profusely, tending the fires and the food. Those that noticed her, as she passed, greeted Nurse with respect, then exchanged glances when they saw that she continued on through the kitchen yard, past the gardens, and out through the small gate. Nurse felt their curiosity, but let it fall away like everything else except her determination.

Outside the gate, she peered to right and left. The stable yard, a hundred feet away, was straight across from her, but it would be no good attempting to get in. Three soldiers worked in the yard, checking gear and grooming the horses. Nurse was glad to see that neither mare belonging to the children was in sight. Just then, however, the young king himself emerged from the barn leading his own black steed in one hand and Deirdre's graceful mare in the other.

He was laughing. A pretty man, Nurse thought. Behind him came the whore Felice, dark and very serious. The king stood at the head of Deirdre's horse talking with one of the men. The mare tossed her head and rolled her eyes. The men soothed and

53

admired her. Felice held Clotaire's horse for him. Absently, she ran one hand gently over its muzzle.

For a moment, Nurse simply stood taking in the scene in front of her without its meaning anything. It was as though her mind sheltered her momentarily from the several realizations that now pushed forward into recognition. Felice was dressed in a fine skirt of dark linen and a tunic that belonged to Lady Sigrid. Seeing the tunic whose design she herself had worked into the fabric over long hours, Nurse was suddenly faced with the fact of Sigrid's death. Not a word had been said of this, nor had Nurse, until now, given it any thought. A wave of regret bordering on grief rose up. With it, the past -- Gudrun's cruel murder, as senseless as Sigrid's -- and the sudden present -- the young Clotaire holding Deirdre's dancing mare with its message that the children had not escaped -- combined inside her like a vine that grew magically fast, twisting around itself to rise up in her throat. Her face contorted with the pain of it. It began deep in her chest, in her heart that had beat so long with its one warm purpose, and traveled up into her throat and down one arm to the fingers that clutched upon themselves convulsively. The storm was sudden and total. Her eyes finally released the water that she had held for so long, and her throat let go, just this once, the curse that a serf kept forever locked behind his heart, hidden even from himself, the unknown dark wish for freedom, for self-mastery.

"May Tollech strike ye down!" The words were garbled, only the yell came out, a screech or high-pitched moan. The king, Felice, and the soldiers looked; Clotaire's and Felice's hands held up in a gesture of comfort aimed at the horses they had been stroking, now turned slightly toward Nurse's rigid figure. The cooks behind her stood awesome in the smoke and sounds of bubbling pots and meat on spits, their strong arms slowly settling to rest on their hips or at their sides or, absently, rubbing the soot onto the already blackened tunics. And down the path, between the walls, Fabian, the two field women, and Deirdre and Lothar all turned to behold the source of this unearthly scream. For a moment it was as if the wind had died, all voices ceased; then the king turned back to his new prize, Felice laughed and shrugged; the cooks clucked their tongues and raised eyebrows at one another, before turning back to their work. Fabian's group all turned back to continue on their way, except Deirdre and Lothar who looked from under their rags with awe at their old nurse. Deirdre's mouth opened involuntarily; she stifled the cry in her own throat and took Lothar firmly by the hand, letting him know by a look that he was to do what Fabian had told them. Fabian would somehow save them; this was the only thought in her mind. She was convinced Clotaire would kill her and Lothar with as quick a blow as the one to her uncle.

The ground slowly reappeared to Nurse. Her senses returned one after another, the silence filling up with the fires behind, with the horses' nervous jingling of their gear, with the small sounds that accompanied the little breeze that stirred everywhere. The king was about to mount the mare. Felice was laughing now, her wide mouth inviting and full as she looked at Clotaire. Nurse turned. She was about to return through the kitchen when she caught sight of the one, long golden swatch of hair that hung down Deirdre's back.

"Child," she murmured. "Child."

The day opened like a butterfly's wings. Suddenly, there were colors, good odors of food and grass, a sweet breeze on her skin. She moved with a grace and speed her heavy body had not known in years. Her joy was so full, she did not pause to wonder at why Deirdre was dressed as though disguised and traveling in such company. She could not run, she was too heavy; and she could not call out because she was already winded and the pain still throbbed in her chest.

The little group was about to turn into a doorway that led into one of the small shops built into the base of the outer castle wall when Lothar peeked up from under his rag, back toward Nurse. She saw the fear in his blue eyes and called out breathlessly.

"Oh! Child, child!"

Fabian stopped abruptly and looked directly at her as she hurried toward him. He shoved his charges roughly down into the cool darkness of the shop and stood, arms across his chest to meet her. Nurse bustled up to him, one hand over her beating heart, the other holding her headpiece in place. She curtsied to Fabian and panted out:

"Forgive...sire...I...oh...I cannot...." She took a deep breath.

Fabian snarled at her in a low voice. "On your way, wench. What is here is no business of yours if you value your life."

"Oh dear...sire...a mistake...the king...."

Nurse looked uncomprehendingly at Fabian who raised his arm. Stunned, she watched as the arm fell in an arc and smacked her full across the mouth in a fist. Nurse fell backward. Blood flowed from her lip.

Deirdre and Lothar together emerged from the shop.

"No!" Deirdre cried. A thousand bees beat their wings just beneath her skin. "No! That is my nurse!"

"Oh, Deirdre! Lothar!" Nurse struggled to rise. They rushed to her side. Fabian swatted both aside.

"Get back in," he ordered. Deirdre could scarcely see him through the tears that streamed from her eyes.

Fabian lifted his spear.

"Please sire. She is our nurse."

"Ye've no need of a nurse now."

In one fluid gesture, he lifted, thrust, and pulled back this weapon. Nurse only grunted, then fell back with a soft thud. Deirdre screamed. Fabian threw her to the ground.

"What goes here?"

In the turmoil, no one had heard the king approach on Deirdre's horse. Fabian stopped, open mouthed, staring in disbelief at his master and the woman who rode behind him and who grinned idiotically now at him. He could find no words. His legs turned to water.

"Why have you killed the good nurse?"

Fabian recovered somewhat when he saw that Dierdre lay quietly on the ground, her head still covered. Fabian reckoned he might get by.

"She would interfere, my king," he said guardedly. "An interfering old woman. I know not what she wanted."

"Then what reason to kill her?" The king's voice indicated disinterest. The mare under him pawed the ground reflecting his restlessness. Fabian took courage.

"She came upon me from behind. With a rock, my lord. She...."

"Ah then, bury her. Get her out of the path. And no more killing no more killing, good Fabian."

"Ai, my king."

The king lifted the reins, ready to go, when Felice suddenly put one hand on his arm.

"Wait, my lord. Would you be interested in the finest prize on Gunther's estate?"

Clotaire was annoyed and showed it in his half-glance back at Felice. She only pointed triumphantly.

"There. That rag pile. Take away the cloth from her head," Felice said. Fabian's blood stopped.

"What is it you want, woman?" Clotaire would ride this fine horse out in the woods. He would have the passionate Felice again. His blood was rising; he felt the heaviness of his desire.

Felice slipped lightly off the horse's back. She stooped and pulled away Deirdre's covering.

"Gunther's brat, the golden Deirdre!" Felice's eyes glistened with triumph. "Just look at her now!"

Clotaire stared at Deirdre who lay still as a stone. He slowly swung one leg over the saddle and dropped to the ground. He stood a moment, then knelt at Deirdre's side and gently touched her shoulder. She cringed and pulled away. Felice laughed.

"And is this the lord Saisson's daughter?"

Clotaire attempted to lift her; she came alive, clawing and striking out at him. Clotaire let her go.

"Dear girl," he said, "I will not harm you. I am here to help you."

Felice touched his shoulder. "Sire, she is Gunther's daughter. She is one of them. And here is her brother." She pulled Lothar up as though he were a sack of carrots.

Deirdre for the first time looked at Clotaire directly. Her eyes were red, her face smudged with dirt, she looked pitiable; yet for all the hate and terror and grief that fleetingly appeared and disappeared in turns across her face, the king had never beheld one so beautiful. He stood up, pulled Deirdre upright with him. Fabian stood shaken and white.

"You knew who these children were?"

"No, my king. I thought they belonged to these women here." He indicated the empty doorway where the two field women stayed out of sight below.

Clotaire struck him. "You deliberately hid them?"

"No, sire. Please, sire. I...."

Clotaire struck him again. His eyes were black with rage.

"Leave him be, you foul leaving!"

The king swung around to see who dared to challenge him so.

"I ordered him to hide us."

Clotaire stopped. "You...?"

"I would rather die than, for a moment, be with you!" Deirdre visibly pulled together into a solid emotion of defiance and hate. Clotaire looked momentarily stunned. No one, least of all a woman, and this one a mere child yet, had ever stood up to dispute him or to interfere in any way with any action he had ever taken.

Deirdre hugged Lothar against her side, one arm around his shoulder. "So now kill me. Kill us!" she said, her voice like his eyes, cold and hard.

All stood breathless. A few flies droned as they circled in the still air.

"Kill you!" The words burst out with a short derisive laugh. "You shall be my wife!"

Had he lowered his ax into her head at that moment, Deirdre would not have been so surprised. She stared in disbelief. Finally, she found her tongue. "Your wife! Never! Never!"

CHAPTER 7

Hoping to understand Clotaire's startling words, Felice went over the events and words of this last hour, each detail, each nuance.

"Come with me," he had said and she had followed him to the cool, pungent-smelling stable. She could not yet believe her luck in her life's having taken such a turning. That a man of high station would use her did not surprise her; but that he would speak with her and treat her kindly, be gentle with her and, of all things, request her to accompany him like a wife or mistress, kept her so off balance she had not uttered one word all morning. She had followed him out of the dark stable into the bright sun. She squinted her eyes against the light. Directly across the wide yard, at the gate to the kitchen yard, stood the heavy, dark-robed nurse with her high, stiff headpiece. Even at that distance, Felice could see her agitation and dismissed it as a justifiable concern for herself and her charges. Felice had overheard Clotaire's early morning interviews with the highly placed household servants from behind the thick curtains that divided the bedchamber from Gunther's receiving room. She had listened more out of the desire to hear Clotaire's deep voice -- to be close to that which had given her so much happiness only hours before, and which she believed would soon be lost to her -- than out of her native curiosity and instinct for survival, though, in Felice, since her coming to this manor, these two elements were necessarily always there. When one survived as precariously as she did, one could never tell when a stray piece of information or gossip might come to one's aid. Thus, taking Clotaire's voice into every recess of her mind and body, storing it up, so to speak, for its future absence, that she might recall its every nuance and shape, she took in also the content. She heard then his anger with Nurse and his impatience to have Gunther's two children brought to him. She understood. Clotaire could not afford to have them survive, particularly the son, who would be bound to vengeance once he achieved

60

manhood.

Clotaire handed her the lead rope to his horse. She ran her hand lightly over the horse's velvety muzzle. The animal rubbed its bony head up against her side and Felice smiled to herself. A good sign that her master's horse should like her. She patted it and spoke caressingly into its ear. She watched Clotaire calm the other black horse; a pretty mare, small, but spirited. Just then an unearthly scream broke the peace Felice had been feeling inside. She turned to see the nurse, whose face was almost unrecognizable, so twisted it was in pain. Felice glanced quickly at Clotaire. The nurse looked directly at him. It seemed as though the cry she uttered was directed at him. Though she could not make out the words, Felice recognized that it was a curse from the depths of the old woman's spirit. Witch that she was, Felice knew the power of such a cry, and a shiver of apprehension ran the length of her spine. She silently vowed to perform a protective ritual for Clotaire as soon as she was able to go again into the forest to be with her special gods. She had never heard that the nurse had any such powers and regarded the woman with a moment's curiosity; then, satisfied by the appearance of helplessness and anguish that overcame the nurse as she stood there, Felice returned her attention to Clotaire who was mounting the mare. He smiled down at her.

"Up here," he said, patting the mare's back. "You too shall ride with me to inspect the fields." His eyes were filled with mischief. She returned the look.

"And other things, dear sire, I have no doubt of that," she answered.

"Up, wench."

He reached down and helped Felice to swing up behind the saddle. Felice had never ridden and grasped the horse's back as tightly as she could with her legs and wrapped her arms tightly around Clotaire.

"You leave me no air to breathe," he laughed. "A strong

woman you are, indeed."

Felice laughed and loosened her hold. In her nervousness to be mounted horseback this first time, she had forgotten that this was a king, a lord. She fairly glowed with her delight and amazement. The soldier would not look at her. He was a foot soldier, a former serf, no doubt a field serf like herself, who had made his way through skill and intelligence to be an aide to such a man. To see one so low as she was with his master this way was a source of shame to the man. It was one thing that his master should use a woman like Felice, another that he should treat her with gallantry and public esteem. Felice threw back her head proudly, only to have it almost jerked off when Clotaire spurred the lively mare and the horse leaped forward.

"Ai, my king," she cried in alarm and grasped him firmly again. Clotaire brought the horse to a halt and her body propelled forward into him. He loosened her arms himself and laughed.

"I tell you, woman, you cannot hold me so. I turn purple for lack of air."

"But I will fall. I cannot stay on."

The mare started more gently, a quick walk, and after a few paces, Felice fell into her rhythm, bouncing lightly up and down.

They had turned down the narrow path between the walls. Clotaire suddenly stiffened. Felice peaked around him to see what slowed them down. Nurse lay like a fallen crow in a heap of black skirts and tunic. After such a cry as Nurse had emitted earlier, this was indeed a bad omen. But Felice could not tell whether the curse had turned its power back onto the old woman, or whether it was now loose in the air. She took in the scene as Clotaire challenged Fabian, and quickly guessed that the one who lay so still against the wall was the girl Deirdre. She saw it too in the tight fear that played over the soldier Fabian's face. The girl, no doubt, had paid the man dearly for his protection. Clotaire's ax, falling through the air, dreamlike, into Gunther's skull, the lifting upward, as of a long-imprisoned bird within her breast, repeated itself in her mind's eye. Deirdre had been brought to the manor at the same time as Felice. During the long, hard trip, Felice had watched from a distance with what care and concern the blonde girl and her brother had been treated. Deirdre stood for the warmth and comfort that Felice had seen destroyed with the loss of her family, and for the immense difference in caste. Already the young Felice had been roughly taken by several of the men; already she had been beaten for her one fierce attempt to protect herself. The golden Deirdre had become the source of a deep rage and pain and was the symbol of all that oppressed Felice.

Clotaire's body signaled he was about to move on. Felice grabbed his arm.

"Wait," she said. "Would you be interested in the finest prize on Gunther's estate?"

She saw his irritation and swelled inwardly to know his wanting her was its cause. But he would be more pleased with her when he understood her intent. She leaped down and triumphantly unveiled the girl Deirdre. She saw his irritation leave. But another emotion, one she could not fathom, quickly took its place as Clotaire knelt at the girl's side and tenderly spoke to her. Felice was confused. She pulled up Lothar as well, and took the liberty to remind Clotaire whose children they were. She did not understand any of what Clotaire was saying. She had never heard the name of Lord Saisson. Perhaps he could not harm children, that was all. She had expected him to cut them down quickly, mercifully. Even now, as Deirdre hurled her icy taunts and insults at him, he only stood open-mouthed and permitted them.

"You shall be my wife!"

The words touched Felice like ice. Now, completely forgotten, she only watched as Clotaire led the small group back along the path toward the courtyard. She held in her hands the reins of Deirdre's mare, a servant again. Her head told her she had no more than this to expect, but her heart yearned already for what it had only barely tasted. Thus, she felt used, yet when she looked at it, she was left with the conclusion that Clotaire owed her nothing, had indeed repaid her with more than she could ever have hoped. But the human heart, once aroused in hope toward something better, cannot return to its former isolation. Felice could not help but believe that she had been given love for the first time in her life and it had been given in a manner so natural that she felt now she had a right to it. Thus her conflict circled in her mind like a dog chasing its own tail endlessly.

She scarcely noticed when the foot soldier at the stable sniggered at her. He had seen his master pass and now saw the defeat and impotence in Felice's face.

"Fallen so soon, my lady?" he taunted.

Felice did not hear him. She walked along the way Clotaire had taken out to the front courtyard. The lottery was over, a sense of order had reestablished itself. The soldiers with their prizes, both human and material, were packing and repairing their gear for departure the next day. The moat gate had been lowered once again and the children played on the banks of the bracken water.

Felice strode quickly through the grasses, feeling them tug against her skirt. Her fine tunic caught on the twigs of low bushes. She pulled it free, snagging and tearing it in a dozen places. The field women did not use the over-tunic for this very reason. They wore short blouse-like tops over their long skirts, and these they often hiked up between their legs in a knot in front so that they could move more freely. Only the fine ladies of the house and the household servants wore the elegant tunic.

She felt the warm sun on her head and shoulders. A fine sweat broke out all over her body. She loved to walk like this through the fields and to feel the grass at its roots beneath her bare feet that were hardened against the stones and sharp spines at the base of the new growth. She carried a flat basket with her, one she had picked up near the gate so that when the soldier challenged her going out, she indicated she had been ordered by the king to collect some sweet-smelling herbs for the lady

Deirdre's bath. Her self-assurance came from the presence again of her gods within her, and the soldier waved her past.

She let the power of the fields, of the earth, and of all growing things to enter her. She became a receptacle for the sun, the air, and the water of her own body. She felt her power growing as she let enter the energy of all that surrounded her.

At the edge of the first copse of trees, she stopped and turned around. The castle walls in the distance embraced the squat, two-story castle like the arms of a mother. The stones had a yellowish cast to them, so that from here, with the sun shining strongly upon the manor, it glowed with a warm, golden light. Felice pushed all remaining thoughts from her mind and concentrated on merely seeing, allowing the scene to come into her. She had to collect power. To do this, she had first to empty herself, to become pure woman, pure receiving.

She could see from here the original dimensions of the walls, which had, as years passed and the manor grew, been broken through with doors and gates and extended to house the growing number of shops and storage rooms that were a necessary adjunct to the swelling population. It looked like a large village. In fact, there were now some three hundred souls in all. The shacks of the field serfs outside the walls looked like small haystacks with their yellowed roofs and walls. Then the fields stretched out green or speckled with small wildflowers of white and yellow and blue. It was a pretty scene. Felice knew when she could see it this way -- without personal rancor, without its being a symbol of injustice and pain -- that she could now enter the wood, that her power was at its height.

Her mind was empty now without effort, the shade was cool and welcome, as were the speckled lights from the sun that lay like stars all over the copse's floor. She went directly to the spot where the mushrooms grew, where once she had seen a spirit rise and pass away through the trees, beckoning her to follow. She sat on her rock in the shadow of a huge, old chestnut and looked down into the small clear pool formed by a hidden spring. She leaned far over and saw her own face framed by her hair. She was surprised to see a line in the middle of her brow.

"Come, O Tollech, come to me. Touch your mistress' brow."

She rocked on her heels back and forth as she chanted. Her voice was barely audible; her chanting was soft, whispering music akin to the sound of wind or water.

"And come, Criace, with your laughing eyes, come to bless my love."

She repeated each chant the required four times, then rolled her head back, eyes closed, and sat very still until she heard the slightest rustling in the tops of the trees above her. She smiled and rolled up in one swift motion to a standing position. She raised her arms upward as in an embrace.

"I hear you," she said. "Now hear me, you who have power over lovers' hearts. Make Clotaire mine. Give me the secret I must have to bind him to me."

She sank down again and closed her eyes. The trees rustled.

"Yea, I hear you. I hear you and obey."

She sank down flat on her back, her arms raised above her head, her legs open, indicating complete submission. The earth smelled rich with decay and damp. She let herself sink down into it, let the god come into her with a desire that was the same as hers for Clotaire. She moaned softly and rocked her body from side to side. She understood that her love for Clotaire would make her the serf she had never yet been in her heart. The love god held her long in his power, but when she sat up, the picture of a tansy came into her mind, clear, with even its sharp odor. Felice laughed.

"You are a warmth yet in my body, oh Criace. I thank you for your power and your secret."

She knew exactly where some tansy grew and walked as

quickly and silently as a deer through the trees to the spot. She knelt in front of one and asked its forgiveness and blessing, telling it she had been directed here by Criace himself. Then she dug down deep all around it with a stick and took it out whole, its root ball intact. She collected another in the same way, then started back toward the manor. She had been gone a long time. Already the sun was low in the sky and the castle walls glowed pink, as did the smoke of a dozen fires that rose up in columns to join their sisters, the clouds above.

And as she neared the walls, the odors of roast pig and chicken and duck greeted her now-aroused appetite. She had taken the precaution of collecting, besides the two tansy plants, some rosemary and wild sage and passed the gate guards without being questioned.

The courtyard atmosphere was festive. For most, death and wounds and losses were clearly forgotten, for the moment at least. Never before had Gunther's serfs even seen so much food let alone partaken of it. Gunther had made sure that they were only strong enough to do their work and they had managed to do that only by stealing from the harvest. Their lot was such that they had grown used to the gnawing in their bellies. Even the dozen mothers and widows who had lost a beloved in yesterday's melee joined in this incredible feast, temporarily putting aside their very real grief for the lean time they fully expected would return once again. So they all had dressed in their few bits of finery for this the soldiers' last night on the manor and the feast that was in their honor. They sat around in small groups gnawing lustily on pieces of meat, stuffing bread and baked apple and greens into their bulging cheeks and washing the lot down with ale. Yorkum, already drunk, leaned against the wheel of one of the packed carts and played the lute. His curly, dark hair fell down over one eye. His cheeks, always red from the sickness in his lungs, were rosier than usual. He smiled absently as he plucked a tune and sang whatever words came into his head.

"...and so the soldiers you see

67

killed the brute with glee

and when Gunther fell

we all knew it was well so...

heigh ho fie dee la fie dee."

The circle that was gathered around him joined in to sing the last line loudly, with laughter and happy tears and slaps on backs. Felice watched enjoying their pleasure. Yorkum spotted her.

"Ah, the king's wench herself! Come, join us with a little song, my pretty."

Yorkum had always been a friend to Felice when he had paid attention to her at all. He was often ill, and other than to labor in the fields, he passed his hours lying on the straw pallet in one corner of his small hut. Felice, out of gratitude for his occasional kindness to her, had sometimes brought him food she had prepared, or mead after harvest time when Gunther passed out the traditional kegs to the field serfs. He had never been rough with her in word or act, and twice she had even slept with him to warm him, for he trembled so from the fever that would grip him. She answered now with a wag of her head. His eyes were bright from the fever.

"Come now. Pay no attention to these here. They have no life in their bones compared to one curl on your fine head."

Felice laughed. Yorkum often praised her in front of the others. To please him now, hands on hips, she sang with her husky voice.

"...and so the king, you see

took just one look at me

and his manhood did swell

why 'twas big as that bell, for...

heigh ho fie dee la fie dee!"

The crowd laughed and applauded her bawdy song. For a

moment, Felice felt the warmth of being part of a community again. Yorkum picked up the verse changing the rhythm.

"...and she laid him so low

he will not soon again know...

heigh ho fie dee la fie dee!"

Cora, an old woman, midwife to everyone in the village, cackled and cracked out her verse:

"...the king he will pay

'til the end of his day for...

heigh ho fie dee la fie dee!"

The merriment reached such a fever that three of the soldiers came over.

"So this is the wench who prettied the young king's night?"

Felice tossed her head, inwardly swelling with pride.

"And to whom then do you now belong?" he asked. "I saw ye not in the lottery."

"To me." These words, said with a seriousness that momentarily stopped the loud calls and whoops from among the crowd, came from behind Felice. Her heart stopped. She felt a rush in her belly and swung around. It was not Clotaire. Villem stood large and tall before her.

"By the king's own order," he said quietly, and carefully watched as Felice rearranged the look of hope that had fallen into a disappointment that had now to be hidden.

"Ai then," she said, and ducked her head so her hair would fall forward to hide the blood that returned suddenly to her face.

"So humble then, Felice?" Yorkum's voice was kind, and he winked when she looked at him. She tossed her head back and signaled him to accompany her.

"...and so this soldier you see

has taken one look at me

and now he will pay

'til the end of his days for...

heigh ho fie dee la fie dee!"

All raucously joined her in the chorus again.

"...heigh ho fie dee la fie dee!"

"Come then," Felice said loudly to Villem, so all could hear. "We have more than a song to make, haven't we?"

"Ai, Felice, we shall miss you," Yorkum called out.

"Miss me? Why, what do you mean, sirrah?"

"Do you not listen when your own master speaks?"

She looked at him questioningly.

"Most of us are to stay on, here with the new master, the lord Dubesque, if you please. Your own handsome king declared this today and ordered this celebration. But you and a few others will move out with the troop." Yorkum looked at Villem. "You, my pretty, will travel, after all, with your king."

"Ai, so be it then. Never were these happy days I spent here, except with thee, Yorkum."

Villem led Felice away. She did not protest. They turned into a wooden shed that housed the sandal-maker's shop. He pushed her roughly up against the back wall.

"You did not return last night," he accused.

Felice pouted prettily.

"And how could I? Your king kept me prisoner with him even unto this morning. I, a poor woman of the fields, what could I do? Or say?"

He pulled her to him, kissed her roughly on the mouth, and began running his hands over her breasts. Felice held her breath. She still had power within her. She raised her arms and ran her fingers lightly through Villem's thick hair. Closing her eyes, she imagined Clotaire in her arms and cooed softly.

"Come, my man Not so harshly. It is much better this way."

She took his hands and guided them to touch her already aroused nipples with the lightest of touches. She felt him swell against her, saw that she was in control this time. "I will teach you to love a woman well."

Villem only gasped as she found the opening in his trousers and caressed him.

"It is gentleness that arouses lust, yours as well, though you would not believe it. Here," she said and gently pushed him back from her. He stood, face flushed, waiting like a boy as she closed the shutters and piled a few old rags into a corner. She pulled off the enclosing tunic, smiled as he ripped at his shirt.

"I will do that for you, sire," she said. "Let it be."

She unlatched the fastenings on his over-shirt, then slipped out of her blouse as he took his shirt off. He pulled his trousers open.

"You will be freer if you take them off," she said. Her breasts stood free now. He lunged at her. She slipped aside.

"Nay, sire. Slowly now. Let me be your guide. You will never want to grab like a young boy again."

Villem finally found his tongue. "You be a fine whoring woman," he said, with real appreciation.

"A woman, ai," she said, "and a whore, if you will. But not every man do I take such pains with."

"Then you like me somewhat?" He was free now of his trousers and foot bindings as she slipped entirely out of her skirts. She only smiled in answer.

"Now lie ye down," she ordered. Villem grinned and lay down as bidden. He stretched the length of his body, which was electric now to her practiced touch. She showed him how to touch her as she had learned so well only yesterday. Even with her eyes open, she could imagine that he was Clotaire who aroused this heat that overtook her. She abandoned herself to Villem as he mounted her, no longer able to control his pulsing passion.

71

"Now hard," she said, between her teeth. "Now you can be rough. My lust is yours as well."

They moaned as they came together. Felice let herself go into the fullness of her heat as it swept wavelike over her.

"Oh, sire," she moaned. "Oh, sire."

Villem lay back down beside her, panting.

Felice recovered first. "And am I then a good teacher?"

"Ai, good," he answered. "Do you so with every man?"

"I told you no. Do you not believe me?"

"I have known whores before."

Felice did not answer. She sensed the conflict in him.

He lay beside her, very still, chewing on his lip. "Ai. I believe you then. It does not matter. You are as no other woman I have known. I would be your student."

They laughed together.

"And what does the teacher get in return for her service?"

"You shall be my woman. I will protect you, if you will, from the others' lust."

"Would you marry me then?" she asked with irony.

"Nay. Not marriage. My woman, that's all. Marriage is for property. Do you agree?"

Felice thought for a moment. "And what besides teaching must I do?"

"The fire, the cooking and the water." He rolled on his side to face her, caressed her hip and back. "But mainly, to warm my night. Like this." He pulled one leg over his side and entered her again before she could protest. He watched her face as now, in control, he brought her to another height of heat. Felice felt weak. Whore though she had been with many a man, she had never once, before yesterday and now today here with Villem, tasted the delights of her own body so fully.

"I agree," she said when he let her go.

72

"Dress then, wench, and fetch us some food."

He slapped her hard as she rose to dress. Felice laughed. Dressed, she turned and regarded Villem for the first time. He stood and began to dress.

"We make a good pair, you and me," she said. "We shall make jealous the moon herself whom the gods love."

Villem looked back with the same candor. "I have been alone long," he said. "You mean well, I know. But you do not deceive me. I know the source of such lust in you. Take heed, Felice. I am your friend if you treat me well. You cannot reach so high as you would. Take heed for yourself and for my goodwill toward thee."

Felice heard his words and knew them to be true. She noticed the tansy plants still among the others in the basket. She had to brew them before they became too wilted and lost their power.

"Ai, sire. Let me fetch the food. And then I shall make you some tea to restore your strength." She took the plants and went out. Villem followed her out and watched her go.

"A good whore ye be after all," he said quietly. Felice suddenly turned and looked at him as if she had heard. From a distance, with her tunic on and with a quiet assurance like an aura around her, she looked, in every way, like a fine lady. Then she smiled, big, bright, bawdy, and turned with a swing of her hips and disappeared behind the smoke of a fire.

Villem looked up at the darkening sky at the first small lights of the stars. Something caught his eye and he lowered his gaze. In the window he saw the young king looking down into the courtyard, following someone with his eyes.

CHAPTER 8

The sun rose behind the morning clouds, a bleary eye in the sky's forehead, looking to those who were awake to see it as though it, too, had partaken of the nightlong debauchery. From its vantage point on the horizon, the bodies of serfs and soldiers looked one and the same, strewn as they were like rag piles all over the courtyard and passages inside the castle walls. The strong ales and wines had worked to erase the very real distinctions between soldier and serf; household serf and field serf and craft serf; men and women and children. As the roosters began to crow, stretching themselves, their necks and beaks reaching for the sky above them, the rag piles became human and rolled over or rearranged themselves; a few even raised themselves up on one elbow. But when Clotaire's foot soldier blared out some notes on the long, gilded horn, distinctions reasserted themselves. Soldiers gave out orders; women drew water, relit the fires, and cooked; men checked the soldiers' gear and the horses and picked up the litter that was strewn all about. Small children withdrew to the walls where they leaned listlessly, bone weary from the night's celebration. The older children scrambled about, gathering the fowl and pigs and lambs back to their pens.

Deirdre had slept in her own bedchamber on the familiar thick straw mattress. Lothar had sneaked in to be with her sometime in the night. When she awakened, in the darkness before the roosters began to crow, she felt a wave of nausea as she experienced again the shock of that moment when her mind registered the sound of Clotaire's ax crushing the bone of her uncle's skull and, later, when Nurse was so brutally slain. But her mind clicked off awareness in a flash. She was in a peculiar state, one in which she perceived only what was within the immediate range of her senses.

She sat up and watched the sky gradually lighten. It was a

cloudy morning. A light fog clung to the trees and bushes like a huge, soft spiderweb. The distant forest was invisible behind a wall of cloud. Lothar also sat up. His eyes were swollen from crying. He sat close to Deirdre and put one thin arm around her waist. Though he felt shame for his long hours of crying, the pain was less in him now. He had taken the first step toward living again, and in his youngness, he recognized that his sister had not -- she was in some kind of cocoon-like state, between living and dying. He stroked her hair. He would have liked to help her, but he could think of no words that might have comforted her. They sat side by side that way just looking straight ahead out the window at a world that was uniformly grey. When the horn sounded, they both rose like obedient children or serfs. Lothar kissed his sister's cheek and left her room, quietly closing the door behind him. Deirdre dressed mechanically in the dress and tunic that the serving woman had laid out for her. The first hint of a sob caught in her throat. This was the first time in her life that anyone other than Nurse had selected her clothing. The daily selection had often been accompanied by a good-natured struggle between Deirdre and Nurse because Deirdre invariably wanted to wear something other than what Nurse had picked. Miffed, Nurse would return from the closets with the desired tunic or skirt or slippers. Now, Deirdre simply put on the clothes without noticing them. The rustle of the fine fabrics served to deepen the silence in the room. Dressed, she sat on the hard chair.

An old woman entered with a tray of light food: an egg, two pasties, an apple and some tea. She bowed before Deirdre, stealing a glance at the girl. Her heart flinched to see the blank, lost look on Deirdre's face.

"Ai, dear girl," she said in a scratchy voice. "Here. A bit of food."

Deirdre looked at the plates. Her body gave no response, no signal of desire. She shook her head.

"Just the tea then. You must travel today. You need

strength."

Deirdre summoned a rag of a smile and drank the tea that was raised to her lips. The old woman's hands trembled and Deirdre herself steadied the cup.

"There now," the woman said and grinned, revealing the gap her missing teeth made. She was satisfied the way countless women have been satisfied to see their charges finally take in some drink or food they have prepared out of their loving concern. The acquiescence to food always represents the first step toward healing.

When the old woman left, the words *you must travel today* penetrated Deirdre's mind. She looked carefully at every wall and piece of furniture in the room and then moved to the window and took in the outside scene as well. Off on the horizon was the forest. She could smell its musk today. A slight wind carried it in like a message of distance. Another sob rose in her throat.

Her door opened. Without turning around to see who had entered, she knew it was time to leave. Lothar came to her side and tugged on her hand. She saw that something was changed. He seemed older, more solicitous toward her. She could not know the great relief that Lothar felt in having this chance to be new, to leave behind the shame he had felt every time he saw the look of judgment in Nurse's or Gunther's eyes.

"You will have to take care of your sister," Clotaire had said to him just moments before. "I shall make you a good soldier, a leader of men. Now go to her and comfort her." Lothar had pulled himself up proud. Clotaire respected him then, boy though he still was. There was no look in the king's eyes, as in Gunther's or Nurse's, that betrayed contempt. Lothar would meet this challenge; the last vestiges of sadness left him. He would be new; he would be brave. With these new feelings he went to his sister. But he himself did not understand this sense of lightening and would always attribute it to the release of his grief through tears. His grief for Nurse was real enough, but most of the tears had been shed for himself: Nurse and Gunther had not believed in him and now would never know that, given the chance, he was as brave as any other man. Gunther had pushed him too hard too soon. Therefore he was cautious and timid. Deirdre was all he had left, and now he was determined to show his sister his capabilities. He stood straight and tall, his eyes directly on hers, not shifting off to one side as they were wont to do. He saw her wonder and a seed of admiration and he felt proud.

"You are not afraid, dear brother?" she asked softly.

"There is nothing to fear. I will myself take care of you."

Deirdre did not scoff at him as she would have in the past.

"And I too, young princess." The voice, deep and resonant and gentle, came from the doorway where Clotaire had courteously remained. But, to Deirdre, the voice was a whip that lashed across her back, bringing her out of her stupor with a cry. She whirled around.

"You! You will not touch me," she cried.

Clotaire drew up. His gentle eyes hardened.

"You forget your manners, young lady. You are in my charge. My prisoner, if you will. Therefore you have little choice but to accept my protection and good will. Though you do not believe it, I have only your best interests at heart."

"My best...!"

Lothar interrupted. "My dear sister, trust me. Come now. No more harsh words. We must leave here; it is no longer our home. The good king Clotaire has done you no harm, on my word."

At these words, the tears, long held, started from her eyes. Deirdre bit hard her lip and fought them back. In an instant, she withdrew the just emerging hope that Lothar was truly a man. Lothar saw it and flinched. She turned proudly then and walked to the door slipping past the now-cool Clotaire out into the hall. They walked the halls and stairways down to the main hall and out into the thin sunlight, their footsteps the only sound breaking the silence.

The serfs who would remain behind stood in a crowd around the now-readied troop. They stared in awe and sorrow at the two young people whose blond heads and fair skin made them shine like lights among all these other dark ones. Deirdre looked straight ahead at no one. Lothar attempted to still his beating heart and to look as proud as he had earlier felt. But it was no good; the fear that had long fluttered within his belly had returned with Deirdre's withering look. He could have sworn she had said aloud the words: *traitor! coward!* His fair face went red with the old shame. He hid it somewhat as he mounted his horse, then kept his eyes on the base of the animal's coarse mane, afraid now only to see it mirrored in the eyes of those looking at him.

Deirdre had already been mounted on Clotaire's horse and the king now swung up behind her. She pulled herself stiffly erect so that no part of her body would touch him and said in a crisp, clear voice, "I can ride alone, sirrah."

It was a public affront, both her gesture of revulsion and calling him "sirrah," a term reserved for the lower classes. Clotaire answered by spurring his horse sharply, causing Deirdre to be thrown back against him. He laughed and turned the horse abruptly, letting all see her now-reddened face as he called out, "Dubesque do your duty here before God, and farewell."

Dubesque bowed, then called back, "For the Lord, our God, and for you, my king, I shall do all in my power for the heathen folk here. Godspeed and farewell."

Clotaire walked his horse with a dignified slow pace, the other horsemen followed, then the wagons and foot soldiers and their prisoners.

Deirdre tried to keep herself forward and could not.

"You are a toad," she said between her teeth.

"Hold your tongue, child, or you will walk with the prisoners in the rear."

"Rather walk than ride with you."

Clotaire stopped his horse.

"You say you can ride?" His voice was derisive. No lady of the nobility rode alone; a lady was always carried by wagon or, in an emergency, as Deirdre was now, seated sidesaddle in front of a gentleman.

He helped her dismount.

"That is my horse," she said, pointing to her mare, which was tethered to one of the pack wagons. Clotaire raised one eyebrow. His good humor seemed to have returned. The whole troop stopped and waited while the mare was saddled. Deirdre swung up, disdaining assistance, skirts and all, and seated herself just like a man. The men all around dared say no word, only permitted themselves the tiniest curl of a lip to show their amusement.

Deirdre sat proudly, then touched the horse with the heels of her soft slippers. The mare responded instantly and the group set off once again with a groaning and creaking of wood and leather.

Deirdre rode forward, ahead even of Clotaire, as though she were riding alone. Clotaire watched her with equal parts amusement, amazement and rage. Indeed, she rode as well as any man he had ever seen; the high-strung mare was calm and alert under the touch of her small, firm hands. The black horse and the blonde girl made a pretty picture, each of them erect and proud and sure of herself.

Clotaire could see only a portion of Dierdre's profile; thus he did not know that she rode ahead to hide the stream of tears rolling down her face; that she urged her mare into a rough trot in order to disguise the sobs that shook her. She would not have him or anyone else pity her; yet without turning around to see, she felt the withdrawal of Gunther's home, of her home, of the life that had, until two mornings ago, stretched out in front of her like a pattern into the future, unknown to her, to be sure, but there, the way the figures of her aunt's unfinished tapestry had been there, ghostlike, waiting to be filled in with color. Twice the life in which she had every right to expect to find fulfillment had been abruptly cut off by violence. She grieved now for that unfulfilled life, for the ghosts of what would have been a different future, just as two mornings ago, in typical human fashion, she had longed for that future to alter.

On a sudden breeze, wisps of dust rose up from the road, surrounding her with its old promises of adventure. Deirdre could no longer bear the pain that consumed her. She dug her heels hard into her mare's sides and lifted the reins. The horse leaped forward and raced down the road toward the river. Deirdre released the controlled sobs, let them go with the waters that streamed from her eyes. *Faster, faster,* she cried within. *Faster. To the river.*

There was no purpose to her bolting, no plan, no aim. She just needed the release, needed to feel speed, needed the movement of muscles that were aching from holding tight, as though, had she relaxed, she would have been washed away by the horror of all that had happened. But she could hold it no more. It was immense, this pain and grief, as large as the sky itself, above her, grey and misty.

But Deirdre's leaving created a wave of excitement behind her. Lothar called out and kicked his own steed. The soldier,

Callon, slightly ahead of Lothar, turned and quickly grabbed the reins, pulling the horse up short and nearly unseating Lothar. Clotaire had signaled for all to hold, not to pursue. After a few moments, he himself leaped forward, giving his horse its head.

Deirdre had enough presence of mind to halt the horse before she reached the sandy riverbank. Now she walked the mare to the river's edge, dismounted and went alone out onto the large rocks in the stream. A soft wind embraced her, wrapping her tunic and skirt tightly against her body. Its voice was a music that engulfed her, and the sound of the rapids further out soothed her. She gasped in the cool, damp air. The sobs were subsiding; her body relaxed; she could not help but feel the returning of that life force within her, that energy uniquely hers, that had made it possible before to begin a life out of ashes, and that would again make that possible. Over the roar of the river and her own pulse that still beat in her ears, she had not heard Clotaire's horse pound the dirt path behind her, nor now, Clotaire walk up within a few feet of her. It was that she became aware of a presence and turned. For a moment, she saw only the rugged face of a handsome young man. She regarded him curiously, noticed the warm, dark eyes that looked at her so openly.

"It is time to mount," he said, moving closer in order to be heard above the river. She leaped back, away from him. He was suddenly Clotaire again.

She strode to her horse, mounted, and rode back to the road to await the troop that was coming slowly up the path. Though she turned her gaze aside, she could not help but catch a glimpse of her home distant up the road. It shimmered briefly in the sun like a jewel or a dream she had had. Deliberately then, she turned to look at it, to allow herself one final look. Clotaire was beside her now.

He sat stonily still on his horse, also watching the troop arrive.

"Your uncle was a cruel man, Lady Deirdre. Therefore, I killed him."

With these puzzling words, Clotaire kicked his horse and rode off ahead, this time making sure Deirdre rode behind him.

Unable to retort, Deirdre let his words simply fall away from her. Gunther had been a good man: he had spoiled her with his fatherly favors and concern. She had never seen him be cruel, though she had seen fear in the eyes of the servants. *No,* she thought, *Gunther was not cruel.* But Clotaire's words kept returning to her, distracting her attention from the scenery. They trembled at the edge of her consciousness the way a moth hovers uncertainly in the circle cast by a single candle.

The morning cleared and grew hot with the sun. They traveled with the meadows to their left, the thick forest and mountain range to their right. When the sun reached its zenith overhead, Clotaire raised his arm to signal encampment. The last hour had been quiet of talk and laughter; all were too tired to do more than put one foot in front of the other.

The troop straggled slowly into the shade of the trees at the edge of the forest. Everyone was weary and covered with the dust of the road. After the animals were unburdened and watered, Clotaire's captain, the long-legged Brut, distributed strips of salted meat and dried fruit. Felice and the other women were put in charge of collecting the drinking water from a nearby stream. It was a simple meal, but satisfying, and all were grateful that no preparations were needed. They flopped down on the thick carpet of leaves to watch the play of the clouds scudding across the deep-blue sky, or to close their eyes and listen to the soft soughing in the trees rising above them..

Deirdre walked wearily to the stream and let the water encircle her wrists, then splashed again and again handfuls over her face and neck. The sun was intense. She could feel its heat already burnt into her face, but it, and the grit of the morning's ride, were swept away in the water's coolness.

And would you have your fair skin burned then to brown?

Deirdre heard Nurse's words from a great distance within herself. She sat perfectly still waiting for the image of Nurse's face to appear. It did not and already she could not summon it. The morning and the adventure of travel, of being out in the world riding her very own horse, had combined with the long hours of silence to put a great distance between her present and this receding past. Deirdre was young enough to be caught up in the magical web that traveling weaves. There were no great cities: only the fields unbroken except by the swifts and songbirds that were everywhere; the trees with their leaves that sparkled in the sun; and the clouds with their ever-changing shapes, each of which told its own story. Her sadness had been taken away from her by each of these with its tugging beauty. She could even now let her eyes come to rest on Clotaire's back across the way without feeling deep revulsion.

Deirdre rose from the stream and looked over the camp for Lothar. She saw him and smiled. From here, he looked the picture of a young god. He leaned against a tree trunk, his eyes closed. A bit of sun and wind played through his hair, making it a bright halo of light around his face. Deirdre walked to him and stood in front of him until he felt her presence and opened his eyes.

"Forgive me, brother, for my earlier sharpness."

She saw the hurt at the back of his eyes, then the immediate and warm forgiveness.

"Oh, you were long forgiven. Sit with me." He patted the earth beside him. Deirdre sat.

We will ride all day, I have heard, and many more," he said. "How are you faring?" He noticed her burnt cheeks and the look of weariness around her eyes.

"I am better now," she said simply. "But I would sleep."

"Ai, and me too. Lie here. I will guard."

Deirdre laughed. "And how will you guard if you are sleeping?"

"Even in my dreams, I will guard over you, dear sister."

Deirdre lay back. "Look at that cloud," she said.

"The one like a horse?"

"No, the one before it. It looks like a soldier's helmet."

"Like the one Clotaire rode into battle?"

"I did not notice that."

She rose on her elbows to look, and found herself looking directly at Clotaire across the way. The blood rushed to her cheeks and she lay back down quickly. She had not noticed any helmet.

83

"Please, Lothar, do not speak of him to me. He is a murderer. I saw the act with my own eyes, though you did not. You are younger than I. You do not understand these things."

Lothar sat up. "I do understand. There are things...."

"Would my lady have water?" Felice stood in front of her former mistress and master and offered them the bowl.

Lothar brushed her aside. "No, no, not here."

"Wait," Deirdre sat up and held out her hands for the bowl. It was withheld a moment, so that Deirdre glanced upward. She was surprised at the intensity with which this woman regarded her. "What is it?" she asked with a frown.

Lothar also looked now at Felice. "Why do you look so at your mistress?" he demanded imperiously.

"Beg your pardon, young sire. I am but tired from the long walking." Felice looked downward and held out the water.

Deirdre drank, then lay back down. She gradually fell into a deep and dreamless sleep. Lothar soon joined her, and though there was no harm to be guarded from for either of them, Clotaire watched them until it was once again time to move on. And though none would have noticed, Clotaire's decision that it was time to move on coincided exactly with Deirdre's first stirring back into wakefulness.

CHAPTER 9

Felice was restless. They would remain here for perhaps two hours until the sun was lower. Everyone else rested quietly, conserving energy for the afternoon ahead. But a strange fire consumed Felice. All day she had observed Clotaire and the maiden Deirdre. She was glad for the girl's rudeness and for Clotaire's obvious anger with her. Yet Felice was too far from him to get his notice, though, for the first hour, she had been loud in her taunts and laughter at the other captive women in hopes that her voice might carry to him and cause him to turn to seek her out. Villem finally came to walk by her side, ordering her to be silent after she made one of the younger women weep from the cruelty of her tongue. Only when she held the earthen bowl in front of Clotaire in camp did he notice her. She kept her eyes modestly downward as she was supposed to do until he had drunk; then she could no longer resist and looked directly at him as he lowered the bowl. He was tired, his face lined with dust, but his eyes regarded her with a combination of warmth and kindness. He touched both of her hands as he returned the bowl to her.

"Come to me this night," he whispered.

Felice's heart leaped. Ducking her head, for all like a shy maiden, she was scarcely able to get out a husky, "Ai, my king."

"Do not forget, sweet lady."

"I will be there, sire."

She served the others, then returned to her place next to Villem. He was already asleep. Felice gathered her skirts around her legs and leaned forward resting her arms on her knees. From here, she could watch Clotaire who sat in profile to her.

His words rang inside her like the small bells the plow horses wore on holidays. She trembled with impatience at the whole, long afternoon in front of her. Villem snored. Felice looked at him and laughed softly to herself. Already he was caught; she knew that the moment he fell back to walk beside her on the road. The other men ignored the women they had taken captive to serve them. Yet here she sat beside this man as though she were his wife, and, across the way sat another man who wanted her for this night.

What pleased her most was her surety that it was the tansy plants that had secured Villem's love and that there was yet double as much of the brew as she had given Villem to be given this night to the king himself. She leaned her chin on her arms and happily watched Clotaire. He lay back on the ground looking up at the sky. Felice wished she could be beside him or that he would sit up and notice her and she sent out her wishes on a wave of desire and in a whispered prayer to Tollech. In fact, Clotaire sat up within moments and propped himself against the tree. But he looked straight across the little stream. Felice followed his gaze to where Deirdre laughed and talked with her brother. Felice felt the first sting of an emotion she had never felt before. All of Clotaire's attention was directed at this blonde young girl, scarcely a woman like herself. Felice rose and walked quickly down to the stream's edge, picking up the water bowl on the way. She glanced at Clotaire. All his attention remained on the girl. Felice watched her too, fascinated. Suddenly she knew she had to stand beside her, to have Clotaire see them together. She slung the wooden bowl up onto her hip and walked to the water's edge. When she stooped to fill the bowl, she glanced back over her shoulder. Clotaire was looking intensely out in front of him. A glance beyond and she saw how Deirdre, sitting up, was also caught in that look; in fact, was returning it. Felice stood up abruptly, spilling some of the water. She felt suddenly heavy, as though she were rising against some great weight. She pushed herself up the bank over to where they were sitting. She scarcely noticed the boy nor that he was speaking to Deirdre.

"Would my lady have water?" she asked. The blue eyes caught hers. They looked startled and pulled back in a mild fear. Felice felt her own heartbeat at this moment and thought it would consume her. It beat with an emotion that was familiar to her, the one emotion she had lived with all her years at Gunther's estate. Except now it was stronger and mixed with confusion. She sensed Clotaire behind her, knew she existed across the stream in the back of his eyes, that he was puzzled by her action.

"Why do you look so at your mistress?"

She heard the boy, then saw the challenge in his face. Just then the vial that held the tansy brew, which she wore on a band around her neck, dropped forward free of her blouse that had hidden it.

"Beg your pardon, young sire. I am but tired from the long walking."

She curtsied then and turned after Deirdre returned the bowl. Walking back to where Villem lay, she knew that in some way she had failed, but she knew neither why nor in what. Weariness overtook her. *Just as well,* she thought. She lay with her eyes closed, the shadows of the giant cottonwood's leaves playing over her closed lids; she would need to be wakeful this night. Sleep came and went the way the slight breeze moved in and out from the forest bringing with it a recurring dream she had had ever since she was a child.

Villem shook her roughly by the shoulder.

"Up, wench! Pack up the gear."

Felice sat up and pouted. But Villem would have none of it.

"Up, I say."

"I'm moving. I'm moving," she said when Villem prodded her with his foot. He laughed and Felice looked down at him. His eyes showed a pride in being her master. *Let him think what he will,* she said to herself. She washed quickly at the stream and straightened her skirts. Deirdre sat in the shade of a tree while a soldier saddled her mare. She looked fresh and alert.

"A curse on you, " Felice murmured on her way back, loud enough for Villem to hear.

"Who be you cursing now?" he asked.

"Ah, the girl, Gunther's brat," Felice answered with a sour look.

"The good Clotaire's young bride?"

"Bride!" Felice's face reddened with her sudden anger that took even herself by surprise in its virulence. "She's a babe, an unfinished piece of embroidery, a bit of handwork, no more!"

Villem looked shrewdly at Felice. "And what be it to you?" he asked seriously. "Are you thinking of her with the king? Did ye so much like the night ye spent with the him?"

Felice snapped her head back and smiled full and wide. "Ah, and be ye jealous?" she said, mimicking the peasant dialect he now fell back into.

"I think not." Villem's seriousness remained. "Ye be but a whore to him. He is of high family, like her." Villem indicated Deirdre with his chin.

Felice laughed mockingly, but even she heard the false ring in it. Villem looked away.

"Better ye pack up," he said. "It be time to go."

Felice gathered the few packs near the stream and tied them down on a small cart. She kept silent, but Villem's words burned inside. She glanced at him now and then, but he too kept to himself and would not look at her. She felt vulnerable, and was angry for having let Villem see into herself. But she also felt surprise that he had seen to her heart so quickly. She was both angry and afraid for that. Her position was not assured, though Tollech and the tansy plants had helped to establish the beginnings of that security.

When they were ready, they moved forward among the others. Felice walked by Villem's side.

"It is not as you think at all," she said, tugging at his sleeve.

The moment he looked at her, she knew she had unwittingly revealed herself again. He said nothing, only looked, but his eyes told her he knew her words were empty.

"I hate the fair wench," Felice went on, trying to cover now, even for herself, what Villem seemed to be mirroring for her. He was right. It was inconceivable that she, a whore and a serf at the lowest rung of the social scale, should, for a moment, have these feelings that Clotaire inspired in her, let alone any pretensions that he could notice her in any way except as an instrument for his use.

"It matters not, wench," Villem said. "Get ye behind with the prisoners."

Felice's eyes stung briefly, not at Villem's words, for these inspired fear only that she might have jeopardized her future, but with the sudden memory of the soft, yellow robe and of that now distant night in Clotaire's arms. Walking in the dusty heat, she thought it impossible that such a night ever occurred. The moment passed; Felice looked around her. She walked with five other women. They were her equals now. They also were involved in an internal struggle for survival. She felt the aura of their fear and uncertainty; it was one she knew she had given off six years earlier on a trip similar to this.

The troop began to move out. It was still hot and dry, though the shadows had begun to lengthen. Felice fell into a rhythm that would sustain her for hours. She felt strong and allowed herself the pleasure of thinking of the night ahead. It did not matter how long they kept walking; she would reserve her real energy for Clotaire.

The dust had already enclosed the women and guards at the rear of the line, so that Felice did not see him until his horse was almost upon her.

Neither he nor she said a word; but she knew immediately that he wanted her now. He leaned down and pulled her up behind him, then set off at a gallop, back the way they had come.

She was surrounded by the sound of their own movement as the air rushed past. Then, when Clotaire slowed the horse to a walk and turned the steed into the forest, even the sound of the horse's hooves ceased on the soft carpet of leaves and pine needles. She closed her eyes and listened to her own heartbeat; she leaned her head against Clotaire's shoulders. He pulled the horse to a halt. Together, they slipped to the ground. Felice felt a heat such as she had never known rise in her.

He was upon her, his mouth soft and moist, but urgent, all over her face, then moving down her throat over her breasts,which she had freed, unfastening the buckles on the bodice of her dress. Clotaire was also filled with his heat. They moved like dancers finding the way to the other, getting past clothing until they lay completely naked and exposed in the dappled shade of the forest. Breathless and gasping one for the other, they came quickly, in moments. Neither spoke a word, and now Clotaire, in the exhaustion of his earlier watch, fell off into sleep. Felice watched him, drinking in every detail of his face and body at her leisure. She felt a swelling in her breast similar to the sexual swelling felt earlier. It was not exactly in his chin with its deep cleft and day's dark growth of beard; nor in the contours of his nose, the way his nostrils flared slightly; nor was it in the large, dark eyes that were closed to her now; and not in the thick, long black hair, nor in his chest and shoulders, nor in his strong neck or arms that she would find the source of this sweet ache. It was in none of these things alone, nor even in all of them together; it was in something indefinable that she knew began somewhere in the depths of his eyes and reached out to embrace her. Felice had no words for what she felt. She could say she wanted him; she could convince herself that she was concerned only with her future and with security or self-pride to be wanted by one at so high a station. A woman such as Felice knew no words to express this weight in her breast. Yet it was the lightest burden she would ever carry; she knew love now for the first time and had only her eyes and body to tell him. Her tongue would never know how, her mind would never find a structure in which to put this warmth that took her over this late afternoon amid the callings of a few birds and insects, just before the evening cool began to fall.

When he awakened, a short time later, she even forgot about her tansy brew. She felt shy and simply looked away from him. They rose and dressed, still without words, mounted the horse, and rode briskly back. Overtaking the troop, Clotaire paused to let Felice slip off back among the prisoners. He smiled for the first time and looked at her with that gentleness that imprisoned her more firmly than any social distinction such as king and subject, master and serf, ever could. He left then, riding to the front.

In the evening, when they camped, he did not come to her and she did not leave Villem's fire. She had remembered her tansy brew, but simply promised herself she would offer it to him at the next opportunity. In the meantime, she had Villem to reckon with. He was deeply silent and distant. Felice fell in with his mood, it being hers as well, and made no further efforts to convince him of anything. She cooked for him, drew the water, and felt a leftover passion for him. She liked Villem: he was not cruel and he was hers. When night fell, she sought his lovemaking and gave him such pleasure that he forgot the source of his pain.

"Ai, Felice," he moaned. "Ye are such a woman."

"I am yours, sire," she whispered. And she meant it, knowing now that this thing that was between her and Clotaire was beyond her comprehension. And certainly beyond what her times would permit, other than as master and whore. She was Villem's, if he would have her, to keep and protect. Felice valued that. But something deep and vital belonged forever with Clotaire. No Villem, for all his kindness or all his manliness, would ever know that part of her. She slept then, exhausted but peaceful. Clotaire was not far away. She knew in her sleep that she would always be close to him.

CHAPTER 10

They kept to the old road that hugged the edge of the forest until late in the afternoon of the next day when Clotaire turned westward across a wide meadow into more forest beyond. There was no distinct path, and they wound their way as best they could through the trees. By dusk, they had reached the end of the forest. Miles of rolling meadowland with stands of trees here and there stretched out in front of them. They camped this second night under the shelter of the trees. The land in front seemed immense. Deirdre had never seen such a vast sky as she did here sitting at the edge of the forest looking up into the night. There was no moon; the stars were myriad and bright, but cast little light on the denseness of the land ahead. There was no castle, no sign of people living here. Further on a lower mountain range rose up.

Deirdre could not help being caught up in the excitement of the adventure of travel; she had nothing to fear, though she was, in reality, a prisoner. Clotaire, though distant and cool, treated her and Lothar with respect and dignity. Each night, he had a canopy stretched for her to protect her from the evening damp, and she knew that Clotaire himself kept a close eye on both of them, so that no harm, however inadvertent, might come to them. She could not help but be drawn in her thoughts to this man. She saw his lustfulness with the woman, Felice, and had seen him ride off that afternoon to return hours later amid the grimaces and snickers of his soldiers.

The soldiers loved him, Deirdre saw. Yet they also feared him. But their fear came not from any cruelty on his part that she could see; he was a stern master, expecting obedience, but not harsh or cruel; it came rather from an unpredictability. In some cases, he was lax, almost absentminded; in other cases, firm, so that his men could never be sure whether their actions would be approved or censured.

Deirdre wondered at her fate. Since that hour when she had

opposed Clotaire's statement that she would be his wife, she had had no indication of where they were heading nor what that might have to do with her. Lothar had somehow discovered they would travel a dozen or more days altogether, so there was some destination in mind. Beyond that, she knew nothing. She wondered now as she sat under the stars what lay ahead for her. She was determined she would never be Clotaire's wife, even if that meant she should die like her aunt and uncle. He was too closely linked in her mind with the murder of her parents. She did not know who had killed them or why. The killings were veiled in secrecy, mystery, never to be spoken of. But by one of those quirks of the human mind, seeing Clotaire kill her uncle had unloosed the bitterness within her, so that, right or wrong, in Deirdre's heart, Clotaire became the murderer of her parents as well. And she hated him all the more because she was somehow, in spite of this, attracted to him, and sensed that her own destiny was now closely linked with his. She was, after all, his prisoner. He could do with her as he willed.

Deirdre rose and walked slowly to the grass mattress that one of the women had been ordered to make for her. Every bone and muscle in her body ached from the long days of riding. She ate the dried fruit and meat that lay waiting for her and drank the warm ale. A delicious weariness took hold, and she lay back on the mattress, into its sweet odor, falling asleep immediately. The camp grew gradually quiet, and soon only crickets and the occasional call of a night bird could be heard.

When all was absolutely still, Clotaire rose and stood above the sleeping girl. Her youth and innocence showed in the way she slept. He looked long at her, at the tousled, long, golden hair, the fair skin, the slender girl's body just beginning to find its womanly form.

"You *shall* be my wife," he said softly to her. He laughed at her silence, which he pretended to be acquiescence. "Yes, and you shall like it," he added.

Then he turned and went to his own bed to sleep the few hours left before dawn. Deirdre never stirred. She slept peacefully through the night.

The next days took them through expanses of rolling meadows and lowlands, and through woods filled with songbirds. It was a gentle land, open and wide. They crossed rivers and low mountains covered with forests. Finally, on this the fourteenth day, they stopped to rest in a grove of young maple trees. The sun fell in bright patterns on the leafy ground.

At the edge of the trees, Clotaire was giving orders to Brut and another mounted soldier, who then rode off at a brisk trot in the direction they had been heading. Lothar, standing behind Clotaire, turned and came toward Deirdre across the grove. He looked healthy and tanned, no more the young, sullen boy; he seemed to be accepted among these men. Deirdre marveled at the change in him, but felt resentment at his obvious pleasure in the company of Clotaire. Just today, he had ridden all the morning by Clotaire's side. She had seen them talking and laughing together like old comrades or brothers. Lothar walked erect, his shoulders thrown back, which made his thin and boyish body appear taller and fuller. He gave Deirdre a wide smile.

"We shall arrive by dusk, milord declares."

Deirdre's anger rose in a rush. "And how are you so privy to our good uncle's murderer?" she challenged.

Lothar blushed and said nothing in his defense. "We are going to a place called Athies," he said.

Deirdre sulked.

"Dear sister, I can no longer allow you to attack our master Clotaire in my presence. You are ignorant of what has occurred."

She laughed deliberately to show her scorn. Lothar blushed again. The old discomfort and vague sense of shame rose with his blood into his eyes and he turned away to hide the quick tears that brightened them. Deirdre felt sorry immediately, but at the same time was glad to have wounded him.

94

"How dare you speak so to me?" she said. "You are but a boy, quick to get into anyone's good graces, even the murderer of your own blood! If you were a man, you would rather die than ride and talk in company with such a cur!"

Deirdre's eyes also filled, but with anger. She could not stop the flow of words that now poured out against her brother.

"You walk so proudly, think yourself quite a man. How did you come to think of yourself so? Where is your honor? You are the only descendant of our blood left to walk this green earth and you make jokes with the killer of that line! Then you dare to come to me to say I am not 'allowed' to speak ill of our 'master'! Ah. You are such a coward, Lothar. You make me feel shame."

She turned away, ashamed herself at the fierceness of her tongue and its results. The small boy, the one who had shaken next to her only two weeks before, reappeared. He touched her arm and looked at her beseechingly.

"You are right. I am a coward. I know not why nor how I became so. But not for the reasons you have named. Clotaire is not as you think. Though two years your younger, I am yet a man, and I know what I am speaking about. Clotaire indeed killed our uncle Gunther, but he is no murderer. I can say no more. Forgive me, Deirdre. I will stay no longer in your company. I do not wish to give you shame."

As he left to sit alone at the edge of the trees, Deirdre felt a heaviness at his words and wanted to retrieve all she had said against him. She despised him for his defense of Clotaire, yet he was all of her blood left to her. She felt all alone, but could not bring herself to go and ask his forgiveness. Each time she wished for that, her anger rose once again at his betrayal.

They rested only long enough to water the animals and eat. Then they started once again on their way. Lothar rode toward the front, but alone this time. He looked small and young, and, after a few hours, Deirdre moved up to ride beside him. They only looked at one another a moment, then rode silently, but with all forgiven between them.

They moved at a faster pace than in previous days -- as fast as those on foot could go, considering their weariness. Clotaire was obviously impatient now and rode far ahead of the rest, stopping on a distant rise in the land to pause and look back.

"What is this place Athies where we are going?" Deirdre finally asked, her curiosity raised beyond bearing.

Lothar looked doubtful. To speak of Athies, he would have to speak of Clotaire.

"It is the place where King Clotaire was raised," he answered guardedly.

"Is it a manor? A castle?" Deirdre's face brightened. "Or is it a town? I have heard of such places from Nurse."

"Ai. But I know not. Only that it is the place of Clotaire's young years and that he yearns to see it again."

Deirdre appreciated Lothar's circumspect manner and controlled the anger that sparked with each mention of the king's name. She decided to ask no more.

"Do you know what is meant by 'Christian'?" Lothar asked.

"Nay, what is it?"

"I am not sure. Clotaire says that is what he is. It has to do with one god."

"One god? How can that be when there are sun and moon, wind and sea, a thousand stars in the sky?"

Lothar shrugged. With his chin, he indicated Clotaire far ahead on the trail. "*He* believes in one god and calls himself this name 'Christian'."

Deirdre dismissed the idea. "What he believes is of no consequence to me."

Clotaire disappeared over the rim of a long, low hill covered with daisies amid new green shoots of barley. Deirdre saw that once again there was a definite path that cut through the barley.

The soldiers ahead had speeded their steeds and those on foot called to one another, pointing at this sign of habitation. It was not nearly dusk, yet it appeared they were nearing their goal. Halfway up the hillside, Deirdre heard from afar the calling of trumpets. She kicked her tired mare and broke into a slow gallop.

From the top of the rise, a long fertile valley spread out lazily under the bright blue of the sky. Trees and shrubs grew along a small river that ran through the land. Deirdre saw long, low houses such as she had never seen before, as well as small huts belonging to the serfs. The manor itself was distinguished not so much by its height as by its size and position on the top of the next hill. It overlooked the valley in all directions and covered almost the entire hill, spilling even over onto the sides. Fields of all sorts of grains and fruit trees and vegetables covered the valley floor. Vineyards climbed up both the side of the hill Deirdre stood upon as well as the side of the opposite hill where the manor shone golden in the sun. Deirdre had never seen such a beautiful sight. Bright banners flew over every gate and trumpets of welcome sounded again and again.

But most beautiful of all was a building that stood alone on a smaller hill across the river and facing the manor house. It was made of dark stone with a tower. At the very top, a gold cross gleamed brightly. Dierdre released the breath she had taken in and held without realizing. She felt almost giddy.

Lothar caught up with her and also looked with awe at the scene below. They followed the others on horseback down the path into the valley. Children with flowers and garlands hastily put together scrambled in packs alongside them. More rustic folk, the peons and serfs, stood back along the buildings and peered at the newcomers with open-mouthed curiosity. Further along, about two dozen or so men, dressed most oddly in a rough brown cloth robe tied with a rope, wearing no shoes, and their hair uniformly cut in tonsures, stood in a line, bowing and smiling a welcome. Deirdre used all of her best breeding to keep from staring. They were certainly a freakish lot, but kind-faced, she noted. When she

97

and Lothar had passed, they stole a look at one another and stifled their laughs. By then, they were among a large crowd. Deirdre had thought Gunther's estate to be large with many souls to be counted there, but this place Athies was many times larger. The folk, artisans and craftsmen, and courtly noblemen and their ladies stared with great interest at both Deirdre and Lothar. Here all the people were of darker complexion with dark eyes and hair, so that Deirdre and her brother shone like bright lights among them. Beyond that, the word had spread like fire that Deirdre was to be Clotaire's queen, so their interest was all the more intense.

The crowd thinned as they made their way up the stone path leading to the manor house. Trees and shrubs and small fountains made lovely resting places along the way. Only those on horseback went as far as the manor, all others stopping below where they were welcomed by the lesser folk. The women here wore odd, small caps and rouged their cheeks and painted their eyes. Deirdre noticed this and wondered if she looked plain by contrast. She tried to look straight ahead to show neither surprise nor fear as she had been schooled to behave according to her class, but it was with great difficulty that she achieved this. She would simply have liked to stop and gape at all the beauty and fineness around her.

Ahead, standing near a low gate, she saw Brut and the other soldier who had gone on before. The lead horseman stopped. Two guards leaped forward to assist Deirdre in dismounting. She was then led, with the others, through the gate into a large, rectangular patio. There was a fountain in the center with flowers growing all around it, and, above that, a large opening in the ceiling that let in the natural light. On the wall opposite was a mosaic portraying Athies in beautiful greens and blues. An old man with white hair to his shoulders sat on a graceful, gilded chair next to an equally old woman, most elegantly dressed. The old man rose and held out both his hands to Deirdre.

"Ah, my child," he said. "You are welcome here at Athies. Let this be your home."

To Deirdre's surprise, he stepped forward and gently embraced her, planting a dry kiss on first one, then the other cheek, and proceeded to do the same with Lothar.

He stood back to survey them again.

"Such beautiful children, eh?" With his hands folded in front of him like a merchant about to make a sale, he spoke to Clotaire, who stood unobtrusively off to one side. "You have chosen well, my son." Turning back to Deirdre, he beamed like a father upon her. "Such a beautiful queen you will make."

Deirdre bristled, visibly reddened. Clotaire stepped forward quickly and bowed.

"Berthaire, the lady Deirdre and young Lothar."

Deirdre stiffly bowed. It was odd to hear him voice her name.

"And Lady Balline. The children of Lord Saisson and Lady Gudrun."

Deirdre bowed again, absently, to Lady Balline, who only smiled and nodded as before. Deirdre felt the names of her parents almost as a blow. Not a soul had spoken their names aloud since as long as she could remember. *And how did Clotaire know this?* she wondered. She had no time to ponder, however. Berthaire, with great courtesy, extended his arm.

"You need rest, dear girl. Come with me, and a serving woman will take you to your quarters. There, you may order what you wish and it shall be yours. And when you are ready, we shall all dine. Again, let me welcome you. Athies is yours."

Deirdre had said nothing, only looked, barely keeping herself from gaping. Within, she entered a world of luxury and elegance such as she had never imagined possible. The walls here at Athies were covered with faded murals and mosaics executed in glass and tiles. The floors were a smooth polished stone with a weblike pattern in pinks and grays. Silken fabrics covered chairs and sofas that stood around in small groupings. Tables were of the finest woods, and polished smooth. She was led up a marble stairway that curved gracefully around up to several rooms that turned out to be, all of them, for her use: a sleeping chamber, a large bath with a hot tub awaiting her; a dressing room; a room with several musical instruments, a loom and a desk; and another room for sitting and looking out three wide windows that took up all of one small interior wall and overlooked one whole side of the valley.

After showing her her rooms, the serving woman opened one of the large trunks in the dressing room and pulled out, one after the other, gowns in every color with finely embroidered tunics and caps, such as the ladies here wore, to match. Helping Deirdre to undress from what she had worn all these three days traveling, she then bathed her and washed her long hair, using the finest-smelling scents and oils. Deirdre let herself relax into the warm water. It was good to have again a nurse to care for her needs. Scrubbed, she slipped into a lavender gown and lay down on the feather mattress, freshly made up with the finest linens. She could not sleep and waited only until the serving woman left to get up and explore again her rooms. Though noble by birth, both of her previous homes were rough by comparison.

Through the windows, she saw the way the manor was built with many wings like the petals of a flower. She walked out onto a balcony. From here, she could see below to the many small patios that were located among the walls.

The serving woman reentered and came to the balcony. "Would you kindly follow me downstairs? Berthaire would give you a tour of the grounds."

"Fix my hair then," Deirdre ordered. "And I shall need slippers for my robe."

The woman disappeared momentarily into the dressing room and returned with a looking glass, a brush, and a pair of delicately embroidered rose-colored slippers.

"Ah, your tunic," she said to herself and left to fetch a tunic in a darker shade of lavender with tiny, bright green flowers all over it. Slipping it over Deirdre's head, she then brushed her hair. Ready now, Deirdre rose and followed the maid down the cool, stone staircase.

The old man paced on the floor below. He looked up as she descended.

"Ah, you were not sleeping. I would spend some time in your company, if you please." He smiled happily and his deeply lined face lost its age in the smile. But, the aged Berthaire, even not smiling, had the eyes and the step of a much younger man. He gave Deirdre his arm, which she lightly took.

"Where is my brother?" she asked.

"Oh, I do not know." He chuckled at her appreciatively. "I only made it my business to discover where you were. No doubt he is in one of the gentlemens' suites. He is also our honored guest."

"Will I be staying here long, milord?"

"Long? Why, what do you mean?"

Deirdre stammered. "Well...I....I do not know my position. I am a prisoner after all."

"A prisoner! My dear, lovely, little lady! A prisoner indeed! You are my most gracious guest. No prisoner at all. You are free to be here as long as you wish."

"And to go, sire?" Deirdre liked Berthaire already. His was a warm and open nature.

"Ah, to go. Why would you wish to go? Do you think you might not be happy here the time you must wait? Do you lack something?"

Deirdre swallowed the tears that suddenly rose in her throat. "I...I am without my family, milord. Except for my brother."

"Yes. Oh dear, yes. I know that. It is terrible. But we shall be your family. Your betrothed wishes that you have everything you need."

They were walking along a path that followed the contours of the manor. It was lined with flowers of all kinds growing in profusion. Berthaire stopped and took Deirdre's hands in his own.

"You will see," he said. "you will like it here."

They resumed walking. In order to please the old man, Deirdre let her anger rest.

"All of this estate," Berthaire said, indicating the sprawling low walls around them, "was built many years ago by a Roman gentleman. Thus, it is in their style. They called it a villa, and so, now, do we. It was in much disrepair, but we saved a good bit of it."

"Roman? What is that?"

Berthaire smiled. "Of course. You would not know that." He frowned to himself. "I do hope your brother also stays with us and has a yen for learning. I do so love to teach young ones. To watch them grow."

"Is it possible my brother would not stay?"

Berthaire patted her hand with a fatherly concern. "Now, now. No doubt he will. I just thought he might have other wishes."

"Where would he go? How could it be he would not be with me?"

"Clotaire wishes to make him a man. To train him in the soldierly path. The boy is, I understand, most anxious to accompany our king on his campaign."

Once again, they stopped on the path. Berthaire looked closely at Deirdre; he sensed her concern. "I shall do my best to keep him here."

"Oh do, sire, I beg of you. I would not be without my dear brother."

Deirdre understood that Clotaire would be leaving and that she would not. Her fate was sure to that extent; she would not be traveling with him. Torn between her relief in that matter and her despair that Lothar might also leave, she pried Berthaire for more information.

"When will King Clotaire be leaving?" She spoke calmly, careful to disguise the contempt she felt when she spoke his name. She sensed that Berthaire loved the young king.

"Ah, I am not sure. But I think in a few days at the least. They must rest a bit."

There would surely be no wedding then.

"And where will they be going?"

"Clotaire has a long campaign ahead of him. His is not an easy task."

"What is that building there across the river?" Deirdre asked, pointing to the building with the tower. She was unable to continue the direction of conversation. She did not wish to hear Clotaire spoken well of.

"That is the church. It was begun only fifteen years ago and is yet unfinished. But it will perhaps be done in your lifetime."

"I don't know what a church is. Nor what Roman is." She smiled at him. "You did not answer my previous question."

Berthaire's eyes twinkled. "Oh there is so much to tell. So many stories. We shall have wonderful walks together." He turned to a circle of stones set to one side of the path. "Here. Let us sit here to rest a moment." He eased himself down. His back hurt him and he let out a big sigh once settled. "Oh, that is good." He patted the flat stone next to him. "Here. Sit. I can answer your questions without getting so winded."

As Deirdre sat, he continued. "It is difficult to be so old when one wishes still to do so much." He looked off across the valley. "The Romans were a people who settled here." He raised one arm and drew a large semicircle in front of him. "All over this land." He looked at her, but his eyes were distant, back in the time of his story. "Gallicia. They called this Gallicia. Before they came, a primitive people lived here. The Romans built roads and

103

bridges and aqueducts; they brought a new language, called Latin." He grew thoughtful. "And war, though we have always had that." He noticed Deirdre's interest and laughed happily. "And it was they who built this house. A Roman family lived there until two hundred years or so ago. My own blood is partly theirs, mixed too with the blood native to the land here."

"The world must be very big, sire is it not?"

"Ai, indeed, though I know not how big it is. I have never left Athies in my lifetime."

"Then you have never seen a town?"

"No, but I have seen drawings of them."

"Oh, I should like to see such a drawing."

"And so you shall."

Deirdre's excitement rose as she sensed the great wealth of stories and knowledge in Berthaire. Nurse had never been able to answer so many of her questions. Berthaire seemed to know everything. Deirdre liked him more and more.

On his part, Berthaire saw how quick and curious Deirdre was. He was amazed because he had never seen it in a woman before. Not that such a distinction mattered to him. He loved only to share learning, and now that he was old, it did not matter who might be his student so long as he had someone to watch develop. It was he who had established the monastery at the foot of the hill, in order to have access to the manuscripts that the monks copied laboriously, day after day.

He pointed again now across the river. "And that over there, is the church, where God lives."

"Which god lives there?" Deirdre's gods were the myriad gods of nature. They would never live inside a house made by men; they occupied trees and rocks, rivers and all sorts of places within the natural world.

"You ask that as the little pagan that you are!"

"Pagan? What is that?"

"There is but one God, though you think there are many. But we cannot learn everything in one day. Let us continue our tour. I want you to feel at home." He rose and indicated she should accompany him.

"Those are the cells where the monks live. See? Here comes one now." He squinted down the path. It was growing toward evening; the light was just falling. "Oh, it is Brother Fortunatus." One of the brown-robed men came toward them from below.

"Good evening, good Brother Fortunatus," Berthaire called out.

The man paused, raising his face up toward them. He was young and he smiled easily.

"My dear Berthaire. Good evening to you as well. And to the...." The monk stopped and stared. He blushed then and bowed deeply to cover his embarrassment. "...lovely young maid," he finished, bent on his bow.

Berthaire laughed. "So, even a young monk can lose his heart. Do not be ashamed, Fortunatus. You have me feel less foolish, an old man such as I."

Fortunatus laughed heartily. His eyes were a deep brown, the softest eyes Deirdre had even seen in a grown man. He looked at her with open admiration and gentleness.

"This young maid is the lady Deirdre, betrothed of Clotaire."

The smile clouded briefly.

"The Lord's blessing upon the union. So be it," Fortunatus said softly.

"So be it indeed," Berthaire chimed in. "Where are you going?"

"I bring Lady Balline her herbs in the hope that she shall spend a more pleasant night than these last."

Berthaire sighed. "Yes, it is difficult. Though I think she does not suffer as much." He waved Fortunatus by absentmindedly. "Go then on your way."

"By your leave." Fortunatus bowed again. "And by yours, young lady." He smiled at Deirdre and she found herself smiling at him in return. "You are most welcome here at Athies."

"Thanks to you," she said, and curtsied. She watched Fortunatus walk briskly up the path.

"Why does he wear that robe?" she asked.

"He is a monk." Berthaire anticipated Deirdre's next question. "A monk is a man of God who serves the Lord through service to others and good works. His robe shows that he has given up all worldly possessions. Fortunatus, like the other monks here, owns nothing."

"How does he serve others?" Deirdre tried to formulate the question. "I mean, my Nurse did the same and she, too, owned nothing. How is this man whom you call a monk different?"

Berthaire looked carefully at her. "A good question. A good question indeed! Perhaps you should learn to read."

"Ai."Deirdre laughed. "There is another question. Berthaire, with you, I have only questions. You speak of so many things I do not know of, not even the names!"

"And what question is it now?"

"Read. What is read?"

"Oh, you will discover soon enough. But let us finish our tour. There, below, are the vineyards; beyond that, the fields for pasture; and further out, those for growing. Our folk live below in those long buildings along the river. What do you think?"

"Oh, it is all very beautiful. But also confusing. It is large like a town. I thought perhaps Athies was a town when I first saw it."

"The shops, the leather-smith, the iron monger, all of those are below, so that we have peace above in our home."

"There is no moat, no walls."

106

Berthaire shrugged. "It has never been necessary. And now we have our Lord to protect us from harm. We do not need walls." He took her arm. "Now let us go back."

They walked slowly, as Berthaire was having difficulty with both his back and breathing. Deirdre took in everything within view. She admired the wide vistas and was pleased that there were no walls to hold her in.

Berthaire led her through a wide gate into a central courtyard. The ground here was covered with large, flat grey stones. Moss grew thick between. And, in the center, as in each of the smaller courts and patios, there was a fountain with its own music made by the falling water. Benches along the walls accommodated perhaps a dozen lords and ladies who visited with one another here. They stood and curtsied or bowed courteously as Deirdre and Berthaire passed through into the large dining hall. The room was high, and the late light streamed in from small windows set in the upper part of the walls. In the center of the room stood a long, table along whose edges were placed benches and at either end of which was placed a plush armchair. Servants in green and gold livery stood about in attendance. Lothar, dressed in a fine robe, smiled at Deirdre from the far end of the room where he stood with Clotaire, Brut, and several other of Clotaire's high officers. Berthaire directed Deirdre to a cushion to his right and called to Clotaire to take the one to his left, thus putting the king and Deirdre face to face with one another. Those in the outer court drifted in and took their places as Berthaire directed. Lothar was seated at the far end of the table. They waited a moment and then a door at the far end of the hall opened and Lady Balline, leaning on the arms of two serving men, entered and took her place at the opposite end next to Lothar. As was her habit, she smiled continuously and nodded her head up and down.

Berthaire greeted her, then put his two hands together in front of his heart and bowed his head. The others did the same. Deirdre and Lothar exchanged a look and followed suit.

107

"We ask thy blessing, oh Lord, for these thy gifts. Amen."

The "amen" passed around the table, spoken in various tones by all those present. The servants then began to serve, and the weary travelers enjoyed something more than dried fruit and meat. It was apparently not the custom of these folk to eat silently as it had been in Gunther's home, each one there engrossed in the simple matter of eating; so the meal progressed slowly as Berthaire and the others conversed. Clotaire was silent and paid all his attention to Berthaire. Deirdre kept her eyes on her plate and was grateful that Clotaire made no attempt to speak to her. Berthaire chattered on and on about this and that and did not notice how cool the space was that separated the king and his "betrothed."

The meal was over after several hours; everyone spoke a soft good-night and retired. Deirdre thanked Berthaire for the lovely walk and curtsied a good night to him. She made no gesture toward Clotaire who stood beside Berthaire. At this, the quick old man did take notice and when Deirdre turned away, he took Clotaire by the arm. But Clotaire would not be questioned.

"I shall leave at dawn tomorrow. Teach her, milord, as only you can. Teach her to read and write. She is a girl yet. When she is grown, I shall return to claim her as my wife. I leave her in your charge."

"You are leaving so soon?" Berthaire momentarily forgot his question in his upset. "You need at least a few days rest, Clotaire. I pray that you stay."

"It is better I go. The boy Lothar will come with me. I shall be his teacher. Good night, Berthaire." Clotaire turned and left the question to remain a puzzle in the old man's eyes.

"Oh," Berthaire sighed to himself. "There is some trouble here, methinks."

Morning brought the sound of trumpets and the jingling of the horses' gear. Clotaire and his men and the women prisoners, all of them, now in wagons rather than on foot, had gathered by the main door of the manor. Berthaire, in a robe as white as his hair, sat in his gilded chair to give the blessing and farewell. Deirdre woke with the noise and stood in the fresh morning breeze on her balcony to watch the scene below. Something in her body returned to an earlier scene and she felt a shiver as her eyes were irresistibly drawn to the black horse and the dark-haired man astride it. She could not hear the words they spoke, but saw Clotaire bow to acknowledge Berthaire, then raise his banner high above him. As he did so, he also raised his eyes to look directly at Deirdre. He grinned, wide, and something wild in him broke free in his voice as he gave the order to proceed. He waved his banner once at her, then turned, astride his horse, and galloped away, never looking back. Deirdre felt violated in some way, as though, in that look, he had truly claimed her as his own. And by not turning away, she felt she had somehow acknowledged him in spite of herself. She stamped her foot in anger.

The band was moving away at a slower pace now. The path down the hill and along the river was lined with many people. They were in a festive mood and waved the troop along. Passing below her balcony clattered one of the wagons carrying three of the women. Deirdre looked down at it. Two of the women looked distraught and haggard, and Deirdre's pity went out to them for the hard journey ahead, and for the uncertainty of their lives. The third was the green-eyed Felice who had offered Deirdre water that first day on the way. She was looking directly at Dierdre, a full smile of either derision or triumph distorting her otherwise beautiful face. Deirdre frowned and turned away, dismissing the woman from her mind. A sudden breeze caught the small cap she was wearing, and before Deirdre could capture it back, it fell, spinning down in the breeze toward the ground. Deirdre watched it fall, a small pretty yellow cap that matched the yellow nightgown and robe she was wearing. Below, Felice also watched as it settled among some white roses that lined the path.

PART 2

CHAPTER 11

"I will not stay here longer!" Felice's green eyes snapped at Villem.

"I am just returned," he said. "You have not greeted me."

Realizing her error, Felice threw her arms around his waist and laughed. But impatience quickly reasserted itself.

"Ai, Villem, but I am crazy with sitting all the days these many seasons only waiting, waiting. You were to return in weeks. Two winters have passed already! What do you think? That I enjoy it? You are gone, out on adventures, traveling, while I but sit and wait with these other women and old men!" In disgust, she waved her arm in a wide arc to indicate the others in the encampment.

"Then ye missed me, eh wench?" Villem was not laughing. Thin, tight lines had worked their way into the skin around his eyes and mouth, and a deeper line gave him a permanent frown.

"Ah, surely sire. I have missed you foremost, and all the travel and excitement as well." She smiled pleasingly.

Felice sensed the question Villem was not asking. She took a deep breath. She too would not ask what, for her, was the most important question. Villem and a dozen other men had ridden in just now. Clotaire was not with with them.

"I am tired," Villem said.

"Ai, sire. I shall fix you a fresh bed. You will sleep while I fetch some restoring herbs and prepare some stew."

He was quietly asleep before she returned with the soft boughs to make up his bed. Felice sat on a stone and watched his face. In the two years she had waited here, she had scarcely thought about him and had forgotten how an uneasiness had grown between them during the time she had travelled with him and Clotaire's band all over the countryside. Felice saw the tightness in his face. She knew he had not once lain with another woman since he had taken her to be his. She liked that, even now. It made her feel the strength of her powers. But she sensed his passion for her was unnatural. All these more than five years since they had left Gunther's land, it had lasted and did not seem to wane; rather, it grew larger, like something within him that consumed him. It was this love for Felice, wanting her for himself alone, set against Villem's deep loyalty and love for Clotaire that engendered a bitter conflict in Villem's heart. He was a man slow to anger, slower to violence. But he ached from his inability to act against either one or the other. He was caught between two loves, each of a different order. Thus he had grown more inward and distant from both Felice and his master. Clotaire half suspected its root, but Felice knew it well. She clung to Villem, using his love as an anchor to Clotaire.

As she watched him now, she smiled. Perhaps it would be all right again, she thought to herself. Indeed, she was fond of him. He was a good man, generous to her. His very existence assured her social protection. He made few demands on her, other than bed and board, and though they both were aware that he knew her secret heart, he said nothing and asked no questions. But she had often suspected that he deeply resented those nights in the past when she slipped out of their bed to be with Clotaire.

At first, she had been open about these meetings, tossing off at him that she was not his wife, that she was a whore, and the king their master to whom they owed obedience. Villem never disputed her arguments and only became more deeply silent, and it was this that gave rise to the unease. Truly, it should not have bothered him; he was a freed serf, not a nobleman; she was his only by his goodwill, and he could cast her off at any time; Clotaire did not make Villem small by either word or look. His use of Felice was a simple matter. These had always been her arguments, but once he had looked at her and simply said, "What you say is not true. You are his, not mine."

111

Villem himself could not understand what power this was that Felice had over him. He had tried, in these two years without her presence, to turn his thoughts to other things, and he had been successful, had felt lighthearted as he had in former days before lying with her. But in these last few days, as he rode closer and closer to where she was, the old burning returned. He kept his heart dark, even to himself, because something hard was growing in him against Clotaire.

Felice prepared his bed anyway and made a stew of rabbit with wild onions and parsley. Villem slept hours, but when he woke, he was still tired. They ate in silence, watching the fire until it was a slight glow in the night that, like a curtain, dropped around them. Then he took her to his bed, only to lie quietly beside her. Felice was amazed at her own cold body, which she could not arouse toward him. Something in her too was tight, waiting now for the other, listening for his voice.

"I am now captain," Villem said.

"Ah," Felice breathed. Perhaps now he would speak of Clotaire.

"Lord Brut was killed with two other officers. It has been a hard campaign. I do not know why Cl...why the king went so far into foreign lands where even the tongue is different."

Felice clenched when Villem started to say Clotaire's name aloud. But when he stopped and spoke, with distance, of Clotaire as "the king", as though the name could no longer be said between them, she felt a new apprehension. She bit her lip. It would be hard to make things right between them now, to be natural.

"You are tired, Villem. Rest now."

Villem was silent again. But it was not a silence of quietude. Lying beside him, she felt the tension in his body.

"He will come in some more days."

Felice touched Villem's hand. A sadness that had hidden

itself away from her for a long time now released and filled every cell of her body. She felt a weight throughout, as though a force pinned her to the ground. She could not have explained it, but she suddenly understood how she and Villem shared this weight; he, because of her; she, because of Clotaire. It was this understanding, engendered by his simple statement, more telling than any question he could have asked, that unbottled the sadness, so that it flowed like a river through her. He too was this sad. Her heart filled with pity for both him and herself.

She lay quietly beside him, until she could stem the tide of emotion that made her want to weep. She only held his hand. His eyes were closed. Finally, she turned to him.

"Ai, Villem, be not sad. What he is to me is not something I can understand. But you, I understand. I am yours, because we are one and the same."

Villem sat up, his whole body a clenched fist.

"Ye be a whore! A slut! Ye are nothing to me! Nothing!"

He slapped her hard. Felice recoiled from the blow, the tears starting to her eyes. She could not see him in the darkness, but he was also crying. She could tell it in his voice.

"Why do ye not fight me, eh?" He slapped her again. "Beware, wench! Beware!"

With these words, he leaped up and strode off into the woods. Felice let out the long held-back tears in great sobs. In doing so, she recalled the one other time she had cried -- that first meeting with Clotaire -- and the sobs were renewed in vigor, nearly choking her. Finally, they subsided. She was lightened somewhat of the weight. And now anger gradually replaced it entirely. Her face stung where Villem had hit her. And there was a tenderness on her arm where his second blow fell when she raised her arm to fend him off. She got up, straightened herself, pushed her hair behind her ears, and, picking up her basket, walked purposefully out into the forest.

There was no moon, but Felice followed the narrow path

without the slightest hesitation. Many were the nights she had walked in these woods on the barely visible paths made by deer and other animals. She was akin to them when outside of human company: silent, swift, sure of herself, and alert to the smallest sound or movement. She gathered her skirts up in a bunch in front of her to keep them from snagging on the shrubs.

She went to her favorite spot, a place of power for her. It was a small clearing in the middle of the trees. The land sloped here, and a tiny trickle of water, an underground spring, broke through the surface and made its way down the slope to a very green place below where it formed into a soggy pool.

Felice lined herself up with the pool and the evening star. She did not know what her own intentions were. She simply sat and waited.

She had come to this spot a number of times during these two years of waiting. At first she had come secretly, fearful the others would discover her worship of the other gods, then openly without fear when she saw how all of them, with Clotaire's influence and teaching gone, fell away from the belief in one God. Felice could not truly believe that all of nature did not seethe with many gods, each with varying powers. When Clotaire spoke to her of Christ and goodness and love, she could accept all of it, even suspected that it was this faith of his that engendered his kindness to her, but when he talked of a single God, Felice, like so many others, listened dumbly, without, for a moment, believing it. Once she had dared argue with him. Clotaire was not terribly distressed and even showed signs of his own doubts. His only insistence was that each of his folk, from the highest to the lowest, be baptized, believer or not. *Christ will work in his own way through you,* he always said. *Your gods will be overcome.*

Such a change had not yet come to Felice, and her own resistance was such that, unknown to Clotaire, she had avoided baptism. She shifted her weight and closed her eyes. She was here to ask Tollech's assistance in her love for Clotaire. Long ago,

114

within the first year of traveling throughout the lands with Clotaire, she had given up the notion that Clotaire would grow to love her, to need her as his own; rather she had come to ask humbly that Clotaire only continue to want her and to ask for her. She had long ago given him the tansy brew, and she believed that its influence kept his desire for her alive. But, until this evening, she had never admitted all of this consciously. The admission that Clotaire could never love her, indeed, that he no doubt did not recognize her heart's existence, let alone its wishes, filled her with this weight, which was a resignation that came close to despair.

"Ah, Tollech, Tollech, all powerful. Bring me your power. But a sliver of your light will show me the way to his heart."

She began the words under her breath, a slow, monotonous chant to which she began to rock, concentrating her whole being into the sounds and rhythms. She was so distraught and engrossed that she did not hear Villem's approach. He waited behind her as she slowly swayed with her chant until she sensed his presence and stopped dead still. She would not turn. She knew it was he and she sensed also his burning for her. He stood directly behind her now and put his hands in her hair which he began to caress roughly. She touched his hands lightly -- her signal that he should be more gentle. He had forgotten in his hunger for her, but he took his schooling well. Kneeling behind her, he ran his fingers down her neck and over her shoulders. Felice closed her eyes and leaned back against him.

"Oh," she moaned when he lightly touched her breasts. A tear rolled down her cheek. Her mind would not let go of its images and kept insisting that this could be the touch of the other. Villem was tender, more than he had ever been before. He pushed her down against the earth and rolled on top of her.

"Ai, Felice, ye are such a woman," he said softly. It was not Clotaire. Villem's words were awkward, pulled from the deep silence into which the peasant is born, a world in which words are rough tools, where the heart must remain mute, only to be given expression in yearning.

"Villem, truly we are friends. Truly." Felice was crying, the tears flowing out of her in silence, so that Villem knew only when he touched her face.

His passion grew strong, then spent itself quickly before she could rid herself of her pain. She lay beneath him, weeping softly.

"Ye will not see him again. Not alone. Ye are my woman now," he declared to Felice's utter amazement. She sat up, pushing him off, and laughed gaily.

"Would you make me your woman? Would you?"

Villem grew awkward and could not answer.

She spoke without laughter. "Would you, Villem?"

"Ai, if ye do not lie with him again. I would tell him myself."

"And do you think he cares?" she asked mockingly.

"I do not know." Villem paused. His nature was not a deceitful one, but he hesitated to share his heart with her, for he had never done so with anyone before. "He whores with many a woman," Villem said with caution.

Felice remained still. She felt as though he had pressed a blade between her breasts.

"But...." Villem paused.

She knew he was watching her face carefully in the dim light that came from the stars. She pouted prettily for him.

"But he has them once perhaps and is done with them. Ye...ye are different, methinks."

Though it was the middle of the night, in the middle of the dark forest, Felice filled with light as though it were midday in summer. She could scarcely sit still. She wanted to run like a young colt its first spring after the long winter. She wanted to laugh, to throw her head back and scream for the sheer delight of it. Her sadness broke, rising like bubbles of air out of deep water.

She chose to laugh in such a way as to hide her joy.

"Oh," she laughed, ducking her head so he could not read her eyes. "Oh, Villem, do you think so? You are crazy, methinks. A mad fool!"

Some of his former edge returned. "What do ye mean? Why do ye laugh like that?"

"You yourself told me long ago how he was a king, I, a whore. You do not believe he thinks me different now."

"He is a man who holds only to his own god -- this Christian god whom he makes us all fight for and kneel to. He breaks all other rules, all traditions, respects no custom. Why should he not prefer you to others?"

"And what of his pretty little maid, the girl, Deirdre?"

"Ah, that's different," Villem said.

"Different, indeed!"

"She is his betrothed. He will marry her."

She dug her nails into her hands.

"Ai. Because she is born of noble parents," she said with barely disguised bitterness.

"Do ye accept me, then?"

Villem stood straight and proud and Felice saw how much this asking her to be his woman cost him.

"I do not understand you," she said, begging for time.

"What I have already said. That you do not see him anymore."

"Ai, that." She would have liked to ask why, to have him admit to jealousy, so she could believe Clotaire loved her. To say aloud that she would not see Clotaire again, even if she lied, would bode ill for her. She hesitated a moment longer.

"All right. I will."

Villem grinned. "Good. It is done then. You will see, Felice, you will not regret this."

Felice shivered. He had not noticed that this was only an apparent acquiescence to his proposal, had not caught the true meaning of the words *I will*.

Perhaps a week passed quietly between them. Felice was content to wait. She clung to Villem's assertion that she was different for Clotaire, talking herself into, at least, his possible love. And Villem was happier and gayer, as he had been formerly. He lost the tension around his eyes and laughed with them as well as with his mouth.

Early one morning, Felice awakened suddenly as though from a dream or a sound that had broken her sleep. Villem lay still beside her. No one was yet stirring in the camp. Yet something in her insisted. She got up and in her bare feet walked to the edge of the encampment. Every sense, every fiber of her being was alert. A mist hung over the camp and forest. There was not yet light enough to see more than the darker lumps of human bodies and their belongings in the darkness. There was nothing. Yet again the hair on her arms prickled. She looked out into the trees. There in the deeper shadows she saw something. Her heart pounding, she walked slowly toward it. She was ready to turn and run, if need be, to scream. It was large and stood perfectly still. Then there was a movement, and she understood, rather than saw, that it was a horse and rider. Now truly her heart began to pound. She walked at the same, slow pace until she stood before him. He slid quietly down the horse's side and in one fluid gesture held her in his arms.

"Ah, lady. the mornings were always kind to you. You are the sun itself."

She could scarcely breathe, so when he pressed his mouth against hers, she had to push him away in order to catch her breath.

"Ai, my king" she gasped. "You are here. Oh, you are here."

Clotaire smiled and looked at her with his head to one side as though her words were most peculiar. Felice blushed, realizing she had let him see, for the first time, the tenderness of her feelings. Always before, she had handled him gaily or been silent, merely acquiescing to his slightest wish.

"Come with me," he laughed. "I have missed you sorely."

He started toward the encampment. Felice pulled on his hand that held hers.

"No, this way, " she said, and she took the lead. It was growing lighter; the woods filled with the early dawn light. Felice led Clotaire to a special place, one in which she had often lain alone, dreaming of the time she would hold him in her arms again. It was a small grass enclosure, invisible from the path, surrounded by mulberry trees and shrubs. No doubt it had once been a deer's nest, though there was no sign it had been used by animals recently.

One had to crawl in to enter, and Felice smiled apologetically as she crouched and then disappeared. But Clotaire only laughed at her and also crouched. Inside, it was a bower of green light with a circle of sky, like a window, overhead.

"You make me crawl, I see," Clotaire began as though their old friendship had never been interrupted. Felice hid her anxiety. Clotaire would talk, she saw. She would be gone hours and with no excuse. She shook off her discomfort. Looking at Clotaire, it did not matter.

"Where have you been?" she asked. "What places? What people have you seen?"

Clotaire shrugged. "So many that I have forgotten. We shall return now. Back home. To Soissons. I am weary."

Felice looked at him sharply, but he made no mention of Deirdre or Athies.

"Are there now many more of your religion, milord?"

Clotaire looked at her seriously. "Perhaps. It is hard to change." His mood shifted and he became playful again. "Would that you could change."

"How do you mean?" A line of a frown crossed her brow.

"You are still pagan. Still with your old and many gods."

"Ah." She was relieved that it was only a question of gods again. "One day perhaps you will speak to me of this god of yours. Then I may understand and change."

He looked at her sternly. "Need I convince you?"

Felice felt again, as she had before, the immense distance between them. In her class, the woman was equal to a man in all ways but physical strength and working duties. She saw that Clotaire expected simply that she do, even in such a matter as this, whatever he wished her to do. She was too strong to go along with his wishes without understanding, and too honest to pretend that she did go along.

"My gods are with me," she said simply. "I cannot cast them off."

"It is not important. You are but a woman. Come. Let us think of other things."

He looked at her, smiling. She felt her thighs suddenly blossom with heat. Her eyes were half closed, her lips softened for the kiss she had so long awaited. She unfastened her blouse and under-blouse; moaned to see his now-bare chest, his tight, smooth muscles, his aroused sex. She was a river of heat and passion and he huskily laughed to see her lust, to feel his own rise to meet hers. Clotaire did not think about Felice when away from her; but in her presence, he experienced her as mystery; as a power he could not explain that made him return to her again and again, ignoring the inner voice that warned him to beware. He was not entirely unaware of Villem's feelings toward Felice, as both she and Villem believed, and had seen the smoldering anger in Villem's eyes on several occasions. Often he had vowed never to lie with her again. Then she would come to his tent or room wherever they might be or come near enough so that her musky odor reached him, and he gave in again. She was like no other woman he had known. With her, not only was his lust satisfied, but some deeper, shadowy thing was fulfilled that made him know his maleness to its depths. With her, he was fully man because she was so fully woman. He sensed Felice as a natural aristocrat in spite of her low birth and called her 'lady' out of that awareness, rather than out of the playfulness she always suspected.

They clung together, tossed back and forth on the silken grasses, could not get enough of each other, kissing again and again, drinking of their passion it its fullest.

"Clotaire, Clotaire," Felice cried out softly. "Enter me, please." He had been teasing her, holding back until she would beg for him, her body tense with longing. He entered her now and began the slow rhythm. Her body reached a peak of ecstasy only to be aroused to a higher peak again and again, until Clotaire rose above her, his head thrown back, a deep cry of pleasure escaping his throat.

He leaned over her then, caressed and held her. Felice wept, in spite of all her efforts not to. She was grateful and humbled by this man's tenderness, but more than that, she felt, for the first time, a deep regret for this betrayal of Villem. But Clotaire made her forget her tears, kissing them away and loving her so sweetly she had no thought in her head but that she wanted him no matter what might come as consequence.

Their passion spent, they lay on their backs looking up at the pale blue sky. Clotaire was quiet and serious.

"We shall rest here some days," he finally said. "It has been a long journey. We are all tired."

"Not I, sire," Felice said with a grimace. "It has been a long waiting for me."

Clotaire laughed. "No doubt it was long. You should have travelled with us." He grew quiet again. She had never seen him so serious. "Lord Brut was killed, may the Lord have mercy on him."

Felice saw the pain in his eyes, felt his sorrow.

"He was long with me, for years, like a father, lately as a brother, a friend. A good man." A look of bitterness crossed his face.

Felice lay quietly looking at him, waiting. She was amazed he was sharing this much of his world and feelings. Always their talking had revolved around themselves and their love making, never about his inner concerns.

"He was my confessor as well, my whole court." He laughed bitterly. "It would take ten Lothars to make just one of him!"

"You mean the Lady Deirdre's brother?" she asked. She watched his face carefully, hoping to be able to read his reaction to hearing Deirdre's name. She was disappointed.

"Ai. Exactly. The son of Lord Saisson, my dear father's kin and friend. Yet I cannot harm him, though he is not more to me now than" -- he flicked a ladybug off the leaf of a mulberry bush -- "that, the small coward."

Felice felt Clotaire's rage. "I do not understand, milord," she ventured when he was silent. Her heart beat with her audacity to discuss his peer with him.

"It was he who killed Lord Brut."

"And is yet alive?" she could not help saying.

"Ah, he did not lay the blow. But he was not there behind the good Brut as he was supposed to be -- and as Brut believed him to be, therefore rushing in only to be felled by three men." He sighed. "But I am Lothar's protector by the deepest of vows." Clotaire sat up. "Ah, I am tired now. Tired of all these campaigns where people become Christian only until I leave them." Felice blushed. "Then fall back into their pagan ways giving only lip service to the one God." He lay back down again. "As I do," he muttered. "Ai, even myself sometimes." He laughed again.

The sun was rising higher. Villem would be up. Felice straightened her dress and hair.

"Milord, I must beg your leave."

Clotaire looked surprised. She had never before taken the liberty of asking to leave.

"Forgive me, milord. I do not wish to part company, but I must go. I have much work to do."

She dared not speak of Villem, out of fear that Clotaire would discover Villem's grudge and either respect it, no longer desiring her, or hold Villem to task for his attitude. She could not predict Clotaire's reaction.

"Ai, go then."

"Beg pardon, milord."

She bowed and crawled out of the enclosure. Before returning to the camp, she hurriedly gathered bunches of herbs, armfuls of them, as an excuse.

Villem was lying in bed. "Breakfast, woman! Where have you been?"

Felice grinned in reply. "Be still or you'll eat nothing, sire."

Villem was in a jovial mood. After this week of rest, his face was more relaxed. He looked years younger.

"Ai, ye'll give me breakfast or something else."

Felice looked around. Others were eating round their fires. She put her hands on her hips and challenged him.

"Breakfast or nothing." But she grinned. Her exuberance was real, even her fondness for Villem, which was, at the moment, an overflow from her joy.

Villem looked at her invitingly. Felice threw up her hands in mock disgust.

"Out with you then. I will come in a minute."

Villem went off to their spot away from the camp, and Felice took the bowl to gather water to wash. She got halfway to the stream when a trumpet sounded not far off. In moments, Clotaire appeared leading the rest of his small troop into the

123

encampment. They stopped in a circle of excitement. Felice could not take her eyes off of Clotaire, who, seeing her, winked and grinned conspiratorially. Just then, Villem appeared at the edge of the forest. He looked at Clotaire in time to catch the wink, then at Felice who turned to regard him, having caught his arrival in her peripheral vision. His face showed something she had never seen in him before, and she knew they would not be making love this morning.

Clotaire must have followed her look, because now he called out in a loud voice.

"Brother Villem! Come to welcome us. We would have your company."

Villem bowed stiffly, then walked to his king's side. Clotaire dismounted.

"Is it all right with you, my captain?"

"Ai, Clotaire," Villem said. "Ai, it is all right, methinks."

Clotaire slapped him hard on the back and began to give orders for unloading the animals and arranging for food. In the bustle, Villem's quiet, stolid presence was unnoticed by all, except Felice. She watched him until he turned to look for her. She bit her lip. His look was accusatory, and she knew that somehow he understood her absence this morning.

"Tollech, be damned, " she muttered under her breath.

CHAPTER 12

"The light is falling. You must stop."

Deirdre looked up from the page she was laboring over. "Is the day so soon over?" she asked.

Berthaire was pleased. "You have worked since midday."

Deirdre looked critically at the delicate lettering and designs. She held the page up so that the light from the window fell full upon it.

"Look," she said, "it is not bad, methinks."

Berthaire looked at the work carefully. "It is exquisite. Indeed, you have a talent for it."

"'Twas I who taught her. She's a dolt really."

Neither Berthaire nor Deirdre had heard Fortunatus enter. But neither was surprised when he voiced his comment jovially.

"No doubt, my son," Berthaire said dryly. "But you must admit the lady has a little talent."

"None whatsoever. Nor brains either. It's impossible, I am told."

Deirdre could not help but laugh.

"Impossible?" Berthaire asked, incredulous.

"Ai," Fortunatus answered. "The lady Deirdre is a freak of nature. Brainless, but she learns. Without talent, yet she can draw if given infinite patience and direction by someone as brilliant and capable as I."

"Ah, you mean because she is a woman."

"Ai, 'tis true." Fortunatus' eyes were filled with mirth. Deirdre sniffed and pretended indignation.

Berthaire, usually the serious teacher, joined in with the prevailing mood. "I have often pondered this very question. How, the lady Deirdre, being a female and therefore brainless as you say -- which is quite true, my boy, quite true, I have many years behind me to have experienced its veracity -- how then does she learn?"

"Gentlemen. Indeed the day's light has failed. You both reflect its passing by the darkness in your minds. Moths chasing their own shadows into the candles! Off with you! I must wash my pens."

"Will you walk with me then?" Fortunatus asked.

"Walk with you? For what purpose if my brains be not present?"

"Even if I help you wash your pens?"

Deirdre was indignant. "Particularly if you help me wash my pens. I will not be treated differently. The pens are my tools, and my good teacher Berthaire has taught me well how to care for my tools."

Fortunatus looked disappointed.

"But I shall gladly walk with you, dear Fortunatus. You need not look so sad. I but wanted a small revenge."

"And well you got it. My day without our walk would be sad indeed."

"I shall leave you two. Fortunatus, will you join us again for our evening meal?" Berthaire asked.

"Ai, it is a great pleasure, sire, though my brothers frown on it. They feel I am not going to make a good monk if I spend so much time in conversations and pleasure."

"Well then, perhaps you will not," Berthaire said quite bluntly. "That would be a pity in some ways, yet in others, not. Your life must become what it will. Follow your inclinations, my boy."

Fortunatus, however, was truly distressed. He spoke of it again as he and Deirdre walked along the river in the long shadows of the afternoon.

"I spend many hours in prayer, dear sister. It is not that I do not love the Lord." Fortunatus hesitated. He was unsure of what

126

he was feeling. "But my brothers say I have too much exuberance. They frown on my friendship with you."

Deirdre stopped and looked at him. "I'm surprised that your brothers frown on friendship when it is a rare occurrence and a beautiful gift. I cannot believe our Lord would not bless our friendship, Fortunatus."

"Ah, Deirdre, it is not the friendship, but the need for it, they say."

"Look." Deirdre pointed to the far hill. "Is it not just a bit greener than yesterday?"

Fortunatus smiled in reply.

"I believe it will all burst out any moment. I would love to be here at just the moment a single leaf opens. If only it happened that way."

"Dear sister, you are not interested in my dilemma."

Deirdre touched his sleeve. "Do you not have need for the spring? Is it wrong to have need for friendship? We are chaste, Fortunatus. We took that vow a long time ago, when first I came here. Do you not remember? You took my hands and told me you would be brother to me in place of my absent brother. Berthaire was present, as was Brother Amien, your superior. And that has not changed for me, not even in thought. That has been the only danger in our friendship -- ever! Since it is not present, why do your brother monks worry and bother you about it? Besides, now I am Christian like you. I would not harm you in any way, least of all endanger your heart's purity."

Fortunatus frowned. "It is not that. You see, as a monk, I am expected to be single, whole unto myself. I love you dearly, Deirdre, though it be a chaste love. I would not be without you."

"Oh, nor I without you, dear brother. What is wrong with that? You do not covet me, do you?" Deirdre asked the question with such surprise that Fortunatus turned away.

"No, I do not covet you. You are not understanding me."

127

Deirdre sat on a rock and indicated one across from her. "Now. I shall listen most carefully. What *is* it that is concerning you?"

"I am in doubt, that is the problem. I am much drawn to a life of pleasure -- good food, music, art, study and song. I enjoy people and their company. That is my nature. I come from a region farther south where the people are boisterous, where dance and gaiety are a part of every day, not reserved for special occasions as here in the north. But I have turned my passion toward God, toward finding my own wholeness -- at least I thought I had -- yet I cannot simply be the austere person my brothers seem to want me to be."

Deirdre laughed. "Yes, your exuberance even shows in your hair, in its springy curls that will not stay in place." Then, more seriously, she said, "'Tis true, Fortunatus, you love this world and you love its beautiful things. But I cannot see that that is wrong. Why can't you still be a renunciant and devote your life to God? It is not only possible, methinks, but easier to laugh and be gay when one gives oneself to God."

Fortunatus grinned. "Ah, little sister, how beautiful you are. How clear."

"Even though brainless."

"Because brainless! Mine gets filled with the dross of my many arguments. You penetrate to the heart of the problem."

"Ah, that is better."

Fortunatus got up. "Of course. I live among these men who seldom laugh. All day is spent in renouncing. They are so afraid of sin, they sin against joy. I cannot be that way."

"There. Now my dear Fortunatus is back without that silly frown." Deirdre took his arm and they resumed their walk.

"How many springs will I have been here?" she asked.

"It seems as though this is but the very first."

"It is five, methinks. Or six."

128

"Why?"

"I only wonder at time's passing and at how much time one needs to learn all that Berthaire has to teach."

"You have learned much."

"Ai, but it is only a beginning. Is it possible, do you think, to understand some things?"

"Like what?" he asked. He was not now in a serious mood, having been relieved of his own burden, and wished only to walk and look at these first signs of spring's imminence.

"Oh, it is hard to put into words," she said. "There is the old history of the land and of the people who came before, of our Lord Christ and the Testaments, both new and old, and yet too of the old religion, which is still near me and hard to cast off. Then the stars and planets and the maths! Oh, Fortunatus! I feel I too could turn to be a monk and spend my days copying old manuscripts and reading and writing."

"And would you like to rise in the middle of the night to kneel in the cold and dark in prayer?" he asked.

Deirdre pouted. "You are mocking me." She was not angry. She admired much about the life of these monks, but she considered the nightly prayer vigils to be silly, unnecessary.

"And what of your marriage?"

Deirdre stopped. She looked hard at Fortunatus who had never once before mentioned this subject -- not that it was taboo between them, just that it was tacitly understood that Clotaire should not be mentioned.

"What marriage?" she asked in measured tones.

"Ah, let us not be silly, my sister." Deirdre had never heard Fortunatus use such a tone with her. "I know we are here forbidden to speak of him to you, but the time draws near when he will return."

"I do not understand you," she said, meaning his tone. But Fortunatus chose to understand differently.

129

"You are Clotaire's betrothed."

"Oh, I hate him!" Deirdre cried, stamping her foot.

"Hate him! Deirdre, he will be your husband."

Tears sprang to her eyes. "Do you think for a moment I had a choice in that? Or that I do now?"

Fortunatus could scarcely believe his ears. "Do you mean that you do not wish to marry him?"

Deirdre looked away. "Oh, what difference does that make? You have spoiled my day entirely. I have not thought of him in so long, he no longer existed for he. Now you speak of him again, bringing his hated memory back to me."

"But I thought of course you wanted to marry. He is a much admired and handsome man."

"Will you stop? Please? I can not bear to think of him."

But Fortunatus pursued his own thought. He had always assumed that Deirdre was delighted to be Clotaire's betrothed. Her present reaction puzzled him.

"My dear sister, forgive me. These years that we have been friends,we have not spoken of the king nor of your coming marriage. I have respected your silence because I believed it came from modesty and from sparing me the painful reminder of our separation when that marriage occurs."

"Separation! Oh, Fortunatus!"

"Please, Deirdre, let me finish."

Deirdre's eyes filled with her distress.

Fortunatus continued. "I never once suspected anything of what you have just spoken in such strong words. Now tell me truly, do you not wish to marry miClotaire?"

"He is a brutal murderer. How could I want to marry such a man?"

"A murderer! Dear Deirdre, do you not know who is this man, your future husband?"

"Indeed I know him well! I have seen him with my own two eyes!"

"Clotaire is the son of the great King Clovis who was the first king to become Christian. It is Clovis we have to thank for our present faith, and Clotaire himself who is tireless in bringing the faith to the folk throughout the land."

"Fortunatus, you are too kind. You carry only the good tales. Please, let us return. I have not heart to continue either this walk or conversation."

Fortunatus looked at her kindly.

"Let me say only one thing more, Deirdre. If your heart is not in this marriage, then do not let it come about."

"Why, how do you mean?"

"You need not marry him."

Deirdre's distress was great. "Please do not speak of this again. I have no peace to think of it. Oh, Fortunatus, truly I had tried to forget his promise to return to claim me. It is the only way I have lived with any happiness. To think he might return gives me the keenest distress. You say so simply 'Do not marry him.' You do not understand what it means to be a woman. And a prisoner!"

Fortunatus seemed to be elsewhere in his thoughts. "I am sorry to have distressed you. Forgive me. I shall never speak of him again."

Deirdre looked up at him. She smiled wanly. "Methinks, dear brother, that it will not matter. Now that it has risen in my thoughts, it will return of its own. But yes, between us, let us share what is joyful. We have two things now we must never speak of."

"Two?"

"Ai. Also your distress about being a dreary monk."

Fortunatus threw back his head and laughed heartily.

"Yes, I, a dreary monk and you -- forgive me the word this

131

one time more -- you, the dreary wife. What a sad pair. How we should remember then these days spent together in study and prayer and such bliss!"

Deirdre looked up at him. "Ai. But I would have these days forever. I shall not easily give you up, my friend."

Fortunatus tossed his head to throw back one curl off his forehead.

"Why do you not yet wear your hair tonsured?" she asked.

"It is my pleasure not to do so," he answered with a cocky air.

"But was it not tonsured when first I met you?"

"Perhaps. I don't recall. When I am sure I shall take my final vows I will cut it so. Until then...."

"You too are a spoiled darling, I see."

"Not as you are," he said, taking her measure.

"Come, let's run back." She lifted her skirt and ran ahead.

Fortunatus called after her. "Ladies do not run."

Deirdre called back over her shoulder. "And do not think! And do not read!" She stopped and shouted back to him. "So I cannot be a lady. I know not what I am. But Fortunatus...."

"What?" he called.

"I *think!* And I *read!* And look! I *run!*"

Fortunatus laughed and, lifting his monk's skirt above his knees, like a boy, took off after her.

CHAPTER 13

They had been three days on the road, heading northwest toward the castle at Soissons where Clotaire's court was. This third day had been the hardest. Now that Clotaire had decided to push on home, he was without mercy. They rose before dawn and rested but an hour at midday, then rode and walked until sundown, by then having energy only enough to eat lightly and go to sleep. It was not like the days when they were *en route* everywhere and nowhere with vague directions as to where the next settlement or manor might be. Then they rode perhaps a day or half a day and rested sometimes weeks between, the men hunting and the women foraging for food. Those had been the good days, with nights of singing and drinking and storytelling. There had been no urgency, no weariness, no irritation between those on horse and those on foot.

Clotaire made no attempt to lighten their day with joviality. He seemed distracted, angry even, keeping to himself. Lord Lothar rode beside him, as was his station, but long ago a rift had appeared between the two and Clotaire rode always slightly ahead on Lothar's left.

Lothar had grown to be a handsome young man, having filled out and grown taller than Clotaire. He was brown skinned from the sun, yet still lighter than all the other men, and his blond hair always seemed to emit its own light compared to the blackness of the others'. He held himself erect on his horse and remained aloof from all the other men, proud and alone, no longer the young, enthusiastic boy who had initially joined them. He had grown quieter still after Villem was appointed captain, thereby being give the place of Lord Brut in Clotaire's hierarchy. Villem was a freed serf, not a nobleman. It was Lothar who should have been appointed. Clotaire's reason that Lothar was yet too young was met with silence from all the men, but Lothar had burned with shame. Though only fifteen, he was yet old enough to take his rightful place as the king's immediate officer. Clotaire himself had been only fourteen when he rode his first campaign.

Villem rode toward the middle of the group as had always been his wont. He was too modest to claim the honor of riding forward, though that now befitted his rank; thus he avoided giving further affront to Lothar. He knew, as everyone knew, why Lothar had been passed over, but held his tongue, like all the other men. The foot soldiers, who were otherwise ruthless about such things, said not a word against the boy, even among themselves. This was out of respect for Clotaire who had taken Lothar on as his protégé and to whose sister he was the bespoken lord. But Lothar felt the pressure of their evaluation of himself as well as their judgment.

I have committed no cowardly act, he would like to have said to the reproach he saw in every man's eyes. *Ai, but ye have,* any one of them would have responded if the truth could be spoken. To himself, he puzzled over his feelings of shame and inadequacy. Had Clotaire chastised him, or even punished him, Lothar would have at least had the respect of the others for an acknowledged mistake. But Clotaire said no word publicly.

"You were not at your post," he accused Lothar privately a few days after Brut's death.

Lothar blushed deeply. "King Clotaire, I believed I was where I was supposed to be."

Clotaire whirled toward him. Lord Brut had not only been his adviser and close companion since boyhood, but also his confidant, the one to whom Clotaire had turned in his private agony of religious doubt. Brut's own ambivalence, together with his ability to give utterance to both his doubt and his faith, had acted as a mirror to Clotaire's position, giving him the needed strength and purpose to continue his promised mission to bring Christianity to his people. For three days since Brut's death, Clotaire had kept to himself and had burned with anger and grief. It was only then when he called Lothar to him.

"You were not at your post, Lothar," Clotaire said again, his

134

anger barely held in check.

Lothar dropped his eyes. A deep silence fell between them.

"You are my charge, as you know, for all the reasons I have told you. Your father was my father's kin, his dearest friend and ally. Therefore I cannot kill you nor publicly shame you, though you deserve no better. Beware, Lothar. Beware. Because of you I am without my dearest friend. I will not lose more."

Clotaire left. Lothar's shame filled him with loathing.

Why was I born this way? he cried silently over and over. *Why haven't I changed as I have so wanted to?* Clotaire's words of long ago came back to him. *Fear is every man's enemy, but one which is his constant companion. Once you learn that, you will become strong and a good soldier.*

How was it that Clotaire had not taught him to be free of fear? In all these years, Lothar felt he had not won a single battle against it. Even the shame that he experienced and that he detested was not great enough to balance the terror that flooded him when in battle. It was as though those original sounds, heard so long ago in his parents' home and which had meant the irreparable loss of his mother's love and his father's protection, had become a part of him, inexplicable, unconscious, so that when he heard their echo now as an adult, that child's fear rose in him to choke him. He would run, or pretend control at the furthest remove from the battle, being careful to stay clear of Clotaire for days after. Worse, he knew that he took advantage of his position with Clotaire as a protected one and that Clotaire would, at worst, chastise him as he did now. He had grown to hate Clotaire for that and for the obvious, seemingly easy, courage Clotaire displayed in every encounter. But his hate was yet mixed with his former habit of gratitude and admiration. Part of Lothar's being was still that of a very young boy; that part emitted a bright sweetness and joy. But a newer part, that of the rapidly maturing young man, was emerging, and where before he had pleased the king and officers with a childish wit and enthusiasm, now he saw how they

135

turned against him, expecting him to be suddenly grown. And since Lord Brut's death, he was treated like a pariah. Their respect he had done without for quite a while now, but this sudden loss of their affection and camaraderie was more than he could bear and made him turn like a snake that curls to devour its own tail. There seemed to be no way out of his dilemma; his mind ran the circles of self-justification, and because he could not face his fear, he looked for an outside source of his shame. Gradually, he was convincing himself that Clotaire was its source and he, Clotaire's victim. It was difficult to acknowledge his self-hate; thus it moved out onto Clotaire to whom Lothar gave the responsibility.

A young soldier, new to Clotaire's band, a volunteer from one of the manors where Clotaire passed this latest winter, guarded that night. It was cloudy and moonless, darker than usual. Only once in their travels had Clotaire's band run into marauders, but Clotaire's band had been so much bigger, they had given rout to the thieves immediately. This night passed quietly. The boy, close to exhaustion, fought to stay awake, but toward dawn, he began dozing. Suddenly he felt his air source cut off. That was the last the boy ever knew. His throat had been cut.

Two more died in silence before the alarm was given by one of the women prisoners when the soldier astride her suddenly slumped on her in a heap. She screamed before she was knocked unconscious with a kick.

Villem was the first to leap up. He let out a war cry that made the chill from the wind a small matter by comparison. He threw his fur wrap over Felice's face and gave her a sharp kick to waken her.

In the morning mist, it was difficult to see how many there were of this enemy, or even who was the enemy, until one came almost face to face with them. Clotaire and his men rose up out of the silence of their sleep as though into a nightmare to confront this screaming band of thieves. The woods filled with the din of battle.

Felice, covered by her fur wrap, scrambled along the ground until she was under the bushes she and Villem had chosen to lie near. Wild-eyed, she peered out from under the fur and branches to see what chances she had for escape. She saw little in the mist, other than the violent scramble of bodies as they hurled themselves upon one another. She heard the thud of an ax as it found flesh and the sudden expulsion of air as one man took a mortal blow and collapsed slowly down onto the ground.

"Ai, Tollech and Criace, come to me now. Protect me and my lord and Villem too," she whispered in rhythm with her pounding blood. She glanced behind. It seemed empty of the battle.

She backed through the bushes until she felt herself free of their clinging branches. Then she rose partway and, bending low, dashed through the trees, across a small meadow to another clump of bushes beyond. She heard the screams of a woman as two men dragged her off, away from the camp. Felice bit her lip hard and tasted blood. She could see their shadows against the greying sky. A third joined them and helped to pull the struggling woman across the little meadow into the woods beyond. Felice crouched low and held her breath.

She was afraid to move farther and afraid to stay so close to the battleground. Suddenly, across from her, two men, both large, broke through the shrubs with a great crashing. One roared with rage. Felice recognized Villem. Without thinking, she dashed to his aid, leaping up on the other's back, scratching at his eyes. She felt the man's body cave in under her and she leaped back. Villem looked at her in amazement.

Felice pointed. "Over there," she said, breathless.

Villem strode, without questioning, across the meadow. Felice followed along its edge; they heard the three men. Felice ran across the final open area and crouched in the shrubs near Villem. Below, they saw two of the men holding the limp body of the woman, while the other struggled to free himself of his

137

clothing.

Felice glanced at Villem. Villem handed his ax to her and nodded. They rose together and moved silently down the slope. The men were engrossed entirely. Just then Villem let out a roar and attacked. Felice also screamed. Together, they felled the two men holding the woman. Felice herself gladly sank the ax into the belly of the third man, who backed away, his trousers around his ankles, a look of utter horror on his face. Villem gave him a final blow, then snarled at Felice. "Now! Go!"

"And her?" she asked.

"She is dead," he said.

Felice looked. A stream of dark blood flowed from the woman's nostrils down her cheek and sank into the rich forest soil. The face was twisted in pain and fear. Felice wanted to forget it, because in it she somehow had seen her own face, as if the woman had mirrored her own past, or worse, her future. She was more frightened by that than by all the brutality of the rape or the killings.

She ran into the woods, fighting her way through the underbrush until her lungs were bursting, to the edge of a small stream. There she fell when her foot sank into the mud, throwing her face-down into the water. Even then she did not stop, but crawled up the opposite bank and huddled inside the leafy branches of a large bush.

She crouched, holding her knees to her chest, and gasped in mouthfuls of air. After some minutes, her breathing was easier. Only her heart did not stop its pounding. But soon, even that slowed down. Then she listened. She had no idea how far she had run nor was she sure even of her direction, but if they were still battling, she was far enough away not to be able to hear them. The wind had died and the sun had just risen. She heard the stream's stony voice, the calls and quick flutter of birds, the chatter of chipmunks, nothing more. She was in a deep forest that stretched as far as she could see in every direction.

138

She ran and walked for hours more, until she found a satisfactory place in which to hide and rest. When she finally lay down, exhaustion, caused mainly by her fear, overcame her, and she fell into a sound, dreamless sleep. She awoke with a start in the long shadows of the early evening. The day came back to her in a rush, and she cursed herself for not having stayed awake. But there was no noise, no prickle in her skin, to warn her of any danger.

She listened and waited until dusk; then she retraced her steps, depending on her instinct and sharp powers of observation to guide her. A broken twig, a flattened clump of grass, a stone out of its place: these were what guided her. She quickly found the stream she had crossed and, by full dark, a path. She walked more easily down the path. She felt better now, rested and less frightened. She was prepared, she thought, to handle whatever destiny might be hers. She knew only that she had to return to Clotaire and Villem.

She fell into a smooth rhythm she always used when walking alone in the woods or fields. She could travel hours this way. The rhythm relaxed her, and she was better able to remain alert without tiring herself. She was amazed that she had travelled so far. She stopped and checked her direction. Assured she was right, she continued on her way. The birds had long since become quiet, except for the owl whose hooting made her uneasy.

Suddenly she heard something, something very definitely not a natural sound. It was a rolling squeak, a sharp and complaining noise. She slipped back among the trees, into the dark shadows, and waited. She was calm; even her heartbeat was regular. Gradually, the sound grew closer and she guessed long before she saw it, that it was a cart pulled by a draft animal. And indeed, in the darkness, she was able to make out the darker shadow of a cart pulled by a large ox. A lone man walked beside it.

She almost called out. His traveling at this hour meant that a manor was relatively near. Perhaps he would have news of Clotaire or his band. But she wanted no part of strangers this night. For the first time, she longed for Villem and his masculine protection, for his large and warm affection and strength. She wanted him so much, she could feel his presence beside her.

The stranger passed, the creak of the cart growing distant. Felice stepped back onto the path and continued a short distance when a moan, soft and nearby, made the hair on her arms stand up. She ducked behind a tree, into its shadow, and listened, her body taut as a drawn bow.

An owl hooted. A tree frog began its insistent night song. Then she heard it again, a long, low moan. It was a man's voice. Felice waited to hear it again in order to determine its location, then moved toward it, careful to make not the slightest sound.

In the dark, she almost tripped over his body and leaped back. Whoever he was, he was unconscious and delirious. Felice circled the whole area and found the bodies of two others, both of whom she quickly ascertained were dead. Seeing there were no others, alive or dead, she went quickly to the wounded one and stooped down, to look at him. What she saw in the dim light caused her heart to jump. It was Clotaire.

She leaned over him and whispered in his ear. "Clotaire...Clotaire...'tis I, Felice."

She ran her hands over his face and head, both caressing and searching for the source of his condition. She felt a wetness on his tunic near his groin and on his right thigh, another near his shoulder. Felice straightened. In the distance, there was the dull roar of thunder. She could smell the rain that was coming; the wind was already increasing. Clotaire would need shelter and care, or he would die. The thunder recalled to her the sound of the cart wheels. She got up and ran along the path. She would have to chance it. This man would have to help her.

She heard him ahead and ran faster until she could see the dark bulk of the cart.

140

"Sire," she called out quietly.

The cart kept moving.

"Sire!" She was almost upon him.

"Ai, the gods!" the man cursed and swung around with a large stick raised between his hands.

"Sire, please. Your help!"

He held the stick above him. "Be ye real?" She reached out and touched his sleeve.

"Ah, a woman." He took a deep breath and let out a great sigh. "What do ye want? I cannot see ye. Damnation and cow dung! Who are ye and what is your trouble?" He seemed to grow angrier and angrier now that his fear withdrew. "Ye frighten the wits out o' me. Blood o' the Lord, sweet Jesus, and Tollech and Blandin, for good measure, what do ye mean comin' up a hind me like that?"

He was a peasant, no doubt a field serf. Felice recognized him by his roughness and the quality of his fear.

"And how should I approach ye," she said, falling into the peasant language, "but from behind when I am not in front of ye?"

"Ye sounds young, by all the gods. Are ye pretty? I have not seen a pretty face in years."

"And ye are old, so think nothing of my face. I need your help. Will ye give it?"

"And what is it, and what might I get out of it?" She heard the quick calculating.

"Depends," she said. "My man has fallen and hurt himself, lies wounded back near the path. Methinks he will die if we do not get to shelter where I can nurse him. Will ye help me?"

He was silent a moment, moved closer. "I know not if ye be real or spirit. Let me touch ye."

Felice understood his intent and stood very still. He touched

141

her arm, then ran his hands over her shoulders. He cackled when his fingers got twisted in her hair. He lightly touched her breasts. Felice pushed him away.

"It is not me ye'll be having," she exclaimed. "Ye spoke of the good Lord, so ye've reason enough for yourself to help me. It is the king himself who is wounded."

The man laughed. "Ai, and if I believe that...." He laughed heartily. "Yer man, ye said," and continued laughing. "With such as ye? The good king Clovis is long dead besides."

"It is his son, the king Clotaire, I be talking about. I am traveling with his band. But if ye don't wish to help him," she started walking away, "then I guess I'll find me another to get the rich reward."

"Nay, woman, wait!" He approached her more respectfully. "Help me turn the beast. We's on our way home and he won't willingly want to turn back."

Indeed, the ox proved stubborn and determined to go forward, but together they got him headed back. The man kept glancing at her.

"Ye're sure I'll get me reward?"

"He is the king, is he not?"

He chortled. "Ai, if what ye say be true. A rich reward, eh?"

Felice smiled. She had been long away from her own kind. She liked the familiarity she felt in his company.

She had laid a branch across the path to mark the place where, further in, Clotaire lay. He made no sound now and she grew frightened. Leaning over him, she was assured when she felt his breath on her cheek. Together, she and the man lifted Clotaire and carried him to the cart, which was filled with hay. Lightning flashed. In that instant, she saw Clotaire's face, drawn tight in pain.

They laid him on the hay, far in, so he could not fall.

"Now we must get him to a safe place where he will be out

142

of the weather and where I can nurse him," Felice said.

"Ai, I knows a wayfarer's station. 'Tis small and open, but has a roof to shelter ye. 'Tis but a ways down." He was silent a moment. "But how will I get me reward then?"

"Ye will know where we are. The king's men will be looking for him, so it will not be long, methinks."

They travelled some time down the path in the rising wind. It was so dark, it was impossible to see more than a few feet ahead. The man stopped.

"Wait here. Methinks it's back in here." Though he was standing right in front of her, he had to shout, the wind was blowing so hard. He left and returned in moments.

They lifted Clotaire carefully and laid him on the ground beneath a rough wood and bark shelter. There was a roof, and two sides were covered. Felice hurried back and grabbed armfuls of hay. While the man stood watching, she deftly made up a soft bed with the hay in the corner where the walls met, then signaled for his help. Once again, they moved Clotaire and laid him on the pallet.

"There." She turned to the old man, then stooped down next to Clotaire. She felt inside his tunic to where she had seen him keep a money bag. She felt his heart beating quickly, then her hand felt the soft fabric of the bag. She turned so the old man could not see what she was doing, then opened the bag and feeling several coins, pulled three out and handed him two.

The old man closed his hand over the coins. "But I cannot see. Be they silver or gold?"

Felice laughed. "I too cannot see, but it will be your luck no matter what they are. More than ye have ever had, I can assure ye. Now, leave us your lamp and I'll give ye another."

"My lamp! How then...?"

"Ye know the way well, methinks. And I need light to help him."

143

The old man left and came back holding the lamp high. He held it above Clotaire and looked hard.

"He be a lord, I see that. But he's way gone, methinks."

Felice grabbed the light. "Curse your tongue, do ye not say such a thing! I will make him whole again."

The old man looked her up and down in the light. He grinned.

"I should asked for an hour with ye. Better than coins, methinks." With that, he held out the three coins in the palm of his hand to look at them in the light. He gasped. "Gold!" He looked at Felice, his eyes big. "G'night to ye then and God save him." With that, he disappeared back into the darkness, but, in moments he came back, carrying a large fur blanket.

"Ye paid too well, methinks. And you'll be needing this." Felice's face lit up with gratitude.

"Thanks, good sire. I will tell the king of ye and your good service. Fare thee well, and good journey."

Felice waited until she heard him turn the ox and cart, then listened as the squeak of the wheels slowly faded away.

It started to rain, the drops coming down hard. In moments, it was pouring and the air was cold. She could do little for Clotaire in the darkness, even with the lamp, so she curled close to him beneath the fur. She lay awake for hours, listening to the wind and rain and occasional thunder, feeling Clotaire's warmth beside her, worrying about his wounds.

She awoke with the first light of day. The rain had ceased. The forest around the small hut glistened. She leaned on one elbow to look at Clotaire. His face was wet with beads of perspiration, his long black hair matted. She gently removed the fur and pulled away the clothing from around the blood stains. One wound still oozed. It was a deep one near his groin. Putting her ear to his chest, she heard with alarm how light his heartbeat was. Felice sat up and let her mind fill with all the herbal and

144

healing knowledge she had ever learned. She had no utensils of any sort. She hung her wet clothes in a small opening over the branches where they might dry. Then she wrapped herself in the fur, which was unneeded now by Clotaire. She walked through the trees looking for, and finally finding, a rock with an impression in it. It was already filled with rainwater, so she carried it back to the hut. She bent over the king and with her teeth, tore the fabric that covered his wounds. With a piece of that fabric, she carefully washed around the wound. She found a spring nearby and collected more water, and stripped Clotaire as best she could so that she could find and clean all of his wounds. She could see by the ugly blue bruises on his arms and shoulders that he had fought fiercely. He had a slight wound on his shoulder, a serious one on his right thigh and the deep and dangerous one near his groin. She put wet leaves on his forehead and cheeks to cool his fever, then opened his lips to insert some wet grasses to get water inside him.

She spent a hurried hour digging special roots and collecting plants. It was impossible to find fresh herbs, but she was able to find some medicinal leaves and some dry herbs from the previous season. When she returned, he was moaning again and speaking in a garbled fashion. She placed the medicinal leaves over the deep wound, then wrapped a long piece of cloth, torn from her skirt, around his body to close the wound and hold the leaves in place. She dressed the other wounds and started a small, smoky fire. She brewed a tea with the herbs. Holding Clotaire's head up, she forced some of this brew between his lips. He moaned and writhed in pain some hours. Felice watched over him, rocking and chanting a prayer to her gods, this time not for help for herself and the fulfillment of her love, but for his health and recovery. In the afternoon, he grew quieter and she left to collect fresh leaves and some bark she recalled as being helpful to open wounds. Again, she cleaned the wounds, bound them with leaves, and put sweet-smelling bark at his elbows, wrists, navel, and forehead. This time, she also drank the bitter tea and realized

145

then her own hunger.

She had kept the fire going and dried her clothes. She dressed, and seeing Clotaire more restful and apparently free of the fever, she covered him with the fur. His eyes fluttered open briefly and he muttered an incoherent phrase. She leaned her mouth to his ear, kissing him on the temple.

"'Tis I, my king. 'Tis Felice, who...who loves you." She dared to say the words for the first time and blushed to hear them in her own mouth, even though she knew he would never remember them. "I shall bring food now."

It took hours of foraging to collect edible roots and bark and one small rabbit, which she stalked for a long time and caught with her bare hands. She skewered the rabbit on a stick after skinning it, and cooked it black over the fire. She put the roots in a basket of sweet leaves, which she then placed on a stick over the fire. As long as she kept the leaves wet, the basket did not burn.

Her hunger was immense now, a pain that doubled her over. But she was patient to let the meat and roots cook. She did not wish to get ill herself. Clotaire was perspiring again, so she removed the fur and placed more cool leaves on his forehead and cheeks. She changed all the dressings again, glad to be busy while the smell of the meat almost drove her to grabbing it from the fire and eating it raw. She had placed another hollowed-out stone beneath it, so some of its juices were saved. With this, she made a broth, which she fed to the barely conscious Clotaire.

With the fire, she was able to spend a good part of the night nursing him, but finally she fell into a restless sleep that lasted well beyond dawn.

The next day passed as the one before, though she was not able to catch any animals for meat. Food was a thin broth she made from the roots and plants she collected. Clotaire vacillated between quiet and a feverish restlessness, but she was happy to notice that his fevers were less frequent and less persistent this day. And his wounds looked less violent. All bleeding had stopped

146

and the deep wound seemed to be closing with the pressure she kept on it. That night, she slept well and awakened with the birds. Something had changed; there was a lightness to the air, a softness. She leaned up on her elbows. Some of the leaves had finally opened fully, putting out a green light that suffused the whole forest. Felice smiled and looked down at Clotaire. To her amazement, his eyes were open and he was looking at her.

"What has happened?" he whispered. He was still pale and weak.

Felice's heart leaped. "Ai, good sire. Rest. Do not speak yet. You are wounded. You are hurt, but I shall make you better. You will soon be strong again."

Clotaire smiled wanly and closed his eyes.

When Felice changed the leaves on his wounds this time, she was aware of his pain. He winced when she pulled away the leaves that drew off the infection. She could tell the infection was subsiding by the amount of pus that clung to the leaves. Once, he opened his eyes when she touched him and she saw the pain in them.

"Forgive me, dear sire," she said. "I do not wish to give you pain, but" -- she bit her lip when she saw how he tried not to cry out -- "I must change these."

He was much relieved when she had bound him again, and his breathing became slow and regular. He no longer had a fever and, in fact, was able to stay awake to drink his brew. He was even well enough to complain about its bitterness. Felice laughed.

"Ah, you are healing," she said.

He looked up at her. "You are a good woman, Felice."

Felice's eyes filled briefly. These were the words Villem used with her, the words she knew came close to an expression of love.

"Sleep, dear one," she said softly. "Tomorrow you will be better."

147

CHAPTER 14

Clotaire regained his strength rapidly. The next morning, with Felice's help, he was able to fashion a crude bow and arrow, which he then taught her to use. She felled a fat squirrel with it, so, once again, they had meat and broth for a meal. Her skill with the weapon was limited, however, and led more to frustration than to meals. In a rage at missing a rabbit, she broke the bow in two.

On the afternoon of the sixth day since the battle, Clotaire called Felice to him.

"How far are we from where we camped?" he asked.

"Maybe a half day, more or less, I am not sure."

"Then we can make it in two days perhaps, with my limping so."

Felice shook her head.

"What do you think?"

She hesitated. It was not her place to contradict him, but he was asking her, it seemed. She made up her mind.

"Methinks you need more rest. That wound," she pointed to his groin, "is barely closed. Walking would open it."

Clotaire listened carefully.

"How many days more?" he asked.

She loved these hours she had spent alone with him, though he had passed most of them sleeping or keeping quietly to himself while she foraged and hunted. His wounds were healing quickly, even the deepest one. In three more days, she felt he would be ready to travel.

"Perhaps five or six." Felice seldom spoke less than the truth, though the truth had sometimes to be stretched to fit the circumstances of her always precarious life. Now, with the lie upon her lips, she blushed scarlet from it. Clotaire did not seem to notice. He frowned.

"I am anxious to go. My men think me dead, perhaps. They will wait some time, but then they will depart." He looked at Felice. "We are still far from Soissons."

Felice kept her eyes on the ground before her.

"If we were to walk slowly...," he began.

"Oh, do not think of it, milord." Felice's distress was real. "You were near dead when I found you. I listened to your heart. It was scarcely beating."

Clotaire was quiet. He seemed occupied with something other than the subject at hand.

"I will sleep now," he said. "I am suddenly weary."

Felice had plenty of food on hand, so she was free until the next meal. She played with a large leaf, tearing patterns in it, and watched Clotaire's face as he slipped off into sleep. He was still very pale.

The sun was already making its way down the slide of the afternoon. It was a crisp, bright day. Felice walked slowly to the place in the woods where she had spent her spare hours praying to her gods for Clotaire's recovery. On the way, she saw the first sprigs of a powerful plant, one used for casting spells. She stooped and looked at it carefully. It was a rare plant and normally hard to find, even when looking for it. Felice took it to be a sign.

"Sweet flowering spirit," she said, speaking low, "you come to me now, offering yourself. Still I beg your leave to take your life. Forgive me and bring me no harm." She repeated this incantation three times, then carefully broke the stems off at the base, leaving the roots so the plant would grow again the following year.

Holding the stems in front of her, she ceremoniously walked to where she knew some pulpit flowers were already sprouting. She collected four of these, roots and all, one for each of the four winds. She bowed deeply in each of the four directions, then went to the stream that flowed further down from their shelter. Dipping the whole of each of the plants into the water, she washed the dirt from the roots.

She collected some thick grasses and sat by the stream to weave them into a small basket. She hurried because the sun was getting low. When the basket was done, she bowed again in the four directions and placed her plants within. She ran then to her praying spot. There would be no bowing or kneeling now. She stood proud and tall; she had power in her hands and had come to challenge her gods to give her what she desired.

"Now!" she called out loud, directing her attention to the west. She held the basket in front of her, turned, repeating her call to the south, then east, then north.

Facing north, she spoke an incantation, which she repeated three times more for each direction. She sat suddenly, cross-legged, facing west, and placed the basket in front of her. She spoke now normally as though to an invisible person.

"You see this sweet spirit that has come to me. I have not sought her, though I have long asked your help without receiving it. Now the spirit of this plant has come to me. I have performed her ritual, bringing to her her good friends, these four flowers, who have gladly left their homes to travel with her. Now you must answer my wish as I eat of her powers."

Felice paused and thoughtfully considered the wording of her wish. "I would have Clotaire's love," she said simply.

She repeated her wish three times more, then slowly chewed the five plants, one after another, roots and all. Though they were bitter, she showed no sign of aversion to them. Finished, she dug a hole with her hands and buried the basket after breaking it to pieces. She stood then, and majestically walked away. When she could no longer see the place of her ritual, she ran, her hand over her mouth, gagging violently. She got to the stream and drank four handfuls of water, then lay down. Though the plants had made her ill, she could not vomit them, or all her power would not only be lost but would turn against her.

150

She lay on her back and concentrated on the leafy patterns against the soft, blue sky. Gradually, her stomach spasms lessened. By dusk, they had ceased.

She was weak when she got back to the hut. Clotaire sat inside. He was moody and withdrawn and ignored Felice entirely. She started a basket of meat and roots and herbs over the fire after wrapping more fresh leaves into the basket. She sat on her heels watching the fire.

"I have had a dream," Clotaire suddenly said from inside the hut. Felice turned to him, surprised. He sat up with a grimace.

"Take care, sire."

"Only sometimes it pains me." He smiled at her. "It gets better each hour. You are a good nursemaid."

He pushed himself back against the wall.

"Come within. I would tell you my dream."

Felice moved inside.

"I sat on a hill in a tall chair." Clotaire told the dream slowly, with frequent pauses. "I was alone at first. The hill sloped down and was covered with long, green grass. It was beautiful. I felt as though the hill were alive. It had its own voice as did the grass."

Felice nodded, smiling.

"Why do you agree?" he asked.

"It is how things are," she answered with a shrug.

"How do you mean?"

It was so plain to her. She shrugged. "The gods; they inhabit everything."

Clotaire did not smile at her the way he usually did whenever she asserted her own beliefs.

"Yes, I felt something like that." He became thoughtful. "Suddenly, below me, I saw a town and it had a church with a beautiful tower. I turned, and in every direction, I could see towns and manors and all of them had churches. Then there was someone beside me -- a man. I could not see his face. He put his hand on my shoulder and I felt a great peace. I understood then that I could go home."

Felice waited, expecting more, but Clotaire was apparently finished.

"Do you understand it?" she finally asked.

"Yes, it is a great dream. I understood immediately upon waking." He looked at Felice, noticing her for the first time.

"You look unwell, lady."

"Nay, I am well, sire."

"Come, sit by me. You have looked too well after me, not enough after yourself."

Such concern for her well-being outside of their love-making was unusual. Was her charm already beginning to work? She silently repeated the four required thanks to the great powers as she moved to sit by Clotaire.

"You know I have a mission, nay?" he asked.

"Ai, though I do not understand what that means."

"Someday I shall explain it all to you so that you can understand. Now I shall tell you the meaning of my dream: it relieves me of that mission."

"Ai! I must look to the stew." She leaped up to douse the leaf basket in water before it would burn and dump their stew into the fire. Clotaire resumed when she had resettled herself.

"My father brought the great truths of Christ to me and to all of this land. But he was already an old man when he came to it, with but a few years left to him. As he lay dying, he called me to his side. 'You must bring the word to all men,' he said. That was my mission. I gave my word that I would do it."

"And so you travel as you do," Felice said. She had never wondered at the purpose of Clotaire's long travels abroad. She was content only to be with him.

"Yes, but I was but a boy then, filled with the dreams all boys have. I did not understand this religion." He sighed. "I am not sure even now that I do. But then it was only words to me and empty acts, which I performed to please my father. I was raised in my early years with the many gods that you know."

Felice's face brightened. "You know my gods then?"

"Ai, I do."

She looked at him in amazement.

"And do you speak with them?" she asked.

"I have never ceased, though I thought I had. I have denied them many times, but lately, I have felt them more and more."

"Ai, thanks to Tollech, Criace, and all the gods!" Felice burst out.

Clotaire looked at her very seriously. "You do not love the Lord Christ yet, nor the truth. But it is all right. You are but a woman."

Felice nodded. She did not say what was in her heart, how, this very moment, her gods were with her and working their powers over him.

"It is difficult to cast away what has belonged to the child. I have been in doubt now these last few months. And tired of the battles, the attempt to bring to others what is no longer a sureness within myself." He stretched. "And so now this dream has come to tell me I will not break my word to my father if I return home. It has released me of my mission."

"Ah. I see now," Felice said. "So, of course, it is good."

"Do you see, sweet lady? Do you?" Clotaire grew excited. "That man in the dream was Christ Himself. The work is done. I need not go out again. The seeds have been planted. Now we must only await the harvest."

Felice would have liked to ask why he always called her 'lady'. She was not concerned much with his dream or his mission. She looked at him now, half closing her eyes.

"Clotaire, I would please you," she said in a tone he could not mistake.

Clotaire smiled. "Methinks I am not well."

"You are well enough," she said, sensing in his mood that he wanted her to be the aggressor.

"Would you bring me medicine? Or change my dressings?"

"It is a kind of medicine I would bring you, yes."

"Then I shall lie quietly. I shall await this medicine of yours."

Because of the ritual with the spirit world, Felice was already aroused herself. Clotaire lay down as if asleep, though the trace of a smile gave him away. She had never taken the initiative with him, but she did not hesitate. Avoiding his wounds, she ran her hands over his arms and shoulders. She loved the hardness of his body, the curves of his taut muscles. She leaned over him, pressed her cheek against his, nibbled his ear, then kissed his neck, the protrusion in his throat. With him, more than with any other man, she was aware of the masculine differences. Touching him -- the bristly facial hair, the flat muscles of his chest, the tight belly and narrow hips -- aroused her to the height of her femaleness. She wanted him desperately, wanted for him to respond, to take over even. But he would tease her, playing the ill man, though she knew indeed that his strength was only half back, his wound still dangerous. And so she made this gift of her own love, demanding nothing in return, arousing him until he was satisfied. Clotaire saw, however, that she was not.

"Lie back," he whispered and leaned over her.

He touched and caressed her until she was more than fulfilled. No man had ever loved her this way with so much giving, so much awareness of her own needs. Even Clotaire had never so much as touched her more than was necessary to arouse her for his own fulfillment. She lay back, her eyes closed until she felt the abandonment and joy of her sex. He lay back laughing.

"Methinks that is all," he said.

She examined his wound and saw it was still closed, but that the blood was pulsing beneath the skin. "Ai, 'tis all, milord." She laughed and Clotaire laughed with her. She looked at him closely. His eyes were closed.

"Ai, sire, sire," she whispered. She could not say the words that lay on her tongue just -- but forever -- out of the reach of her courage.

"Ai, lady, lady," he mimicked softly, as was part of their love game together. He was sinking into sleep. She covered him, then straightened her skirts, and watched after the stew. She knew now that indeed he loved her. But, for her, a great puzzle existed. If he loved her, why did she continue to feel as if he did not? Why was she so certain that he would never be truly hers when their hearts and bodies were as one?

CHAPTER 15

Villem watched as the soldiers finished burying the enemy dead. Their own they had buried the second day, and would have left these for the flies and rodents, except Clotaire had not yet been found and these had begun to stink. Villem wanted to wait until he was certain Clotaire could not be found before he gave the order to depart. He glanced around the encampment.

Lothar sat under a tree, his arms resting on his knees, a leaf in his hands. He shredded one, then picked up another and shredded that also. Villem felt a twinge of guilt. Lothar's position was to do no other than direct, but now that Villem was in charge, Lothar had no duties to perform. At the same time, Villem could not help but feel a surge of pride in this power his position gave him, particularly in relation to Lothar. The men unanimously supported Villem in his new role, though more than one, he could see, resented his unprecedented rise. Born and raised a serf, freed only six years before by Clotaire, and now, against all tradition and expectation, he stood in rank above a nobleman. Aware of how keenly Lothar felt the ignominy of this relationship, Villem was most careful, therefore, to avoid giving any orders to him directly.

Lothar stood up. He looked at Villem a moment. Then, some kind of decision made, he crossed the short distance between them.

"Methinks we should leave for Athies," Lothar said.

Villem looked away.

Lothar continued. "Clotaire is dead, be assured. It is now some seven days since the battle."

Villem still held his tongue.

"Our men have scoured the countryside for him in every direction." Lothar laughed. "What kind of king is he to disappear if he is not dead?"

Villem's loyalty rose into his face in a rush of heat. His own conflict regarding Clotaire dissipated beneath Lothar's hinted accusation. Still he held his tongue. But Lothar had noticed.

"I do not say Clotaire is a coward, nay, not that. It is why I believe he is dead, forgive me for saying so, sire. We only waste away waiting here as a result of your indecision."

Villem noted the subtle shift in Lothar's attack.

"Ai," he said noncommittally. "We await now only the return of three who set out through the woods yesterday to search farther."

Lothar scowled. "Did you not give them orders to return at a specific time?"

"Nay, sire. They are good men. They will only stay away in order to follow a certain path."

"What path might that be?"

"A clue, some sign that the king be yet alive."

Villem used his utmost in tact -- the gift, born to a serf, of not directly confronting a master, the ability to shift attention away from oneself in order not to earn a beating.

Lothar guffawed, but did not say anything further. He was satisfied with Villem's response, with the surface of respect Villem showed him. Lothar could not help but respect Villem. He had seen him, always one of the first, to rise up in battle without the least concern for his personal safety, yet be neither cruel nor wanton in the fight. Villem was a natural warrior, a man of spirit, a born leader. Next to Clotaire even, he held his own as a natural aristocrat, but with a humility that masked his power, so that he seldom aroused envy in others. Lothar liked testing that humility, enjoyed the game of being above Villem, because he could depend on Villem's humble virtue.

When Lothar was done, Villem returned to his own thoughts, to his inner conflict of emotions which kept him in such a state of tension that his neck ached, feeling as though it were

157

locked in a vise. A part of him grieved for the loss of both his master and his woman. Another part was relieved with the loss of alternately one, then the other. He kept expecting Felice to materialize suddenly out of the trees, a wanton smile on her lips to tell him she wanted him. He himself had searched each day in the direction he had last seen her going. There were signs of her passage, then they disappeared; he would lose the trail. He wanted her back, yet felt the weight of his love for her lessening, as though, each day without her, he became freer of the prison he had built for himself. Dread and hope coexisted; dread that she would not release him, that she would return and he would feel caged again, hopelessly caught in the mesh of his desire to possess her; hope that she would return because she was a flower of life to him, a challenge that she could be caught as he was caught, that finally, he could make her his alone.

He was as confused in regard to Clotaire as well. He had deep gratitude and affection for the man Clotaire was. Though he did not consciously recognize it, he and Clotaire were brothers in spirit, equals in courage and worth. But Clotaire had the added advantage of inherited power, and it was Clotaire who broke the chains of tradition to free Villem from a life of brutal servitude and so to deliver him into the possibility of fulfilling an inner destiny. Yet Clotaire had also become the enemy, the hindrance to Villem's possession of his beloved. As with Felice, Villem wanted Clotaire both dead and alive, lost and found. His being was torn by the uncertainty of the waiting.

"Sire! Sire!" The soldier Arlick came running into the woods where Villem had wandered. Villem turned. His heart leaped. One of them had been found. He could tell by the joy in the soldier's voice.

"He is found. They are bringing him. He is alive."

Villem followed the man, then overtook him with his long strides. Gregorious, a freed serf like himself, but older, grinned toothlessly at him.

"I came ahead with the tidings. Our king, Clotaire, is alive, though he has been wounded. We made a pallet for him. Goran and Tolsten are coming along with him."

Villem said nothing. A ghostlike smile played over his lips.

Gregorious patted Villem hard on the back. "And for you, sire, a double blessing, may all the gods be thanked!" Gregorious caught himself falling back into the heresy of many gods and made a quick sign of the cross. "I mean, thanks be to the lord Jesus. I forget me-self."

"What more?" Villem asked, his heart rising again.

"Your woman, sire. She too be found. 'Twas she who discovered the king and nursed him back to health."

Villem felt the blood rush to his face. He turned quickly aside.

"Ai," he said hoarsely. "So be it."

"Ah, it's a good day. You were wise to tarry here, though many of us wanted to push on. Think where we would be had we done so, leaving the king wounded behind. You have done well, Villem."

Villem was pleased to receive praise from the lips of one of his own. Even in his confusion and the slow pain that now grew inside his chest, almost smothering him, he recognized the rare value of Gregorious' words.

"Go to your rest now, Gregorious. And thanks to ye. Ye also have done well."

The torturous waiting was over. Now that void was filled with an unreasoning brewing anger that Villem could only release by mounting his horse and riding at breakneck speed through the forest toward Clotaire and Felice. He would have to mask what he felt in front of Clotaire, but he knew also that something inside him had broken. He could no longer bear the burden of this love. He rode until his horse, in spite of Villem's violent urging, slowed to a more possible speed, its sides heaving, its flanks soaked to a

159

wet darkness. Villem realized then what he was doing and allowed the horse to slow to a walk. He would reach his destination soon enough. His anger spent itself temporarily; it moved into the grayer region of despair.

Until he saw them. Felice was laughing, all aglow, striding with her peasant strength alongside the pallet on which a pale, but also laughing, Clotaire lay. Villem's rage became an animal with its own dimensions, a presence that was simply there, dumb, and numbing to the features of his face. Felice saw him then, ahead on the path, and saw it too when she saw him; saw it in the peculiar stance he maintained, in the rigidity of his torso; saw it again, and finally, when they came upon one another and she looked into his eyes, and had to drop hers first. That was all the answer he needed.

"My king," Villem said formally. "I am at your service."

Clotaire did not see Villem's rage. "Villem!" His warmth was genuine. Villem was a good soldier. Clotaire valued him. It was a mystery to Clotaire that Villem should have feelings of tenderness for a woman. Those belonging to the lower classes were considered by the nobility to be somewhat bestial in the range of their emotions; they could hate, but not love; they could be angry or mirthful, but never tender. While Clotaire gave a great deal of credit to Villem for his warrior abilities and his intelligence, he made the assumptions of his class.

Villem heard the affection and responded with a pained smile. He would not look at Felice, underlining what he had already made clear to her -- that he would no longer have anything to do with her.

"Ah, it is good you are well, Clotaire," he said. He heard the difference in his own voice. He was lying from the core of his being for the first time in his life. It hurt, but he knew that would pass, that he had instincts for survival at all levels of his being, and that he could wall in his very heart, if needed.

Clotaire looked very serious. "Ai, but we have suffered

160

many losses. Ten men, Villem, and myself wounded. We must get on with our journey out of this land. We are only eighteen now, scarcely enough of a band to protect ourselves against another attack such as this last."

"They surprised us in our sleep, milord. Therefore we lost so many. They were mere ruffians as such bands are. Two men shall stand guard henceforth."

"Good, but I no longer want my men to die. We are done with our mission. We are going home to stay."

"And where might home be, my king?" Villem knew the answer. He wanted only to have Clotaire say it aloud, so Felice would hear it and suffer.

"Soissons, of course." He looked at Villem and saw the puzzlement. "But Athies first, as you well know."

Villem glanced at Felice. The words had touched her, he saw, even though she looked off into the trees as if unconcerned. But he gained no pleasure from her pain, as he thought he would. Instead, he found himself siding with her, and felt hate when he looked back at Clotaire's smooth face, in whose eyes there was only gaiety, no sign of pain.

Clotaire looked at Villem, seeing something. And he did not ask this time. At some level, he understood what was in Villem's heart and was able to guess with a sense of amazement at its source. He looked then at Felice, but her eyes were dull, devoid of any sign that might verify his perception. Yet he had known this all along, had simply denied the truth of it. Clotaire took all this in in a moment. He was not a cruel man; he wished only that the world be filled with pleasure. It was a puzzle to him now that he could have, in some way, robbed Villem of his pleasure. It made him vaguely sad and uncomfortable. They continued back to camp in silence, Clotaire lying back with his eyes closed.

A tent had been prepared for Clotaire in the camp. Two women had been put to making a roast, so that all was in readiness by the time the small group arrived. Felice slipped away

161

from the commotion to the small area she and Villem had shared. There, she gathered her few possessions in a basket. She did not know what she would do, but she could no longer stay with Villem, that was clear. She sat on the edge of the camp scarcely watching the others in the hours of festivities that followed. She considered making a last plea, but when she saw Villem grab the woman Triane and dance her off into the woods amid the laughter and cheers of the others, she saw it would be useless. If only she had been able to hold his eyes back there on the road. But wishing was past. She felt dull and empty. Her gods had deserted her.

Gradually, the celebration quieted. Clotaire withdrew to his tent; one by one the men drifted off to their own sleeping places. When all was quiet, Felice walked to Clotaire's tent and slipped inside.

"King Clotaire," she whispered. "By your leave."

"You did not celebrate with us, Felice." Clotaire's voice was soft.

Felice bit her lip. "I beg your leave, sire, to let me depart."

Clotaire sat up in the darkness and reached for her hand.

"I did not realize your relation with Villem," he said, pulling her down to sit beside him. "I have brought you harm, I fear."

"Nay, sire. Just...just that I must go. I cannot stay longer if you will permit me."

Clotaire was silent. "And where would you be going?" he finally asked.

Felice had no answer. "I will make my way, sire. I can make my own way, but not now among these." She could no longer hide the tears in her voice that broke now. Clotaire pulled her down to lie beside him and held her in his arms.

"Felice, my lady, you saved my life. Now, you shall have my protection. You shall have a tent by mine. No man will touch you."

Felice could not believe her ears. She lay a long time in silence as though all of her being, in shock, needed time to take in Clotaire's words.

"Sire," she said finally. "is that possible, truly?"

Felice felt at first a wave of incredible joy; then the thought of Villem came to her and her happiness broke against a rock of sorrow. She knew, in that moment, that her life was cast: she had lost the one man whose love she truly had; she would now have to live in the shadow of that loss and in the kindness of this kingly man without the kind of love she so wanted. She did not weep; she lay perfectly still, looking at it from all directions. She had won Clotaire's gratitude. That was not enough and never would be. And now she had lost even the dream of that impossible love. She had only the truth of this moment and the truth brought pain. Out of that pain, she understood that she could indeed have loved Villem and that now it was too late.

"Thanks to you, good king," she said softly. And meant it.

CHAPTER 16

Deirdre knew this was herself, but there was a difference to her. She walked down a long, dark corridor. She would stop and look into one of the rooms that lined the hall. She was looking for something. It was not clear what, but she was certain she would know when she came upon it. She was aware of this difference in herself as being in something she lacked, some part of her being that needed filling. It was this that she was looking for. In one hand, she held a fresh willow twig; the other was empty. The hall was endless, but she slowed now as she came to a door that seemed to emanate its own light. She saw then how the hinges and knob were made of gold. It was from these that the light came. She also noticed an odor, like musk. She stood in front of the door. She was afraid, yet knew she would have to open it. She did.

The room was furnished luxuriously in the manner to which she had already become accustomed at Athies. A window was open on the opposite wall. The wind filled the silken sheer fabric that covered it, billowing out. She felt here the presence of what it was she was seeking. She walked in, looking carefully at everything, in a state of inner waiting, letting herself simply explore. Yet there was nothing extraordinary. Then she noticed a figure behind the curtains, standing on the balcony beyond the windows. Trancelike, a great anticipation filling her, she walked toward it. The. curtain wrapped itself around her, its touch arousing a sensual response. She closed her eyes to better experience the sensations on her skin. When she opened them again, she was looking into the eyes of another. The face was so close, she could see nothing but the eyes, which were the strangest and most beautiful she had ever seen. They seemed to look far back into themselves as an extension of herself or a mirror of her own looking inward. She closed her eyes again and felt the solidity of this other's body against hers. She arched upward to meet this one. Opening her eyes again, she recognized

164

Clotaire and felt a thrill in the pit of her stomach. Those eyes were his. When she looked into them now, she felt as though she were falling into him, or he into her, she could not tell. All of her being was aglow in a kind of ecstasy. Then she heard her name, once, like a bell from inside her skull. Turning, she saw a woman falling backward against the bed, her hair like a cloud rising up to surround her....

Dierdre rose up with a scream, found herself in bed in her own suite of rooms at Athies, her hair fallen loose over her shoulders. She trembled, then released the breath she hadn't been aware she was holding.

"Oh!" she said, pushing the horror out.

"Lady called?" Her serving woman stood at the doorway of the sleeping chamber.

Deirdre looked at her, pulled in her breath now, and sighed deeply.

"Nay," she said. "I was dreaming."

"It is nearly dawn, milady."

"Draw my water then," she said. "I will get up."

She would not sleep anymore, she knew. And at this hour, she would be able to find Fortunatus just going out to the fields to work. Her dream had terrified her. It was the same dream she had had for years, except in this, she seemed to have become her mother falling back onto the bed. And while she yet knew no man's body, she could not mistake the sexual feeling she had experienced in the dream; she had thrilled to have Clotaire's body touch hers. She had wanted to fall into his eyes. This gave her such a fright, she had to speak of it.

She threw on her gown, a tunic over it, and started out.

"Lady Deirdre" her serving woman called out in surprise after her, but Deirdre did not stop to answer.

It was chilly when she stepped outside into the still, dark air. Below, by the river, she heard the slightest gong of the monastery bell that signaled the end of matins and the beginning of the monks' workday. She hurried along the path, wishing she had thought to bring a wrap. Birds began to sing now, at first only a few chirps, then, as more and more awoke, a symphony of greetings to the sun, even before the sun had appeared. The sky grew slowly lighter; the first hint of a soft yellow glow touched the horizon by the time she reached the river path that led out into the fields. Two monks walked slowly ahead of her.

"Brother monk," she called and broke into a run. From behind, she could not tell which of the eight brothers these two might be. She knew neither was Fortunatus because the heads of both were tonsured. They stopped and turned.

"Lady Deirdre," Brother Laurent said with a smile to greet her, "you are up most early. Ah, but you are distressed."

"I need to find Fortunatus," she said, trying to catch her breath.

The two brothers exchanged a look.

"Sister Deirdre," the older brother, Paulus, said. "Brother Fortunatus is readying his departure. Did he not tell you he was leaving?"

Deirdre felt as though they had hit her with something. She stood dumb a moment.

"Leaving?"

Brother Paulus was the monk who had most strongly opposed Fortunatus' spending so many hours with Deirdre. He took her hand in his now.

"Dear sister, we know Brother Fortunatus is your dearest friend. I cannot imagine he would have neglected to tell you."

"Nay, I neither," she said and, forgetting her courtesy, pulled free and ran back along the path to the monastery. She rushed into the courtyard through the wide gate and stood in confusion a moment. She had not entered these precincts before; it was wrong that she do so. Nor did she have the slightest idea

166

where Fortunatus' cell might be.

"Fortunatus!" There was a tremble in her voice.

She waited. She heard footsteps hurrying somewhere. Finally, he appeared from down a hallway.

"Sister Deirdre, my sweet lady!" He crossed the courtyard and picked up her two hands, then checked himself and bowed low.

"Forgive me. It was that I could not bear to even think of departing from you, let alone permit the words to cross my lips."

"Then it is true?" She felt her throat close on something that caught there. She stamped her foot both out of anger and to cover the power of her emotion. She turned and fled.

"Deirdre, dear sister." Fortunatus caught her at the gate. "Please, forgive me, I beg you. I only leave...!" He stopped himself. Deirdre broke free and turned to face him.

"Tell me!" she commanded. The tears were freely flowing down her cheeks.

Fortunatus looked away. "I leave because I will become a priest." He said this with unaccustomed severity.

"You are my friend!" she challenged. "You have no right to leave!"

Fortunatus smiled at her. His eyes too were full.

"I *am* your friend, Deirdre. It is why I must go."

"Go! How dare you? Oh!" She gasped, looking at Fortunatus' newly tonsured hair.

Fortunatus shifted uncomfortably from one foot to the other.

"You have done it." Deirdre took him in from head to toe in a quick glance. "Oh, Fortunatus, forgive me." Impulsively, she threw herself against him for comfort. He held her lightly.

"Dear sister, it is I who should ask forgiveness. You are right. I should have spoken of it. It was just that I put it off -- it was so difficult, and I wanted to spend these last days with you

167

happily."

"Oh, it would be terrible in any fashion. Oh, dear brother, what shall I do without you?"

Fortunatus patted her shoulder gently.

She pulled back from him. Wiping the tears from her eyes, she raised the fine linen cloth to catch those about to fall from his.

"When must you go?" she asked more calmly.

"Now...anytime."

"Can you spare me a few moments?"

"To be sure. Whatever you wish, dear sister."

"Let's sit by the river, shall we?"

Fortunatus moved out through the gate to indicate his willingness. His face brightened. "Oh, wait, I have something for you."

He ran back inside the monastery. Deirdre listened to his steps echo behind him. She fought off a wave of sadness that rose up once again.

He returned with his lute. "I have a song for you."

"Oh, I may weep then," Deirdre cried out with equal parts of pleasure and distress. "Where are you going, Fortunatus?"

"To a town called Tours, to the south. Where the bishop is. I will take my vows there."

Deirdre looked puzzled. "It is wonderful, I suppose. It's...it's that I'm selfish, dear brother. I would have you with me always."

"Ah, Deirdre, if only that could be!" Deirdre looked at him sharply. "But we must each find our own lives, that is certain," he said more calmly.

"Yours is certain perhaps, but what of mine? I know not what is my future. Oh, that brings me to my dream. It's why I have come seeking you."

"And good you did or, coward that I am, I might have

sneaked off."

"No! Would you have truly?"

"But I did not. I don't know. My heart has been broken these past few days with just the thinking of it."

"Did *they* make you go?" Deirdre asked suddenly.

"They?"

"Brother Paulus, the others?"

"Nay. I have lived here now eight years. I have learned all I can, read every manuscript. I am now a man. It is time to decide my future."

"Why couldn't you stay here?"

"I could except...well, I told you...it's time for me to commit myself...I am more needed.... Look, what of your dream? Let us speak not of me, I beg you." Deirdre felt sure the brothers had coerced him and now he was keeping that from her. That, at least, explained his strange behavior. He acted as though he was hiding something from her.

"Tell me your dream," he prodded.

"Oh that. It seems not so terrible now as this." Deirdre looked down at her hands. She was most unhappy.

"But what was it, that you, of all people, would leave your bed at dawn so willingly?"

Deirdre shuddered. "Not so willingly, as necessarily. I dreamed of *him*." She blushed scarlet and covered her face with her hands as though in horror in order to hide the rush of blood that came in thinking of how she had felt toward Clotaire in the dream.

"Do you mean" -- Fortunatus paused -- "the man whose name I'm forbidden to speak?"

His tact was so roundabout, so searching, Deirdre could not help but giggle.

"Yes. Oh, I don't think now that I can speak of it with you --

it's too awful. Yet I would not to anyone else and so I must."

"Do not, if it gives you pain or embarrassment."

"No, I will." She rushed through her words. "I am not sure what it means, but he stood near me with the most beautiful eyes I've ever seen and I...I desired him, or at least I felt pleasure to be near him. I have not known any man, Fortunatus, yet my dream body understood and desired him. And then" -- she glanced at her friend to ascertain his reaction thus far -- "then I dreamed again of my mother and somehow I *became* her."

Fortunatus was quiet.

"I felt such a traitor."

"But Clotaire is your betrothed," he finally said.

"I have told you..." Deirdre began, but Fortunatus held up his hand to stop her.

"Your betrothed is not responsible for your mother's death."

"But...."

"I know, Deirdre, I know what you will say, but he did not kill your mother. He was a mere boy when that occurred."

"But why would I dream of him together with that dream?"

Fortunatus sighed. "Perhaps the dream is a good omen, a sign that you may even find love for Clotaire. I have long hoped that, as a Christian now, you might find the love in your heart to forgive him, that you would even grow to love him. I don't know him myself, but the folk here speak only fine things of him." He touched Deirdre's hand. "And for myself, I would see you happy."

They sat quietly by the river. She would have liked to find a hundred things to engage him, so he would postpone his leaving, but she could not now find a single word. Fortunatus finally broke the silence.

"Shall I sing our song?" he asked quietly.

"Ai. Please. Sing."

He smiled at her. Deirdre looked away to watch the river flow past.

He sang sweetly then of flowers and angels, of seasons and the stars. She sang with him at last and laughed at his wit and charm. The tunes were gay, familiar; they had sung them many times together. Deirdre suddenly stood.

"I must go now, Fortunatus. I am hungry and would do my lessons. Fare thee well and Godspeed." She stood on her toes and kissed him lightly on the cheek, then strode off across the field toward the path.

Fortunatus watched her until she disappeared into the trees beyond. Picking up his lute, one more time, in almost a whisper, he sang three small verses of a song he had written days before, one he had never sung to her, never would.

PART 3

CHAPTER 17

At the end of each day, Deirdre still half expected Fortunatus to appear at the door to the library to entice her out into the sun. The least noise caused her to raise her head to listen the more carefully. It was hard to believe that he was really gone. Friend that he was, she had never realized the extent to which she had depended upon him. These several weeks since he left had been the loneliest she had ever passed. Half the enjoyment she had taken in her studies had been because she was able to share it with someone of equal enthusiasm. Berthaire imparted; he did not share. The other monks kept to themselves; no one else on the manor could read or write nor showed the slightest inclination in those directions. Among the few noblewomen, Deirdre was treated with courtesy and respect, but not with friendship. She was considered freakish for her intellectual pursuits. On her part, she found these women silly and empty-headed.

This time, the sound that caused her to lift her attention from her studies was the call of a bugle -- far off, from perhaps the top of the most distant hill. Deirdre rushed to the balcony where she could see for miles. She stood momentarily transfixed into the past. The serfs and serving folk bustled below her; there was a moment's hesitation before arms were decided against. The home bugle sounded and was quickly answered by the visiting band. A small voice inside her called a warning: *Be not fooled! They are enemy! Arm! Arm!*

Deirdre stood watching, her heart fiercely beating. She returned to the present. This call could mean only one thing: Clotaire had returned. She had to prod herself now in order to really hate him. Her years here at Athies with Berthaire and the gentle Fortunatus had passed so peacefully, so idyllically, it was difficult to feel an emotion so strong as hatred. But she fanned the spark of it with her quick memory. She recalled the lost Gunther and her aunt. Fortunatus had been wrong about her dream, she decided. Her aunt had also been a mother to her and Clotaire was directly responsible for that death even if he did not do the killing of her himself. Deirdre had to hate him, regardless of her Christianity. The old god beliefs called for vengeance, for balances to be returned by hate, not love.

Dazed, she watched as the household bustled back and forth, in and out. She was engrossed in a fear that made her tremble. The two other arrivals that had occurred in her life in just this manner had ended in death and grief and loss. She was chilled; yet she watched, fascinated, as the small band in the distance made a thin ribbon of dust rise above the horizon. Even that was familiar. As they drew closer, she could make out tiny figures on horseback. They came fast now and from the east, so that the late afternoon sun fell full upon them, causing flashes of light to shoot off from their various metals like sparks. Soon she could make out details and recognized Clotaire from his hair, black and long. She strained to see his face; once he arrived she would refuse to look at him at all; yet, she was deeply curious to see what the face that she so hated was like now. She was surprised to see that it was quieter and, in some way, more manly. She glanced over the others, still small in the distance.

Her heart stopped. She leaned forward over the balcony, eyes half-shut, to better see. It was true. That hair! Lothar was alive! He was real. Several years ago, she had somehow assumed the worst for her brother; with such a man as Clotaire, he would surely have been killed. And so, mourning quietly in order that no one might know of it, Deirdre had slowly beaten out of herself any expectation that her brother would return alive. The losses of two sets of parents had left a chasm of mistrust. She could not afford the loss of her last beloved, so she had gradually erased him, and Fortunatus had grown in her affections.

Lothar's presence took away the evil portent of this arrival. Clotaire meant one thing; Lothar quite another. Deirdre rushed inside.

"Claria, Claria," she called to her serving woman.

"Ai, I have all in readiness, milady," Claria said, rushing into the room. She held up a pale blue gown. "The blue one, nay? With the rose tunic. Oh, you will look so beautiful!"

Claria helped Deirdre to dress. Both women hurried with excitement, though for different reasons. Each assumed the source of the other's pleasure was the same as her own. Deirdre had forgotten Clotaire entirely. Claria knew nothing of Lothar.

"Ah, let me braid your hair," Claria suggested.

"Nay, I would have it free," Deirdre answered, pulling away.

"But it hides all the handwork on your tunic," Claria protested.

"Then let it. Brush me, please. Oh, listen! They must be here. Go see!" Deirdre did not wish to show herself on the balcony if they were already approaching the manor house. She would be perfect for Lothar to see her.

"Ai, they are arriving! And one, golden like you!"

"Quickly! Brush!"

Claria ran the brush through Deirdre's hair, which fell down her back below her waist.

"You are right, milady. No embroidery could be so fine an adornment as your own hair."

Deirdre looked at herself and smiled. Perhaps it was her happiness; she fairly glowed; since Fortunatus' departure she had not looked so happy. Claria painted her lips with the slightest blush of rose. Now she was ready.

"Go down. When they are in the large court and have done with their greetings, come to me."

"Ai, Lady Dierdre." Claria rushed out.

Deirdre listened from inside her chamber to the sounds of

welcome that rose up to her -- bugles and clarions, voices and laughter, all in celebration of the return of these men. Though her rooms were quite apart, in their own wing, she felt the surge of life and energy all around her, as though everyone who lived here, and all the servants, raced back and forth and up and down the way ants did when their nest was disturbed. Deirdre dismissed any realization about Clotaire until later. She was filled completely with the joy of her brother's return, and she would not have that joy marred by anything.

Claria returned breathless.

"He is so handsome, so courtly, forgive my liberty, Lady!" Claria bowed quickly.

Deirdre only smiled at her enthusiasm, thinking that Lothar was meant. "And where is he?"

"In the court below. All are there awaiting you."

She took one last glance at herself in the mirror, then, holding herself proudly erect, she descended the stairway. The lower hall was dark and cool; other than the soft sound her long skirts made, she made no sound walking.

She paused a moment near the door in order to find him among the others. She saw him right away. He stood almost directly across from her, off by himself. His face was in shadow from the heavy vines that grew along the opposite wall and roof, but his fairness cast its own light. She gasped, felt her throat constrict with a sob of joy, then, controlling herself, she glided out through the door into the light. She stopped. He was looking at her, as was everyone else, though she only saw Lothar. Her beauty at this moment transfixed all who saw her. Clotaire caught his breath. He had forgotten her hatred of him, forgotten the few words she had ever spoken to him, all of them in fury and out of revulsion. In the years he had been gone, he had had his own image of a very young and beautiful woman who would become his wife and queen. Before him, this woman now stood, real, emanating a radiance such as he had never beheld in any person before. It was the light she stood in perhaps, or the abundance of her hair, or the love that was clearly seen by all and directed toward Lothar. She stood like that only a moment. To Clotaire, it was a moment in which he could scarcely breathe; she was the fulfillment of his deepest dreams of feminine perfection.

"Lothar!" she whispered in a gasp of joy, her face a portrait of tenderness. It was then everyone realized she had not even glanced at Clotaire. Lothar stepped forward.

"Dear sister," he said and held out his hands to her. Deirdre ran into his arms, held him, the tears streaming down her face. They embraced long, amid the nervous smiles of Berthaire and his small entourage, all of whom were embarrassed by her not greeting Clotaire first. Clotaire suddenly came to his senses, recalling that fierce girl from the past and understood that she would snub him. With a quick gesture, he told all to leave, pretending to allow this reunion to have the intimacy that it deserved. He would win her on his own terms; she must never know his truth until she was his entirely.

Deirdre pulled back to look at Lothar. They smiled, each of them, finding words finally.

"How often I have thought of you, dear sister. How often I have longed to see you again."

"Ai, Lothar, I am ashamed. My thoughts of you died some years ago. I could not believe you would ever return to me. To see you now is like seeing a dead man come back to life."

Lothar laughed. "Truly? And why?" He turned toward Clotaire whom he now noticed. Deirdre turned with him and found herself looking directly into Clotaire's eyes.

"Ah! King Clotaire," said Lothar, sensing anger in the king. "Forgive us. We forget our manners."

Clotaire saw the joy in Deirdre's eyes before she could find another emotion to take its place. She was so filled with it, she was not able to summon an angry feeling immediately. Contrary to her earlier determination not to even look at him, she now held

176

his eyes and spoke quietly.

"Indeed, sire" she said, "do forgive us. And I beg you to forgive my indisposition to attend the many celebrations that accompany your arrival here. I am near ill due to a recent sadness. It is only the great love I have for my brother that has brought me from my chamber." As she spoke, her demeanor became increasingly cool. Clotaire felt her reserve, the cool politeness, and returned it with a slight bow.

"I expect that, by tomorrow, you shall be well enough to participate in the festivities." He paused. "By my side, as is your duty." He enjoyed seeing her reserve dissolve in the rush of blood that reddened her face. "We shall stay here a month perhaps, then we shall return to my home in Soissons. You shall ready your trousseau. When we arrive in Soissons, we shall be married."

So saying, he turned on his heel, leaving Deirdre open-mouthed, with a fury mounting in her like a sudden summer storm. Except she had no outlet for her storm. Clotaire left that space for her brother to fill. Deirdre could not inflict the force of her anger on Lothar.

"Come to my chambers in an hour," she ordered out of confusion. "I shall be calmer then. We can visit and talk." She ran to the door and turned.

"Forgive me, Lothar, I am too upset to see you now. Please come." She pleaded with her eyes, then ran inside.

Lothar listened to her soft, quick footsteps disappear within. The strength of her feelings served to justify his own growing dislike for the king. What she felt and expressed would not be disadvantageous to him in the future, he felt. He smiled. It had been a long time since he had experienced the warmth of another's affection for him. It was good to be home.

CHAPTER 18

Felice closed the door and leaned against it. She looked around the room. There was a small chest for clothing below the one high window. It was simple and unadorned, and on it stood a single candle, a water basin and a pitcher for washing; a straight-backed chair was placed near the opposite wall, and in between, there was a narrow bed with a white coverlet and two blankets. The wooden floor was of wide, ancient planks, worn smooth through the years. Felice dropped her basket of possessions and took the few steps necessary to get first to one side of the room, then to the other. She hugged herself and laughed.

"Lucky woman, lucky wench," she said softly aloud, and giggled again. She flopped on the bed with a cry of pleasure. The bed responded with a great creaking and one sharp crack. But it held. Felice had never slept in a real bed before, always having used a pallet on the ground. In fact, other than the few times with Clotaire, she had never slept in a real room. Her quarters at Gunther's estate had consisted of a lean-to, which she managed to cover with scraps of fabric, skins, and fir boughs to keep out the wind and rain. With a fire inside, she stayed cozy enough. But here was a room with stone walls, a wood floor, and wood ceiling, a window, and actual furniture in which to put herself and her few things.

There was a knock on the door. Felice jumped up and simply looked at the door until she realized it was her room and she should answer.

"Enter," she called out.

A serving woman entered with an armful of clothing. The woman smiled pleasantly.

"Ye are Felice, nay?"

Felice nodded.

"I am Gaile," the woman said. "I bring ye fresh clothes --

skirts, tunics, all that ye need. Ye can give me all that ye have on and I'll see it gets washed." She looked closer at Felice's torn skirts and laughed. "Or mended, eh?" She looked at Felice directly. Her eyes were happy and soft, not the eyes of the usual serf. Felice smiled back awkwardly.

Gaile flopped on the chair. "I'll wait," she said.

"Wait?"

"Yer clothes, as I said," she answered.

"Ai."

Gaile chattered on about the excitement at Athies because of Clotaire's return. Felice dropped her clothes one by one on the floor.

"Ah, but I wish the wedding could be here," Gaile sighed. "Ye are the king's mistress, I hear?"

Felice looked at Gaile suspiciously. But there was only a pleasant mischief in her eyes, no rancor, no malice.

"I don't know about that," Felice said.

Gaile raised an eyebrow and grinned. "It's what we be hearing the last hours from the other women. And they get to be sleeping down in the serf's quarters, while ye are singled out to sleep here."

Felice grinned. "Ai," she said simply.

"Besides, we got special orders."

It was Felice's turn to raise her eyebrows.

"The room, clothes, a bath." She got up suddenly. "Here. Put this on. I'll take ye down to the tub." She watched Felice slip into the dressing gown. "Were ye a house serf where ye come from?"

"Nay, I worked the fields."

Gaile was stupefied. "I'd hardly a-believed it. Ye are very comely."

It was not a bath to compare with the one she had taken the

179

first time at Clotaire's orders. It was a rough wooden tub. But the water was warm and sweetly scented. Gaile kept her company, helping her to wash her hair. She told Felice all the stories about Clotaire that she could remember having heard over the years. Clotaire had been raised and educated at Athies by Berthaire. He was loved by all, and jealously pampered by his former servants. Gaile herself had never served him and asked Felice many personal questions about him. Felice was disarmed by her openness, but avoided answering the intimate questions that Gaile put to her without the slightest embarrassment. Felice was not accustomed to the ways of household serfs, the manner in which they thought of and treated a master or mistress as a kind of object under their care and jurisdiction, not as a human being like themselves.

"Ye will eat with us," Gaile said as Felice got back into her dressing gown.

"In the kitchen."

Felice was amazed, but said nothing.

"Ye can rest an hour or more," Gaile said as she led Felice back to her room. "We eat then. The kitchen's around that way." She patted Felice affectionately on the arm. "If ye need anything, I am back there in the laundry next to the bath. I am to serve ye."

She said this without the repugnance Felice would have expected from a house serf who had been put to serve a field worker. And she smiled. Felice liked her, though her own native reserve and suspicion held her from showing her feelings. Gaile was short, round, no more than eighteen, with a wide face, wide-set deep eyes, brown and gay. Her skin was fair and rosy. She was simple in her ways, innocent of rancor, Felice sensed. She could perhaps become a friend -- the first woman Felice would ever have had to be a friend.

In her room, she went through the several gowns and tunics that had been given to her, and selected to wear a deep rose-colored gown with a bright red tunic. She brushed her hair a long

180

time, enjoying its softness and cleanness. It surrounded her face like a great, soft cloud. To her delight, a small mirror was hung inside the cover of the clothes chest, so she could see herself again as she had six long years ago; though, with this mirror, she could only see herself in pieces. She was surprised by her face. There was now a line between her brows and a pout to her mouth which clearly reflected the sorrow she suffered from now almost daily. She scolded herself for it.

"Stupid wench," she whispered, shaking her head at her reflection. "You have all that there is. He gives you this room, this dress. Still you are not satisfied."

The face with the sad mouth looked back at her. "Ai, because he has not touched me once since the night he saved me."

"He treats you with respect now, like a lady?"

By letting her reflection answer, Felice expressed her conflict. "Oh, with such distance. We used to play together, to laugh. Now he only thinks of the trip."

"But he took you in!"

"Ai, and for what?"

Her reflection did not respond.

"He will come to me here."

"Or I shall go to him."

The face smiled sadly.

"*She* is here. Do you think he will even notice you now?"

"Shut up, fool!" Felice slammed shut the lid and sat back on her heels. It was perfectly natural for her to see her reflection as someone nearly separate, another part of herself who could see differently. She rose, irritated, and walked to the door.

She knew that she had to see the girl, Deirdre. By seeing her, she would dispel some of her own anxiety. Clotaire did love her, she kept telling herself. Besides, what did she care? He gave her a room, clothing, and food without her having to lift a finger at work. What more could she ask, she a whore and a field serf?

181

She followed the path that meandered along the walls around to where the house rose up to a second story. This was the main section where Berthaire and the nobility lived. She walked more slowly. On one of these balconies Deirdre had stood on that last day so long ago. Felice hoped to receive some sign; so far her gods had played a terrible trick on her. She had gained what she had asked for, but it was not what she wanted. Clotaire loved her, but she was not his woman.

She walked completely around the sprawling estate without a glimpse of anyone. When she had passed the high walls of the dining hall, she heard from within the music and laughter of celebration. She imagined Clotaire, happy, smiling, healed now, surrounded by people who loved him, and she longed to be by his side. She began the walk again, taking long strides, stretching out the tight ball of envy, a coldness she felt in her chest, whenever her mind slipped back to the picture she had of a smiling Deirdre sitting at Clotaire's side.

From somewhere above her, on a balcony, came two voices: a woman's and a man's, quiet, urgent. She caught only a few words.

"Nay...hateful...," the woman said. Felice strained. The voice was clearly a noblewoman's.

"...come back...." She heard distress in the man's voice; something in its timbre made her suspect it was Lothar.

"I hate him!" This was clear enough. Surely it was Deirdre who spoke. Felice relaxed the tension in her body and smiled.

"There," she said to herself. "It is the sign." With a jaunty step, she hurried along the path. She was hungry, a good, solid hunger she had not felt for weeks.

The kitchen was filled with smoke, tables, a rowdy bunch of servants, and the smell of mutton. The noise created pockets of intimacy. Felice smiled widely. She felt her former vigor, her lust for life, for passion, for men. Someone grabbed her by her waist. She laughed as in former days, and leaned back into the rough embrace to look up into the man's face. She was startled to see Villem, whose surprise, blunted by drunkenness, did not show as quickly. She did not pull away, but poised herself, ready for his withdrawal. But that did not happen. He looked long into her face. Anger supplanted surprise, but lasted only a moment. She saw it pass through his eyes, over his lips, and then disappear as pain moved in, then desire. His mouth was on hers; his arms around her, tight, but tender. She leaned into him and felt her own pain dimly in some recess of her body. He pulled back. His mouth tasted of ale.

Felice grinned at him. "Eat with me first," she said, patting her stomach. "I am hungry."

Villem was too drunk not to be led. He made a face as she pulled him to a table loaded with meats and vegetables. She tore a large chunk of meat off of one of the roasts and took a big bite. The juice ran down her chin. Villem laughed. Felice cringed. The laugh was close to a sob.

"Ai, sit down, man," she said, pulling him down beside her with her free hand. "Be not a fool. Ye are drunk."

"Ai," said Villem. He looked at her long. "Are ye happy now, wench?"

Felice decided it did not matter. She would no more lie to this man who still loved her.

"Nay," she said.

Villem hesitated, his pause the exaggeration of the drunk. "I, neither," he finally said.

Felice took another bite and grabbed some grapes. She stuffed food into Villem's mouth, laughing at his difficulty in chewing it. But soon his appetite matched hers and he began to feed himself. They said nothing, only ate, enjoying one another's pleasure in the goodness of the food and drink. Felice drank faster and faster until her head was spinning. They made faces and laughed harder and harder at the greater efforts each made to outdo the other in contortions.

Finally, they were full and stood shakily. Felice belched. Villem laughed. The room was a chaos of celebration; most were drunk and rowdy. But, for Felice and Villem, it was as though no one else were in the room. They still said no words, but each knew exactly what the other was saying. They made it to the door, holding each other's arms and bumping with laughter into furniture and people.

Outside, Felice's head cleared a little in the night air. She pulled on Villem's arm. It was very dark; an overcast hid the stars. But Felice knew her way. It was simple: just follow the walls. She led Villem out beyond the end of the manor. There she stopped and waited. It was for him to decide, though she made it clear that she wanted him. He pulled her to him. They sank down, their mouths together. They made love slowly, sensuously; in complete silence; each of them, in turns, fighting away a sob that would change halfway out to a whispered laugh; each involved in giving some part of the self to the other, seeking solace and giving it at the same time. They were too drunk to reach any conclusion, or any clarity, either within themselves or to the other. They felt the earth receive their bodies; it gave way into softness as it will when a body completely relaxes. They fell asleep like children, wrapped around one another.

In the morning, in the hour before light, they finished their lovemaking and parted without a word or a smile. But Felice looked back, once, and Villem understood that he could never banish her from his life again.

CHAPTER 19

Lothar was expected to participate in the welcoming festivities, so, after his hour-long talk with Deirdre at dusk, he was able to slip back to her rooms for only a moment.

"These will be too big for you," he said, handing her some men's clothing. "But perhaps they will afford you some protection."

Deirdre looked grim. "Did you manage to saddle my horse, Mani?"

"Nay. I told the stable boy to do so."

Deirdre began to protest, but Lothar held up his hand.

"It is less suspicious. I said you wished to ride in the summer night." He smiled. "The lower folk know nothing of your feud with Clotaire. I let him believe it had to do with a lovers' tryst. He was delighted to assist."

"Oh, you are wonderful!" Deirdre exclaimed, and threw her arms impetuously around his neck.

"Ah, dear sister, I am afraid for you. The roads are dangerous. You have no idea...and a woman alone! You must give up this plan."

"My fate here is worse, I am sure, than any I could meet out there. You yourself have told me what sort of man he is, and you were drawn to him at first."

"I was very young," Lothar said in justification.

"Ai, but now you know better, as I have always known. I will be all right. In a week perhaps, I will be in Tours -- may the good Lord guide me -- and will find my dear friend, Fortunatus."

"Oh, let me go with you."

"We have already been over that a dozen times. If you were to go, all would be immediately suspicious. As it is, they will know by morning. I hope, by then, to be too far to be pursued."

185

Lothar sighed. He was most unhappy. Deirdre caressed his cheek.

"Once I am in Tours, I will send a message back. Then you may come to join me. Only do not allow anyone to discover your destination. Now go, sweet Lothar. Celebrate and show neither concern nor worry. If anyone asks of me, tell them the story we've decided. Go!" She pushed him toward the door. "Pray for me, dear brother."

"Ai, all night and day. Farewell. Godspeed."

No servants were below, so it was not difficult for Lothar to get back unobserved to the festivities in the dining hall. He stayed back among the shadows by the walls, though twice he slowly crossed the wide room so that all would know he was present.

A dais had been set up at one end of the room. There, Clotaire, Berthaire, and several ladies and gentlemen -- relatives of Berthaire -- sat eating and watching the entertainment. A trio of musicians played the pipes; they played sweet, high-pitched shepherd songs, one after another. A fourth accompanied them on a crude drum. The lesser folk of the household and the good brothers had also been invited to the grand evening. Some of the servants began to dance, while others accompanied them by clapping and stomping their feet.

"Ah, good! Good!" shouted Clotaire. He was red-faced and beaming with pleasure. Berthaire, beside him, looked less gay, as though some burden weighed him down. Lothar was sure he was deeply disturbed by the obvious breech between Clotaire and Deirdre. Both of them were his dearest pupils, nearly his own blood if love and pride were the measures. Right now, Lothar had in his wide sleeve the brief letter Deirdre had written begging Berthaire to forgive her. For him she had wept. She loved the old man more than she had realized, and she recognized that her flight would be a severe blow to him.

I pray you understand, she had written, *and forgive me. But I saw him, with my own eyes, strike down my own and only uncle.*

*I cannot live my life, which you have taught me so to cherish,
with a murderer, though he be a king and call himself a Christian.
Farewell.*

"Lothar! Young Lothar!"

Lothar looked up to the dais whence the calling came. The
old man gesticulated.

"Join us here, my son," Berthaire continued. """Servant!
More wine! More ale! We shall drink and laugh the night away!"

Lothar remembered to smile as Deirdre had bidden him, but
his heart was heavy with worry.

"Sire," he said upon reaching the dais, "it is my honor to
join you. I thank you."

"And your sister, my student?" Berthaire asked less
publicly, leaning toward Lothar.

"Did she not tell you she was indisposed?"

"Ai." The old man looked directly at him.

Lothar saw that Berthaire would not be easily fooled.
Lothar blushed. "When I saw her, perhaps an hour before dinner,
she looked not well...."

"All must dance!" Clotaire was on his feet, bellowing to the
folk below who happily obeyed him. Clotaire leaped down among
them, grabbed a young serving girl, and began to dance. The hall
erupted in cheers.

Lothar looked back at Berthaire. "...and she asked me to,
again, beg her pardon, that she would rest."

"Perhaps it is her friend's departure, the monk, Fortunatus,"
Berthaire suggested. "She has been sad...."

The whole dais, somewhat flimsy anyway, shook as
Clotaire leaped back up to take his seat. He had drunk too much
and was winded from the dancing. He sank into his chair and
looked out across the room morosely. Lothar felt a wave of
satisfaction to think that, in some way, he had participated in
Deirdre's plan to thwart the king.

187

"Sire" Lothar said to him now, "a good evening for you, nay?"

Clotaire looked at him in silence a moment. "Ai," he said without looking away, as if he were reading Lothar's thoughts. "I should think you would be with your sister -- Lady Dierdre -- who loves you so."

Lothar felt himself go pale. "I was, indeed. She has retired for the night, I believe."

Clotaire sat up and looked around, mischief in his eye. "And is she still feeling badly?"

Lothar wished now he had kept silent. He knew that Clotaire bothered with few conventions, that he was capable of anything.

"Ai, I believe so."

Just then, by the entrance, Lothar caught sight of the stable boy to whom he had spoken earlier. The old door servant was listening to the young man. The servant glanced once up at Clotaire, then nodded, and sent the boy away. Lothar felt panic rise in his chest.

"I asked a question, sire!"

Lothar turned back to Clotaire who was looking at him with irritation.

"Sire, I beg your pardon? I was momentarily distracted."

The old servant was approaching the dais.

"I said she will be well by tomorrow, will she not?"

"I sincerely hope so"

The servant stood quietly below the dais in front of Clotaire, awaiting his attention.

"Good. It is strange...." Clotaire broke off, noticing the old man. "What is it, old man?"

The servant leaned forward to indicate that he had a private message. Clotaire leaned down to him.

"My horse?" he asked, looking at the old man with puzzlement.

"'Tis what he said, sire."

Clotaire laughed. "I have no need of my horse this night." He frowned. "Whence came these orders?"

"I know not," the old man answered. His wrinkled face showed concern that whatever mistake had been made, its results might now fall upon his shoulders.

"Go to the stables. My orders are to unsaddle my horse and bed him down for the night. And inquire who ordered him to be readied." The servant disappeared. Clotaire, laughing, then leaped off the dais and joined again in the dancing.

Lothar was apparently forgotten. He leaned back tensely.

"Will the young Lothar accompany the king to Soissons?" This was politely put to him by Berthaire's oldest daughter who had returned to Athies to take care of her father after the death of her mother, Lady Balline. She was a widow, a matronly woman with her father's kind eyes, though with none of their liveliness.

"Yes, yes, of course, I shall go to Soissons."

Berthaire's daughter smiled. "Ah, it should be a lovely affair. They are both so young, so handsome. I remember my own wedding. It was here at Athies."

Lothar was grateful for the woman's chatter, another trait of her father's, because it made no demands upon him and he could watch the door. Finally, it opened to the old servant who looked up at the dais. Lothar signaled to him. As the servant approached, he excused himself momentarily and kneeled at the edge of the dais so none could hear his conversation. "And what happened?"

The servant thought what Lothar hoped he would: that the king expected Lothar to receive the message. "The boy was confused. Tell milord he had no orders; only he was given to understand his master might wish to ride this night."

"And who gave him to understand that?" Lothar asked.

189

"He did not say."

"Good." Lothar smiled and looked around. "There. He is dancing with the young maid. Tell him the message yourself."

The servant bowed and waited at the edge of the circle of dancers. Lothar sat back on his cushion and gave his attention back to Berthaire's daughter.

"Please continue, dear lady," he said.

Lothar felt a pull on his sleeve. Berthaire was looking at him fiercely, holding out in front of him Deirdre's note. Lothar looked blankly at it. Berthaire hissed, "What is this?"

"I...sire...I...."

"'Twas found down there." Berthaire pointed to the floor just below the point where Lothar had knelt. Lothar felt his sleeve. It must have fallen out when he leaned over.

Berthaire turned to an attendant. "Fetch the king and send him immediately to my office. Hurry!" He turned back to Lothar. "Did you know of this, Lothar?"

"Ai" Lothar answered and bowed his head.

"Fool!" Berthaire said this more gently, shaking his head. He was assisted down from the dais and walked quickly from the dining hall.

Lothar looked around. He estimated it had been almost two hours since Deirdre had fled. Clotaire was still dancing, though the attendant was trying to interrupt. Perhaps she could still get away. He sent up a fervent prayer.

Clotaire stopped now and was finally listening to the attendant. Then, he too, left the room. Berthaire's daughter had resumed her recollections for Lothar's amusement. Dismayed, feeling like a traitor to his sister, he sat listening mutely, paralyzed into inaction.

Berthaire simply handed the note to Clotaire when, drunk, he staggered into his old mentor's office.

"Eh?" he said only at first. "What?"

190

"Clear your head, my boy." Berthaire ordered. "You are about to lose your woman and your honor, methinks."

Clotaire laughed. "You mean?" He looked at Berthaire in bewilderment, then laughed again. "She left? She is out there attempting to flee?"

Berthaire only nodded.

"Alone?"

"It is unsafe, sire."

Clotaire shook his head in disbelief. "She is crazy." He looked at Berthaire. "Perhaps I should let her go." He laughed again.

Berthaire turned away in disgust. "You are drunk."

"Ai, I am indeed quite drunk. But it's coming to me now." He spoke slowly, as if trying to penetrate his befogged mind. "The good lady Deirdre, my betrothed, has taken to the road, this night, alone, in order to avoid becoming my queen and wife." Clotaire could not help but laugh. He sat down and slapped his knees.

"Ah, Berthaire..." he said, catching his breath. "She is a lady of spirit, eh? Do you realize how many women I have known? And how many of those women would ride all night to *find* me, and she would brave the night to *escape* me?" Again, he went into gales of laughter.

Berthaire remained serious. "I would also find it amusing, my dear young king, if I did not love the lady as my own daughter. She endangers herself out there. She is young and beautiful *and alone*." He emphasized the last two words. "I will go myself then if you will not take action."

"Ah! Woman be damned!" Clotaire stood up now in a rage. "I shall go after her myself. Ah, the wench, the stupid twit, the blasted, damnable feisty she-dog! My first night to be merry and she destroys all. I shall marry her off to one of the commoners, teach her a lesson!" He strode to the door, tore it open.

191

"Saddle my horse!" he roared. Three servants raced down the hall.

"Good Berthaire, forgive me. She is a beautiful woman indeed, but a woman to be broken, I fear. A shrew, no doubt. If I wife her, I shall have to beat her or keep her locked up."

Berthaire smiled sadly. "She is very wonderful. You must be patient with her, Clotaire. She is headstrong, but not so strong altogether, as you might think."

Clotaire turned away and as quickly turned back again, asking, "Did her brother know of this plan or in any way help her, milord?"

"Oh, dear no! Lothar is a man of honor, I am sure," Berthaire lied without hesitation. "I but found her note moments ago here in my office."

Clotaire walked to the stables taking deep breaths of the cool night air to clear his head. He said not a word to anyone, only mounted his horse, which had been once again saddled. The poor stable boy, wide-eyed and trembling, stood at the horse's head.

"Which way?" Clotaire bellowed. The boy raised one shaking arm and pointed toward the path leading south. Clotaire dug his heels into the horse's side and quickly disappeared into the night.

CHAPTER 20

Deirdre had no idea how long she had pushed the horse to her fullest capacity, but it had been too long for Mani. The mare was soaked from the fast pace. Deirdre's own anxiety and fear had been the spurs, and while these had lessened as the night passed uneventfully, she had continued to push. It was Mani who awakened her to the realization that the horse would be ruined if she continued to push her. A spirited mare, she had kept going as her mistress wished until she simply could not continue and nearly fell from her own fatigue. It was that which made Deirdre slow her. Mani's sides heaved from the effort. Deirdre slipped off and walked beside her. The road, lined with poplars and pines, was like a dark canyon on this moonless night. Mani's breathing gradually quieted. The only other sounds to break the silence were the soft clopping of the horse's hooves on the dirt road, and the occasional hoot of an owl or rustle in the forest of a small night animal. Deirdre listened for sounds of riders, of pursuit, and wondered if she would ever be able to put enough distance between herself and Clotaire and Athies. Her throat constricted. Athies: where she had been so happy and made a life of joy and fulfillment. Athies: which she now was forced to leave. She made herself swallow. She would not permit herself to look back. Fortunatus was ahead of her. She would get to him and to sanctuary safely. Lothar would join her later. She would make a new life. She stopped and put her open hand over Mani's muzzle. There was a slight breeze just beginning. Deirdre thought she had heard hooves, that the breeze had carried the sound to her from the distance. She heard it again. It was still far off. She hesitated. Not sure even of the direction it was coming from, she simply could not mount and ride. She had only one direction in which to go. She pulled Mani with her into the bushes among the trees. There was no path, no opening, and the branches raked her skin and caught her clothes. There was a small clearing a short way in. There was no doubt now; horsemen were approaching. Deirdre's heart beat almost as fast as the sound of the hooves that pounded the road. Reaching the clearing, she turned and stood quite still beside Mani. Gently and surely, she ran her hand back and forth over the horse's neck to soothe her. Mani snorted softly.

"Hush," Deirdre whispered. The hoofbeats were close now. There were more than she had thought. She kept soothing Mani for fear the mare would shy or whinny. She dared not allow herself to think for even a moment what her fate would be if she were captured by highwaymen. Until now, even with Lothar's many warnings, and arguments against her plan, her only fear had been that she would be discovered and brought back to Athies. But now her blood ran cold with the proximity of these strangers. They were passing by. She could just see the movement of darker shadows through the foliage, could hear the gear and feel the presence of each horse and rider as they passed. She counted six. Her only consolation was that they were heading north, in the direction opposite hers. She waited until there was no longer any sound of them before leading Mani back to the road. Mounting, she hardly had to persuade Mani to a brisk trot, which she kept up easily for several miles. Deirdre had just begun to relax into Mani's rhythm when she pulled her to a sudden stop. Ahead on the road was a dim light. Deirdre was stunned. For a moment she felt trapped, with no way to go. Then she started again, at a slow walk, approaching carefully. The light was coming from a fire to one side of the road in a clearing. Deirdre stayed mounted. She would have to bolt if anyone attempted to stop her.

Three horses were grazing off to the side. Each raised its head as she passed, but none made a sound. Deirdre saw three sleeping forms around the fire. They remained still as she passed no more than ten yards from them. Her legs felt as though, of their own accord, they would kick Mani to race away, but Deirdre restrained herself. She would run when she was out of earshot. From behind, she heard one of the horses whinny. Mani's head shot up, her ears forward. Before the mare could answer, Deirdre kicked her. Mani broke into a gallop. Deirdre cursed within. If anyone pursued her, she was lost; she would not be able to outrun them. She pushed Mani for only a couple of miles, then veered off the road into an opening. Deirdre slipped off before Mani had completely stopped and led the horse behind a dark clump of bushes. Then she used all her self control to calm herself as well as the animal. Finally, Mani stood quite still. Deirdre listened. It was quiet; she heard nothing but the crickets, an owl, and her own breathing. The woods offered shelter; she felt safe here.

"We will rest in the woods all day," she whispered in Mani's ear. The mare lifted her head a little and whinnied softly.

On the road again, Deirdre let Mani find her own pace, a fairly slow walk. She herself was beginning to feel sleepy and Mani's walk rocked her toward sleep and dream. The night was endless. She had almost decided to stop when she heard again the sound of hoofbeats. Deirdre looked around. The road here was thickly lined with bushes and trees. Twice she tried to force Mani through, but the mare shied back from the thorny bushes. The sound was getting closer. Deirdre panicked. She would run for it. She kicked Mani hard. The mare leaped forward, racing along as fast as she could. Deirdre hung on, all her senses alert again. So intent was she on the road ahead that she was startled when, in the periphery of her vision, she suddenly saw someone coming up alongside. Instinctively, she turned and struck at him with her riding crop. It was grabbed out of her hand, almost unseating her. She leaned forward, kicked Mani hard. But the rider was upon her; his horse was large and fast. He brought his horse close to hers; Deirdre felt herself held around the waist, pulled from Mani's back, and lifted into the air. The rider's horse came to an abrupt stop, and the next thing Deirdre knew, she lay in a heap on the ground, stunned. Vaguely, she sensed a presence like a large bird of prey above her. She looked up at the shadow of a man.

"I should break every bone in your body," he muttered through his teeth.

Deirdre was up. She was electric. The voice was Clotaire's.

195

Throughout the chase, she had made no sound; now, she shrieked. She ran madly through the bushes, felt herself grabbed by the skirts, and fell forward, face-down, onto the slippery pine needles. She was roughly turned onto her back and saw the arm, brutal and hard, raised like a club over her.

"Ai," she gasped, her fear distilling itself into this tiny sound. The arm hesitated, softened, lowered. She could scarcely breathe. And now not at all. Her mouth, half-opened, was covered over with his. She felt the moist softness of his lips. They were alive. His tongue tingled her own lips and the inside of her mouth. She pulled away in order to take a breath. His body was on hers; she felt a warmth moving up her arm to her shoulder, down over her breast, felt the rush of pleasure in her nipple and its echo in the other, untouched, breast. His body was heavy and pushed against her; she felt her own arms reaching up now to caress him. It was then she realized her own body's betrayal.

"No!" And her arms turned into weapons, beating against his head, his shoulders. He was kissing the opening of her tunic. She twisted halfway out from under him; one arm was caught beneath his body. He grabbed the other and leaned to kiss her again. She jerked away.

"Ah, the lady's changed her mind," he taunted.

"Filthy toad!"

He held her fast now, lay upon her, his face only inches from hers. They could only sense the other's look; it was too dark to truly see. Clotaire's body relaxed somewhat. She felt a spasm run through him.

"Aghh!" Deirdre exclaimed in disgust, trying to pull away again.

He was laughing. His whole body shook with it. Clotaire rolled off her onto his back, helpless with laughter. Deirdre moved away from him, still trying to calm her breath and blood.

"Ai, ai, ai," Clotaire said, catching his own breath. He leaned up on his elbow. "You need not worry, milady. I have yet to force myself on any woman. I have no need of that." He laughed again. "No, indeed not."

"Ah, you are a dirty, foul-mouthed beast, a crumb left in a basket of stale loaves! You are fish skin, toad eyes! Cur!"

Deirdre's curses were met with greater laughter. Each name seemed to tickle him more. Finally she shouted at him, "Why are you laughing so, like an imbecile?"

Clotaire quieted and sat up. "Methinks you know, Lady Dierdre. I am a gentleman. I would not say it aloud."

Deirdre blushed and bit her tongue. "I hate you," she said quietly, with conviction.

"You shall make a wonderful bride," he answered, not disguising the irony in his voice. "May I assist you up?"

"I can get up myself," she said, spitting out the words.

They walked back to the road. The two horses grazed on the grasses by the side. The sky was lightening. Deirdre pulled at Mani's reins and mounted.

"My horse is tired," she said proudly, after Clotaire mounted.

Clotaire looked at her. In the grey light, the first light of the day, she sat erect on her small horse. Her hair framed her face the way Felice's hair always did -- a wild cloud, electric with energy. Her face was set in anger and coldness. She looked like a statue of a very young girl. Her eyes flicked toward him and stopped on his for a moment. Clotaire felt a surge. She had wanted him. She had the cool eyes of a cat at this moment, but he felt again the surge in his own sex as surely as he had felt it in her. She had wanted him.

"We shall ride slowly, my lady, to spare your horse."

They turned then, back down the road, heading north. Clotaire rode beside her.

CHAPTER 21

"I am resigned. I see no hope at all."

Lothar leaped up and settled next to Deirdre on the low couch. "How can you say that? How can you just give in to him?"

Deirdre raised one eyebrow. "Give in to him? Never! But I see I will be forced into marriage."

Lothar looked around the library. Deirdre laughed haughtily at his caution. "You may say what you wish whether anyone is here or not. I have at least the satisfaction that everyone knows I despise him and am forced to marry him. He has that dishonor to bear."

"Dishonor means nothing to him. He is born of our class, but partakes of the lowest levels. He calls himself Christian, but breaks all the laws of God and man. Right here, at Athies, under his teacher's roof, he keeps a common whore for his pleasure."

Deirdre looked at Lothar with irony. "Would you rather he keep a lady? Or an uncommon whore?"

Lothar squirmed. "At least that would not be so scandalous. This woman is a field serf! She is unclean."

Deirdre laughed. "It interests me not at all what his escapades might be -- ladies or whores. Of what significance is that to me?"

Lothar looked shocked. "Sister, he will be your husband."

"In name only. He shall never touch me. I would die first."

Lothar looked at her seriously. "I believe you mean that."

Deirdre looked away, out the window. "Dear brother, when I finally embraced this new faith, I embraced it fully." She looked at him. "It was not easy. I disputed and argued all the way." She smiled. "That is my nature, as you know. But now, I try to live the precepts taught me. I would not lightly take my life, but I would die nevertheless."

Lothar looked at her, puzzled.

"It's like the birds we used to capture as children. Do you remember?"

"Ai, but I fail to see any connection."

"We would try to save them. We would make them a cage, bring them grasses and threads, give them food and water. They always died before morning, though nothing would be wrong with them. Lady Gudrun once told me how they simply chose to die like that. After that, I never tried to catch any. That is what I mean. I would simply choose to die and it would happen."

"I will never permit it!"

Deirdre looked at him, the question in her eyes.

Lothar leaned closer and whispered, "I shall make certain that you do not have to die."

She took his hand in hers. "Dear Lothar, take care of your own soul and body. Be not concerned about me. I shall fight him in my way. Perhaps, after all, I shall win."

Lothar was quiet, then spoke softly. "His captain, Villem by name, also bears him a grudge."

"It does not surprise me, after all you have told me, that anyone associated with him should hate him."

"It would not be difficult...."

"What? What would not be difficult?"

"With Villem's help, I could kill him."

Caught by surprise and disbelief, Deirdre laughed. Lothar scowled. "You do not believe in me."

"Oh, dear Lothar, I do not wish to believe in you. Are you not Christian?"

"Ai, but such a brute deserves to die in the eyes of God."

Deirdre looked at him in amazement. "I believe you are serious."

Lothar did not answer.

Deirdre said sternly, "If you are Christian, look into your heart as I must daily do. Never speak to me of such a thing again." She looked hard at him. "It is murder you speak of," she said.

"How can I bear it?" he cried.

"It is not your pain," she answered. "It is mine." She clasped his hand. "Believe me, I will find a way. I will not have you jeopardize yourself for my sake."

"Ah, I hate him. I would do it for myself only, but this thing with you makes it an ache in my heart."

"You have never spoken of what made you change toward him."

Lothar looked at his hands.

"I must confess that when you left here six years ago, I was very angry with you," she continued. "You rode beside him, conversed and laughed as though he were a brother."

"I blush to think of that." Lothar looked directly at Dierdre. In these many hours they had spent together, he had basked in the warmth of her love and respect for him. After so long a deprivation, his need for these was such that he allowed himself the indulgences of what he privately called 'small stories'. He told Deirdre completely invented adventures in which he figured prominently, if not heroically. Her growing respect for him filled such an abyss of wanting that his tales became bolder, he braver. He was careful not to exaggerate, watching where her belief was about to give way, and he inwardly hated himself for his lies as they accumulated, until, lately, unable to bear the guilt, he could find justification for them in his sister's firm belief that Clotaire had murdered their uncle in cold blood. Clotaire had told him quite another story, but Lothar now preferred to believe his own version. Why should not Clotaire try to justify that act to Lothar? No doubt he had hoped the boy would tell the story to Deirdre and so break down her resistance to the king. For this reason, and for others unknown to him, Lothar had never told her. He was glad now that he had not.

"It was that I was so young," he said. "I had lost you, our uncle, my home; and Clotaire seemed kind at first. Perhaps he was. But...you recall how I was once...perhaps frightened is the word...not brave at any rate. Clotaire began to test me, to put me in dangerous positions. Now I see that he wished me dead without taking his hand to the act directly."

"No! It is just as I believed."

Lothar watched Deirdre's reaction, fascinated. If only what he told her were true. And yet, Clotaire had put him in dangerous situation. Perhaps his perceptions were true. Who was to know? Thus his mind circled, finding a way through the maze of his wishes.

"As my bravery grew, he tested me more. Thus, once I lay as near to death as ever I care to."

"Ai, Lothar! Say no more. He is a beast."

"Indeed. Therefore I have spoken to you of his death."

"No, Lothar! Do not think such things. You endanger yourself."

They sat quietly for a while, then Lothar smiled. "Forgive me, I shall never speak of it to you again."

But already an idea was forming in his mind, one that would win the real admiration and respect of his sister, one that would free her of this burden she faced. He thought he knew how he might carry it off without much danger to himself. Lothar smiled again.

"We leave tomorrow."

"Ai, so soon?" She looked around the library. "Oh, what shall I do with no manuscripts, with no Berthaire? What life will I have?" She felt close to tears.

Lothar got up and walked to the window. He turned to face Deirdre. "If Clotaire ever harms you in any way beyond this insult of a marriage, only say one word and I shall avenge you. Promise me that, Deirdre." Lothar was sincere. At this moment, he would have died for her.

Deirdre sighed. "Ai, I promise. I am tired now and would be alone if this be my last day here at Athies."

"I shall ride with you tomorrow."

"Good. Until then."

Lothar gently kissed her hand and left. Deirdre closed her eyes. She would not cry. Somehow she would escape again. Only this time she would succeed. She would wait until the time was right.

To her surprise, she was able to sleep that night, and she woke before dawn feeling rested, happy even. She lay quietly a moment, then remembered the dream responsible for her pleasant feelings.

Everything will be all right. She had heard these words in her dream, clear, though from far away. All else had faded already, but the words were to her like the clapper inside a bell. She trusted the voice, the source of the words. *It will be all right. It will be all right.* She lay there chanting to herself over and over until she heard the light knock of her maid, Claria.

"Ai, come in," Deirdre called out. Claria entered. She laid out Deirdre's clothes and stood silently waiting as Deirdre got up. Her disappointment in Deirdre showed itself in her silent servitude. Where before she chattered and suggested and took delight in assisting Deirdre, now she was sullen, kept her eyes on the floor, and spoke only when directly addressed. It irritated Deirdre, and she decided not to have Claria accompany her to Soissons. Claria was not much older than Deirdre. All Deirdre's years at Athies, Claria had served her. She was married to a sickly man with constantly infected eyes. Her lot was not easy, yet she had always maintained a cheerfulness around her mistress.

"You need not pack your things," Deirdre said coldly.

Tears sprang to Claria's eyes. "As ye wish," she said softly.

Deirdre looked at her angrily. "You need not look so sad. You have been most unkind all these weeks now. I know clearly where your heart is."

"Ai, Lady Dierdre, forgive me. It is not my business; it is just I would see ye happy and now...."

"Now?"

"Now he won't even talk to ye."

"Stupid wench." Deirdre grabbed the brush from Claria's hand. "Get my bath prepared."

Claria was openly weeping now. "It is ready,." She threw herself on her knees. "Please forgive me, Lady Deirdre. I am indeed stupid. I shall never do so again."

"Indeed you shall not!"

Claria turned pale with her own audacity. On her knees, she touched Deirdre's robe. "Oh, lady," she whispered. "I would go with you, please!"

Deirdre looked down at her with irritation, but softened when she saw the desperation in Claria's eyes. "Are you mistreated here?" she asked.

"Nay, not by the masters, nay. 'Tis my husband." Her eyes opened wide. "Oh, I hate him."

Deirdre laughed coldly. "Then how can you condemn me when you feel the same as I?"

"But Clotaire is a king and good. He is a gentleman."

Deirdre looked at her. Claria was a good servant. But she was not a friend, never could be. Deirdre held her tongue. She would not reveal anything of Clotaire; anything she might say now in a moment's confidence would travel all over Athies and again at Soissons. Already the necessary reserve between mistress and servant had been breeched.

"You may come then. And now my bath."

It was difficult for the household folk of both classes to

celebrate the wedding party's departure. Berthaire had been quiet and sad for weeks. Several times, he had approached Deirdre as though to tell her something, then stopped himself.

"Ah, I would that you be happy," he had lamented to her over and over, rubbing his hands together as was his wont when distressed.

Now he embraced her tenderly. His eyes were moist with the farewell. Deirdre sat astride Mani with the resigned air of a captive, taking away from all any thought for well-wishing.

As the wedding party rode off, the folk of Athies silently watched the unhappy bride and the angry bridegroom. Clotaire rode in front with Felice mounted behind him. For the first time, Felice felt shame rather than pride. She recognized that Clotaire was publicly using her to chastise Deirdre. That she would not have minded, but all these weeks at Athies, Clotaire had only come to her once, and his loving had been brief and cool.

The day was warm, and they travelled in a leisurely fashion, resting for several hours at midday. Then they continued on their way until dusk when they arrived at a low hill covered with trees. There, they set up camp. Clotaire ordered a shelter for himself and Felice, but not for Deirdre. She had Claria make a rough bed for her off at the edge of the hill, as far away from Clotaire as possible. Mani was tethered nearby. Lothar ordered a pallet for himself not far from Deirdre. He was enraged that he and Deirdre should have to sleep out in the open, but when he had ordered one of the foot soldiers to set up a shelter, he had been sheepishly told that Clotaire expressly forbade it.

"Sleep well, dear sister. I shall be by your side."

Deirdre smiled at him. "I am not concerned. The stars are our friends."

She lay in the open. At first it was strange; then she thought how she liked it. She felt it was a small test compared to what was ahead for her. She fell into a light sleep. Gradually, the encampment quieted.

Inside the tent, Felice lay on her side, feigning sleep. She watched Clotaire's face. He lay on his back wide awake. His eyes betrayed a restlessness and a coldness she had never seen in him. He had not touched her this night either, nor even spoken other than to wish her a goodnight. Felice was very unhappy, and a worried part of her nagged constantly so that her mind gave her no peace. She was like a hungry dog, circling the dried bone of Clotaire's love. And she worried also about Villem. He hid well his anger toward Clotaire in front of others, but twice now she had heard him give vent to a hate she could only begin to fathom. Villem had always been a gentle man, though gruff and rough in his ways. It was with dismay that she saw him too grow a hardness in his eyes and around his mouth. Off in the distance, she heard a howl. She started. Clotaire turned toward her.

"It is nothing. A wolf. I have heard how sometimes they come down to the lowlands here."

"Ai, sire. I am not afraid."

"They will not come near us. They attack sheep or cows."

In her sleep, Deirdre also heard the howl. She had never heard such an unearthly cry and she half woke. All was still. She rose on her elbows sleepily and looked around. Lothar lay further off, unmoving. She lay back down and closed her eyes, drifting off into sleep. Not far away she heard a horse whinny softly.

As in a nightmare, she heard a scream. It was surrounded by snarls and growls. She sat bolt upright, a like scream coming out of her own mouth. Not ten yards away, a pack of wolves were upon Mani, who rose, front hooves helplessly flailing. The scream had come from her.

"Ai, Lothar!" Deirdre screamed out. She saw him across from her. He was sitting up. He was not moving.

"Lothar, help! Help her!" Deirdre leaped up, but her knees collapsed beneath her. Mani fell heavily with another horrible scream. Suddenly Deirdre was grabbed and thrown down. She heard a snarl matched by another, this one made by a human in

205

pain. There were more men now and three of the wolves were quickly downed. The others raced away.

Deirdre sat up. Clotaire was surrounded by his men. Lothar still sat frozen on his bed.

"It is nothing," she heard Clotaire say with a growl. "Bury her after you kill her."

Deirdre leaped up.

"No!" she cried. "No, let me go to her. You will not kill her!"

The men stepped aside for Deirdre. Mani lay on one side, her belly torn open. She breathed heavily, her visible eye rimmed with pain and terror.

"Oh," Deirdre exclaimed. Mani blurred suddenly. Deirdre was caught as her legs caved in and all went black.

CHAPTER 22

For the remainder of the trip, Deirdre was treated with the utmost courtesy, being given a tent for shelter at night and a spirited young mare to ride. But her own spirits plummeted. She rode as if in a stupor, ate little, slept almost not at all, and spoke to no one. Had anyone asked what thoughts passed through her mind, she would not have been able to answer; she would not have known. All was black, hopeless.

Clotaire watched her from a distance, as did Lothar from nearby; no one knew how to approach her. Claria chattered to her as usual, but when Deirdre did not respond, even the dauntless Claria grew quiet. And when they finally approached their destination, the view of Soissons -- a huge castle that rose up a cliff above the river like a fist of grey stone cut out of a darker stone -- could not have inspired joy in even the lightest of hearts. From a distance, it looked dreary, cold, devoid of the grace and beauty that had been the heart of Athies. Closer, it did not lack warmth, but Deirdre scarcely noticed. In her soul, she was bleaker than any castle.

Their entrance into Soissons was met with long and boisterous cheer. The steep path was lined with women and children waving banners and throwing flowers. Men stood at attention, their lances and swords held high in salute to their king. Talk went quickly among the folk and flew up to the inner court that the bride of Clotaire looked dismal and wan, though outwardly pretty.

Gossip flew in all directions; hands went up over mouths to hide the words spoken in one another's ears; eyes sent glances that even Deirdre noticed. She refused to acknowledge any of them or to show the least concern, but being now in the public view had a visible effect on her. She sat straight, kept her eyes ahead on the path, and masked her pain. Lothar saw it first and was glad for it; she was yet in life if she responded so. He also felt the loss of Mani. The little mare had been a last tie with their childhood and with happier days. But he did not comprehend the depth of Deirdre's reaction to the horse's death. He had understood without her saying so that she would have had him protect Mani even if such an effort had meant his death. This was a profound puzzle to him, a source of hurt.

"Long live the king! Long live the queen!" the crowd cheered. The chant was picked up and echoed out among the hills. Deirdre felt the power of their voices with an unexpected thrill. She was born to rule, to direct; she had not known this about herself until now, hearing her name called out by a hundred voices. But when she recalled that her leadership depended upon her marriage, the momentary luster of it died. What was left, however, was a spark that rekindled her determination.

I shall escape, she thought anew. She looked around. These people were no different from those of her childhood, though rougher than the folk at Athies. And certainly the noble folk in the inner court were cruder than those in Berthaire's court. Deirdre felt some satisfaction in this. Clotaire's court reflected him; it was primitive, dark, draughty-looking, and without charm. She was not wrong about his base nature, she felt sure.

Musicians played in the central court; ladies stood about, obviously pleased to have their master home again. Deirdre could not help but notice their attention given to Clotaire.

"Ai, good Clotaire" one thin woman with red hair said. "We have missed you sorely." She had once been pretty, Deirdre could see. Now she looked pasty beneath her paint, as did most of these women. They looked as though they had stayed for years in darkened rooms. They all stole anxious glances over at Deirdre.

Clotaire was enjoying himself immensely, laughing and teasing the women back. Felice, proud and haughty, sat until Clotaire did the public honor of helping her dismount. Then she laughed, and the color came up high in her cheeks.

"Claria," Deirdre said sharply. Claria looked at her,

surprised.

"Discover my quarters, quickly, and lead me there."

Claria was clever enough to pick one of the old servants and returned before Lothar had had time to help Deirdre dismount.

"Sister, I shall accompany you," he said as Deirdre began to follow Claria through the crowd.

"'Tis unnecessary," Deirdre snapped.

Lothar followed anyway.

They were led by an old woman through a long, narrow hallway to a narrower staircase that circled the walls of a corner tower. The old woman stopped before a low door and fumbled with a key in the lock. Finally, the door opened. The rooms were plain with simple furniture, sufficient only for one's basic needs. There was a large bed, a few chests, a table, some chairs and one small loom in the first room; a few chairs and dressing table in the second. The third and last contained the bath. The windows were high; there was no balcony.

The servant smiled and bowed. "Your quarters, Lady.Dierdre. And welcome to Soissons. If you need anything, we are at your service." She indicated a bell-pull near the door.

Deirdre answered. "I have my own servant who shall take care of all my needs."

"As you wish," the old woman said. She bowed again and departed.

"But where am I to sleep?" Claria asked, looking about.

"For now, you need not be concerned," Lothar said, having followed them into the apartment. "I would speak to my sister now."

Claria bowed to Lothar and Deirdre and left the room. She sat halfway down the circular staircase in case Deirdre should need her.

"Well?" Deirdre asked finally, when Lothar said nothing.

"Well, indeed!" Lothar said indignantly. His face was flushed. "My dear lady, you have my sympathy for all you are going through, but pray tell me one thing."

"Ai?"

"Why do you shun me?"

Deirdre turned her back. "I do not shun you."

"Indeed, you have not spoken a word to me in three days."

Deirdre shrugged. "What is there to say?"

"How have I wronged you?"

Deirdre slowly turned to face him. She too flushed with the slow rise in her blood.

"Wronged me! My dear brother, you allowed my Mani to be destroyed by wolves in front of your very eyes!"

"What?"

"You sat there, simply sat and watched them rip her open." Her eyes filled with tears. "You said you would protect me. Dear God, it took *him* to do that. I could have been eaten alive."

Lothar's face burned a deep red. "'Tis not true! I would never have allowed them to touch you! It was already too late with Mani. When I awakened, they were upon her."

"You could have saved her! You could have! You never once stirred."

"Deirdre! I had no means. What is one man against six wolves? Would you have me die?"

"Better die than live with the shame of a coward!"

Lothar became quite pale. His voice shook when he again spoke.

"I am ashamed only that you think me so. And I am sorry that you would have me die before your horse!" Thus saying, he turned on his heel and left. Deirdre flung herself on the bed. She released the long-held tears of shame and sorrow and told herself she would make it up with him on the morrow.

210

Claria tiptoed to the door, which Lothar had left open. Seeing her mistress in such a state, she quietly pulled the door to and descended the stairs. Deirdre would not want her for several hours perhaps. She would explore this new home.

Born and raised at Athies, Claria was used to a grace and lightness in the appointment of a room. Here, at Soissons, things seemed haphazard, dark, heavy. The walls were built of thick stones, and no attempt was made to cover them with rugs or tapestries. And there was no marble here; again, stone only, or, in some places, rough and wide planks for the floors. Doors were low and small, passages narrow; torches has to be lit even in the day due to the lack of windows. A dampness hung in the air. Claria explored the wing where Deirdre's rooms were located, then found her way back out to the central court where the noisy celebration continued. She sat on the threshold and watched.

Several clowns, their faces made up with powder and paint, cavorted and somersaulted to the laughter and cheers of the crowd. Clotaire sat on a low throne in the center of the court. He held in one hand a glass of ale; in the other, a large piece of juicy meat. He was surrounded by the women of the court, young and old. He beamed with pleasure. The whore Felice sat on the ground to one side of the throne. She was smiling happily. Clotaire had personally shown her her quarters: two large, airy rooms with long windows opening onto a narrow balcony that overlooked the river and all of the valley. To her, the furnishings, the utter luxury of two whole rooms and a small bath to herself were the fulfillment of a fantasy she would scarcely have had the audacity to invent. Gowns, in the style worn here at Soissons and in every imaginable color, had been prepared for her; oils stood on the shelf in her bath; fine sheets covered her bed. Clotaire had kissed her gently on her forehead and asked if the rooms made her happy and assured her that, above all, he wished to make her happy.

"If you wish," he had said, "I shall make it all right again with Villem."

Felice looked surprised. "Clotaire!?"

Clotaire shrugged. "Methinks perhaps you would be with him as you once were."

"Ai no, sire, I am happy as I am. How could I wish for more than you?" Her heart fairly overflowed with love for him.

And so as the celebration continued into the small hours of the morning, and exhaustion overcame one after another of the revelers, Felice stayed on, filled with the glow of her love, and with simple awe at her good fortune.

One by one, the dancers sank into heaps around the courtyard; the clowns had long since departed; only the musicians carried bravely on until the cocks began to crow. Then Clotaire rose. He clapped his hands. "It is over," he said, dismissing the musicians. He had drunk all night, yet now he got up as though perfectly sober. Felice rose with him.

"Methinks you should sleep," he said gallantly. He saw the disappointment in her eyes. "I shall accompany you to your door." With a hand on her elbow, he guided her. When they reached the hall, he leaned close to her ear and whispered, "In a while, I shall return." She looked up at him with surprise and undisguised delight. "I have some business first that I must attend. It should take but a while."

He left her then. Felice chose a sleeping gown of yellow, the color she knew he liked most. Sitting in front of the small mirror, she brushed her hair. She was lost in her own dreams.

Clotaire crossed the courtyard in the shadows at the back, so none saw him enter the door into Deirdre's wing. He ran up the stairs, pulled out a key, and let himself into the room.

Inside, he stood a moment to accustom himself to the darkness. He crossed to the bed where Deirdre lay, and stood above her simply watching her sleeping form until, even in her deep sleep, she sensed his presence and woke with a start.

"Claria?" she said with the slightest intonation of alarm in her voice.

"'Tis I, your husband," Clotaire said and smiled to himself at these words.

Deirdre was silent. Finally she said, "What is it you want?"

"I came to speak with you only; to make peace perhaps, if you will."

"My only peace with you will come when you release me of this destiny."

"Of becoming my wife?" he asked ironically.

"It is a travesty," she said without rancor, hoping to appeal to what small good she hoped might be in him.

"For you. Not for me. I like my women strong. You shall make a good wife after you are broken."

"Broken!" Deirdre sat up, her ire aroused.

Clotaire laughed. "Ai. Just a bit, my pretty. I'd not want you without spirit."

"Get out of my room! Do you only wish to torture me?"

"I shall torture you soon enough since that is what you wish. I truly came to see if you wished to make peace between us."

Deirdre withdrew silently into herself.

"You give me no quarter then? Fine, so be it. We shall be married on the morrow. Any resistance in front of my court and I shall have you stripped and publicly flogged."

Clotaire turned and was gone in a moment. Deirdre, mouth open, heard the key turn in the lock.

"Claria!" she called. But Claria was not in the rooms. Deirdre got up to pace the darkened rooms in a futile attempt to calm herself. *I will get him*, she vowed to herself. *In some way, I will make sure he regrets these words of his and this marriage.*

Outside, Clotaire bounded down the steps. The morning had begun. Servants were up and about and picking up the debris from the night's welcoming celebration. They greeted the young and happy king who emerged from Deirdre's quarters with a grin. They giggled among themselves when, later, they heard he had gone straight to his mistress's rooms after telling his steward to prepare for the wedding at midday.

"Such a rogue," his ancient nursery maid said as she took the sun on her old bones out in the courtyard. "He always was such a rascal." She clucked like a hen, then burst out into a cackling peal of laughter. "Such a terrible rascal."

CHAPTER 23

Deirdre braced herself when, shortly after Clotaire left, there was a great commotion outside her door. Four exuberant young serving girls burst in.

"Oh, Lady Deirdre! Forgive us!"

All four deeply bowed. Deirdre saw how they stifled giggles and exchanged glances as they rose.

"We are here to draw yer bath, milady," the youngest said.

"It is yer wedding day," beamed the tall one. A third popped out from behind the other two.

"And we've brought yer gown. Oh, milady, it is so beautiful."

"Ai, like you. So very beautiful. Here, we shall show it to ye."

Deirdre clapped her hands. "A little order, please. Which one of you is in charge?"

The girls drew back, embarrassed at their lack of manners. Finally, the tall one spoke up.

"Forgive us. Not one of us is in charge. We expect Gertrude will be along. She is our head. We...we did not intend offense." She curtsied.

Deirdre had come to a decision regarding Clotaire. She had no doubt he would delight in publicly humiliating her, so she would have to be most compliant in the court. In fact, she had decided to be more than compliant. She sensed that he loved her; she would then drive him to distraction by being lovely and sweet in front of others, while, in private, giving him the treatment he deserved. She was as pleased with this as with anything so far. Until she could escape, she had little other recourse. But her temper was not so calm as she knew it would have to be, and the degree to which she was irritated showed now with the young maids. She saw it and attempted to control herself. She smiled.

"'Tis all right. You may draw my bath."

They seemed to fill the room with their energy. At neither Athies nor at Gunther's had Dierdre seen such undisciplined servants. It was yet another example of Clotaire's ignoble state of being. He could not even keep order among the household serfs. Deirdre settled in a chair. Two of the girls laid the wedding dress across the bed. They kept glancing at Deirdre to see if she were noticing. Deirdre would not give them the pleasure, though it was hard not to, there being little to distract her in these plainly furnished rooms. She rose.

"I shall walk outside. Fetch me when the bath is ready."

One girl gasped. The other showed alarm. Deirdre's irritation returned.

"What is the matter?" she snapped.

Both girls looked down. "Nothing, dear lady," the one said. An older woman now entered. She bowed to Deirdre.

"At your service," she said most graciously.

"Where is my Claria?" Deirdre asked.

"She is in the maids' quarters, my lady. We have been asked to serve ye. The king's orders."

"Ah, I see," Deirdre said. She suddenly realized that, at all times since she had arrived the day before, the door to her chamber had been kept locked. Now, when she had moved toward the open door, the two girls' reactions showed she was a prisoner here. They had been too embarrassed to stop her, but feared the outcome had Deirdre left. Deirdre walked into the other room, pretending to have forgotten her original intention.

"I should like a manuscript, if such a thing is available here," she said, turning to the door. The older maid looked uncomprehending.

"A manuscript -- something to read," she elucidated.

The woman reddened. "Lady Deirdre, I wish to serve, but I am not familiar with what ye wish."

216

"I see." So there was no library here at Soissons. Deirdre felt a wave of self-pity. She turned away and walked into the second room. "Is there a chapel?" she called out.

"Ai, indeed there is. A very beautiful one. 'Tis where ye shall be married today." The maid followed Deirdre into the room. "I am Gertrude, milady." She bowed again. "It is a great honor to serve ye."

"You should keep better order among your girls," Deirdre said, indicating the two fussing with the wedding gown. Gertrude looked chastised.

"Indeed. I shall take your words to heart and train them better. But I believe part of their misbehavior is that they are excited to be serving ye, and especially on this day."

The youngest now popped into the room. She always seemed out of breath. "My lady! Your bath awaits!"

Gertrude lightly clapped her hands. "Rosina, no words!"

Rosina curtsied. "Ai, madam," she said. Her eyes sparkled. She blushed.

It was a long bath scented with a lovely fragrance. Gertrude took special care of Deirdre's hair, washing it three times and using special oils after each rinse. Then, relaxed from the heat, Deirdre rested on a divan while refreshment was brought to her. She ate well for the first time in days, and gave herself over as they lightly painted her and coiffed her hair. Gertrude was an artist in both makeup and hair, and Deirdre was amazed at her own reflection as her hair was piled up in delicate curls and waves, looking, for all to see, like a crown. With a little paint, her lips were rosy and her eyes larger and softer-looking than normal. Deirdre had always shunned painting her face; today she needed it and was grateful to have this mask.

Finally, it was done, and two of the girls carried the dress to her. She felt its weight as they slipped it over her head. After it was buttoned, she turned and viewed herself in the mirror. She gasped. The fabric was a sheer, soft linen, almost white, but tinted

217

with the softest hint of rose that showed in the deep folds. The dress fell full from the bodice, loose and soft, with a long train. Full sleeves of the finest lace with pearls and a gold filigree gave the dress its weight. The tunic, short, as was the custom here at Soissons, was a slightly darker shade of rose. It was of velvet. Pearls and gold threads embroidered into flower patterns lay on the soft fabric as if they were pebbles lying half-buried in moss. It was the most elegant gown Deirdre had ever seen. Pale slippers embroidered to match the tunic, and a small gold and pearl crown completed her attire. Deirdre had never been aware of herself as beautiful, though all her life she had been told she was so. But today she saw it. She smiled now, and the serving girls burst into giggles. Even Gertrude smiled with pride. She had overseen the handwork on this gown these past months. Deirdre was her handwork, from head to toe, as Gertrude saw it.

"You are grand," the youngest maid whispered with the greatest respect.

"It is time," Gertrude said. "Your brother, Lothar, awaits below to escort ye to the king."

Gertrude led the way down the narrow stairs. The four girls followed, holding Deirdre's train. Lothar was stunned when he saw her. All the fine words he had prepared to show Deirdre his Christian forgiveness for her rudeness to him the previous evening evaporated in the vision of this woman who now smiled down at him as if she were indeed the happy bride.

"My dear!" he finally said, when she stood in front of him. Deirdre lightly kissed his cheek.

"Forgive my late temper," she whispered. She saw her power, the power that beauty gives, in Lothar's immediate forgiveness and his inability to take his eyes from her. If her own brother were in awe, so should be Clotaire. She would torture him with this new-found weapon of hers. She took Lothar's arm. She was ready for whatever was to come and even looked forward to it.

218

But when she saw Clotaire at the chapel entrance, she nearly fainted. Outwardly, she showed only the slightest hesitation in her step and Lothar felt her hand grip his arm. Clotaire, though not having slept all night, looked as though he had just risen from a long rest. He was clean-shaven; his long, straight hair shone blue like that of a crow's blackness. He looked alert and alive with an electric energy. He was dressed in a long tunic decorated with gold and pearl like Deirdre's; only his colors were ivory and soft yellow. In the moment before she saw him, he was smiling and had not yet seen her. She felt a shiver of fear. She saw it immediately, as did Lothar, when he caught the look on her face. Clotaire was handsome; indeed she was attracted to him and felt the power of his manliness, which was somehow of the same strength and capacity as her own power. She had looked at him first in order to watch him succumb to her; now she dropped her eyes before he turned, so he would not read what she had not time to mask. He turned when he saw how the man he was speaking with simply lost all interest in his conversation. Thus, she did not see the look in his eyes before it was masked with a cool calm. It passed like the shadow of a bird crossing over the courtyard, that quickly.

"Lady Dierdre," he said with the slightest tinge of irony.

"Sire," she said simply.

Several musicians played lutes as they walked in. A simple monk, one who lived at Soissons to officiate at the little chapel, awaited them in front of the simply carved, but elegant, altar. Flowers of all kinds decorated the whole of the interior in garlands and chains. The nobles of Clotaire's court, both gentlemen and ladies, stood on either side. Together, Clotaire and Deirdre were so beautiful, people audibly caught their breath.

The service was conducted in Latin, and Deirdre was surprised when she heard Clotaire answer in well-schooled accents without prompting. It was her first indication that he was anything other than a high-born brigand. A part of her was alive with rebellion; another with a sadness at such a travesty of a marriage before both God and man. In her heart, she asked forgiveness and told herself and God privately: *It shall not be consummated.*

The service was soon over; she walked by Clotaire's side out to the hall where she expected they would no doubt greet the guests. She had anticipated this moment, one of power for her, one in which to charm the court and, indirectly, Clotaire. Thus, she was surprised when Clotaire simply kept walking. He crossed the courtyard leading her to the tower stairway. He stood aside to let her go first, and held her train. Without a word, he followed her into the chamber, closing the door behind him.

"And now, my wife," he said, emphasizing the last word.

Deirdre turned. Her heart was beating furiously, but she looked at him out of a haughty reserve she had been born to.

"In name only. As you are husband. Or am I to be flogged for *any* reason?"

"No, I shall give you some rein."

"I see. Like a horse. Then why did you not get yourself a horse if you wanted to train one? I am a free soul in God's eyes."

Clotaire looked at her, his eyes softer. "You are so beautiful," he said, his tone suddenly different. He moved toward her. Deirdre backed away before she realized that she had expected this and had planned to stand her ground.

"You may admire me, if you wish," she said, trying to retain her reserve.

"Ai, and I shall. Take off that dress, woman." He reached out for her tunic.

"Nay!" She backed away again.

"Nay? You are my wife, my property, my bit of flesh, my garden. Take off your dress!"

This time she did not back away. "Keep away from me," she said, summoning all her power.

220

Clotaire stopped. He looked at her long.

"I want you," he said, finally. "I want to touch your skin, feel your soft breasts as they melt under my touch. I want to kiss them, nibble your beautiful ears, run my hands over your back, your thighs, that mystery between your legs."

Deirdre was appalled. "Stop!" She held her hands over her ears. "In the name of God, do not speak so. Leave, please!"

"Oh, I shall make you want me." He had his arms around her waist. She felt him fumbling with her buttons.

"Nay!" she cried. "Do not touch me, you filthy toad! Oh, you are horrible!"

"You shall speak of me differently, you shall see. I shall make your blood so hot, your lust so deep, you will plead with me to come to you." He was kissing her ear as he spoke, pulling her tight against him with one arm. With the other, he lightly touched her breast. Deirdre struggled, but he held her tight. She fought two enemies -- him, and her own body that felt the thrill beneath his touch. She pushed him hard and broke free.

"I hate you," she hissed. "How can you think for a moment I would want you? You disgust me."

Clotaire's eyes were laughing. The slightest smile played at his lips. "Ah, my beauty, my sweet, my turtledove. Methinks you know not how to love. Be patient, I shall teach you." He slowly walked toward her as he spoke.

Deirdre held her ground. "Why do you make me a prisoner?" she challenged suddenly.

Clotaire stopped in his tracks and laughed out loud. "You are a comic, my love. Why indeed?"

"If I gave my word?"

"I would not trust it. You are a scoundrel. I learned that at Athies."

"Sire!" Deirdre was desperate. If she could but engage him in talk, he might spare her this further humiliation. "Let us be sensible. Will you listen?"

He was standing directly in front of her. He lifted his hands to embrace her.

"Do not touch me!"

Clotaire dropped his hands.

"I shall listen." He looked around. "Here," he said, indicating the bed behind her. "Sit down."

Without realizing, Deirdre sat on the bed, then immediately jumped up. Clotaire laughed.

"I gave my word I should listen. Please sit."

Deirdre did not trust the look in his eyes. She felt he was amusing himself only, but she sat, a bit off from him.

"I despise you," she said with the equanimity of a judge. Clotaire raised one eyebrow at her. "As for you, I do not know your heart, but you wish me to be your wife. That I have become, just now, in this ceremony. I will not do more or I shall kill myself." She blushed with these words.

"You are most generous, I see."

"Please, listen." Deirdre was not sure herself what she would say. She only knew she must not let him touch her, that, by talking, she might be able to avoid that. Her mind raced.

"I am willing, however, to be publicly your wife, your queen. I will not disgrace you by rudeness. I do not object to your leading your private life as you wish. You see, I promised God I would remain chaste. I...I would be a nun." Such a thought had never once occurred to her, but she felt now as though that might not be a poor choice. She blushed again with her lie. "You see how it is. I am Christian like you, in fact, as a result of your having" -- she fumbled for kind words -- "having met me and taken me to Athies. I appeal to your Christian charity to let me keep my soul's promise."

Deirdre's heart pounded. She watched his face as he sat quietly opposite her. When he looked up, his eyes were full of mischief.

"Indeed, you offer me so much, I am overwhelmed with your goodness. A nun. Indeed!" He stood and paced. "Why did you not say so before?" He looked at Deirdre as though he actually expected an answer. He suddenly knelt before her. Deirdre drew back.

"I shall grant you your wish. Gladly." He looked at her with the deepest understanding.

Deirdre was astounded. Her eyes grew big. She almost liked him at this moment. "Ai, sire, I thank you from the bottom of my heart."

He held her hands in his. "I beg you, dear sister of God, only one small thing, a favor."

Deirdre saw again the irony in his look. "What is that?" she asked suspiciously.

"I am but a poor, lustful man. And my heart, indeed, belongs to you, though you wish it not." He paused and looked down. "I shall grant you this good wish of yours if I am but convinced you truly want me not."

"Oh, I can assure you," Deirdre said quickly. "From the bottom of my heart, I do not want you."

Clotaire looked at her. "Thank you, that is most kind, but no. You must prove it."

Deirdre did not comprehend. Finally, she asked, "And how, may I ask, can I prove it?"

He put his hands around her small waist. She felt his fingers caressing gently as he spoke.

"I shall test you," he said. "Not every woman is worthy to be a nun. Perhaps your blood is too thick -- and you too passionate and lusty a woman. And perhaps, as I suspect, you truly want me and know it not."

"No, that is not true. Take your hands away."

"A real nun, a truly chaste being, is not tempted by the flesh regardless. Now I shall touch you. I shall love you and we shall see."

Deirdre tried to leap across the bed. "No!" she cried. "You are a trickster. This is no test at all. Oh! Stop! You are vile!"

He was upon her on the bed, his one hand already up her skirts, caressing her thigh. He was kissing her, crushing her beneath his weight. She could not move, could barely struggle. He whispered to her passionately through his kisses.

"I will make you want me. Here!" He ripped her tunic and pulled the thin fabric of her dress away from her shoulder, revealing her breast. He kissed her nipple gently.

"No!" she cried. "Stop!"

"You see, you are perhaps lying. You are already waiting. Your breast does not lie." She felt his breath on her skin. He licked her breast. "Look. See for yourself how it has grown hard for me, how it stands at attention." He pulled her tunic off, tearing it more as he did, then slipped her gown down to her waist. She tried to roll out from under him; her arms were pinned.

"You mock me! You mock God! Please, in His name...!"

"Oh, such beautiful breasts. Ye gods, I have never beheld such beautiful breasts. Such white skin and so soft. Oh, my wife!" He was kissing her neck and ears, caressing her torso. Deirdre closed her eyes. She would close him out. But doing so, she could only exist within her feeling, and her body was indeed growing in desire. His one hand pushed her dress lower, she felt his warmth now against her belly.

"Ah, you see, you are wanting me. Oh, how I love you. How I want you too. Yes. Here."

"Nay, please don't," Deirdre pleaded, but she felt weak with desire now. Her one hand allowed to go free lifted of his own volition and began to lightly caress his shoulder.

Clotaire laughed softly. "You see, my beauty, my lovely wife, my darling. We shall make beautiful lovers. Your body is moist for mine. Let me show you."

Deirdre moaned. It was true. She wanted him. He allowed her the freedom of her other hand. She did not strike him.

"Oh, you are not fair, you are evil," she said without conviction.

"I would only save you from the folly of a poor decision." He sat up suddenly. Deirdre felt the sudden cool. She waited, her eyes still closed, her body yearning for him. But he stood. She opened her eyes and looked. He smiled at her.

"You are so beautiful, so desirable, but I must leave you now."

She looked at him out of a semi-stupor.

"Leave me?" she asked.

"Ai. I said I should make you want me. You see how I have succeeded. Now I must go." He leaned down and kissed her reddening cheek. "Oh, you shall dream of me, you shall long for me. My darling lady, when you are in an absolute fever, then I shall come to you and love you as I should like to do right now. But I want you to cry for me, to beg me, hmm?"

Deirdre was in such a state, she simply lay unmoving until he had closed and locked the door. Then she leapt up.

"Oh, my god! Lord Criace! All the gods and the single God! May he be plagued with blindness! May he burn in his loins! May he...!" She stammered, looking for the curse that would most express the rage and disappointment that overpowered her, spilling out down her cheeks. None came that was strong enough.

"Oh! He is the foulest beast!" She paced up and down, pulling her torn wedding gown from her, tearing it to shreds. She grabbed a bath gown and put it on, all the while railing aloud. "And I, oh my sweet God, how utterly base I am. How stupid! Oh!" She pulled at her hair. The lovely curls fell free. "How could I let him fool me! Oh, Lord how could this body betray me! I disgust myself. Oh, I would jump in the river and drown." She raged long and loud, until she grew tired. She would not lie on the bed, however, but sat on the divan. She kept bursting out with curses and self-recrimination until, gradually, her energy spent, she dozed.

She was up in an instant when a key turned in the lock. It was Gertrude. Deirdre sat back down.

"Lady Dierdre," Gertrude said, with the greatest formality, stepping over the ruined wedding dress that lay in pieces all over the floor, acting as though she did not notice it. She carried a tray of fine foods brought from the wedding feast. Putting it down on a small crude table, she bowed again, and left the room without any further words. Deirdre heard the key turn in the lock. She kicked the tray, tipping it. Like a small child, she felt a deep satisfaction in watching the food ooze over the floor. She lay back down and closed her eyes. She would not eat; she would die.

The day gradually waned. No one, not even Gertrude, reappeared to bring light or more food. Deirdre grew chilled and finally gave in to her needs enough to bring the blanket from the hated bed to cover herself. She lay, half-sitting, trying to stay awake, sure Clotaire would return to attempt to seduce her again. From a great distance, she heard, far into the night, the music and laughter of the celebration of her own wedding.

She was awakened early by the four young maids and Gertrude, who came in, utterly silent, acknowledging Dierdre with bows and lowered eyes. They wordlessly cleaned up the room, bathed Deirdre, and left another tray of delicacies to tempt her. She was very hungry, but left the food untouched. She did not, however, throw it on the floor again.

The day passed endlessly. Deirdre alternately lay on the divan and paced. She listened at the door and tried the knob, but no one was nearby, and there was no way out. She stood on a chair, but could barely see out the high windows. It was a beautiful, sunny day. Deirdre felt desperate; already it felt like weeks since she had walked in the fresh air under the sun. There were no manuscripts here, no pens or brushes, no lute, no view, even, to distract her. The one activity she might do here was one she had never had patience for. She felt sure Clotaire must have known this and deliberately put the loom there as a further torture. She wished the maids had left the tub filled with water; she might at least have tried to drown herself. She felt, by turns, tides of rage and despair.

Toward evening, Gertrude appeared with a tray. The food smelled good, and Deirdre was hungry. Gertrude bowed, removed the other tray, and left, wishing Deirdre a good sleep. Deirdre did not respond. If she were to be treated so malevolently, she would not give Clotaire or anyone else the satisfaction of knowing she suffered. As evening settled into night and the world grew quiet, she heard again the sounds of revelry. How she hated this place and these people. She fell into a fitful sleep.

Two more days passed and Deirdre felt near to madness. Other than the servants who appeared twice a day with food and drink and to bathe and dress her, there was no letup in the utter emptiness of the day. On the second day, she ate, and now ate quite regularly, not knowing why she did so, except that she could not bear the pain in her belly. She would have liked to request something for amusement, but was too proud to speak to even these women who served her. Her thoughts circled again and again the same concerns: how to escape, how to avenge herself; how to be worthy of her Christian faith and not avenge herself.

On the evening of the third day, Deirdre did not glance up at the sound of the key in the lock. It was time for Gertrude to bring her her supper. She stared straight ahead at the grey stone wall facing the divan. The door opened. Deirdre heard the clink of the metal serving pieces and smelled the food and ale.

"Good evening, my love."

Deirdre felt his voice like a stone breaking the surface of a deep pond. She pulled back on the divan, truly frightened. She saw pity in his eyes.

"I did not intend to frighten you. Are you all right?"

Her fear was quickly replaced by anger.

"I hate you," she spat out at him.

Pity withdrew.

"I had thought to see if you wished company, some distraction," he said. He grinned. "I could make love to you, if you'd like. But you must ask me nicely."

She glared at him. She would have liked to say how he would never touch her again, but she sensed he would turn her words into a challenge -- use them as an excuse to abuse her again. She looked away, holding her tongue.

"Well, I am happy to see your self-sufficiency. You look well, healthy, and well fed. I shall not visit you again until you have asked for me." He stood a moment, as though awaiting her response, then left.

Deirdre threw down the food. Then, feeling the weight of a despair, the depths of which she could not sustain, she threw herself face down on the bed, crying softly. No one heard her. From below, the voices of lutes carried gently up, like the first birds of morning, from a distant hill. Deirdre cried herself out. She fell asleep listening to the soft melodies of the lutes. Their distance was appropriate: any hope of a life like the one she had lived at Athies was that distant, that small.

CHAPTER 24

The curtain billowed, filled with the wind, or a presence. She felt its touch against her skin, silky and soft. She closed her eyes, letting herself go into the experience. She had been lost in an endless hall of doors; now she was within reach of her destination. She felt another touch against her cheek, light, but firm. She sighed and opened her eyes. On the other side of the curtain stood the figure of a man, his features masked by the fabric. It had been he who touched her; now she felt his hands in her hair, the weight of his body upon hers. She arched upward to meet him, filled with waves of sensuous delight. She moaned and heard a laugh, soft, close to her ear. "Deirdre, beautiful, darling Deirdre," the voice said. Her whole body came alive; he was in her arms. She opened her eyes.

This was not a dream. Clotaire lay on top of her.

"Ai!" she cried out.

"'Tis all right, my love. I have come to you. I heard you call."

"I did not call you. Leave me. Now!"

He breathed in her ear. "You called me. 'Tis why I came here. In your sleep, you moaned with my name on your lips." He kissed her though she struggled and used her struggle to incapacitate her further, holding her arms down. But she was already aroused from the dream and did not struggle more after he caressed her breasts, moved down her belly. When he released her, she raised both arms as though to strike him, stopped midway, held them there as a wave of heat pulsed through her.

"Ai," she breathed. Her arms became sinuous, wrapped around his smooth, warm body. He held her more lightly. Some part of her knew she could break free, but she no longer wished to. She felt wave after wave of desire rising. She did not think, did not want to; she wanted only to ride this wave to its crest. She dug her nails into her palms, into his back; every part of her yearned

229

for him. His entering her was strange; she had known no man other than the one of her dream; yet it was not painful as Nurse had told her long ago. Clotaire was gentle with her, patient, so that her body gradually accepted him. She moaned with this strange fulfillment.

"Ai, milord. Oh, I betray myself." She tasted the salt of her own tears in surprise. She had not known she was crying.

"You betray nothing, you shall see. Is it good? Do you like me a little now?"

Deirdre turned away. In a corner of her mind, she knew she was using her dream and sleepiness to allow this wondrous sensuality to overcome her. She wanted it, and she wanted him, but she could not allow the want to be consciously acknowledged. She only moaned with the pleasure of it. He kissed her shoulders, her neck; she kissed him back. They rolled together, clinging one to the other; she allowed his tongue in her mouth. She experienced the miracle of her own body that opened to him, and opened, and opened, until the crest of the wave was reached. She closed upon him with a cry as her desire reached its trembling conclusion in smaller waves that ran over her thighs, over her belly, radiating out from her womb. He cried out too, rising up just after she did, then fell back down to lie quietly upon her.

She lay quite still, watching her desire gradually wane, feeling a wonder at her own body. Clotaire lifted up and leaned on his elbows. Deirdre was wide awake now; she could not pretend a dullness of wits due to being just aroused from sleep. There was a light next to the bed, a candle she had not noticed. It flickered, casting shadows over his face and chest. He smiled down at her and leaned to kiss her mouth. Deirdre turned her head.

"Nay," she said coldly. "You have taken me as you did, like a coward, out of my sleep. You used dream and unconsciousness to have your lust."

Clotaire got up. She watched him out of the corner of her eyes. Without a word, he dressed. Deirdre lay rigid. He did not look at her. He picked up the candle, walked to the door, and let it close quietly behind him. At first, Deirdre felt the slap of his silence that testified to the lie of her accusation. She had indeed consciously acquiesced, and, for a moment, she admitted it to herself. Then the rest of the dream, how she and her mother became one and fell backward onto the bed aroused her disbelief that she would have given in to him with such passion. *What woman could marry her father's murderer? And then could desire the hands that...oh!* She covered her face and cried. It was a cruel trick that the fates had played on her. She got down on her knees.

Dear God, she whispered, *forgive me. I am lost.* As she prayed, feeling an immense pity for herself, she grew confused as to whether she had really acquiesced, or whether she had been forcefully taken. By dawn, she had determined it was the latter.

Fatigued from her mind's endless rationalizations, doubts, and arguments, she fell into a restless sleep. When she awoke a few hours later to the room's silence, her thoughts drifted back to the morning, trying to revive the sensations in all their deliciousness. But they were pale ghosts, echoes only, and she rode the wave but part way. She sat up, irritable, again filled with self-recrimination.

"I shall go mad!" she said out loud. "Oh, I would die!"

The days passed so, with Deirdre falling off into sensual reveries, then chastising herself for doing so. In bed at night she lay listening, both afraid and wanting that he should come. The hours hung on her like the heat that clung tenaciously to the land outside. She no longer knew how long she had been here at Soissons. It seemed like months.

She awoke one morning to a cloud-darkened room. The heat would break. A storm was hovering above Soissons. Deirdre felt its weight in her heart. As Gertrude washed her in her bath, she had to bite her lip in order to stop herself from asking to see Clotaire.

"I should like to soak this morning," she said instead.

231

"I shall draw fresh water then," Gertrude said, and pulled the bell cord. Deirdre heard her at the door giving the order. She leaned back in the tub. The warm water soothed her and she almost fell asleep.

"The other tub is here. Let me assist you."

Deirdre sank into the fresh hot water. She was very sleepy.

"I shall wait out here," Gertrude said. Deirdre was vaguely surprised. She had not been left alone in her bath for even a moment before this.

She let the warmth relax her, and closed her eyes, sinking into the silky realms of half-wakefulness.

"My dear lady." The voice was like a command. Clotaire stood above her. Deirdre tried to cover herself with the cloth that lay on the stool next to the tub. Clotaire grabbed it away.

"Are you awake?" he demanded.

Deirdre's heart began to pound. "I...I am in my tub."

Clotaire pulled his tunic over his head.

"Ai, I see that with my own eyes."

"You would not...!" Deirdre's words drifted off. Clotaire was pulling at his slippers.

"If you are quite awake and aware of what you are doing, I would not have you miss what is about to occur."

Deirdre tried to get up. The tub was slippery. Clotaire simply had to touch her to keep her down. Her throat went dry; her blood raced. She recognized her dilemma. She both did and did not want him. He was completely naked now.

"You see in front of you, a man. He is naked, and, as you can see, he is erotically aroused. Now you cannot fail to notice that, eh?" He grinned at her. Deirdre blushed and hid her face in her hands. He pulled them down.

"Now, do not hide your eyes because, later, you will say I took you while you were blinded." He was in the tub with her. He lay upon her.

"'Twill be difficult here, but you cannot say you were sleeping. Do you recognize me? Answer!" He was half-playful, half-angry. Deirdre was as if in a trance, shocked, admiring and amazed. She nodded.

"Now I shall kiss you on your mouth." He leaned toward her. She felt his lips, soft and moist; his arms wrapped around her. She did not respond, nor did she resist.

He stopped taunting her, kissed her over and over, caressed her until she finally responded.

"Do you know what you are doing?" he asked.

Deirdre hated him for this, but she acknowledged him with a nod.

"And do you like it?" he insisted. Deirdre only moaned.

"Answer." He pulled her head back by the hair.

"I do not like your questions! You treat me like a whore."

"And how do you, a lady, know how a man treats a whore, eh? Now, do you like it?" He was entering her. She was in a passion again and felt the waves of erotic desire overpower her.

"Ai, damn you, ai. I like it, though I hate you!"

He kissed her, came into her, matching her passion with his. He lifted her, standing in the tub, then climbed out. He did not stop kissing her, whispering words of love. She was limp with the bath and his lovemaking. He carried her to the bed and lay beside her until both their desires and energies were completely exhausted. Deirdre fell asleep in his arms. Clotaire lay a long time watching her, then awakened her with his hands that knew exactly how to arouse her. He loved her again without words, with the greatest tenderness.

"My beautiful queen," he murmured when the storm outside finally broke and a startled Deirdre snuggled closer to him. They watched the rain and lightning through the high window. Deirdre felt a great peace. She would never tell him, but she had finally

233

found a way through the maze of her thoughts to justify the feelings she had for him. It had come to her in the tub.

I shall save him by loving him. She was not sure what she would save him from, but with this final rationalization, she was able to let her natural desire and attraction for him move into her heart. She would mask that by never openly seeking him out, but this permitted her a quietness to lie in his arms.

He kissed her lightly on the brow. There was such tenderness in him, she could scarcely believe this was the same Clotaire she had seen let fall the axe into her uncle's skull.

Forgive him, O Lord, she prayed, and she swelled with pride that she had moved herself toward that forgiveness.

Clotaire stood up and quickly dressed. He moved with grace, the kind animals have, being perfectly comfortable with themselves.

"Farewell, my love." He paused at the door to look at her, then left. He left the door wide open. Deirdre fell back into a restful sleep.

CHAPTER 25

When Deirdre awoke several hours later, a tray of food stood on a table next to the bed. She stretched voluptuously.

"Ah, ye are awake." Rosina popped up from a chair and shook Gertrude who was dozing in another chair. The sky was clear now, the sun shining. Deirdre checked the door. It stood open. Gertrude noticed the movement and smiled.

"Perhaps ye would like to walk in the court below, or the gardens. We are to show ye to your new quarters, but it is so beautiful out, ye might prefer to wait."

"I should like first to take some air."

It was a glorious day, everything fresh and watered from the storm; a coolness rose from the wet earth; a soft breeze rolled through the trees and grasses on the neighboring hills. Deirdre felt as though she had been imprisoned for years. She took deep breaths and let her gaze wander freely out to the horizon. Until today, Soissons had simply been grey stone, cold, damp, without grace, or light. Now, suddenly, as she beheld the view in front of her, she was amazed. To one side, there were open fields that sloped gently up to the sky above, filled with tall grasses and wildflowers. Farther down were the cultivated fields, neat, well cared-for; and close to the castle walls were the vineyards. The small huts of the field serfs were thatched and looked to Deirdre like haystacks. She was enchanted with all this newness.

She followed a path up around the castle walls. It was good to be alone, to be moving, feeling the pull in her calves against the slope. She had asked Gertrude to wait in the courtyard; she preferred to walk alone. She walked with a sense that all this was hers, she its queen, and it made her glad. At the crest of the hill, all out of breath, she turned to survey her kingdom. The castle, huge as it was, was below her. It stood like a crown above these softly rolling hills that gently embraced the horizon. They gleamed with greenness, flecked with white and yellow flowers like stars. Deirdre laughed to herself. She felt happy, really happy. She fell upon her knees and closed her eyes.

"Dear God," she said aloud, "bless this foolishness of mine. Let me not be the fool, but wise. Let me be the bearer of love and forgiveness. Let life be mine and all of ours, as a gift of joy. Let there be an end to this suffering and grief." As she opened her eyes and said her "Amen," she thought of Lothar. *Oh dear, I must see him. I fear what his thoughts might be.* She looked below her a few moments longer. She did not want to think of anything, particularly not of herself and Clotaire, because her thoughts might once again begin to circle as they had so painfully these past five days. She could not bear that; better to have made the decision -- any decision -- and meet its challenges than to keep weighing first one side of her doubts, then the other. She took a deep breath and ran down the path until her chest heaved. She would see her new quarters first, then seek out Lothar for a talk. Everything would work out, she was sure. Together, they would find the way to make peace finally.

Gertrude was again dozing when Deirdre returned. She sat, leaning back against the wall in the full sun, her mouth open, snoring lightly. Rosina was nowhere in sight, nor were the other girls. Deirdre lightly clapped her hands. Gertrude awoke with a start. She leaped up.

"I beg your pardon, I know not why I am so sleepy. Follow me."

She passed through a wide and elegant courtyard. Its floor was of flat stones arranged in intricate patterns. Long windows of the main rooms -- dining, sitting and music -- opened on to it; and above, balconies of more private quarters overlooked it. Roses grew around the edges in narrow border gardens. Their sweet smell filled the air. Gertrude turned off under a wide arch that led to a smaller, more intimate, court. She stopped.

"Here is your suite." She pointed to the left. "And there is the king's, just across." Gertrude led the way through a narrow door. Inside was a small hallway. Its floor was marble, smooth and cool. Deirdre was surprised. Here there were tapestries of the finest threads and weaves. She had grown to suspect Clotaire's house to be of the most primitive nature; she realized now that, indeed, she had been kept in a virtual prison. This was every bit as lovely as Athies.

"These are the public rooms," Gertrude went on, showing, to one side, a receiving room, large and well-furnished; to the other, a music room with instruments of many kinds. Gertrude smiled. "There might be dances here if you should wish."

They went up a curved staircase. It was ornately carved with small figures. At the top, a small chamber contained an altar: Deirdre's own private chapel.

"These rooms belonged to the queen, Clotaire's mother. His father, King Clovis, resided where Clotaire now resides. This was a weaving room until Queen Clotilde turned it into this chapel. The king has one, a twin to this, in his rooms." They both curtsied before the door as they passed. "Here is your sleeping chamber." Deirdre smiled. It was a glorious room. Everything glowed in ivories and soft yellows. "King Clotaire loves these colors. He asked us to weave these furnishings especially for you.

"And here is your bath. And now, here is what, I believe, you most wish for. The good Berthaire had all of these sent up just after you arrived. It is his wedding gift to you. This was a sitting room. Now, I understand, it is called a library."

Deirdre gasped. A desk stood in the middle of the room with an open manuscript lying on it. The rest of the room was lined with tables and shelves holding ancient rolled scrolls and flat, book-type manuscripts. The one on the desk was the last she had been copying. Deirdre's eyes overflowed with happiness and gratitude.

"You may go, Gertrude," Deirdre said. Gertrude left and Deirdre sat on the small divan and let her tears flow. Perhaps she would find a life here after all. Already God was blessing her. It was good of Clotaire to allow her this great gift.

"I see you are not pleased."

Deirdre looked up. His voice always caused her to jump. She wiped away her tears and stood.

"I cry not out of displeasure," she said. "I am so grateful. This was the manuscript I was studying last."

Clotaire came to stand beside her.

"And you copy well. Berthaire says as much himself. He is very proud of you, you know."

"For a woman, as he would say." It felt odd to her to stand beside him this way, to talk so calmly.

Clotaire turned one page. "I remember this one well." He laughed. "I was not Berthaire's best student, though, because I am my father's son, he would never say so. I gave him a lot of mischief."

"You were his student??" Deirdre stifled the surprise she felt so that he would not hear it in her voice.

"Ai. I lived at Athies for ten years." He smiled. "Did Berthaire not tell you?"

"Nay. Not a word." She blushed. "But I did not speak of you to anyone."

Clotaire walked across the room. He picked up a scroll. "Nor would it have done you any good had you asked."

"I do not understand."

"No one was permitted to tell you aught of me."

"Why not?"

He shrugged. "My orders."

"Then why did you ask, just now, if Berthaire ever did so?"

Clotaire laughed. "Oh, 'tis good to discover whether one's orders are obeyed."

"But why?"

He looked at her. "I wanted you to meet me on your own terms, not through the eyes of others. No more."

His words puzzled her, but she let it drop.

"Are your rooms comfortable?"

A moment of indignation rose in her cheeks, causing them to color. She suppressed it. She would not mention the dull prison he had put her in. "Ai. They are most gracious," she said simply.

Clotaire brought to the desk the old scroll he was holding.

"Have you ever seen this?" His eyes sparkled with excitement. She looked down. It was in a script she did not recognize.

"It is very old; even Berthaire does not know how old it is, nor what language it is, though he suspects it comes from long before the time of the Romans. See how beautiful it is."

Deirdre only glanced at the scroll. She was amazed at this Clotaire; she was seeing a side to him that was never before visible. He was actually excited by this writing. She watched his face.

"Has anyone any idea what it is about?"

"How could one?"

Deirdre laughed. "I hoped perhaps Berthaire had guessed. He has great intuition."

Clotaire looked very serious. "I suspect, at times, that we are on the edge of something, or between. The influence of the Romans, with their great empire, ended more than three hundred years ago. Some of what they brought to us remains. Yet we have discovered so much through the new church. It is exciting, as though we are also at a beginning. It is wonderful for me to feel a part of that. Do you know what I mean?"

"Oh, yes, I do. I have often thought that. When Berthaire told me of the great library at Alexandria, how I longed for it to be still there. To think of what was lost! But then here are these books, all of this, and we keep that culture alive as we keep alive

239

the languages of the Romans and Greeks in order to keep in touch with what was. We are a bridge into the future. Things *must* change."

Clotaire looked at her. Deirdre lowered her eyes.

"I am so pleased you studied with Berthaire."

"Do you also have a library?"

"It is all here now."

"You put it here, all of it?"

Clotaire smiled. "It gives me more reason to pass my hours here in your company."

Deirdre again felt a wave of discomfort with this new relationship. "Sire, I know not my heart truly," she said, looking down at the lace cuff she played with in her hands. "I cannot say how I feel, except that what is between us is strange, and only time will tell if such friendliness will grow into a true marriage."

He took her hands into his. "Would you wish for that -- a true marriage?"

"I would indeed since all that has happened." She looked up at him. "I mean, we are married, and though I did not want it so, that marriage is now consummated."

"Happily methinks, no?"

Deirdre avoided answering by taking her hands away to pick up the old scroll.

"What I wished to say is that I am not yet comfortable in your company. There are wounds...."

"There are things that words cannot deal with. I suggest we allow ourselves time and tolerance, and not spend words on the past, on what perhaps is better left alone. Someday...but enough! I must leave you for a while. May I suggest you dine in your rooms here tonight? I shall return later in the evening." He took Deirdre in his arms. "I shall try my best to make you comfortable with me." She felt his leaving as a sudden withdrawal from around her body.

Recalling her need to talk with Lothar, she shook off the heaviness that suddenly overcame her, making her sleepy. Facing Lothar would not be easy, she suspected. From all that he had told her of Clotaire, Lothar knew nothing of his background nor of his very real capacity for tenderness. She pulled the bell. Gertrude appeared shortly.

"Lead me to Lothar," she ordered.

Lothar's rooms were smaller, though also elegantly appointed. His servant seated her. Lothar appeared after a few moments, unshaven, his clothes rumpled. He had been sleeping.

"Oh, how I have worried about you!" he exclaimed upon seeing her. "He would not permit me to see you, and I feared night and day for your life."

Deirdre kissed him. "But you look well!" he said, holding her at arm's length.

"I was not mistreated," she said, preferring to ignore the trial she had undergone.

Lothar narrowed his eyes.

"What has happened?"

Deirdre felt her face go hot. She walked to a window and looked out. "It is important we talk," she said.

"Ai, sit here."

Deirdre turned and looked at him. She saw what his expectation was.

"Lothar, it is not as you think. I fear you will be angry with me."

"Sit by me. We shall talk. Have I ever been angry with you?"

Deirdre laughed. "Ai. Once, that I remember. We were hiding from Nurse. Oh, Lothar, how I have missed her over these years." Her face reflected the quick change from gaiety to pain. "I...but let us not look back at that time."

241

Lothar grew quiet. "Why not? It was a day that yet burns in me. We must not avoid what has been."

Deirdre watched his face. "What have you been doing? You look tired, pale."

It was his turn to redden. "Oh, nothing. I spent some time with Villem. I have mostly worried about you and tried to find ways to get to you." He looked at her. "But it is you I want to talk about. Tell me what you have to say."

"I want to make peace," she said suddenly. Lothar looked puzzled. "Can you understand that?" she asked when he offered no objection.

"You and I long ago made peace." He took her hands in his. "We are as one. No matter what words might pass between us, we are as one."

Deirdre stood up. This was more difficult than she had thought it would be.

"It is not you and I whom I speak of. It is he."

"He? Clotaire?"

"Ai."

There was silence.

"He has seduced even you, I see." Lothar's voice carried bitterness. "I have heard how he bewitches women. You are just one more."

"No! Do not speak so. It...I am...." She groped for the right words. "It is confusing, but it is not that. He is kind, gentle."

Lothar leaped up. His face was livid, his eyes like sparks.

"Kind! Gentle! Ai, indeed! Our dear dead uncle would attest to that! How can you say such a thing?"

"Lothar! You said you would listen!"

Lothar glared at her. Deirdre went on.

"I want peace! We cannot bring our uncle back to life. We are Christian. Do you not believe in what you profess? What is forgiveness? He does not seduce me. It is that I would save my soul. And his. And yours! What have we to gain by hate and revenge?" She saw his face was closed, his thoughts angry and private. She grabbed his arm. "Lothar! Listen! I want to live. I want my life and I want yours! Don't you understand? I want to forget the past. I am his wife, though it was against my inmost wish. But now that is what I am, and I want to live fully. I want to forgive. Can't you also?" She was pleading. Lothar pulled free.

"Never!" She heard the finality in his voice. She twisted her handkerchief in her hands. When he spoke, it was more quietly. "It is exactly as Villem predicted."

"Oh, who is this Villem after all? He was a serf, as I understand, whom Clotaire freed and let climb to a position of respect. What of him?"

"Indeed. Only that his woman, the woman with whom Clotaire has had many a long night, also turned against him, even as you turn now against me, as a result of being bewitched by this man."

"Nonsense! I am your sister. You know my heart and mind better than that."

Lothar was quite pale. "If you wish, I shall go away from here. It disgusts me that you speak kindly of him. That you are his wife and share his bed is enough to bear, but that you speak of gentleness, my God! He is a boor. He is cruel. He takes whatever he wants without regard for the consequences. He is a brute, a pig! He sleeps with many women. He is a murderer. How can you allow him to even touch you?"

Dierdre ran out of the room and rushed down the stairs and back across the courtyard to her own rooms. She threw herself on the bed, all faith and hope destroyed. She was empty again, torn between loyalty to her brother and to this man who was now her husband. All her logic and her reasons fell apart. She was lost in an avalanche of confusion and despair. She prayed fervently.

"Dear Lord, do not desert me. O God, help me find a way. I

cannot be entirely wrong. Clotaire seems kind. It must be so, yet...." She could not continue. She bowed her head into her hands. Lothar burst in upon her.

"Deirdre," he cried. "Please do not weep. Please." He knelt beside the bed and embraced her. "Look, you do not love him, I am sure of that. I understand your difficulty. You feel you have no other choice. But you do. You will see."

"No, Lothar," she gasped. "No, I cannot escape now."

He smoothed her hair and held her close. "Do not weep. I am here. You shall see. It is not as you think, so hopeless as now. You shall see."

Lothar stayed with her until she quieted.

"Then there is hope for peace among us?" she asked.

"There are always solutions," he answered.

"Lothar...."

"No more. Let's not speak of it. I shall never let him come between us."

Deirdre let it go. It would take time before Lothar would accept these new circumstances. She would wait.

"All right then." She smiled. "Let time take care of things, shall we?"

He stood. "So be it, I must go now. Rest easy. I assure you everything will be all right. You have no reason to cry."

A valet knocked.

"Where would you have your dinner?" he asked.

"Here in this room." She turned to Lothar. "Will you stay and dine with me?"

"I cannot, to my regret. I have made other arrangements." He kissed her brow and left.

The valet carried in a large tray filled with foods and drinks of all sorts. Deirdre smiled.

"So much for me?"

The servant only bowed. Clotaire strode in.

"Will you invite me for dinner?" he asked, smiling.

Deirdre felt the familiar shock. She looked at him hard. He awaited her answer.

"Ai, sit down."

"Are you sure? You look not well."

Deirdre dropped her eyes. "'Tis my brother. We had a small disagreement."

"I saw him on the stairs. He seemed quite gay."

Deirdre looked at him with surprise.

"Indeed, he even greeted me with warmth, which is not like him for a long time now." He smiled. "I fear he likes me not." Deirdre watched his face. He shrugged and smiled rakishly. "But perhaps I can win him over. I did, methinks, with you."

She could not help but smile. He was like quicksilver, the way he changed from man to boy to man again. And it was his smile that was the door through which he slipped from one state to the other. She found it charming.

They ate leisurely, chatting of one thing and another. Clotaire had known Fortunatus, though not well. Deirdre found herself telling Clotaire story after story about the young monk. Clotaire listened appreciatively. When she had finished one and was lost in reverie, he looked at her askance.

"It sounds as though perhaps you loved him," he said in a teasing tone.

"Indeed I did, and do," she answered openly. Then she understood and blushed. "Oh, not like that. He was a brother to me. He was a monk."

Dinner over, they went into the library where Clotaire read to her his favorite tale, one that had been also one of hers. Deirdre found herself wishing he would look at her and touch her. She cursed herself within, feeling she was a traitor to Lothar, yet she recognized how much pleasure she felt in Clotaire's company, in his mere presence, and in this world that they shared. The tale over, she rose.

"Forgive me, Clotaire. I should like to retire, though I am enjoying this time with you."

Clotaire stood with her and bowed. She felt a thrill seeing his ironic smile. "After you," he said.

"I should like to sleep alone," she said.

"Alone? Nay, I shall sleep with you, but I promise I shall not molest you, 'tis a promise," he repeated, when he saw the objection in her eyes.

"I trust you not."

"'Tis no matter since I am your husband." He grinned. Deirdre stamped her foot as her anger rose. She was not accustomed to being crossed.

"I beg you, please!"

"Never stamp your foot at me, " he said, and scooping her up, he strode into the bedchamber and unceremoniously dumped her on the bed.

"Now, you shall sleep here, and with me." He began to undress. Deirdre got up. She was annoyed, but she did not know how to handle her feelings with this man. She started toward her clothes chest.

"Where are you going?" he demanded.

"I shall dress in my bath, if you please!"

He shook his head. "Nay. Here."

She stamped her foot before she realized. Clotaire dropped the top he had just pulled off. Slowly, he moved toward her.

"Nay," she said. "I forgot, that's all." She backed away.

Clotaire stopped his advance.

"Here," he said, pointing in front of him.

"I am not a dog!" she cried out. "I shall not obey you like one."

Clotaire laughed and sat down. "Dress where you like then, but you shall sleep here." Deirdre was surprised at her small victory. His behavior was too erratic to be predicted.

Undressing, she felt again a shiver of pleasure and quickly suppressed it. She chose the most sedate sleeping gown and put it on.

He lay naked in her bed, his hands behind his head.

"Sire, I do not want to sleep with you."

"Quiet. If you say another word of that, I shall attack you like a maddened lover." He rolled his eyes wildly. Deirdre had to laugh.

"Now, I said I shall not touch you. Do you not believe me?"

"Nay, I do not."

"Then you shall soon learn that Clotaire is a man of his word. He is a king, after all, and cherishes honor." He winked.

She climbed dubiously into the bed and lay perfectly still on her back, as far to one side as she could get without falling out. Clotaire got up and extinguished the candles. He also lay still and far over on his side.

"I may not be here for a while," he said quietly. "'Tis why I would just lie with you tonight."

"Why? What do you mean?"

"I have reason to go out again on a campaign. It may take some time."

She wrestled with conflicting feelings as he spoke. She should have been glad and relieved, but her body and heart felt a wave of acute disappointment. She did not speak of it.

"So be it," she said softly.

They lay quietly for a long time.

"I shall miss you," he said after a time.

"Why must you go?"

"Only I must."

Deirdre turned on her side to look at his profile in the dim light. "Can I not know?"

He glanced over at her. "Nay."

"Are you always so secret?"

"Nay."

Deirdre leaned across the space that separated them. She kissed his cheek. He turned, surprised.

"I said I would not touch you," he said softly. "I gave my word."

"Ai." Deirdre whispered. "But I made no such promise."

She kissed him again. Then his arms were around her. He was kissing her back.

"I shall miss you too," she said so softly he never heard the words.

CHAPTER 26

Felice awoke early, with the first light. She shook Villem. He did not stir.

"Up, drunkard! It is dawn. Up!"

Villem groaned.

"Up, I say." Felice beat on his back. "No one must see you here. Up!"

"Ai, I'll go."

She watched him. Every movement was irritatingly slow. She grew more impatient as the sky lightened.

"Villem, please. Move quickly."

He growled at her. "Be ye so afraid of him?"

"I fear him not. I do not wish to give others reason to speak to him against me. I would not give him pain."

He glared at her. "Would that ye had felt so about me."

"Agh," she said with disgust. "I gave you as much. Just you always watched so close. You gave me no room in which to spare you."

He began to argue.

"Nay, go! You have fast become a drunkard, Villem. You think like one with so much pity for yourself. You reek of the bottle."

"Then why did ye lie with me this night?"

She shrugged. "You know why. We do each other good, not harm. Between us, it was always good."

"Then come back to me."

"I cannot."

He pulled her close. "Someday soon ye will be begging for me, ye'll see."

"Agh. Dreaming again."

His face grew hard, his eyes dark. "I not be fooling ye this time."

Felice looked at him shrewdly. "What is on your mind?"

He saw her curiosity and withdrew. "Nothing ye might be knowing."

"I see you often now in the company of Lord Lothar."

"'Tis not yer affair who I accompany."

"No good will come of that, Villem."

"No more than for ye with a king. We all be done in with the likes of them."

"Beware, Villem. Lothar is not a brave man. Such a one will hide behind the likes of you."

He finished dressing and prepared to leave.

"Be careful none of the kitchen maids see you," Felice cautioned.

"Are ye sure ye won't come back with me? Ye could save me a lot of trouble."

"There you go again with your dreaming. You even dream of trouble."

Villem winked. "Someday...." But he would say no more. He jauntily tipped his head toward her and stumbled out the low door.

Felice dressed quickly. If she could get to Clotaire's rooms before the servants were too active, he would not be angry with her.

His courtyard was empty, still deep in shadow. She ran lightly up his stairway. The door to the bedchamber stood ajar. That meant Clotaire had not slept there this night. Felice felt a rush of anguish. She could not help it; she desired Clotaire for herself. She hated any woman with whom he slept, and she suspected all and any of them as having gained his favor. She was careful, however, not to show these feelings in front of him. He gave her much; she would not jeopardize any of that.

She entered his bedroom. Indeed the bed lay untouched. Closing the door behind her, she looked around. Then, pulling herself up tall, she strode around the room as though it belonged to her. She opened a chest, took out a pale silken shirt. She sniffed it and held it against her cheek, feeling its softness. She thought of him and of his touch, and yearned for him. Though he had lain with her several times since their arrival here at Soissons, she wanted him constantly, and her hours, in which she was required to do nothing but wait for one to flow into the other, were filled with this endless wanting. Sometimes she passed the day wandering in the hills surrounding the castle, or in her room, just watching the square of sun travel across the floor. At the sound of footsteps, she would become all listening, until the person appeared to whom the footsteps belonged and they passed off into the distance. She had grown paler, like the other women at Soissons who avoided the air and sun and stayed indoors for days at a time. She combed her hair down, pulling it tight around her face, wore the more fashionable clothes that were given to her, so that she looked less wild and certainly unlike a serf at all, let alone of the lowest class. But she had lost something in the kind of energy she had always emitted, which had been the source of her beauty. Her eyes were dulled from the constant yearning; her full mouth pouted more often now than not. She was more serious, quieter, lively now only in the company of Clotaire.

She stood by the chest, her eyes closed, the cloth pressed against her cheek, lost in a dream of Clotaire when she felt the dream suddenly become real as she was taken into his arms.

"Oh," she breathed. She leaned into his embrace, into the soft kiss he planted on her brow.

"And what is my lady Felice doing breathing into my chemise?"

Felice frowned, recalling the purpose of her visit. "I came, because I have something I must tell you."

251

He smiled and moved away to lounge on his bed. "You look so serious," he said.

Felice bit her lip. She had waited several days now to deliver to him what had grown to be a deep suspicion. She feared for the consequences if she was mistaken.

"Sire," she began, searching for the right words, "if I am wrong, and I might be, you know 'tis only that I *feel* it's right and my feeling is usually apt, but if I'm wrong, will you forgive me?"

Clotaire laughed. "You speak so roundabout, but if I understand you, ai, I shall forgive you."

"And will you take care to be certain of what I tell you before you act against any that I speak about?"

Clotaire sat up, looking more attentive.

"Indeed. What is it?"

"I am not certain, milord, but methinks there is a plot against you."

"Ai, I know that to be true. Already some indications have shown themselves."

Felice raised her eyebrows. "Ai? Have you any idea who might be behind them?"

"Of one, yes, but I suspect there's more than he."

"Villem?"

"Villem?" Clotaire stood. "Nay, I did not suspect him. He is my captain. What do you know?"

Felice felt a surge of pride that she could be of help to him. At the same time, she felt a horror -- as though she stood at the edge of a precipice -- that she should bring dishonor on Villem.

"I am not sure, only that he has dropped hints."

"Tell me what exactly."

Felice watched his face. She had decided to tell the truth exactly as he now asked her to do, both for him to evaluate the potential danger to himself, as well as to see what his reaction toward her would be, so she could know the depth of his caring for her.

"Villem lay with me this night." His face remained calm, showing only the intensity with which he listened to each word. "In his sleep, he seemed disturbed, tossing about from side to side and muttering, though I caught no word or meaning." She paused. Still he showed no surprise, no emotion. She dropped her eyes. "This morning he asked me to come back with him -- you know, as his woman. I said no and he said twice that I would have reason soon to want to do that. It was as though...as though he had planned something." Felice waited while Clotaire pondered. He scowled.

"That is not much to be suspicious of, methinks."

"Nay, but I know Villem well. He has taken to drinking much these last months and he spends much time in the company of milord Lothar."

"Lothar? That would seem odd, nay?"

"Ai, methinks as well."

Clotaire laughed at the thought of it. "Villem and Lothar? They are so different."

Felice said quietly, "If you will forgive me, I think it is more what Lothar might want with Villem."

Clotaire embraced her. "Of course. You have solved my mystery. I thank you. And I shall take care with Villem. I know that you two once shared lives, that you risk much to speak of him like this. Thank you, Felice. I should like to repay you. Tell me if there is anything you lack or desire. It shall be yours."

Felice looked at him. She saw the sincerity of his words in his eyes. "Ah, sire, you have already given me so much. What more could I ask?" She saw also that what she most wanted he would never be able to give her. She felt suddenly weary, defeated. Perhaps Villem was right. But she could not think of that; she wanted only to rest, to sleep.

253

"You look unwell," Clotaire said, leading her to his bed. "Methinks you should rest here. Stay with me this night, will you?"

Felice nodded.

"You sleep now. This takes much out of you. I see that and appreciate it, more than you can know." He helped her to lie on the bed. She was feeling weak; it was hard to keep her eyes open. "Sleep. Perhaps you are wrong and everything will turn out all right. We shall soon find out. Sleep. I shall return later."

Clotaire ran down the stairs to his office below.

"Ring the summons bell," he called out to his clerk.

He opened the long, low chest that held his king's garments, and slipped on the ring his father and his father's father had worn before him, then the crown, the cloak, and the scepter. The bell was ringing; one could almost feel the hurrying of all the castle's occupants toward the large, central courtyard where the throne was. Clotaire, dressed now in his official garments, strode across the court into Deirdre's quarters. Gertrude stood in the hall, looking confused. She bowed, obviously relieved to see the master.

"My orders, if you please, sire."

"Dress the queen in her courtly garb."

"Ai, sire." She took up to Dierdre the crown and robe and ring.

Some minutes later, Clotaire watched his queen descend the stairs. When she stood in front of him, he said so only she could hear, "You were born to wear those robes. You are truly a queen."

Deirdre dismissed Gertrude. "What am I to do?" she asked when they were alone.

"What you are doing now -- only to look like a queen."

"What is the purpose of the summons?"

He took her arm and started out. "I wish to formally present you to the court as my wife and my queen." He grinned at her.

254

"Then I shall announce my plans."

"Oh," she said. "You mean your campaign."

"Ai. If all turns out well, I shall not be gone long."

Clotaire escorted Deirdre to the throne room. She had never seen a room of such proportions. Beams the size of mature trees supported the roof twenty feet above. They were inlaid with jewels and delicately painted patterns and scenes. The walls were windowless except for one large, round, colored window above the dais where the two thrones stood; long, richly woven tapestries hung from the height of the ceiling all the way down to the floor. A long velvet cloth, deep violet, lay on the floor from the door to the dais for the king and queen to walk upon. The rest of the floor was a smooth, silky, cool marble, ivory in tone. All of Clotaire's court, gentlemen and ladies, descendants of his clan, filled the great room. A hush fell as Deirdre and Clotaire entered the room and slowly walked to the dais to take their places in front of the ornately carved thrones.

As they turned to face the court, Deirdre felt a rush of nervousness and masked it by looking straight out the arched doorway into the sunlit courtyard.

Clotaire raised his scepter, at which all present cried out in the ancient Frankish tongue: " Long live the King! Long live the Queen!" He raised the scepter three times, then turned to Deirdre and told her she might sit. He strode forward to the edge of the dais.

"Dear members of this royal court, hear your king. I, Clotaire, son of Clovis, present you to your queen, the lady Deirdre, daughter of Lord Saisson and Lady Gudrun. Let God's blessing be upon our marriage. Let God's blessing be upon our reign. Let God's blessing be upon our harvests, our vineyards, and our homes. Raise your voices for Queen Deirdre.

Deirdre felt terror. All their eyes, though friendly, or merely curious, were upon her. Their voices surrounded her, an ocean of sound mixed with blaring trumpets and a roar of drums. She

255

forced her lips to smile, her eyes to move from side to side, from front to back as though she saw each one. Yet she saw no one and nothing, she was so filled with a sudden shyness and fright at so public a position. She scarcely heard Clotaire's words until, by chance, she caught a glimpse of Lothar who stood halfway toward the back of the hall. She saw how pale he was; then he grew suddenly paler. She felt alarm. Clotaire had pronounced Lothar's name.

"...to remain in order to look after the queen, his sister. And Villem..."

Villem strode forward.

"...you shall remain also as my honored captain to look after my affairs here, to keep peace against any outside intruders."

Deirdre watched as one after another of the named men stepped forward to receive their orders. She had missed his earlier announcements, but now she relaxed as attention was shifted completely onto Clotaire and the men whose names he called. Deirdre noticed how, when the order was given to Lothar and three men to remain at Soissons, there was a wave of emotion, an unseen judgment that passed among all those present. She watched carefully, but saw no reason for it.

"So be it," Clotaire concluded.

"So be it," the court answered back in one voice.

"We leave in the morning," Clotaire told her as they walked back to their quarters.

Deirdre was too excited from what had preceded to hear him. "Am I not to be presented more pleasantly to your court?" she asked. "If I am to be left here, it would be nice to know someone by name."

Clotaire glanced at her. "If you wish, but I see no reason for it. The folk here are primitive compared to Athies. You would share little with them. And of course, Lothar will remain here to be company for you."

"What did it mean when you called his and the others' names?"

Clotaire looked out over the wall into the hills. "It meant what it meant for all, that they were to hear their orders."

Deirdre stopped walking. "Nay. There was something different when you called Lothar's and three others' names and gave orders for them to remain."

Clotaire faced her. "Nay. Only that they were disappointed perhaps not to be included. Some men feel cheated of the adventure."

They had reached their small court.

"Will you dine with me this evening?" she asked suddenly.

"You mean I need not force myself upon you?" he teased.

Deirdre looked him squarely in the eye. "Nay, " she said simply.

"All's the pity then, for I must ask you to excuse me. I have much business to attend if I leave on the morrow."

Deirdre could not hide her disappointment. "Tomorrow? Oh, I did not realize it was so soon."

Clotaire laughed. "You did not listen to my announcements in court."

Suddenly his mood changed. He became very formal and bowed to kiss her hand. "Forgive me. I shall not disturb you in the morning. Farewell, my queen." Without further words, he left her.

Deirdre stood amazed. She entered her own quarters with a sense of something imminent, but fell asleep that evening with his name on her lips, the pillow he had slept on clutched tightly in her arms.

CHAPTER 27

When Felice awoke, the light outside was already failing; it took some moments for her to realize where she was. She sighed. Her sleep had been restless, with dreams in which she was unable to accomplish the smallest task set before her. She was alone again, working in the fields, but, as she attempted to plant a seed, or pull a weed, she would find the seed had disappeared, or the weed was impossible to dislodge, though she would pull and pull. She lay on her back, her eyes closed, gathering her thoughts. More and more lately, she was faced with the fact of her own unhappiness. Always before, she had fought it off, had lived from one moment with Clotaire to the next. Either the moments with him had grown fewer, or her desire had grown beyond normal proportion, because she spent nearly all of her time now unhappy and dissatisfied. She wondered if, perhaps, someone stronger than herself had cast a spell upon her.

She opened her eyes. The room was quite dark now. Clotaire was standing at the window, looking out over the hills. The quarter-hour bell was rung, its sad sound carrying up over the castle for all to hear.

"Sire,...." she called out softly. He made a gesture of surprise.

"Ah, Felice, I forgot you were here. You startled me."

"Shall I leave? Do I disturb you?"

He thought a moment before answering. "Nay, stay, but...nay, perhaps you should go."

"As you wish, sire" Felice had long ago discovered that the best way round Clotaire was to acquiesce to his every wish. Any effort on her part to obtain her way and he became a wall of resistance; when she apparently accepted his way, he would let his go, and she invariably got what she wanted. It was as if he needed resistance from her in order to insist on his demands. Felice manipulated this trait in him both ways; it was why, all these years, he had never yet tired of her. She artfully resisted him in their lovemaking, but acquiesced when he would send her away or deny her some small wish. Now, she wanted to stay; she wanted him to make love to her. Thus, she slipped on her slippers and, bowing to him with eyes downcast, moved without hesitation toward the door. She turned and smiled at him. "Good night. May the gods give you a good rest."

"Felice...."

"Ai, sire?"

"Wait. Perhaps you could stay a little longer. I do not mean to send you away."

"Only if I am not in your way. I would not want to disturb you."

"Come here."

She stood her ground. "Oh, I believe you ask me now to stay only out of pity."

"Pity! What an absurdity." He grinned. "If you do not come this instant, I shall come after you."

Felice grinned back. "And if I come?"

"Here, woman!" he commanded.

She took her time to tease him. When she stood in front of him, he put his hands on her shoulders.

"I want you to understand. I asked you to leave only because I suspect they will come this very night."

Felice's mind was on lovemaking. This remark caught her entirely by surprise. "They? I do not understand, milord."

"Sit here by me."

They sat on a divan. The room was quite dark now.

"I summoned all to court today and announced a new campaign to be ready to leave by dawn...."

"Truly? Are you going again? May I...?

"I shall go only if need be. I did so to force action. If there

259

is a plot against me by any or all of the four I suspect, they will have only this night in which to carry it out."

Felice frowned. "Forgive me, sire. I still do not understand."

"I named four men -- Villem and Lothar are two of them -- to stay behind. I have reason to believe one or any combination of these four are in the plot, *if* there is a plot at all. Thus, with the promise of my departure early tomorrow, they must act this night. If nothing occurs, then I have wronged them all. And so, my dear lady, do you at last understand why I do not wish you here with me this night?"

"Indeed, and I thank you for your consideration, but if you'll give me some credit for knowing Villem, if it is he, then you may be sure he'll not be here 'til he's had a bottle or two."

"Villem is a true soldier, Felice. You know him not at all."

"But if he is planning to murder you, he'll feel as though his heart were in his boots."

"Does he hate me so that he would kill me?" Clotaire asked quietly.

Felice suddenly recognized that yes, Villem did hate Clotaire so.

"Methinks he does," she replied, "and I know 'tis not his fault." She looked at Clotaire suddenly with her former energy and passion. "Perhaps I can yet stop him. Let me stay here with you. Let me try."

"You would be in danger if anyone came."

"Why don't you only put a guard?"

Clotaire was quiet. "I need to know. I will be sorry if it is Villem."

"Oh, I hope it is not Villem," she said with passion. "But if it is, it is because I drove him to it."

"You? What have you to do with it?"

"Oh. It is a long time ago, but Villem loved me truly. He

was good to me. I gained his heart wholly. I used magic, a spell I cast. He lost his heart to me."

Clotaire held her face and looked deep into her eyes. "Do you believe that?"

"I know it, sire. I say it not out of vanity."

"I asked not for that reason. I do not believe in such magic myself. If you became Christian, you would understand."

She answered quickly. "I would become Christian if you wished it of me, sire, truly. But I could not lose what I know to be true. There are powers. I know how to use them."

Clotaire smiled.

She continued. "But Villem alone would never strike you. That I also know. He loved you truly, cherished you. I...I should not accuse one above me, sire, but I fear it is Lothar. I fear he uses Villem and Villem's anger because of me."

"I would to God that were not so. It will cause much harm." Clotaire looked pained.

"I do not know why I feel it so, but I have seen how he sometimes looks at you with evil in his heart."

Clotaire walked to the window and looked out. "It grows late. You should go."

Felice almost objected out of the strength of her desire to remain, but caught herself in time.

"As you wish," she said abjectly.

Clotaire turned. "But if you wish to stay, then do. I can not give you love tonight, as my mind is elsewhere. But I shall not let harm come to you either."

Felice brightened. "Ah, I should like to help you keep your vigil. I have already slept; you may rest. I shall keep guard."

"No woman shall guard me, so, if that is your intention, off with you. But I sorely need company to help me stay alert as the night drags itself through its hours."

Felice threw off her shawl and joined him again on the divan. "With great pleasure. I am without peer in making empty hours pass."

"Indeed you are," he said, looking at her appreciatively. "But we must be quiet and stay here in darkness in case someone comes. I have sent all my servants to ready our journey, so anyone we hear will be coming with other intentions than to assist me."

The evening was very still, without wind; only the night frogs and the many insect singers which inhabited the hills and every corner of the castle kept the night from falling into complete silence. Clotaire lounged on one end of the divan, looking off into the distance. At his feet lay a sword and a mace. Felice alternated between watching the stars through the open windows, and watching him.

His face was no longer a boy's, as it had been when she first saw him so long ago. It was sterner and sadder, from having lived through battles and losses. The boy in him still broke through on occasion, the way the sun will sometimes break through a cloudy sky. Then he was carefree and gallant, filled with mischief and teasing, traits Felice found irresistibly attractive.

They sat quietly several hours; the night was passing well. Felice did not chat -- that was not her nature; she communicated her energy out to him in the silence between them, charging it, as it were, almost electrically. But at last the night reached its zenith, that mysterious point at which minutes lengthen, and an hour stretches itself out like a cat. Both of them felt it; their bodies drooped with weariness. Clotaire's jaw hung slack; Felice felt as though her eyes had dried up, and caught herself, several times, nodding off into sleep. She stood and stretched. Clotaire sat up; she caught his eyes.

The sky was just lightening -- the long hours of night had been crossed. Clotaire smiled; Felice returned it with an open tenderness. They shared this moment that united all the levels of their beings, so that, though each felt desire for the other, there

262

was no thought of fulfilling it now. Clotaire bowed to her and excused himself -- he wanted to give his God thanks. Felice lay back on the divan. She felt a greater and greater relief as the sky greyed. No one had come to harm Clotaire. They had both been mercifully mistaken.

Clotaire had left the door open when he went to pray in his chapel, so Felice heard his cry and the crash. She leaped up, grabbing the sword and mace, and ran into the hall. She caught a glimpse of Lothar's golden head just before he turned the bend to the stairway. Hearing the struggle in the chapel, she rushed in. Clotaire was circling, unarmed, facing Villem who held his ax high. Blood streamed down Clotaire's arm from a wound in his shoulder. Villem turned at the sound of Felice entering; his face was twisted in a confused pain.

"Coward!" Felice screamed and rushed him with the mace, throwing down the sword so Clotaire could grab it. Villem hesitated; she saw he might indeed kill her; his ax was still raised; he looked trapped. Then his face turned white and blood filled his mouth. Clotaire had run him through. Villem slowly sank to the floor. Felice cried out as if the sword had cut her to the core. In her mind's eye, she saw Lothar running down the stairs, disappearing, safe, alive, while Villem lay slowly dying in a pool of blood. Through her tears, she saw Clotaire leaning against the wall, holding his shoulder, his face also a mask of pain. The mace was still in her hands. She caught the cry in her throat and ran out of Clotaire's quarters into the dawn's first light.

She vaguely remembered once seeing Lothar going toward a door near the large, central court. She raced along the halls until she came near it. There were three doors, Lothar's could be any one of them. Felice stood close to the first one and listened. Someone was hurrying around inside; she suspected it was Lothar readying himself for escape. Felice's mind was very clear. She used all the instincts of her years as a survivor. Lothar would run because he had not stayed in the chapel long enough to ascertain the outcome of his and Villem's ambush. She had no idea why he had bolted, but imagined it was because the initial attack had only wounded Clotaire and then he had heard Felice in the other room. Not knowing it was she, he fled, leaving Villem to handle all comers.

She moved back along the wall. She suspected she would not have to wait long. She stood in a recess where he would not be able to see her until he was directly in front of her. Carefully, she pulled back the hem of her skirt. Within moments, the door opened. Felice held her breath. He was listening too. There was a clank of his sword in its scabbard; he was closing the door. Felice gripped the mace hard; her hands were wet, but she was very calm. Suddenly he was in front of her and had not even seen her. The mace struck him. He half turned, a look of wonder in his eyes. Felice made no sound and struck him again with all her strength, then again after he fell with a soft thud. His body shivered once, as though he were casting it off like a piece of clothing, leaving it to lie in an awkward heap on the marble floor. Felice stood above him, for a moment fascinated with the silent horror of it.

And now it was her turn to flee. Unlike Lothar, she would not be foolish enough to try to take anything with her. She dropped the mace and ran, barefoot still, down the endless halls out into the courtyard.

Roosters were crowing, their shrill voices carrying up from the valley below. The sun was a promise in the apricot light on the horizon. The hills around Soissons were still a deep blue with darker canyons. Felice saw it all in a moment. This dawn with its calm entrance of light into darkness was just like yesterday's except that the whole world had changed. She had killed Lothar and Clotaire would not be able to pardon her. There were limits even to a king's powers: a serf's killing of a noble was the equivalent of patricide. She would be a refugee all the rest of her days. She lifted her skirt slightly and walked quickly along the narrow path next to the outside wall. When she reached the gate, she grinned, as in the old days, at the guard. He knew her well

264

and grinned back, then waved at her when, from the valley road, she later turned to take a last look at Soissons.

CHAPTER 28

The call of a rooster, joyous and insistent, carried up from the valley to Deirdre's window. She turned onto her back beneath the smooth sheets, stretched, then lay still, recalling the events of the day before. The morning bell had sounded below. She sat up with a cry.

"Oh, he is leaving!"

She leapt from the bed, barefoot, and ran out onto the narrow balcony just outside her bedchamber. She had expected to see activity -- soldiers, pack animals, carts -- but the courtyard lay in deep silence and shadow. Deirdre ran back inside and grabbed a wrap, drawing it around her as she hurried to the balcony that overlooked the other courtyard.

He has already gone, she thought in panic. There was no sign of activity here either, no horns, no hint that Clotaire's band was even slightly prepared to depart. A sliver of the day's first sunlight cut across the wall. Deirdre looked out to where the sun was just rising above the edge of the horizon. She took a deep breath. *Perhaps he hasn't gone. Perhaps he has changed his mind. Oh, but....*

Deirdre suddenly realized the nature of her thoughts. But she did not want to stop them anymore, despite Lothar's objections. *It is not bad to love; only bad to hate, as he does. Oh, I believe I do begin to love Clotaire.* The morning bell sounded again from below, its voice small, but distinct. The air distorted the sound, so that it broke into two parts: to Deirdre it sounded now perfectly with the two syllables of his name: Clo-taire, Clo-taire. She closed her eyes and gave in to the luxury of her feelings.

He can't be gone! She turned and ran back to her chamber. Seeing Gertrude, who patiently awaited her, Deirdre realized she did not like this woman. *She always looks so dismal,* Deirdre thought.

"Where is my Claria?" she snapped.

Gertrude's eyes showed alarm.

"She is at your service anytime you wish," Gertrude said. A slight blush rose in her cheeks.

"Fetch her after you dress me. I would wear yellow today."

Gertrude bowed and left. Deirdre pushed aside her bad feelings toward the woman. Standing at her window, she looked across at its twin. Curtains were pulled across it. Deirdre could scarcely contain the exuberance that filled her. She wanted to sing or dance. Feeling someone's presence, she turned. Gertrude had returned, Deirdre's clothes over her arm.

"Would the queen prefer Claria to dress her?" she asked. Her face was a mask, her voice even and calm.

"No you may do so," Deirdre said lightly, refusing to let Gertrude's heaviness drag her down, "but I do wish her back as my personal maid." As irritating as Deirdre remembered Claria could be, she was a bubble of happiness compared to Gertrude.

Dressed, she ignored Gertrude's suggestion that she eat and hurried down the staircase across the court to Clotaire's apartment. She paused at the door.

What am I doing? she suddenly thought, and would have retraced her steps, but Clotaire's clerk emerged from the shadows.

"Ah, dear lady! Good morning."

"Oh. Good morning. Announce me to the king, if you please."

"I would, but the king still sleeps. Of course, I shall, if you order me to do so, but, permit me to say" -- the old clerk winked humorously -- "he is a terrible grouch when thus awakened."

Deirdre laughed. "Then, he is yet here."

"Ai, milady. I understand the orders have been changed. There will be no departing today."

At these words, Deirdre turned to hide the smile that

suddenly appeared. Her heart was like a bird, just learning to fly. She crossed the courtyard, passed through the arch into the larger one, then made her way down the path to the gate. She could scarcely keep from bounding and leaping like the two young pups who played along the path in front of her, but she forced herself to walk with queenly dignity until she was out of sight of the gate guard, on her way up the trail that climbed above the castle walls. Then she hugged herself and giggled like a girl, and ran up the path until she was breathless.

No day had ever been this beautiful. Colors were clear and distinct, lines and forms of plants and trees were so tender and beautiful, it was as though she had simply overlooked all of nature until today. *Oh, this is what it is to love.* She ran again, then hugged a tree that seemed so alive she could have sworn that it spoke to her. Pressed against its wide, rough trunk, her arms barely reaching around its girth, she laughed at the feeling of energy that emanated from the tree.

"No wonder we have believed so long in many gods!" she exclaimed aloud. "You are so alive!"

She looked down at the castle. This morning it gleamed like the crown she had worn in court the day before. Deirdre tried to see which were the windows of Clotaire's and her adjoining quarters, and she closed her eyes and sent the sleeping Clotaire a fervent message.

"Wake up!" she whispered. "Wake up and come to me here."

Every cell in her body willed him to her, but when she opened her eyes, there was the landscape, glowing, filled with life, yet empty of him.

She passed several hours of the morning tramping the hills, resting in the meadows, hidden by the tall grass when she lay back to watch the clouds sail past in the sky's ocean, while she dreamed of him. His name became a silent chant; she saw him in everything. Finally, her stomach rumbled with sudden hunger.

She ran most of the way down the hill, so that her eyes were bright, her cheeks pink when she came to the gate. She had to stand aside to let a small, mournful group pass. They were carrying two covered pallets. Deirdre lowered her eyes when she realized these were the bodies of two that were dead. She felt a shiver of apprehension. There should be no sorrow on such a day, no death.

She walked quickly to her quarters, her hunger scarcely bearable. Claria beamed when Deirdre entered. The young maid fell upon her knees.

"Ai, Lady Dierdre, thank ye for asking me back."

Deirdre smiled. The room's atmosphere was distinctly lighter with Gertrude gone.

"Where have you been?" Deirdre asked.

Claria pouted and rolled her eyes. "In the scullery. They had me scrubbing pots. Just look at my hands. It will take weeks before they are smooth again."

Deirdre laughed. "Fetch me some food. I am starving."

Clotaire's curtains were still drawn. Deirdre frowned. *Why doesn't he get up?* It was already midmorning. While no sound of activity reached their protected courtyard, the whole castle bustled with servants working. Deirdre had seen the scrubbers, launderers, cooks, and artisans, all of them busy with their duties and hammering and clanging, a whole symphony of sound. She decided, while eating, to have Clotaire awakened. After three bites of a fruit pasty, she pushed her tray aside.

"I thought ye were hungry," Claria chided.

"No more," Deirdre said absently. "Go over to the king's apartment and inquire if he is yet awake."

"Ai, gladly." Claria grinned and dashed out of the bedchamber.

A short while later she returned all out of breath. "He is indisposed, his office clerk told me."

269

Deirdre frowned.

Claria continued. "Forgive the impertinence of my taking the liberty, but the clerk seemed unduly upset as if something terrible had happened. I saw the doctor there."

Deirdre ran down the stairs, her heart pounding. This time she did not hesitate at the entrance, but ran inside and up the stairs to his bedchamber. Two soldiers stood at either side of the door.

"Announce me," she commanded.

The soldier instantly obeyed, knocking at the door. Deirdre pushed him aside and opened the door before anyone had a chance to move toward it. She went in.

Clotaire was in bed, propped up by many pillows. He had a bandage over his shoulder. He was pale and did not smile.

"Leave us," Deirdre ordered the three attendants who waited upon him.

"Why have you come?" Clotaire asked. His voice expressed pain and sorrow.

"You did not go on your campaign, yet you did not get up. I know not your habits, sire, and would have let you sleep the day, but my servant discovered you were ill. Forgive me if I disturb you."

Clotaire looked at her. "You do not disturb me."

Deirdre picked up the spoon with which one attendant had been feeding him.

"Do not talk," she said. "Here, I shall feed you myself."

Clotaire held her wrist with his good hand. "Nay. I must talk. Terrible things have happened. You see I am wounded."

"Oh? 'Tis not from illness, then?"

"Nay."

A foreboding filled Deirdre's chest. She sat down on a chair near the bed. She was trembling.

"Tell me," she whispered.

Clotaire hesitated. Then he took a deep breath. "This morning, I was attacked in my chapel."

Deirdre watched his face as he spoke. Some part of her wanted to stop his words. She wanted to retain the morning's happiness, to keep locked away from herself whatever event made him look so stern right now. But his voice went on. The words came together in a chain of meaning.

"Villem was one. I was unarmed and he struck me here." He indicated his shoulder. "Missed my head." He too would have liked to stop his words. Dierdre had come into his room just moments ago flushed with concern and love. He had seen in that moment that she did not yet know about Lothar. He had also recognized that she had changed, and Clotaire dared to believe that finally she loved him. It was in her eyes, in the flush of her skin, in her choice of the yellow gown. Now, as he spoke, he saw how her terror grew. Her eyes searched his face and the corners of the room; her hands twisted a fold in her gown.

"My servant got my sword to me and I felled Villem. The...the other with him was Lothar, who ran out after I received the first blow. I...I pursued him to his room, where we fought. Both are dead."

The room filled with silence as Deirdre sat motionless. Wave after wave of a force she would never be able to give a name to rolled over her. She saw nothing, heard only silence, felt the world around her shrivel away. Clotaire watched her. For the first time since he was a young boy, he felt tears hot in the back of his throat. He tried to sit up; a sharp pain, like a knife, knocked him back down.

"Deirdre," he said through the pain. He heard her voice, cold and clear.

"You did not have to kill him!"

When he opened his eyes, she was already passing through the door, her shoulders erect, her head held proud. He closed his eyes again and sighed. He did not wish for it, but if Felice were

271

found dead, he would tell Deirdre the truth, he decided. Until that happened, no one must know that she had killed Lothar, or even he would not be able to save her. He would bear the burden of Deirdre's grief and blame because he could never allow Felice to be hanged for a deed of vengeance done out of love for himself and Villem. He cared too deeply for her and already missed her presence, her loyalty and devotion, which only she had ever given him. But he grieved too, for what was lost between himself and Deirdre, that love that he had just seen rising in her, answering the love for her that he had long nourished in his heart.

Deirdre went down the stairs like someone stunned by a physical blow, but already some force was coalescing. A bitterness filled her. All of her love was now cruelly destroyed. She crossed the courtyard, paused outside the small room that held her queen's robes, then went inside. She took the ring, symbol of her queen's authority, and put it inside her tunic. With this, no servant at Soissons would dare to question her. She knew what she would do. Calmly, she informed Claria that they both were to travel. She showed her the ring.

"The king orders it. He will join us later. To the stables then. Five horses, one for each of us, one for supplies and two for soldiers to accompany us. Show the stable man this ring and tell him to have all ready in half an hour. Tell him we return to Athies."

Claria opened her mouth to ask a question, but Deirdre held her hand up to silence her.

"Do not lose that ring," she warned the sometimes forgetful servant.

Deirdre removed her gown herself and dressed in black from head to toe. She put a violet veil over her head and face. Claria was amazed to see her mistress thus when she returned, but said nothing. Hurriedly, she gathered a few bits of clothing to be packed along with the blankets and food. Her curiosity was almost more than she could bear.

They hurried down to the large courtyard where the soldiers and horses were waiting. Deirdre had put on her queen's ring. They mounted and slowly made their way to the gate. The guard there asked nothing when he saw them. The word had already spread among the servants and artisans: Lord Lothar was dead. Seeing the new queen in mourning, he bowed respectfully when she passed.

They took the road toward the west for several miles until it forked off to the north and south. They did not hurry. Deirdre felt safe this time and sure that Clotaire would give her some time to forgive him and would think she was still inside the castle walls. By the time he realized she was gone, she would have put many miles between them. Lothar had been right this time, she wrong. But she would not cry, not regret. She had nothing left but her love for God. In Tours, she would see the bishop; she would leave this life that brought her nothing but sorrow. She would give herself to God and would never again allow Clotaire even into her thoughts. She would transcend hate and love both. She would become a nun. Perhaps she might even see Fortunatus once more. With such thoughts, she rode on and never once looked back at the castle, which shrank in the distance to a size no bigger than her ring.

PART 4

CHAPTER 29

Though she had been instructed not to, Deirdre let her eyes wander from her folded hands as she chanted the prayer of the hours; thus she saw the first crocus that had this day pushed its way through the slowly softening earth. She stopped both her walk and her prayer and bent down to simply look at it. The winter had been hard, with cold winds and long, dreary days of overcast weather and, though this had exactly suited her mood, in these last weeks, she had begun to long for spring and color.

You must wait, the bishop had told her. *You are in no state to make such a decision. I could never accept it.*

When, then? she had asked.

He had studied her thoughtfully. *In the spring, perhaps,* he finally said.

All the fall and winter, she had felt rootless, uncommitted. The bishop would not accept her decision to take her temporary vows; yet the cathedral was the only place where she could go. It offered her asylum in the event Clotaire should come to force her back to Soissons with him; it also offered her peace, sanctuary from her past, and a library to divert her. She had spent long hours in study: the church's history, dogma, the Scriptures. She had even learned to weave, though she despised handwork, in order to convince the bishop of the sincerity of her wish.

You have known the love of a man. It is more difficult to renounce the flesh after carnal knowledge than before. Wait.

Nothing she said or did could convince him.

I hate him, she said once in desperation.

It is un-Christian to hate.

I do not hate him, but I desire him not.

274

You cannot know yet what you desire. You are trying to escape.

His words surrounded her like a fog she had to penetrate. She needed to find the argument, the exact words, to break through his caution. Only this past week she had approached him again.

Monseigneur, I beg an audience with you.

You are too impatient. You cannot make a good nun. Go!

She had stamped her foot. *But it is spring!*

The bishop had laughed. *You see?*

She looked down. One stem of the crocus lay on the ground. Lost in her thoughts, she had broken it. "Forgive me," she whispered. Unaccountably, she began to weep.

In all the time since she had left Soissons, through the summer, fall and now the winter, she had kept a calm reserve; not once had she cried, neither for her brother, nor for herself. She wanted to move forward out of her past and had believed she could do it. Now she sank down on the ground next to this broken crocus and cried pitifully.

"Sister Deirdre! What is it?"

Deirdre looked up through her tears at the bishop's old housekeeper, a bit of a wizened woman who bent over her with motherly concern. Deirdre could not answer, but let herself be helped back to her small room. She lay on the hard bed and let the tears flow.

"Now, that is better," she heard the bishop say moments later.

She buried her face deeper into the pillow. He put his hand on her head and stroked her hair.

"Ah yes, yes, cry little lady. Let out the grief and disappointment; it is the only way."

"I brought some broth," the housekeeper said. "Ai, poor thing. Such terrible things happen."

275

Deirdre gradually gained control of her sobs and sat up.

"Forgive me," she managed to say.

The bishop patted her hand. "What sin have you committed that I should forgive?" He smiled. "I have waited all this year to see those tears break through. Without them, there can be no healing."

"Oh, monseigneur, I have cried so many days in my life. My history is a long series of losses. But it is safe now; I am the only one left. I can lose no more. That is why I wish to become a nun."

"Dierdre, now I can speak openly. Your position is most strange. I doubt not your sincerity, and your motives are only yours and God's to judge. But you are a married woman, and married by a priest in the eyes of God."

"But I have told you, when I said those words, I meant them not. I was a prisoner. He forced me."

"Yes, yes, and I believe you. What is most awkward is that your husband happens to be the king of the Franks, and also happens to be the young church's greatest champion. I fear for the outcome if I should anger King Clotaire."

"I could change my name. I could disappear. He might think me dead."

The bishop laughed. "Oh, you have thought of everything, have you? And when he arrives asking your whereabouts, as he will one day, I, a bishop, should simply shrug and answer with lies?" He rose. "Relax your duties for the rest of the day. Try to sleep. You have been keeping more than a nun's hours. Overzealousness does not impress me, nor does it make a good nun. Sleep, dear girl. We shall talk later." The bishop left.

Deirdre looked out at the bright blue patch of sky. Feeling had finally returned tumultuously, as if in vengeance for having been so long denied. That now Clotaire should be responsible for keeping her from the fulfillment of her deepest wish was more than she could bear. She paced her room, most un-nun-like, raging within.

"Oh, I hate him! I hate him!" she cried out over and over.

But that night she once again dreamed of him and woke before dawn with an ache in her heart. She was mortified to think that, even in her sleep, she should desire him. She worked especially hard that day and the next in order to purge herself. But two nights later, though she was exhausted and fell immediately asleep, she had the dream again and woke up in a sweat.

He sill drives me mad. He comes even in my sleep. Lothar's words returned to her. *I have heard he bewitches women. You are just one more!* The sound of her brother's voice rose like a ghost from some recess of her memory. She cried again, until dawn. More than a month passed in this way. At times Deirdre seemed close to madness. All her dead returned to her -- in dreams, in vacant moments. She tried to keep every hour occupied; she wore a hair shirt, flagellated herself on three occasions; none of it stopped the desire that rose in her during sleep. But by the time the spring had reached its peak, the madness, of itself, began to lessen. Mercifully, she slept three nights in a row without any dreams that she could recall. She felt, as days passed and her dead lay buried along with desire, that she had come through it, that now she could sincerely ask the bishop to act in her case. He had seen how she had passed through hell itself; he had been witness, had sat with her during the nights it had been at its worst, and had prayed with her long evening vigils after all the work was done.

"You are very brave," he said, when she returned to his office.

Deirdre looked modestly at the floor.

"All right then. You must win one more battle, and it shall be yours alone to fight. I will be the arbiter." He took both her hands in his. "I shall send for Clotaire. You must meet him and present your case. If he gives you his permission to enter a convent, then I shall support you. Otherwise" -- the bishop

277

shrugged -- "my hands are tied."

Deirdre's face reddened with the old anger. "Permission!?"

The bishop laughed. "Oh, my dear, the life of a nun will be most difficult for you. You have more spirit than is good, more pride than you can handle. I would wish your mother superior the best of luck. Ten hair shirts could never hold back that temper of yours." His eyes filled with tears of mirth. "Such a silly girl. I know of Clotaire. He is not a bad man. Your brother attacked him; he fought back. It is terrible, indeed, but 'tis not for you to stand as judge. If you could find it in your heart to forgive him, methinks you'd have a fruitful life." He gazed at her appreciatively. "Indeed, you'd make the people a fine and strong queen. Think on it. Now you may go."

Deirdre went directly to the cathedral where she knelt to pray. She calmed herself first, both the quick anger and her beating heart. The thought of seeing Clotaire again frightened her. She was not sure she could hold her emotions in check; she was yet very vulnerable.

The weeks passed smoothly. Deirdre was busy working in the bishop's garden, planting vegetables and tending the young plants. Hours of bending and weeding left her tired at night, and her sleep was as smooth as her days, blessed with no dark dreams. She felt stronger, calmer.

I think I can make it. With God's help, I shall win. She felt more and more sure of herself.

"He is here, Lady Dierdre."

Deirdre's heart jumped. No one had called her *my lady* for all the time she had been here. The term put her in immediate connection with Clotaire, who, she understood, was here now. She rose slowly and slipped off her gardening gloves. Absently, her hands went to her hair, her bosom, her skirt, straightening, arranging.

"Oh, you always look beautiful; you need not mind," the old housekeeper said, smiling. She put her cool, wrinkled palm against Deirdre's cheek. "You went so pale just now. Are you all right?"

"Ai. Where is he?"

"In the bishop's office. They are expecting you."

Deirdre ducked into the nave for a moment to say a quick prayer. Her hands trembled; she took in a deep breath and slowly exhaled. Eyes closed, she was surprised that she could not imagine him, no detail of his features. She smiled. Perhaps he was truly gone from within her and her only fear now was that she might not win. She bowed deeply to the altar.

"Be with me," she prayed.

She saw him from the entrance to the hall that led to the bishop's office. His back was to her. His black hair glistened. He was speaking and his voice rang like a familiar bell inside her. She was afraid, but did not hesitate. She bowed just as he turned, thus avoiding his eyes.

"It has been a long time, my dear wife."

Her head shot up. Before she could catch herself, anger rose in her eyes.

"Wife, indeed!" she snapped.

He winked humorously. Turning to the bishop, he asked with irony. "A nun? May the Lord bless the good sisters who get her." Turning back to Deirdre, he continued with the same irony in both his expression and voice. "Don't you think you are going too far, you, a lusty wench with so much temper?"

Deirdre bit her tongue. He knew how to defeat her, knew the exact weaknesses, and was using them. Looking at the floor, she listened to the intonation in his voice more than his words, caught herself doing so, and forced herself to listen carefully.

"Ai, sire. You are quite right. Lusty and willful!" She met his gaze full on. "It has already been difficult, and no doubt will be not easy for me ever. But you mistake our Lord if you think he only wishes the life of monk or nun for those without feelings and appetites. You no doubt know of his tests of truly great men. I, only a woman, and of such lesser worth, feel honored that he should test me at all."

Clotaire watched her and, watching her, wanted her. He missed her dearly, particularly because Felice was also gone, apparently for good. He had heard of her here and there, but she had not yet been found, and his search for Deirdre had been equally fruitless until now. It had never occurred to him to search for her here in Tours. By Deirdre's orders, the two soldiers and Claria had been freed, under the condition that they never return to Clotaire's service or speak of her whereabouts to any other person. The two soldiers had disappeared with the gifts of gold Deirdre had given them. Claria still lived in Tours and came on occasion to visit her former mistress.

"You still dream of me and call for me, I know that," he said softly when she was finished.

Deirdre felt the blood rush to her face. "No longer, sire," she said.

Clotaire turned to the bishop. "If you would leave us, I could convince her in a moment, monseigneur."

The bishop was uncomfortable. "Sire, I am present to hear your arguments. The queen would become a sister, taking the first vows here, then to train in a convent. Because you are her husband, you must needs enforce your will or let her go. That you are both Christian, it is my duty to arbitrate between false and real desires. Please continue."

Clotaire slammed his fist on the table. "She is my wife! She is my property!"

"In the eyes of God, I am a free soul and belong to no man!" Deirdre cried out passionately.

Clotaire glared at her. "You have carnal knowledge. You are not chaste. You are not a virgin! How can you be a nun?"

There was a moment's silence. Deirdre answered shakily.

"I am a virgin in my heart. And I am indeed chaste! How dare you say otherwise? A nun need only be chaste, not virginal." She appealed to the bishop. "Is that not true?"

"Ai," he said solemnly. "A nun takes the vow of chastity. A virgin is preferred only because it is infinitely easier for such a one to dwell within God without conflict. But it is not a requirement."

Clotaire had regained control of his temper. Now he smiled.

"Have you not thought of me during all this time? Nay? You never once wished for me as I did for you? You wish to be a nun, yet you close your heart to me, will not forgive me?"

It was Deirdre's turn for anger. "Ai, indeed, I forgave you the first murder, did I not? You saw how I..." she considered only a moment, then blurted out, "yes, how I began to love you..." her eyes filled briefly; she fought her weakness,"...believing love better than hate or vengeance, and you...you turned to murder again!"

"Murder!" Clotaire was furious.

"Ai! What pretty name would you have for it?"

"And what name do you give for his act? Eh?"

They were nearly nose to nose. Deirdre suddenly realized her position and drew back.

"He was a boy. A child, almost. He was wrong. I did not justify him, but his death was also wrong, and you committed that act."

Clotaire bit his lip. He was quite white.

"But we are not here for that. That is over with," she continued evenly. "I wish to be a nun, to devote my life to prayer and the service of others. That is why we are here, not to unearth the dead."

"You and I -- if you remember, and I believe you will when I refresh your memory -- were married."

"Against my will, if you recall! I was your prisoner. You

threatened to strip and publicly flog me if I disobeyed you."

Clotaire laughed. "A pretty sight it would have been, too," he said.

Deirdre turned away in disgust.

"But it was not the ceremony I referred to. A ceremony is but an empty ritual when the heart is not in it. And I accept that you were not with me in your heart at that ceremony." He paused significantly. Deirdre squirmed. She knew what was coming.

"It was later, when the true marriage occurred. I did not force you, my dear, in any way, as you no doubt will remember."

Her face was burning. She glared at him and noticed that the bishop, too, was blushing, though his eyes twinkled with laughter.

"We very happily consummated that marriage a little later; in fact, on one occasion, you rather forced *me*, made *me* break my promise not to arouse *you*, but you were so much more than willing, you seduced me. Do you remember?"

"Have you no shame? Such things are not for the bishop's ears!"

"Indeed the good bishop is a man, as well as a man of the cloth. He knows of lust as well as another."

"I want to be a nun! I cannot be your wife! I cannot ever forgive you!" she cried.

The bishop intervened. "That is perhaps the nub of the difficulty between you. I suggest you speak of that death, though it brings pain to you both." He rose. "Because Deirdre, my child, if, in some way, you could come to peace with that, if you understood your husband's motives for that, and thus forgave him, then perhaps your wish to be a sister might not prove so strong."

"Ai, monseigneur. Then, let him tell me, in plain words, how he could justify killing his wife's only living blood, the young brother she dearly loved."

Clotaire walked to the narrow window. His back was to them. He said nothing for several, long minutes. Finally, he turned.

"Nay. I could never justify that act to you. Nothing I could say would convince you." He picked up his cape and flung it over one shoulder. He was quite pale. "Hence, my wife, my dear love, my queen, you are free. Do as you wish."

He turned on his heel and left. Deirdre's mouth fell open. She had not expected such an easy victory. She heard the bishop's words to her as from a great distance.

"I hope you are happy with your choice, my dear. In the morning, we shall have the ceremony. Then you shall go to the sisters in Poitiers. There is a new, and very small, convent there with a need for more hands. Go to the housekeeper for your robes, and be ready to depart on the morrow." He smiled kindly and gave her a light, fatherly embrace. "I hope you will be happy. May God bless you, my girl."

CHAPTER 30

Deirdre had no time to think on what had happened, nor whether she might, as the bishop wished her, be happy as a nun or not. She carefully selected a few needed possessions and disposed of the rest among the poor who came every day to the cathedral steps to beg for alms. The rest of the day she had her robes to make from the half-finished ones the housekeeper had given her. She worked into the late evening stitching the seams and hems. Her fingers were quite sore by the time she climbed into bed well after the evening bell had sounded for the last time.

She lay in the silence of her small room, her eyes open, seeing nothing, only listening to the mournful hooting of a nearby owl. The singleness of the bird underlined her own singleness, the way in which, now, she was detached from any other living person. It was an aloneness so complete, she heard the bird's insistent call as if it came from within herself.

In the grey light of dawn, after the brief ceremony at the main altar of the cathedral where, dressed as a bride, she received her habit and the bishop's formal blessing. Deirdre hurried in her new, black robes to the main marketplace in the center of town. She was a little frightened; she was not sure of her new role nor of this new independence. She was no longer Lady Deirdre, but Sister Deirdre. The lady Dierdre had had the advantages of privilege and of authority that were immediately recognized by all, and strongly supported by those born to her own caste. Sister Deirdre was yet unknown, and her only visible source of support, so far as Deirdre could see, was this rather shaky young church, personified in the bishop. She was mainly ignored as she hurried along, and that already was a difference. Usually, she commanded attention and respect. But the only attention she now aroused was gawking and a few unkind remarks.

"The lady's not for having," a woman who glanced up at her from her sweeping said in sarcastic tones.

"Ai, but look at her. There be nothing to have," her neighbor responded. Both women laughed.

Deirdre bristled, but bit her tongue and kept walking.

She found a small caravan that would travel down to Poitiers, but only with great difficulty. She was accustomed to giving orders, not seeking assistance.

"Please, sire, I need the way to Poitiers"

The man looked down at her. Seeing her robes, his eyes grew hard with contempt.

"How dare ye turn against the gods, eh?" His face was in hers. Deirdre reeled. His breath almost knocked her over. "It's the likes of ye that brings bad harvests. Get ye home to your fathers! Let them teach ye the true gods." She was backing away, her heart thumping. When he reached out at her, she bolted. The small crowd that had gathered broke into laughter. She ran down the narrow street until she came to a small courtyard. There, she leaned against the wall to catch her breath. Her mind was in a quandary. All of her courage was gone. She wanted only to run back to the cathedral to seek refuge. From its earlier safety, the life of a sister of God had seemed simple. She would have God's and the bishop's protection.

An older man bowed in front of her. Deirdre recoiled.

"Young nun," he said politely. "Be not afraid. I too shall travel to Poitiers. Follow me; I shall lead ye to the caravan that leaves this morning."

"Are...are you Christian?" she asked.

He smiled kindly. "Nay. But I know of the sisters of Poitiers One of them nursed my youngest back to life. He was surely dead otherwise. So ye be safe with me."

There was something reassuring about him. His face was that of a peon, of a man who had worked hard and long days all of his life, and he spoke with respect to her.

"Ai, then," she said. "Lead the way."

She walked slightly behind him and had to hurry in order to keep up with his long strides. By the time they reached the marketplace where the small group of travelers to Poitiers was gathering, she was damp with perspiration. It was already a warm day; yet the sun hung just above the horizon. Deirdre's black robe soaked up its warmth, making her extremely uncomfortable. She sat down, breathless, on a sack of flour.

"We leave in an hour," her guide told her. "Be ye hungry?"

"Nay, not hungry, but thirsty. I could drink some water."

"Ye be high-born is my guess. I be happy to get ye some water, but methinks it will not be clean enough for ye. Then ye'll get sick."

Deirdre was pleased with his concern and did not dispute him regarding her birth, knowing that such an observation would bring with it many favors. In fact, she smiled to acknowledge it, the smile carrying a hint of later payment for any services he might render her. He fetched her some warm ale and returned again some minutes later, obviously pleased with himself.

"I have arranged for ye to ride in the wagon," he announced proudly.

"Ah, but I should walk, like any other," Deirdre protested.

"'Tis almost two days to Poitiers," the man said. "In this heat, with those robes, ye will suffer much, even in the wagon. Be not so proud, young sister. It is a humble cart to be sure, but ye will be under a cloth out of the sun. Besides, I have already paid, and would be ashamed to ride me-self."

The crude axle and rough wooden wheels made riding a dubious blessing. Deirdre lay back in the hay in a half-stupor; the heat was tremendous; the caravan moved slowly. Two horsemen rode guard; a small family of peasants, Deirdre's guide, and three younger men made up the rest of the caravan. The countryside was level, with trees scattered in the wild grass, giving a moment here and there of shade when the narrow road mercifully passed under one. No one spoke once they got under way. Gradually,

Deirdre's uneasiness passed. The protection of this man, who called himself Gendrun, seemed sincere, and her former habit of self-confidence reasserted itself, so that, without a word, the others in the group fell in with Gendrun's attitude of respect toward her. Only the woman who carried a small babe in a shawl tied to her back kept glancing at Deirdre with misgiving. Deirdre, however, did not notice, and this lack of awareness toward her was enough to reassure the woman that Deirdre was indeed one of the nobility.

Toward afternoon, the sky clouded, promising a storm. At first, the loss of the sun was most welcome. But the air became sultry and oppressive; the sky was a fist of darkness from which an occasional stab of lightning shot, accompanied by a distant angry rumble. They were on an open plain with no shelter in sight. The animals became restive: the horses rolled their eyes and whinnied nervously. Only the ox pulling the cart kept placidly moving. The horses' anxiety communicated itself to the people; they looked around at one another in search of the one who would take command. Suddenly, a wind came up. They watched it coming toward them from the distance, saw it flatten the long grass as if an invisible herd of animals were approaching. It hit as a force, cooling suddenly, and catching the cloth that had partially shaded Deirdre from the sun, so that it flapped wildly on the cart like a caged bird.

Gendrun yelled to the guards.

"Come! Give us a hand!"

He signaled Deirdre to get down from the cart. The men then unloaded it, unhitched the ox, and heaving with all their strength, turned the cart upside down. Deirdre, the peasant women and children were pushed under it. The men then tied the animals to the cart, and they huddled around its edge on the side that best sheltered them from the wind.

Suddenly, everything was water. Deirdre cried out in alarm. This had to be a flood, not just rain. In moments, even under the cart, they were sitting in water; water came down through the spaces between the floor boards of the cart and ran in small rivers in the road's ruts. Deirdre's robes soaked it up, becoming heavier and heavier. Her veil was wet so quickly, she removed it. Water ran down her back tickling her into chills. The peasant woman sat still. In contrast to Deirdre's nervous fidgeting, she was like a rock, accustomed to such events as this, her two children and baby like smaller rocks leaning against her bulk. Their four pairs of dark eyes watched Deirdre, offering neither comfort nor judgment, only watching. Deirdre finally saw the futility of alarm, of movement, of any reaction whatever, and settled into the puddle of her clothes, apparently resigned. Outside the cart's small and dubious shelter, the storm raged with lightning bolts striking the ground in every direction, sometimes quite nearby. The horses nervously danced. Deirdre watched their feet prance and felt them pull at the cart, intent on the one thing that might give them relief: to run.

The storm left almost as quickly as it had come. First the wind, then the lightning ceased; the rain, for a while, fell straight down in a steady drone, then slowed and stopped. The women and children crawled out from under the cart. They were more splattered with mud than were the men and animals who, at least, got somewhat washed by the rain. Deirdre's hair hung wet and loose in long, dark strands down her back. Her robes were immensely heavy, pulling down on her as if the hems were weighted with chains.

The men righted the cart, loaded it with the soggy bags of clothing and flour and what hay could be salvaged from the muddy road, and hitched up the ox. The sun suddenly broke through, and within moments, Deirdre felt the humidity as an additional weight. She made a conscious effort to remain good-natured, said a quick prayer of thanks, then, as the heat grew, wondered testily what she should be thankful for, and wondered more, with a growing sense of worry, if she had not made a terrible mistake in judgment in having chosen such a path.

288

Another violent storm broke over them that night while they camped. In the darkness, it was even more frightening. The sky was a constant display of fire, the thunder sounded like the wrath of God Himself, the rain was a flood. A nearby tree, hit by the lightning, fell nearly on top of Gendrun and one of the young men. Deirdre was so frightened, she could not sleep even after it was over, and the next day's journey, with her nerves jangling from exhaustion and the heat upon them once again, was a nightmare. She felt triply oppressed, because she sensed an antagonism growing toward her. They were all believers in Tollech and the many gods. The weather for the time of year was most unusual, the flour was no doubt ruined, the trip the hardest any of them could remember, or had even heard of. She was the significantly different detail, as each of them went over their many possible offenses to the gods. The woman whispered to her husband who looked at Deirdre with open dislike. Soon the feeling had affected all of them, except Gendrun who only looked uneasy.

"Have ye any gold?" he whispered when they stopped by a stream for water and Deirdre was separate from the others.

She looked at him suspiciously.

"They are against ye, can't ye feel it?" he said with urgency.

"Ai," she answered, and realized the danger of her position.

"Ye can trust me," he insisted.

"Ai, I know that," she said slowly. "My family will see that I am cared for. They will be most grateful to you."

He caught the meaning behind her words and blushed. Deirdre felt keenly the irony of her having to use her position of class after she had renounced it, but saw immediately how it was now necessary. Gendrun had become the acknowledged leader from when he had taken charge during the storm, but the tide of feeling was shifting as he continued to protect Deirdre after the bad luck of the second storm. The group's support was slowly changing in favor of the sturdy peasant husband. Gendrun felt the loss and feared that, if another bit of bad weather or luck befell them before they reached Poitiers, he would be abandoned along with Deirdre. All the roads that led into Tours up to a distance of three days were traversed by highwaymen and brigands who thought nothing of killing a man for only his foot wrappings. Even in a group with guards, it was not unusual to be attacked; alone with Deirdre, Gendrun would have no chance. He had hoped, with what gold the young maid might have, to assure his position within the group. Now he would have to do without it.

He saw the others talking and walked down to join them by the stream.

"She is of royal blood," he said, approaching them with a swagger.

"Ah, I believe it not," the woman said. She was the firmest in her dislike of Deirdre.

"What do ye know of her?" one of the guards asked.

"Only she is a noblewoman, and her family assures her safety to the sisters in Poitiers."

Gendrun's words fell upon them like the pebble he threw into the stream. They immediately understood his meaning. The woman muttered out of the side of her mouth: "One more bit of luck like we've had, noble or not, I'll see to it she be with us no more." The men shifted uneasily. The woman's husband spat.

"Another word, woman...."

Husband and wife glared.

Gendrun changed his tone and spoke loudly. "Let's be on our way then. We'll be in Poitiers in some hours more. We can all drink and laugh then, safe in our homes."

"Ai, if we make it." The woman was on the ground before she finished the last syllable. She fell with a soft thud and lay silent, looking up with a sullen hatred at her husband. The baby screamed, his one arm pinned under his mother. She made no move to free him. The two other children looked down at the

290

small pebbles they kicked with their bare feet.

Deirdre watched all this from the road. Sweat ran down her body in small streams, tickling her and burning her eyes. When the group came up, one of the young men offered her water from his pouch. She shook her head. She would not get back in the cart either and, with shaking legs, followed the group at some distance. Gendrun kept looking around to see that she followed. Finally, he halted and waited for her.

"Ye make us go slower, that is no way to behave."

"I am afraid," she admitted.

"I promised ye I'd take care of ye, didn't I? They would have left ye back there, but ye see that they didn't."

The group also stopped and stood watching as Deirdre approached. "Why do they hate me?" Deirdre's sense of herself had shrunk so small, she scarcely had a voice.

"Now, that is not it. They see ye are different, that's all. Come on, up with ye now." He glared at the woman. "Methinks she is ill. Ye see how white she is."

The woman looked at her husband, opened her lips as if it speak, then closed them again without a sound. Silently, the group pushed on.

Exhausted, Deirdre looked out through half-opened lids at a world that appeared to be floating in water. She fell asleep that way, with her eyes half-opened, as though she dared not, for a moment, give herself over to darkness. She awoke, hours later, with a start and then relaxed when she saw the faces of two women who were dressed in robes exactly like hers.

"Oh, my dear," the older one exclaimed. "What a terrible journey. Gendrun, lift her. Take her inside. Sister Catherine will lead the way."

Deirdre felt herself lifted. She was swimming again, then she knew no more.

CHAPTER 31

"I am sorry you must serve me," Deirdre said when the door opened and Sister Catherine entered, carrying the heavy tray.

The young nun smiled. Her cheeks, rosy anyway, blushed deeper with pleasure.

"Oh, 'tis the nicest service I've had to do since I got here," she answered.

"Ai? Is that true?"

"Indeed. At least you...oh, forgive me, Sister, I should not speak so." She tossed her head. Her veil slipped to one side and she righted it with a laugh. "I was not made for this life."

Deirdre smiled. "What was it you were going to say?"

"Oh, that..." she shrugged prettily "...that you are clean. *They* stink and often have lice. The first week I was here I was sick to my stomach all the time."

"Who are *they*?"

"All of the people here. The poor, the serfs, all of them. I hate them." She laughed gaily at Deirdre's look of shocked surprise.

"I am not a good nun," Catherine said. "But none expects me to be, either." She thought a moment. "At least I hope not." She sighed. "I expect I'll be here perhaps a year."

"I don't know if I am good either," Deirdre said, half in jest.

"Oh, you? My goodness. You were, or are, the wife of a king!" Catherine looked at Deirdre with admiration. "You see, dear Sister, I don't understand this life. God is God, that is fine. But Catherine is a woman; she needs a man, not a spirit."

Deirdre had to laugh at Catherine's gestures that accompanied her speech; they expressed a complete sense of logic.

"Then why are you here at all?" Deirdre asked.

"Oh! La, la! It is a family tragedy, you see. But why are *you*? You must either be a saint or a castoff!" Her hand flew up over her mouth. "Oh! I did it again. I should not say that."

"Nay, you should not. But I sense you often say what you should not." Deirdre laughed, and Catherine joined in.

"Tell me, I am curious," Dierdre said, "why must I either be a saint or a castoff?"

Catherine rolled up her eyes. "Ai, to be the wife of Clotaire, not only a king, but a wonderful and beautiful man as well." She sat on the bed and leaned toward Deirdre familiarly. "Do you know, once, when I was much younger, he came to our home and stayed three weeks." She flung herself back on the bed and threw up her arms. "Oh! I fell madly in love, but he would not look at me."

Deirdre sat up in consternation. "Please, Sister Catherine, do not speak of him to me." Catherine sat up also. "Oh. Then, it is castoff. I am sorry." She looked at Deirdre carefully. "You are so beautiful. I don't understand."

Deirdre felt her patience leaving. She wanted to leave Clotaire forever behind her.

"It is not so simple as you think, and neither thing you say is true. Now, no more!"

Catherine stood. "But you must have your broth." She pouted. "If you can be so firm with me, then indeed you have regained your strength."

While Catherine was about Deirdre's age, she behaved younger, like a girl. Deirdre could not help but be charmed by her.

"You bring me strength with your laughter and bright eyes, dear Sister."

Catherine smiled. "Oh, I have been so lonely here. The others spend all their hours in prayer, making long faces, and oh God! They come back scratching with lice the poor folk give them. You have no idea how it is. All of us are more in the bath

293

and the laundry than anywhere else."

Deirdre frowned. "Is it not good to help others? I mean, does it not make you feel good?"

Catherine shrugged. "Ai, when it is an idea only. But when you enter the room of a sick man or woman..."she made a ghastly face "...one who has not bathed in weeks, and then only in cold water, well, it is terrible! Enough to make one retch!"

"Then, I ask you again, why are you here? Can't you go back to your family?" Deirdre stopped. She feared suddenly that she might tread upon a tragedy as painful as her own. She stuttered an apology.

"Oh nay. 'Tis not a death or such that brings me here. You see my age. I should already be married. In the last three years, our vineyards and harvests failed, and much of our lands and fortunes were lost. My dowry also went. It is terrible. So here I am like a serf! My father hopes this year to recoup his losses and my dowry. Then I shall be free again, and shall marry. So...." She shrugged again. Deirdre did not know whether to feel gaiety or sorrow. No matter what Sister Catherine expressed, it was done with such a lightness, it invited smiles and laughter, not pity or sorrow.

"Then you are not a nun, really," Deirdre finally decided to say.

"Ai, but I am. They made me take my vows in order to stay here."

Deirdre protested. "But only the first ones, nay?"

"What does it matter? I am to act like one! I must clean and cook and harvest and do all that the others must do who have chosen for reasons other than mine. It is a dull and dreary life. The only man I ever see is the old priest who comes once a month to confess us. Goodness knows, I have only thoughts to confess, no deeds."

"Will you have some food with me?" Deirdre asked

politely.

"Ai, with pleasure. That is another thing. I am nearly starved."

Catherine happily perched on the edge of Deirdre's narrow bed. Together, they ate and chatted like family sisters rather than spiritual sisters.

"Is there a library here?" Deirdre asked.

"What? A what?" Catherine screwed up her face to show her ignorance.

"Scrolls. Manuscripts."

"Oh, that. Nay, thank the Lord. It would be yet another task for me to do. Mother has one old, yellowing collection of prayers or something. That is all. And she does not know how to read any more than I. But she sits in front of it long hours as if she did." Catherine sniffed haughtily. "Methinks 'tis her way of getting out of the labor." Catherine giggled. "But how have you come to be here?"

Considering for a moment, Deirdre decided to tell Catherine all of her story after all. The young nun listened and exclaimed and comforted.

"You see how it is not difficult for me to renounce the world." Deirdre finished.

"Ai, it seems the world renounced you first."

"When I feel that, I am in despair."

"I sometimes feel that too." Catherine looked out the window. "I worry that my father will forget me and leave me here. I want to die then."

Deirdre watched Catherine's profile. "How strange life is," she sighed.

Catherine looked at her, the question in her eyes.

"That you came here wanting what I ran away from; that you met Clotaire and believed you loved him; that if you could

295

have changed places with me, we could both have been happier perhaps."

"But tell me something." Catherine hesitated. "I should not ask, but you are right. I often speak or ask of things I should not."

Deirdre smiled at Catherine's preparation. "Only ask it then, since you will anyway."

"Did you ever love him?"

"Is that all?"

"Ai. Except I should tell you why."

"Why?"

"All this week during your fever, you spoke his name perhaps a dozen times. Once you even raised your arms, like this, as though you reached for him."

Deirdre felt the blood rush to her face.

"Oh! I have embarrassed you."

Deirdre covered her face with both hands. "Nay, not for that. Only I don't remember any of it. I don't recall a dream, nothing. I used to dream of him. It was a terrible time." She looked at Catherine. "I wish to be honest, with you and myself as well, but I do not know. I do not love him now. I don't know if I ever loved him before."

The door opened. Catherine jumped up guiltily.

"Good day, Mother, " she chirped.

"Catherine. You have been neglecting your duties again. Off with you!"

The mother superior watched Catherine as she passed with a curtsy and a pout. Mother shook her head.

"A nun, I fear, she will never make."

Deirdre protested. "Mother, 'twas not her fault. I detained her with talk. She does my spirit so good. It was selfish of me."

The old nun smiled. Her face was so wrinkled and pale, she looked like a cauliflower. But when she smiled, the muscles

296

redistributed themselves into a kindly, human, face.

"It's good to see you awake again."

"Have I really been here a week?"

The old woman nodded. She cleared the dishes and moved the tray off the bed. Deirdre felt how the woman was used to silence. She made almost no sound in her movements and kept her eyes cast downward as though she rarely came out of herself. She was such a sharp contrast to Sister Catherine that Deirdre felt her silence almost as a rebuff.

"Mother...," Deirdre began. The old nun looked up. Her eyes were bright and alert.

"Why did I get so sick?"

The mother superior reflected a few moments. She smiled. "It is often so in the beginning. Do not dwell on anything. Let it go and you will recover."

"I worry that I may not make a good sister. Those...those people I traveled with...they were so coarse. I...I did not like them. Nor did they like me."

"Ai. Only let it go," Mother said with a smile. "Did you eat enough?"

"Thank you, yes." Deirdre watched her move slowly around the room, putting everything in order.

"When you are strong," Mother said when she reached the door, "spend a little time in the garden. Rest, then come to me for your duties." She was gone before Deirdre could respond.

That day, Deirdre walked a while inside the convent courtyard. The convent stood at the edge of the town. It consisted of a tiny chapel, a modest dining hall and kitchen, an office with an adjoining receiving room and visitors' dining room, and ten cells, only seven of which were at present occupied. All the rooms were arranged around the courtyard, which was filled with flowers and herbs of all kinds that the sisters cultivated. Beyond the building walls were the fields. The sisters had to grow and

297

preserve all their own food. Thus, they had several goats, a cow, some sheep, chickens, a large vegetable garden, and a small vineyard. In order to survive, they depended on these and on occasional gifts from a townsman or the local nobleman. The church was yet too small and poor to give them anything substantial.

The sister's duties consisted of gardening, cleaning, cooking, scrubbing, sewing, weaving, laundering, and caring for the animals in addition to the hours spent in prayer and chanting. And when a towns-person was ill or dying, it was one of the sisters who went. When that happened, the others had to perform any duties which that one had to neglect in order to perform an act of charity.

After a few more days of rest, Deirdre's strength returned and she went to the mother's office.

"It will be best for you to work in the air and sunshine," Mother said upon seeing her. "But beware you do not overwork at first. The bishop tells me in the letter you brought that you tend toward overzealousness." The old woman stood up and walked to the tiny window cut in the thick outside wall of her office.

"There is Sister Catherine. Work with her and let her not slack by letting you do more." She looked at Deirdre curiously. "Can you hoe?"

"Ai. It is a chore I most enjoy."

"Remember to be patient with yourself. You were not raised for this life. It is very difficult. When you have trouble, be not afraid to admit it, and come to me." She looked out the window again and shook her head. "Poor Sister Catherine. Be kind to her. Befriend her, and help her to make peace with this life, if you can. You both are of the same age and background." She looked at Deirdre. "Her father has informed me that his affairs have gone from bad to worse, and he has no hopes now of recovering Catherine's dowry. She will have to stay here with us. It is a burden for all of us, and most of all, for her. But don't speak of

298

this yet. I shall tell her when the time is right." She looked at Deirdre with concern. "Do you feel truly strong enough now?"

Deirdre nodded. "Yes, Mother. I am anxious to begin my work here."

"Good. Go then."

The old nun waited at the window until Deirdre appeared from around the outer wall. Sister Catherine stopped her hoeing and smiled happily to see Deirdre. Mother shook her head. She knew she would have to make exceptions for these two young noblewomen and give them certain privileges the other sisters could not have. It was the reason why she had given them both the gardening to do. That was as hard work as such women could be expected to perform. But it was hard for her and the others who saw the privilege and could not speak without breaking their vow of perfect obedience to the superior. Mother Corita hoped that by being lenient, she might win Catherine over to this life, since that was now the young woman's destiny. She also hoped to please the bishop so that word might get back to the king in Deirdre's case, to Catherine's family in the other; help from either quarter could mean the convent's survival. Mother turned away from the window. She wished she could concern herself merely with spiritual matters rather than these earthly ones that her duties as superior imposed on her. She returned to her desk, opening the large prayer book to mark the day's lesson.

CHAPTER 32

As the weeks passed, Deirdre grew accustomed to the daily routines. She rose with the others at four in the morning to the sound of a bell; dressed in silence, kissing each layer of her habit as she put it on; wrapped her head in the stiff cloth of the veil; then, making as little sound as possible, went to the chapel to chant matins with the other six women who shared this life with her. She had a difficult time staying awake in the hour that followed matins when they knelt in meditation without moving. Stiff, she would rise from the floor to chant the lauds at sunrise and was glad when, then, she could be involved with the physical labor that filled the rest of the morning.

Though she was the youngest in terms of her life in the convent, her noble birth, and former marriage to one so high as Clotaire, influenced the mother superior in subtle ways, so that Deirdre always found herself out in the gardens doing jobs she enjoyed working at. Before noon, the bell sounded again, and the sisters all hurried to the chapel to again chant prayers of prime. Prime was followed by another hour in which the nuns were to concern themselves with their faults and on ways to improve themselves. Each knelt, her veils drawn over her face, and whispered over and over the faults she was trying to improve, counting out each hour's infractions, conscious or not. The chapel echoed with the whispers that sounded like the rustling of leaves. Lunch followed, a meal most welcome, since it was the first of the day. Deirdre quickly understood Catherine's complaint about being starved. There was an abundance of good food at the lunch meal, and Deirdre always left the table feeling more than satisfied, but with the day's work as demanding as it was, she was hungry all the time except for those first two hours after lunch.

The chanting of terce followed lunch; then the afternoon hours alternated between laboring and two more shorter sessions of chanting -- sext and none. Dinner was a light meal and was followed by a half hour of free conversing, the only time of the day in which the rules allowed the sisters to talk simply for its own sake. Even meals were taken in silence while Mother Corita and Sister Briandor took turns reading from the one book the convent could boast of. The chanting of compline occurred at sunset, and, at that point, until matins the next morning, the sisters observed the Great Silence, which could not be broken for any reason whatsoever, even one of life and death.

The days flowed together one after another like the water in a stream. There was little to distinguish one from the next, except for the half hour free period in which Deirdre talked with the other sisters, and an hour's instruction with Mother Corita on Sundays, the one day of rest when no work of any sort, even cooking, occurred. The sisters prayed and fasted most of that day.

Mother Corita was a wise and gentle superior who initiated Deirdre into the rigors of convent life with patience and love. Each week Deirdre was taught another aspect of self-limitation and given specific instructions and exercises in its practice.

"Modesty of the eyes is most important," Mother said, as Deirdre knelt in front of her. "It is through the eyes, more than any other sense, that temptation comes." Deirdre watched the hem of Mother Corita's robes where it met the floor. By its movement, she could guess at Mother's gestures. It was worn and stained by many years of dragging around after the nun busy at her various chores.

"But temptation is not often the issue, because, gradually, the large temptations pass. They are the easy ones to conquer. It is distraction, the little things, which are hardest to dispense with. One wants to daydream or watch another in order to compare oneself, or judge. Or we want to engage ourselves within another's attention, and so we look at her. We cling for a long time to the things of this earth and to this earthly life."

Deirdre worked hard at keeping her eyes downward, of seeing little else than the row she hoed or the floor of the room, or the plate from which she ate. The deep silence into which she felt herself sinking was not half so difficult to practice as this narrowing down of her vision. She broke the rule many times in a day. With the call of a bird, her eyes flew up, seeking, flying off on their own wings, grateful for the space of the blue sky reaching for the horizon. In the hour of défi, in which she whispered her mistakes and faults, she spent most of her examining upon the breaking of this one rule. It was the one she was most frequently accused of, both by herself and the others, during the public acknowledgment of faults in the chapel on Sunday afternoons. Mother Corita was patient with her, admonished her gently, and rather than punish, Mother encouraged and gave advice on how to hold oneself in. Deirdre took it upon herself to punish, and took to wearing a hair shirt and other punishing devices in order to help herself remember.

"It is not wrong to punish oneself," Mother told her when Deirdre confessed one day that her own punishments had not worked, that she yearned for the freedom of her eyes, and had finally succumbed and looked up at sunset to see, for a moment, the day's flames dying on the distant hills. "But it is not my way, nor the way of our founder. If we are to love others, then we must love ourselves as well. Would you beat a child for a small infraction? Be the mother to your self, which is yet a child. Save punishment for real sins, not for the breaking of the rules. You will make greater progress if you forgive yourself, let go of the error and move on."

Another time, she told Deirdre, "Our Lord's words: 'Love thy neighbor as thyself,' could as well be said: 'Love thyself as thy neighbor.' In these two years you will be here as a novice, I would rather you discover your true heart to God than that you become rigid in the following of the rules."

Deirdre was learning how to keep herself still: her hands clasped together inside her sleeves when not productively occupied; her feet quiet on the floor; no part of her body moving. None of it was easy, but Mother guided her carefully, gently, making it a loving goal to be accomplished.

"Mother, may I have permission to speak with you?" Deirdre's knees ached with all the kneeling; she was discouraged and vaguely angry.

"Ai, what is it?" Mother Corita asked. Deirdre's eyes raised before she could stop them, and she stared a moment in shock at this woman whose face she had not looked at in the many weeks since she had arrived. Corita's face was absolutely white, and there were two bright red spots on either cheek, making her look like a court jester in his bright makeup.

"Mother!" Deirdre cried out. "You are ill."

"The eyes," Mother chided, and Deirdre dropped her gaze to the floor. Her irritation flared.

"You came for something else, not my health."

"I am troubled," Deirdre said. "I feel an anger growing inside me, and I don't know its cause. I long for friendship, for laughter. I long to study and read. I am no longer sure that I can be a nun."

"That is not unusual, particularly with someone like you." Deirdre waited. Mother Corita was slow with her words, as if they came from deep within her, traveling up from a great distance. "You are too harsh with yourself, thus you crush the tender feelings, crush even your own love for God and for man."

"But how can I improve? I must try." Deirdre felt close to tears, but the tears were of this unexpressed anger, not of self-pity.

"You are only a novice, barely three months in this life. You need some time to rest, to rethink your decision. I would release you to the bishop entirely, but we need you here to help with the work, especially now that harvest time is coming. Do your labor, pray the hours with us, but I release you temporarily from défi, from the daily silence, except, of course, the Great Silence. You and Catherine will be free to talk together while working, only you must not let the others hear you or know I have released you

303

in any way. Let your eyes roam, all of this for one week. Then I shall talk to you again. Now go."

Sister Catherine had grown quieter in the time Dierdre had been at Poitiers, and spoke less about the possibility of leaving and marrying. She was often criticized on Sundays, and her own confessions of her faults in front of the others had grown briefer and more abrupt. Now, meeting Deirdre out in the gardens, her spirits rose.

"So you are having trouble too," she said. They looked at one another with some difficulty, after these months of practicing modesty of the eyes. Deirdre was shocked to see how much less animated Catherine had become.

"It is indeed more difficult than I thought."

"Ai, you made it so for me," Catherine said with some bitterness.

"I? What do you mean?"

Catherine shrugged. "After meeting you that one day, and speaking with you in such a human way, I felt hope that I might be able to make a life of some sort here. Then you withdrew like the rest of them, as a turtle pulls back into its shell, and I was more alone than before. That was unkind."

Deirdre bit her tongue to hold back this unaccountable anger she felt. She answered evenly, "I did not know the rules. I am here by choice, not by the fate of my family's misfortunes. I have wanted to fulfill my duty, to grow in my spirit and love."

Sister Catherine made no attempt to disguise the sarcasm in her voice. "Ai, and you have come so far, have grown so in love that now you chide me for my reasons for being here."

"Chide you! I said not a word!" Deirdre had completely forgotten the rule of the eyes and looked at Catherine straight on, challenging her.

"Oh, not in words, indeed! Nay, such directness never suits. You have learned well how to avoid the words, yet your tone goes

304

straight to the spirit! 'I am here by my choice, not by the fate of my family's misfortunes,'" Catherine mocked. "Oh, you are so good!"

Deirdre felt as though her face had been slapped and she suddenly awakened from a long sleep.

"You are right," she admitted candidly. Catherine's face registered her surprise. "Sister Catherine, thank you. You have made me see the source of my trouble."

Catherine looked at Deirdre with suspicion. "Have I, indeed?"

Deirdre smiled. "Yes, truly. Forgive me. I have been trying so hard to *look* perfect, to prove to myself and the others that I *can* be perfect, in fact, already am!" She laughed with the relief her perception gave her. "Oh, I am not, and that is a great relief to know."

Catherine did not smile. "Not one of them is, except maybe Corita, yet that is their burden. I get most of it thrown at me, since I am the only one who admits to being a sinner."

"Oh, a sinner you are not. You are the most honest of all of us."

Catherine laughed. Her liveliness began to reassert itself. "No, oh dear no, don't do that to me! I am a great sinner and liar! Each Sunday, I pretend to these small infractions. In fact, each day during défi, I whisper out my wishes, not my faults!" Catherine pulled her veils forward over her face and whispered rapidly, "Oh dear father, hurry and release me from the horror of this life. Dear lover, dear husband, whoever you are, wherever you wait for me, dream of me, wait, as I dream of you and your kisses, come to me soon, take me with passion and deliver me from this dullness." Catherine threw back her veils and laughed. "You see how terrible I am? And it grows worse, I feel. It is almost harvest time, yet I have heard no word of our fortunes."

Deirdre dropped her eyes to hide her surprise that Mother Corita had not yet spoken to Catherine of the truth.

305

"For me, the difficulty lies in the bringing together of my own need for companionship, for study, and, of course, for fulfilling my old habits of being in this world. I want to *see*; I want to be alive in the old way. Yet I long for the growth of my spirit. All of me is in conflict; thus I grow angry. It is such a relief merely to speak of it to you now."

"Let us hurry and finish the weeding. I have sometimes slipped off...." Catherine giggled at Deirdre's look of amazement. "It is the one advantage of your hard practice because you never looked up and saw me." Deirdre had to laugh now with her. "I have found a wonderful place back there in the wood, where I sometimes pass an hour with a laughing brook. Do not look so horrified. Sometimes I feel as though I will die or go mad with longing. That place has given me a little peace. You will see. It's wonderful."

"But we do not have permission."

"Oh, then confess it, if you will, later. Mother said we had to do our work. If we hurry, why can't we have a free hour? It is no sin, no harm that we are doing."

Deirdre felt the desire for freedom so strongly that it was like an ache within her. She offered no further objection, and they both hurried with the weeding, working over the rim of the hill so that none could see them from the convent; then, dropping their hoes, they hiked up their robes and ran, giggling like girls, across the open field into the trees beyond. They stopped to catch their breath and laughter, then walked, winding their way through shrubs and trees to a small, open meadow cut through by a brook.

"The stream is like you are -- noisy," Deirdre said when they settled in their skirts beside it. She felt like a child again, when, so long ago, she and Lothar would sneak away from Nurse and hide. Deirdre giggled with the feeling of naughtiness; she was delighted with herself and this transgression; she knew it was small, not evil, and wondered at the spirit of denial, how there is nothing it asserts, and how that was the spirit that the convent at

Poitiers inspired, in spite of Mother Corita's attitude of compromise. She felt full of rebellion suddenly; it felt good to her to have her old self back, if only for this short time, which she would, no doubt, later regret.

"How is there love if no joy accompanies one?" Deirdre asked, feeling the question deep in her bones. She looked at the now-quiet Catherine who leaned back against a tree. Catherine only smiled vaguely, as though far away. Deirdre continued, "I feel we do not love there. We never laugh, seldom smile. If loving God is such a grim business, then I am not sure it is the right thing for me at all."

Catherine sat up, alert; her mouth became a thin, hard line.

"Ai, but even so, if it is not right, then what will you do? Have you somewhere to go?"

Deirdre was amazed. "I...I have only thought so far, no further."

Catherine looked off across the trees into the open space of the sky. "I have thought all the way, many times." She looked back at Deirdre. She suddenly had the face of a very old woman. The look was there for only an instant, then faded. "I do not love this life. If the other does not come to be" -- she shrugged -- "then I have no life at all."

Deirdre and Catherine slipped off every morning of that week. It was a delectable freedom, but Deirdre grieved each night, as she lay tucked into the complete silence of the convent, for what she felt was her betrayal of Mother Corita's confidence in her. Yet each day was now delicious again, and happy. She felt herself expanding.

Her grief exploded on the last morning of the week, when Sister Briandor announced that their Mother had slipped off beyond this life, and that she, Briandor, by order of the bishop, as the next oldest in the community, was now the convent's spiritual leader. That day passed like a Sunday, in prayer and fasting, and, at sunset, the six remaining sisters carried Mother Corita's body out into the courtyard to lower it into the deep grave which Sister Charitas had dug. They all helped to fill in the grave. The Great Silence was broken that night by the sound of earth hitting wood, then earth on earth. When it was a mound, the six women stood a moment in silence, heads bowed. Out of the silence came the sudden, soft call of an owl.

"Hoo, hoo," it called. Deirdre lifted her eyes. She was startled to see Sister Briandor, eyes also raised, looking directly at her.

CHAPTER 33

The change occurred so quickly and completely, none questioned it other than Deirdre and Catherine in the hour each day they continued to sneak off.

"I *hate* her," Catherine exclaimed. "She is evil."

"Nay," Deirdre said in Briandor's defense. "Methinks she pushes us for our own good."

"Good! Look at my hands! Three weeks of scouring, and my hands look exactly like Felicity's after five years. And now Felicity is near mad, always looking over her shoulder, terrified that a demon will take her."

Deirdre frowned. "She has an instinct for what it is that each of us can't stand. But still, I believe she means well. She wishes us to face what is most awful, to transcend simple likes and dislikes."

"Ah, Deirdre, you are too kind. You try too hard to find good where none is. Do you not see her?"

"Nay, I observe the rules except for this one hour with you."

"Well, I no longer do. She watches. Like a night bird, her eyes glittering like any falcon's does when it sees a prey. Corita was a saint, truly, now I see it. This one's a devil."

"Oh!" Do not say such words!" Deirdre was deeply distressed.

"Then, why so many changes? Five times in three weeks you have had public penance! And I! Oh, she wishes to drive me out. She wasted no time to tell me how she found my father's letter. Oh, how her face glowed as she told me. 'There'll be no marriage for you, my dear, except here with our Lord Jesus Christ.'" Catherine's bitterness was keen and deep.

Deirdre said no more, not wanting to continue what was a fruitless conversation.

"I could kill her, I could," Catherine muttered.

309

"That is a mortal sin," Deirdre whispered. "Blame her not for what is now your lot. You had best to look to your own soul.'

"Ai, and my body as well!" Catherine blushed with her own words. Deirdre looked away. Catherine's duties were lately poorly done, and Deirdre suspected that Catherine slipped away more often than this one hour. Deirdre did not want to know more. Mother Briandor had established public confession of one's faults on a daily basis, and one's duty consisted also in accusing another before her sisters. The sisters under Briandor's guidance were becoming sweetly vicious, or cringing.

Each sister was called once a week into the mother's office for an hour of daily instruction. Deirdre never looked up, but she heard sometimes the hardness in Briandor's tone.

"Here," she said, handing Deirdre a leather strap that separated into five strands, each with a knot that tied around a rose thorn. "This will be your friend. This will help you remember your eyes, never to look up. 'Tis your greatest weakness. Each strand is for one of Christ's wounds. Take your beating well, and hit hard on your legs and back. 'Twill save your soul."

Deirdre felt split. She obeyed the rules for all the hours of the day, except this one with Catherine. She could no more give up this hour than she could cease breathing, yet she dared confess nothing of it, even to herself, and justified it to herself as the single event of the day that gave her the emotional thrust of love and strength to complete the rest of her tasks. In short, she ignored it, somehow slipped through her own conscience the way a fish sometimes slips through a net. She thought often of Mother Corita and prayed for that kind of guidance, though it was so far from her now.

Catherine's words, *Have you somewhere to go?* echoed in her like the chants of the hours. *Have you somewhere to go?* The bells rang, and she heard the question in the overtones. She had nowhere to go. That was also the answer, contained in the question, which caused Catherine such bitterness. Deirdre was of one nature: she had decided to grow in this direction; she had a will of iron and would shape herself according to that will. Catherine was of another, and she slipped further and further into self-deceit, along with the deceit she consciously practiced in front of Briandor.

"I accuse Sister Catherine," Briandor said on Sunday in chapel.

Deirdre saw the floor sway under her gaze, felt her own heart stop. She glanced up; Catherine was hidden behind her veils.

"She has had desires of carnal knowledge. I heard her speak of them," Briandor continued.

The usual silence inside the chapel was shallow compared to this one now. Deirdre felt the others, like herself, shrink back into themselves. Who could not be accused of desires? Who had not known the torture of one's sexuality, the heat of the thighs, the meanderings of one's thoughts?

"*Domine, non sum dignus*," the sisters murmured. There was a flurry of robes. Catherine rose.

"Yes, and if I could have a man in place of my own hand, I would, as would you, dear Mother!"

The words fell like ice upon the stone floor. No one breathed. Deirdre heard the rustle of robes as Catherine strode toward the door. "You are a filthy hypocrite!"

Deirdre also gasped. To question the authority of the superior was forbidden. The mother was absolute -- given wisdom by the Holy Spirit through the authority of the bishop; none had the right to question her; all took the vow of total obedience.

"On your knees!" Briandor's voice was cold.

Deirdre heard the quick, soft steps of Catherine's slippers as they left the chapel. The door slammed.

Deirdre threw herself forward, veils pulled over, like the

311

others: Felicity, Charitas and Melinda. She heard Mother Briandor rise. The door closed quietly behind her.

That afternoon, Deirdre was called once again to administer to a village woman who was sick, so she missed her hour with Catherine. Deirdre worried as she walked the village road to her patient's house. Catherine had not been anywhere that Deirdre could see and she had not dared to ask of her. *Have you anywhere to go?* Deirdre knocked on the rough, wooden door.

"Ai. Enter." Deirdre pushed open the door and the odor hit her full on. She gasped.

"Oh, 'tis ye. Good. 'Tis bad." The woman had a large, festering wound on her leg and foot, and would only allow the wrapping to be changed on it when she was clear from drinking -- a brief moment that occurred about every two weeks when she then called one of the sisters to do it. Dierdre went to the basket of rags.

"In a minute," she said, taking a quick breath over the less foul-smelling rags.

"It hurts so much," the woman whined. "Methinks I'll never work for my master again."

"It would help if we could change the dressing at least once a day."

"Then why don't ye do that? Ye say that all the time."

"Well, you lock the door and curse at me each time I've come between."

"Oh, ye say such things. Here, hurry and change it. It hurts like the furies."

Deirdre took a deep breath and began unwrapping the wound. She had to stop midway and rush to the door to breathe.

"Ai," she said to the woman from the door. "How can you stand it? It smells so, I cannot breathe."

'Tis because ye are one of them highborns," she cackled. "None of mine complain."

312

Deirdre took a deep breath and hurried with the dressing. Finally it was off. She felt a deep anger at the woman's slovenly attitude.

"It's best to let it air awhile," Deirdre said. "I'll help you outside."

Indeed, if for only this, I deserve to go straight to Heaven, Deirdre thought as she supported the fat and smelly woman to a stump outside. The leg was a dark greyish green, the woman pale.

"Will ye clean up a bit?" the woman asked, as she always did when Deirdre came. It was the only time the small hut got cleaned. Deirdre smiled and suddenly recalled Catherine's words to Mother Briandor: *Filthy hypocrite!*

"Why can't you be clean?" Deirdre suddenly asked, surprising herself with her own candor. "Why must you drink so much?"

"Ye forget your manners, sister Deirdre," the woman said slowly, enjoying her power. "Now, do your Christian duty, as ye call it, and mind your tongue."

Deirdre wanted to walk away, to say what truly filled her mouth. *I despise you. I hate your filth.* She went back inside and opened the one window in the hope that air might begin to circulate. She moved quickly around the room picking up one thing after another, pushing the growing mound of dirt with her broom.

Suddenly, she was aware that she was humming. She stopped. The tune was familiar and she hummed it again, but could not place its sweetness. Then she seemed to be hearing it. Somewhere there was the soft, distant, playing of the tune on an instrument.

Deirdre dropped her broom with a bang and raced outside. She looked up and down the narrow path. On the horizon of the road that travelled toward Tours, a man in brown robes came walking. Deirdre felt the cry first in her heart, then it leapt out of her mouth.

313

"Fortunatus! My God! Fortunatus!"

She was running, her skirts hiked up, and she ran more than halfway before she was overcome with a shyness that slowed her. The man had stopped, his mouth open, as if he were viewing a mirage. Her shyness turned into self-consciousness: *I am a nun, a woman of the veil; I should not behave so*. She stopped. Then she saw his smile. He began to run, and she, too, forgot all. Arms outstretched, their throats open with laughter, Fortunatus and Deirdre ran to one another like two children.

"Fortunatus!"

"Deirdre! My God! And look at you! A nun!"

They embraced, broke, laughed, looked at one another up and down, blushed and laughed again.

"You were singing my song," Deirdre accused.

"Ai, I sing it often. 'Twas a sad day when I left Athies. I think of you often."

"Oh, I looked for you in Tours. I waited there about one year."

"Yes. I come from there now. I saw the bishop and he told me of your trouble. I came this way in the hope of finding you."

They laughed again, each feeling the awkwardness of being monk and nun, at the same time old friends who loved each other dearly.

"Then, you know of him?" Deirdre asked, falling into her former caution of not using his name.

"Ai, and I was deeply sorry to hear of it, and to think that I ever tried to convince you to make peace with the notion of marrying him. Forgive me that."

"Oh, 'tis over. I am happy now. I am free."

"Are you truly?"

They looked at each other for a long moment. Deirdre broke her gaze first with a smile.

314

"You are a monk, so can be housed at the convent. Oh, Fortunatus, how good it is to see you again! How I have longed for your friendship."

They walked back along the path, Deirdre's patient entirely forgotten by her. The woman had fallen into a doze under a tree, so was left there until evening, when neighbors returning from the fields, helped her back inside, and wrapped her wound.

To Deirdre's amazement, Mother Briandor graciously received Fortunatus and gave Deirdre permission to serve him supper in the guest refectory. Deirdre carefully explained who he was, but Briandor only waved her away.

"You have permission. He may stay three days. You may pass your free time with him after you have finished your chores."

Deirdre did not know that Fortunatus had already presented himself with a terse letter from the bishop himself, requesting the mother's hospitality to Fortunatus as well as Deirdre's temporary freedom.

Fortunatus joined the sisters for the afternoon chanting, though he had to do so from outside the convent walls. With a thrill, Deirdre heard his deep voice, along with hers and her sisters', praising the Lord. Catherine was present in the chapel and managed a look to Deirdre meaning she wished to speak with her. They slipped outside the walls just before dinner.

"Something has happened," Catherine whispered excitedly.

"What is it?"

"I know not, but when I returned this afternoon, Mother Briandor came to my cell." Catherine peeked around the wall to make sure no one approached. "She actually begged my forgiveness."

"You see?" Deirdre felt a sadness for Catherine. It came from some inexplicable source. "Oh, Sister," she whispered back, "believe me when I say I love you as one of my own, and thus do not take my words badly. I fear for you. I do not wish to know

315

where you go besides that hour with me, but take heed. Do nothing that jeopardizes your soul. It is enough to break the rules of the convent, something terrible to break the laws of God." Deirdre raised her gaze. Catherine looked away.

"I do no one harm." She tossed her head in a way that was characteristic. "You yourself wondered how there could be love if one felt no joy." She squeezed Deirdre's hand. "Don't worry about me. I am fine."

Deirdre told Catherine about Fortunatus' visit and suggested Catherine gain permission to join them for dinner. Catherine was about to run off, but stopped.

"I suspect my father has sent a message. That's what's different, I suspect," she whispered in Deirdre's ear. Then she was gone.

Sister Melinda gave Deirdre the simple fare that would be their dinner. Catherine and she carried the tray into the guest refectory. They beamed at Fortunatus.

"Sister Catherine, our brother Fortunatus, a poet and singer and scholar and monk," Deirdre announced.

Fortunatus bowed. Catherine was delighted.

"What a pleasure to have a man among us," Catherine said, and winked naughtily at Deirdre.

"Sister Catherine is a novice like myself. You must forgive her, dear brother. She is not exactly sure of her future here as a sister."

"And are you?" Fortunatus challenged.

Have you somewhere to go?

"It is difficult, to be sure," Deirdre said, "but I have progressed."

"It does you no harm, that I can see," he said. "You look very well."

After dinner, they walked in the courtyard, talking of Fortunatus' long travels and adventures. Deirdre felt the old,

316

familiar tug of her heart for new places. She sighed.

"I have four books with me, Lady Dier..., excuse me, *Sister Deirdre*...." He smiled. "Would you care to look at one?"

Deirdre felt as though the sun had burst through the clouds, which hung like a heavy curtain in the early evening sky.

"Oh," she exclaimed. "it is my deepest wish."

Fortunatus laughed. "It has been difficult indeed for you, dear sister. I shall see to it that that much gets lightened. You shall have all four before I leave."

"Oh, dear Fortunatus! Don't speak of leaving!" Deirdre blushed at Fortunatus' kind smile, and Catherine's significant rolling of her eyes. "I *said* it was difficult," Deirdre admitted to them. Catherine and Fortunatus looked at one another. Both burst out into laughter, which mixed at that moment with the evening bell that rang out over the courtyard announcing compline and the beginning of the night's Great Silence. Deirdre and Catherine pulled their veils over their faces. All three wordlessly bowed. Fortunatus watched them hurry across the stones into the hallway that led to the chapel. Catherine looked back once, and smiled. Fortunatus bowed his head for the evening prayer.

That night Deirdre broke the Great Silence with a scream. She had again had the dream of Clotaire, of her mother falling backward into the lake of her hair.

CHAPTER 34

Mother Briandor did not appear for matins the next morning, and when she did not appear for lauds, Sister Felicity went to her cell.

"Mother answers that she is unwell and would rest today," Felicity said when she returned.

Deirdre breathed a silent prayer of thanksgiving. She fully expected that she would receive punishment for breaking the Silence and, further, that the punishment would be severe. But that, in itself, did not concern her; what had kept her awake until dawn was the fear that her punishment might preclude her seeing Fortunatus for the rest of the time he visited. That so worried her, she was not much concerned even about the return of the dream. After lauds, she prayed for Mother Briandor's recovery, aware of the discrepancy between this prayer that wished Mother well, and her earlier one in which she thanked God for saving her via the identical illness.

She hurried through her morning chores, doubling up on them, so that her afternoon hours might be free.

"If you need, I can take your charities this afternoon," Catherine whispered as they passed one another crossing the courtyard.

"Ai, many thanks," Deirdre whispered back.

For once lunch seemed too long, and terce before it was endless. Finally, the bell rang, and Deirdre was free for nearly two hours. She met Fortunatus in the small receiving room.

"Shall we walk as we used to?" Deirdre suggested.

"Are you allowed such freedom?" Fortunatus asked with surprise.

"Not usually, but this is a very special occasion, and I have been given permission."

"How extraordinary."

"I think it is because Mother knows I have no other family, that you are the only person left to me, and since you are a monk...." She shrugged.

"It may also have to do with my carrying with me a fair-sized gift to the convent from an unknown donor."

Deirdre looked at him quizzically.

"I suspect it's he," Fortunatus said, "but I have no notion what might be his motives other than charity."

Deirdre also wondered, but said nothing. She understood that Clotaire was meant.

"So, let us walk. The land is beautiful now with the first traces of autumn in the leaves."

They tramped across the convent fields over the hill and down into the wood. Deirdre guiltily led Fortunatus in a direction away from the spot where she and Catherine went, but they came upon the brook further along.

"This is the brook that passes the convent walls," Deirdre said. "Out here in the woods, it is noisy. Where it flows by us, it is quite silent, as if out of respect for our ways." Deirdre laughed. Fortunatus sat on a rock. Deirdre watched him. He seemed lost in thought.

"How strange to be with you like this again," Deirdre said. "I feel almost like before, at Athies, almost as if I could be that young woman. She feels very long ago, very distant.

Fortunatus smiled. "She is not very distant; I can see her in your eyes still, and in your smile."

"Fortunatus," Deirdre said. She watched a yellow leaf break free where it had caught on a rock in the stream. It glided quickly downstream. "Was it difficult for you when first you studied to be a monk?"

"From the way you ask me, I see you make the mistake of believing it someday gets easy."

Deirdre's head snapped up. "You mean!...But!...."

Fortunatus also watched the stream. "It was not easy then. It is not easy now. My nature makes it doubly difficult because I am a lover of music, of poetry, of people. Some are, by nature, more reclusive. I know not if it's easier for them, but for me, for you...." He threw up his hands and laughed. "I was amazed when the bishop told me of your choice."

"You always seemed so easy with yours. Even now you seem comfortable and happy."

"I am, and am not. One does not cease being human when one puts on the robe."

Deirdre thought for a long time. "Mother Corita, methinks, was one for whom it was easy."

"Ai. She was a good woman, a great teacher. I met her here before, when I first left Athies. She helped me then at a time I felt most lost. But, Deirdre, do not mistake desire for ease. You strongly wish to be perfect in the eyes of God. Even the strongest wish does not make it easy. Mother Corita had many years of difficulty here at Poitiers-- with the villagers and with her own nuns. No doubt, she had trouble with her own spirit as well. She was too deep to have had it easy."

To Deirdre this came as a great revelation. "I thought...."

"I know. 'Tis what we all think. 'Tis difficult now because I am young. It will change. A little time more, and I will be perfect. No more desire, no more temptation, no more longing. It will be so easy. Nay?"

"Ai." Deirdre shook her head.

Fortunatus laughed. "Do not look so sad. No one's path in life is easy. You are not alone in that."

"Hallo! Hallo!" Fortunatus and Deirdre turned in surprise. Catherine came toward them through the trees. She was winded; her cheeks glowed with running. Fortunatus rose from his rock and bowed.

"Catherine!" Deirdre cried out.

320

"I am here by permission." She ginned at Fortunatus. "I sometimes sneak off. Good Sister Deirdre was concerned."

"Mother Briandor gave permission?"

"Ai. Oh, what a beautiful day! But let me only join you. I would not interrupt."

"Then, you are our chaperone, is that not so?" Fortunatus asked with a wry smile.

"Ah, methinks the man's privy to the thoughts of mothers superior."

"Chaperone!" Deirdre looked at Fortunatus and blushed slightly. "But how silly! All those years you and I tramped around, hours, at all times of day and night, and now, suddenly, we are not to be trusted alone."

Catherine pursed her lips. "One can never be sure." Fortunatus laughed. "But you could at least be grateful. I could have been Felicity, or Charitas, or, God forbid, Briandor herself!"

"Methinks the convent is not to your liking," Fortunatus said ironically.

"Indeed not. Has Deirdre not told you? I await deliverance in the form of a dowry."

"We were speaking of the difficulties of our paths."

"'Tis not so difficult if one knows how to manage."

"And you do, no doubt. I see that, " Fortunatus said with admiration.

"Oh, she's shameless!"

Catherine grew serious. "If the way is not chosen, then it is not the way. I harm no person but myself, if I do that at all. I must find a way to live without becoming bitter and dour. That, to me, is the most important thing. I am like a songbird caught by winter. I must find some way to sing, or I'll die."

Fortunatus looked at Deirdre. "You see? Catherine does as you do, what I do. In my travels, I have met many men and women. Some have committed the most terrible acts. Others are saints. I have learned one great lesson, and that is not to judge, even myself, particularly myself. I take each day as a gift. I then let it go, let everything pass as it needs will. But let us walk. Let us enjoy this day."

They walked and talked like three young people who had known one another since they were children. By the time it was the hour for sext, and they approached the convent, Deirdre felt again as she had before; she was alive with curiosity, alive without the guilt and constant worry that she might be neglecting her spiritual duties.

"Perhaps I shall not make a nun, after all," she announced when they reached the gate. "This somehow feels better."

The bell rang. "We shall see you at dinner," Deirdre whispered to Fortunatus, and, out of her old custom, affectionately squeezed his arm. He pulled back, and she looked at him questioningly.

"Forgive me, Sister," he whispered, dropping his eyes, "but it is as I told you: we do not cease to be human." Deirdre saw that he was quite serious. The chant had started. Deirdre had to run to the chapel, stifling the puzzlement his words aroused in her.

After sext, she had only an hour, and it was spent with Catherine in helping to prepare the evening meal and set up the guest refectory. Catherine had by now established herself as chaperone, so that she would also enjoy the hours of temporary freedom as well.

"I shall clean and set up the refectory. You help with the food," Catherine suggested.

When the last of the food was ready, the bell rang for none. At last, Deirdre found herself hurrying with the tray to the refectory where Catherine awaited her. The odor of roses filled the room and hit Deirdre full on when she opened the door. Deirdre gasped. Catherine clapped her hands and jumped up and down.

"Oh! Do you like it?" she asked with scarcely concealed delight.

The table was covered with a layer of pink and yellow rose petals arranged in patterns as if they were woven together as one cloth. A dish in the center held a small, beautifully arranged bouquet of deep red roses. On either side, Catherine had placed some white altar candles.

"But what is this?" Deirdre asked in amazement.

"'Tis that we have a guest, no more. Is it not mere courtesy to treat a guest finely?"

Deirdre laughed. "Methinks you have gone too far. No wonder you came late to none, but Catherine! Did you leave any of Mother's roses?"

Catherine tossed her head. "A few, I think. Enough for her to smell one now and again. She has nothing of which to complain."

There was a knock and Fortunatus entered. His mouth fell open and his eyes grew big. Seeing his utter amazement, Deirdre joined Catherine and together they laughed like two young girls.

"It smells as though a king has died," Fortunatus said. He looked quite overwhelmed. "I thought I was to dine with two serious young nuns." Each thing he said made them clasp each other and laugh even harder. "Instead, I see I am to dine with two young maids, like shepherd girls...."

Catherine bowed, holding in her smile behind one hand. "Kind sire, it was done but for your pleasure. Does it not please you?" She curtsied prettily once more.

Fortunatus smiled. "Your father had best find you a dowry, girl; I fear Mother Briandor will have much to rue otherwise."

Catherine giggled. "And look!" Dramatically, when she had both of their attentions, she pulled a large bottle of wine from beneath her robes. Deirdre gasped. Fortunatus shook his head.

323

Catherine's eyes danced.

"Nay, I did not steal it," she said with glee. "And nay, 'tis not the altar wine, and nay, I do not have permission, but it's allowed anyway, and ai, 'tis wonderful wine."

Deirdre sat down. Her stomach hurt with the laughing. She felt weak. "Where did you get it?"

"'Twas sent with me, with other things, when I came. I kept this fine bottle hidden in one of my blankets. I had saved it for the day I would get to leave. 'Twas my father's promise, really, but tonight's as good a celebration as any. Please sit down," Catherine said, indicating a chair to Fortunatus.

"Oh, dear brother, please forgive us if we shock you. Mother Corita gave both of us permission to take a small respite from our duties."

"But Corita is now dead," Fortunatus said.

Deirdre and Catherine exchanged a look.

"Ai...," Deirdre said.

Catherine interrupted her. "It is that Mother Briandor does not know of that permission, which Corita specified we should not divulge, so we are caught betwixt -- no matter what we do, we both obey and disobey."

Fortunatus could no longer take their madness. He leaned back in his chair letting his laughter out until the tears ran down his face. Deirdre watched him happily. At this moment, he was exactly the way he had been at Athies. Her only sadness was that he would leave her once again, and now she felt that leaving heavily.

"No wonder Eve's to blame," he said when he could finally speak. "Such double-talk I've never heard, miladies. What's best is that you both believe it!"

"Nay, Fortunatus, that's not fair. We know our duty. I feel somewhat what Catherine feels. I am not sure that this is my path. The bit of freedom -- and Fortunatus, 'tis only in the small rules,

324

not in anything serious -- lets me taste of what the path without that freedom might be. 'Tis necessary. Did you never cheat?"

Fortunatus smiled and looked down at the floor. "Ai, many times. All those years at Athies when I sneaked off to be with you, dear sister. I was in much trouble all the time, doing long penances. 'Twas the root of why I had to leave."

Catherine was serving. "Let us not dwell in the past, Brother Fortunatus. Let us first toast our futures, then eat."

"To each of us," Fortunatus said, raising his glass. "May you, lovely Sister Catherine, regain your dowry and find a lucky husband! And for Sister Deirdre, may you find the truth of your heart!"

"And for you, Fortunatus," Catherine broke in, "may you find the flower of your dreams; may your laughter always be as free as I heard it tonight; may you have great happiness and ease on your path!"

Fortunatus laughed and blushed. All three raised their glasses and drank.

"'Tis fine, nay?" Catherine asked. "My father once had the finest vineyards in all the land. We had great feasts and celebrations each year after the harvest." She turned to Deirdre. "That was how I first saw Clotaire. He came with his men. I was very young, but I remember him so well. 'Twas after he left, we became Christian. He left there with us a monk who instructed all the folk in the new religion." She made a face. "'Tis so hard to think he could kill any man for malice."

"That was what I meant earlier," Fortunatus broke in. He saw Deirdre's growing unease and wished to turn the conversation away from Clotaire. "When I spoke of judging," he said by way of explanation. "Each of us is mixed with good and bad. The greater the good a man is able to do, also the greater the bad, it seems. It is no simple thing. A man is not all one way or the other. Our old religions were perhaps more tolerant in that regard. Both good and bad were represented in the many gods."

325

"Ai, 'tis what I have noticed in our faith, what makes things so difficult for me sometimes. We lean much on only the good. It becomes confusing," Deirdre agreed. She was grateful to him for moving into more theoretical territory.

Fortunatus smiled at Catherine. "Look even at ourselves just now. We are here drinking wine, enjoying our company, while your sisters eat without laughter, no doubt listening to a reading; a small event, but some might think us wrong."

"Ai," Catherine laughed, clapping her hands. "I shall never miss such readings! If I do not escape here, I shall ask my father's influence to make me mother superior. Then we shall have some fun."

Fortunatus looked rueful. "In that case, you would convert every last pagan and rogue here to the new church!"

"So, what you say," Catherine said, serious again, "is that Deirdre should not have judged Clotaire." Deirdre reddened.

"We must be careful of our sister Deirdre's feelings," Fortunatus warned. "But, in answer, nay, I do not say that, or I would be guilty of the very offense I would accuse her of."

"But we must make some decisions," Deirdre said. "How can we?"

There was a knock on the door. Felicity stuck her head in. She whispered, not for a moment missing the flowers, the candles, the wine.

"Brother Fortunatus, forgive us. We have a call from the village. A stranger there lies dying they say. They heard you were a priest and she keeps calling for one. I tried to tell them you are a monk, but...." She shrugged helplessly.

A rough peasant pushed around her.

"She keeps a-crying. Been calling all this evening since we found her."

"He says she's been living way back in the woods like an animal," Felicity said, poking her head back in.

326

"'Felice will be a Christian. Get her a priest. Tollech's dead,' over and over like that she keeps a-calling near enough to drive a one crazy."

Fortunatus rose. "Forgive me, dear Sisters." Catherine and Deirdre followed him to the door.

"Who is she?" Deirdre asked. Some faint recollection made her ask almost against her will.

"Don't know, never seen her. Says she ain't but a whore, but has lain with a king. Names herself Felice, but I suspect she's crazy, no more. Living like that." He shook his head.

Fortunatus returned with a torch and a small book of prayers.

"She's in no more than rags," the man said, looking back over his shoulder. The two men went out the front gate. Catherine took hold of Deirdre's arm.

"What is it, Sister Deirdre?"

"I know not."

"Are you ill?" Felicity asked.

"Nay, I...I needs must pray." She walked slowly to the chapel where she knelt on the cool stones. She could not pray. Somewhere inside her breast, her heart was a small bird.

Felice. It was the name of the woman Lothar had spoken of. *Clotaire.* She closed her eyes, felt his hand on her neck, his lips on her own. She gasped and opened her eyes, remembering the dream. She covered her face with her hands. Indeed she wanted him. She felt the desire in her chest like a fist, in her belly like an emptiness, and suddenly in her thighs, like a fire.

"Lord, Lord, help me," she cried. "Lead me not into temptation." Somewhere in the falling dusk, a woman who had known him, lay dying. Her nearness brought Clotaire back to Deirdre with a force she had never experienced even in the worst times at Tours. She took a deep breath and began chanting with the other sisters, who had filed in now for compline, the last

327

prayer of the day.

We do not cease to be human when we put on the robe.

Her lips moved with the words of the prayer, but her heart sang with other words. Fortunatus' wisdom was the bridge between them.

CHAPTER 35

Fortunatus followed the man along a narrow path. It was that moment of evening when the trees were blackly silhouetted against the last light and filled with a thousand birds, which made the trees' foliage tremble as if it were the leaves that sang the day's final song. The moon hung low on the horizon, large and heavy and pale, reminding Fortunatus of the silver pendant Berthaire used to wear around his neck, thus keenly reviving memories of his days spent at Athies.

How strange to be with you like this again, Dierdre had said. Fortunatus shook his head. Strange indeed. That Deirdre should be here just beginning the life of a renunciant as he had been at the beginning of that choice in his life when they had first met so long ago at Athies -- that was the oddest thing for him. She did not fit, as Catherine did not fit, and for that matter, he thought with a brief laugh, as he himself did not fit.

"We are here, sire," the man said. "Beware your head."

He allowed Fortunatus to enter first through the low door. The hut consisted of one small room. A fire burned under the roof hole at the back, casting the only light. Fortunatus made out a woman seated near the fire. She watched him curiously, but when he took a stride toward her, she signaled him toward a mound lying near the wall. He saw then that the mound was a human heap of rags with two very bright eyes. He knelt beside her.

Are you a priest?" the woman asked. Her cheeks were flaming even against her dark, weathered skin. Her hair was wild and matted. In the dark, he could not tell if she was young or old.

Fortunatus hesitated. "I am priest enough," he finally said.

"Can you teach me to be a Christian?"

"Indeed, if you wish. But would you not rather have first a nurse?"

She shook her head.

329

"She won't let no one touch her," the peasant's wife said from her place by the fire. "Won't eat nor drink, either."

Felice smiled briefly, and Fortunatus saw in it how once she bad been pretty. He also smelled the illness on her breath, a heavy, sweetish odor.

She whispered hoarsely. "They are afraid I'll die here in their house, so they want to strengthen me to get me out. I will stay here. I want to die among people, not out there."

"Perhaps you need not die. You look young, strong."

Felice only watched him. "Teach me," she said.

Fortunatus closed his eyes. "It is different if you are dying than if you are...."

"I am dying. Can you not see? Only get on with what needs doing."

Fortunatus smiled. "So be it, sister. Tell me first why you wish to convert."

Felice looked off across the hut toward the fire. Her gaze was dreamy and sad. "'Tis a long story. Only that I wish to be Christian." She looked at Fortunatus. "And Tollech," she said. He saw she would have liked to spit, but could not. "Tollech is dead."

"Tollech was one of your gods?"

"Ai, and Criace, too. They were good to me for many years. Then...."

"They deserted you," he finished. "But how do you know?"

"I know," she said.

"I ask to be sure you are sincere."

"I am sincere."

"Then, you need only cleanse your heart of any ills you hold against another. 'Tis called confession. I am not priest enough to cleanse you, but, since I am the best there is, I am sure our Lord will come to us and forgive you. Do you wish to confess?"

330

"I am not to hate, is that what you are saying?"

"Ai."

"'Tis hard, that," she said slowly. "I have good reason to hold ill in my heart against some." She watched him. "I hate Tollech," she finally admitted. "He let me down. He was to help me always, and let me down."

"Anyone else?"

"A woman."

"You need not name her to me. Only cleanse yourself of that hate."

Felice's face showed a quick anger. "Why? 'Twas her and her brother who ruined me." Indeed she spat now, turning her head away from him, into the straw. "I had everything! Everything! Then she came and took it all away. How can I not hate her?"

"It is difficult sometimes," Fortunatus said vigorously. "But you have asked me to come and teach you. I am here, missing my dinner, and you are fighting my lesson. Do you want to be Christianized or not?"

Felice's anger faded visibly. "Ai," she said with a small voice. "'Tis for him."

Fortunatus understood that she meant Christ. "Then you love Him?"

"Ai," she said. "Indeed, I have always loved him."

"I thought Tollech was your god." Fortunatus frowned in puzzlement.

"Tollech was the god I could not see. My lord was the god I could see."

"You *saw* Him?"

It was Felice's turn to look puzzled. "And why not? He took care of me until...until I had to leave. Then he forgot me. Now he lives happily with her, never once thinking of me."

"I misunderstood you, methinks. Do you not speak of our Lord, Jesus Christ?"

"Nay. That is his god, he says. I speak of Clotaire, the king."

Fortunatus had travelled enough, and lived enough among all kinds of folk to recognize that Felice was of a peasant mentality. Thus he masked his amazement and curiosity, knowing that should she see his interest, she would say no more.

"Ah," he chuckled. "Only a mortal man you speak of."

Felice's cheeks reddened more deeply. "Mortal! He is the king!" She looked at him triumphantly. "And he loved me! Me! A whore! A common serf of the fields! Do you not believe it?"

"It does not matter what I believe, eh?"

She tried to sit up. He saw that the effort was too much.

"You should not talk. Only confess."

"Nay. I would but one person hear it before I die. And 'tis in that story anyway I have all to confess. 'Tis she, his queen, who I hate, who took him from me."

"Ah, sire," the old peasant broke in. He, too, wanted to hear the story, true or not. "She be mad. Only do what is necessary."

Fortunatus thought. "What is necessary is to listen. Believing is of no consequence."

"You will believe when you hear."

"If what ye be saying were true, then why be ye here now?" the old wife asked sarcastically. She had moved closer.

Felice looked at each of them to be sure she had their complete attention.

"I be here now," she said with emphasis, "because 'twas I who killed the queen's brother."

The peasant guffawed. "Aw, now I be hearing it all," he said, laughing.

"Wait," Fortunatus said. His heart was in his throat. "I had heard the story that the king himself killed his queen's brother. 'Twas told me in Tours by the bishop who heard it from the king himself."

"There, ye see?" the wife put in.

"Clotaire? The bishop saw him then?" Felice asked excitedly.

"I know only that he saw the bishop some months ago."

Felice's eyes were big. "And he said he himself had killed Lord Lothar?"

Fortunatus turned to the peasant couple. "That was the brother's name. She speaks some truth."

"A woman kill a man?" The peasant made a face.

"I have heard of it happening," his wife said.

"Then he yet loves me," Felice said softly. "And I...I need not have...." She bit her lip, closed her eyes tight.

"How could you kill him, you, a woman?" the peasant insisted.

She lay very still, eyes tightly closed, lips compressed in an effort not to cry. Finally, her features relaxed and she looked at them.

""'Twas a plot. He knew of it and was ready all the night. I know, because I was with him in his rooms. He asked me to stay to help him keep awake. He was such a man he would not warn his guards. He alone would defend himself." She spat again. "The cowards! They waited 'til dawn, and when he, thinking he'd been mistaken about them, went to his chapel to thank his God, they attacked him -- the two -- my own Villem and her brother, the coward Lothar." The fire crackled. Fortunatus and the peasant couple listened intently. "Clotaire was wounded. 'Twas my Villem did it. The coward Lothar never raised a hand. He ran, I know not why, but I saw him as I came out the room bringing Clotaire his weapons." She was quiet awhile, living the moment over again, lost in the shadows of that event.

333

"There they were, both of them, my Villem and the king. I got Clotaire his weapon and he fought bravely." She bit her lip again. "When I saw my Villem fall, I could not stand it. He -- the king had no choice. Villem would have gladly killed him, and that was my fault. But 'twas the coward Lothar's doing, all of it. He set him on, then ran away himself. I tell you I could not stand it. I took the mace and ran after him. Ah, so many times have I killed that man." She looked at them, coming out of her reverie. "And I would do it again. And again. Still I hate him, though he lives not."

Fortunatus bowed his head. "Hate lives on forever. It never stops."

There was a long silence. Finally, the old peasant, wanting to keep on with the tale or hear it repeated, asked in a skeptical tone, "Then tell me, woman, how it is that he here with us now tells another tale?"

"You mean that Clotaire said he did the killing?" she asked.

"Ai. That exactly."

Felice smiled and closed her eyes. She was perspiring. "That I cannot explain to you," she said. "'Twas just his kindness. That is the sort of man he is."

"Ai, kind, I have also heard; and cruel as kind," Fortunatus said.

Her eyes opened. She glared at him.

"Lies! I have never seen him raise his hand except as fair."

"Nay. He killed Gunther, who never raised his hand. And Gunther was his lady's own uncle. Then he took the girl and her brother with him by force, later married the lady Deirdre against her will."

Felice's face went white. "Oh, do not say her name in my hearing! She is loathsome, a toad. I wish my spells had worked on her!"

"You worked spells on her?" Fortunatus was suddenly

angry. Felice looked at him curiously.

"Is that a terrible thing to do in your religion?"

Fortunatus caught himself.

"Nay, just that I have heard of the poor queen. She has lived a life as if indeed a witch had cast a terrible spell."

"She? She was never less than spoiled! Had everything and always did! What spells indeed!"

Fortunatus' anger was barely under his control. He had no grudge against this Felice, but when she attacked Deirdre, he lost his temper.

"What do you know of her out of your hating that blinds you! Ye gods! She was forced to marry him, her own uncle's murderer.!"

"Ai. Indeed, and *he* being her own father's murderer! Do you not speak of that?"

Fortunatus turned white. He recalled Deirdre's dream told to him the day they parted at Athies.

"I don't understand. You speak of a tale I do not know."

"Indeed. That Gunther, her dear and only uncle, was a madman, a whoremonger, a pig -- I knew him well! He killed that girl's own father and mother and took the girl and boy as his own. Clotaire avenged that the day he struck Gunther down. That he did as his duty, the lady's father being kin to Clotaire's own father. We, all of us at Gunther's, knew the whole terrible story. Only those two children did not know. It was spoken of secretly though I only half believed it until the king told me so himself. That he took the girl and married her was an act of charity. She, the prig, gave him nothing but meanness and ugly words. How can I not hate her? She haunts my every moment!"

Fortunatus' head reeled. "How do you know all this?"

Felice looked at him triumphantly. Her cheeks were brighter. "The king himself told me. And Villem too. 'Twas Lothar told him! The filthy coward. Clotaire told the boy the truth early on. Even then, the coward turned against him."

Fortunatus noticed that Felice was perspiring profusely now; her eyes kept closing, and except for the two bright spots on her cheeks, she had lost all color.

"One last question," Fortunatus said quietly. "Do you say the brother Lothar also knew the truth of his uncle's death?"

"Ai," said Felice.

"Sire," the woman pulled at Fortunatus' arm and nodded at Felice, "get on with what you needs must do."

Fortunatus took Felice's hand in his. He squeezed it gently.

"Are you holding my hand?" she asked.

"I am," he answered.

"It feels so far away," Felice said. "'Tis how it happens. 'Tis not bad, methinks."

"Can you let your hate leave, also?" he asked.

She was silent for a few minutes. "To know now that he does still love me...." She turned her head toward Fortunatus, but did not open her eyes. "You swear he said so? That he killed the boy?"

"'Tis what the bishop told me."

Felice sighed. "Then, ai, I can let all my hating go."

"Bring me some water," Fortunatus instructed the peasant wife. To Felice, he said, "I shall make you Christian now. I cannot absolve your sins because I am only a brother, not a priest. But I can baptize you now that you make yourself clean."

The woman put down a shallow pan. Fortunatus blessed the water, then lifted Felice's head slightly with one hand, indicating that the wife should hold it so. He dipped his right hand into the water and gently sprinkled it over Felice's forehead as he made the sign of the cross over her and spoke the words of baptism in Latin.

"I baptize thee, Felice, in the name of the Father, of the Son, and of the Holy Spirit, Amen."

The wife gently lowered Felice's head. Fortunatus knelt at her side and prayed.

Felice said weakly, "Is that all there is to it?"

"Ye be clean as a newborn babe," Fortunatus said, falling into the peasant dialect. "And ai, ye be Christian now."

"If e'er you see the king, will you tell him I was Christian when I died. Methinks it will make him glad. Will you do that for me?"

She asked so shyly, Fortunatus was sure she had never asked a favor of anyone before in her life.

"I shall do it gladly," he said. Felice was quiet then, her breathing soft. Her paleness seemed almost like a light that emanated from her. Fortunatus rose.

"Will you see she is buried proper?" he asked the peasant.

"Will she die here, then?" the woman asked. She looked worried.

"Ai, but you need not worry that the death will harm you. Look at her. She is in peace." He tried to assure the woman with his eyes. "Such spirits never come back to harm."

"He be right," the man said. "We will not be moving her. And ai, sire, I will dig the grave myself. But will ye not stay?"

Fortunatus looked at Felice. "It could be yet many hours more. She needs me no longer."

Fortunatus walked outside and took a deep breath. The moon had climbed higher and cast a glow over all the land. He looked up at the stars that seemed so distant tonight. He started walking toward the convent on the other side of the village, but when he got halfway, he stopped and looked back. He could just see the hut where he had been. It was the only one left in the village with smoke yet coming from its chimney. A dog barked; another came up to him, sniffed the hem of his robe, then trotted off, satisfied that he was not unwelcome. Fortunatus started walking then, faster, and passed the silent convent walls. The moon seemed to follow him as he crossed the fields and entered the deep shadows of the wood. There he stopped to wipe the tears from his face. He leaned against a tree, felt its energy the length of his back.

"Lord," he prayed out loud. "Let me have the silent strength of this tree." At that moment, he longed only to have another touch him. He turned, embraced the tree, let himself cry like a child. The moon, like a stranger, watched coolly from above.

CHAPTER 36

"Sister Catherine."

Catherine looked up from her scrubbing. Sister Charitas was peeking around the door to the refectory.

"Mother would see you in her office," Charitas said and disappeared.

Catherine straightened. "Ai. The roses," she muttered to herself. She dried her hands on her apron and slipped it off. The yard did look bare this morning, with most of the roses gone. The early morning sun just lit the dew on their leaves -- tiny candles that flickered on and off as she passed.

She entered Mother Briandor's office on her knees as was the custom. When she could see the legs of the table, she prostrated herself, her forehead on the cool floor. Already she felt her body bristling with what she sensed was coming.

"Go to the receiving room," Mother said curtly, to Catherine's surprise. "You are wanted there." There was a pause. "We shall deal with the question of the roses after you have swept and scoured the guest refectory from top to bottom, and that, after all your other duties are done. You are dismissed."

Catherine backed out on her knees, bowing again at the door. She shook out her robes and straightened her veil, crossed the small hall to the receiving room. Fortunatus waited for her there.

"Dear sister," he said, "I must speak with you. Do I interrupt too much?"

Catherine smiled happily. "Nay, from scrubbing I am interrupted with pleasure. But you look unwell. Is something wrong, Fortunatus?" Catherine blushed at her omission of his title.

Fortunatus did not seem to notice it. He sighed and paced the small room. Catherine watched his agitation.

Finally, he stopped pacing and threw up his hands. "It's that I know not how to begin."

"Sit down. If you but give me some hint wherein your trouble lies," she suggested helpfully.

"That is my greatest trouble. As a brother all these years, it has been I who listened, comforted, advised. I know not how to do the other."

"Are you truly a monk?" Catherine asked.

Fortunatus looked at her blankly.

"Have you taken your final vows is what I mean."

"Ai." He thought. "That's as good a beginning as another," he said. "I took them when I left Athies some time ago. I thought I'd made my decision then." He shook his head.

Catherine rose and walked to the window. "Now something has changed that decision?" she asked, her back to him.

Fortunatus was silent.

"Has it to do with the heart?" Catherine finally asked, remaining at the window.

"How quick you are," he said, sounding miserable.

Catherine turned. Her cheeks were flushed, her eyes bright. "'Tis not such a terrible thing, dear sire."

"'Tis terrible!" Fortunatus cried out. "Indeed, I risk my soul, my eternal life, perhaps hers as well!"

Catherine turned pale suddenly. Fortunatus was too agitated to notice the change. She turned to look out upon the garden again. "Perhaps you had better tell me right out," she said. "I would not misunderstand you."

"Sister Catherine, forgive me. I am like a boy again. It comes from what happened last night."

"Our dinner?" She turned and faced him.

"Nay, the woman Felice," he explained. "When Deirdre came to Athies, I was very young. I had determined to be a monk

340

early on, had already studied two years. The next six I was torn between that original desire and a...a love for her. But, truly, I did not recognize my lust, nor my love. She was so young, so happy, so sweet, so much a mere girl. And so I left Athies, feeling the pressure of it too much, both for myself and her. I have travelled since then, grown, and I thought before I came here, even unto last night, that I...." He stopped.

"What? What is it?" Catherine asked.

"What I say to you, dear sister, must be considered a confession, for no one else's ears but yours."

"Of course, dear brother. I would only that...that you trust me."

He laughed. "It's so strange. Only yesterday she was asking me about how hard it was for me. She assumed it was easy. Can you imagine?"

Catherine only nodded.

"And I -- this is what is truly ironic -- I lectured her." His laugh was halfway between that and a cry of anguish. "I came here, Sister, thinking only to comfort her on the circumstances of her life, to aid her, support her in this new choice." He reflected. "Or so I thought." He shook his head in wonderment. "When I saw her, even then I did not know, even then I thought 'twas truly but a brotherly interest. Oh, how wrong I was!"

Catherine was watching him intently..

Fortunatus cleared his throat. "Forgive me. I wax too eloquent."

"Dear brother," Catherine said coolly, "believe me when I say I but wish I were the subject of your confession."

"Then you understand! Oh, Sister Catherine, I knew a large heart when I saw you. But I am foolish."

"Ai. And so? Lovers are few, and they are all fools. I, too, was one."

"You? Tell me."

341

"Nay. 'tis but a sad tale. It ended with a lost dowry and now, who knows?"

She shrugged. "I know only that he awaits me not, so it makes no good tale."

"Ah, Sister, I am sorry. But my tale is more foolish than any I have heard. I, a monk, with final vows, what can I do?"

"It makes no difference to me, vows or no. I follow only my own heart, be it right or wrong."

"The heart is complex. It wants both this and that, and often both at once, though they can be against one another."

"What happened last night?"

"It was most strange. I saw myself as a result of this woman and her tale. That's what awakened me to both my hope and my anguish." He stood and paced again. "She confessed that she had been Clotaire's mistress. She loved him and blamed Deirdre for taking him away from her."

"Go slowly, if you please."

"Ai. If what she says is so, then I must confess it all to Deirdre. It...it could change her heart, yet...."

"Oh, Brother, please, I cannot follow all your meanderings."

"Ai." He sat down. "So. Clotaire told her, and Deirdre's brother, Lothar, told a man named Villem, who also told Felice...."

"Felice is this woman?"

"Ai."

"I am working very hard, dear sire, I hope you see that." Catherine laughed. Her good spirits had returned with the complexity of the situation, particularly of Fortunatus' feelings.

He smiled. "Indeed, you are. I shall try to be more clear. This woman, Felice, was told that Clotaire originally killed milady Deirdre's uncle, named Gunther, as an act of vengeance. Unbeknownst to Deirdre, Gunther had killed her own mother and father in order to claim not only their estates and land, but also Deirdre and her brother as his own. 'Twas for that Clotaire killed her uncle, not out of cold murder."

"She has said she mostly forgave him that, that she could have lived with it," Catherine said. "She had begun to love him."

Fortunatus turned quite pale. "Oh," he said quietly. "She had begun to love him?"

Catherine looked away. "'Twas what she told me. But never mind, that doesn't change what makes her hate him now."

"Ah, but it does." He looked at Catherine. His eyes showed pain. "This woman also confessed to killing Deirdre's brother herself. And 'tis plausible. She tells a tale of murder and cowardice; she defends the king."

"Forgive me, but it's easy to claim things on one's deathbed."

"But she hates Deirdre. She had no need to confess such things if they were lies, nor did she know the lady Deirdre is Sister Deirdre here at Poitiers, and my old and dear friend."

Catherine nodded slowly. "Perhaps it could make a difference."

Fortunatus got up and paced again. "The final thing I must confess is how, there at the side of this woman, I suddenly realized what I had all these years evaded." He turned and faced Catherine. "I love her," he said quietly, jubilantly. "I quite simply love her and would that she be my wife."

"Ai, Fortunatus!" Catherine turned away.

Fortunatus sat and looked at his hands. "Dare I tell her?" he asked.

Catherine looked out at the garden, at the many empty rose bushes. "That you love her? Nay. That would give her pain." Catherine turned. "You are a monk. Even if she loved you -- as a man, I mean, for surely she loves you dearly as her friend -- Deirdre is sincere in her religious quest. Like me, she is not truly meant for it, thus it is hard. But, unlike me, 'tis something she wants and works toward. To know she was the source of what would be for you a mortal sin -- in thought only, dear brother, let alone in deed! -- that would hurt her heart deeply. She would feel she had betrayed both you and God. Do you not see that?"

Fortunatus turned his hands from palm to back, over and over, looking intently at them, as if an answer might lie therein.

"But to tell her of this woman's confession, ai. That you are bound to do. It could make a difference." Catherine sighed. "I never understood that she did not love him. My memories of him were so clear, though they were those of a child. I could not imagine that he was so cold in his heart."

"But 'tis a wonder he never told her himself."

"'Tis indeed that."

Fortunatus held Sister Catherine's hand a moment, smiled wanly. "I asked to speak with you, because I'd hoped you would encourage me to confess my love. You surprise me, Catherine. You are more than meets the eye. Mother Corita herself could not have spoken more wisely than you just now."

"Oh, dear brother, do not make me better than I am. My only thought is to escape from here!" She laughed. "I, too, have a confession. It will embarrass you, methinks, but I shall say it anyhow. When first you spoke of your trouble, I had hoped 'twas I you meant."

Fortunatus was stunned. Catherine laughed at his astonishment.

"Be not afraid. But you see how then I would not have advised you so. For me, your soul and mine might burn in Hell, so long as I got out of here."

"Sister!"

"Sister indeed. Do not make me into something else."

"Nay. You are again right. I wish my heart had been as you would have liked. But Catherine, methinks now something that

344

was not there before."

"What is that?"

"I always believed one was 'chosen' to be monk or nun, that, in being so, one had to fit." He laughed. "I do not fit, yet will be a monk, thanks to your wise words just now. But if I do not fit, nor you, nor Deirdre, then perhaps such fitting is but a dream."

"I do not know," Catherine said with a sigh.

"I will not endanger Deirdre, nor give her pain because of me. I shall only tell her this woman's words. If she be glad, then I have done right, and she may return to Clotaire. If she be not glad, then...." He hesitated to say what was in his mind.

"Then you can tell her your heart, if you wish, but methinks it is a mistake. She would not leave for you, even if she loved you in that way, because that would bring you harm. I am sorry to speak so plain."

"I sense, dear Catherine, that you might yet make as fine a nun as Corita."

"You will make me angry," Catherine said. "You would not wish to do that, sire. My temper, when aroused, is keen."

Fortunatus laughed. "I feel a weight is gone."

"Methinks you have only now just picked it up."

"But, knowing that, I can perhaps begin to put it down." He paused. "Catherine, when I leave here, I could visit your home, if you wish. I could discover what hope there is and return to tell you. What is it?"

Catherine was looking down at the toe of her foot, which she tapped absently. "Nay," she said. "Please do not go. I would rather always hang on the thread of hope that I invent, than to know surely that I can never leave." She tossed her head. "'Tis stupid, of course, but that is the way I am."

She turned on her heel then and dashed out. Fortunatus watched her in the moment it took for her to cross the yard.

345

The afternoon turned warm. Two nights of chilly weather had started the trees to giving up their green. Deirdre felt particularly gay as she and Fortunatus walked side by side.

"Oh, 'tis a beautiful day!" she exclaimed. "How I love the autumn."

Fortunatus smiled.

She scrutinized him. "But you seem distracted," she said.

"Nay," he answered. In fact, he was still trying to make his own decision. He had walked for hours alone again in the wood feeling the desire for both worlds. Even now, his heart was torn.

"I have peculiar feelings on days like this when I feel quite content again," she said.

"Why?" he asked. He enjoyed watching her face. It was beautiful, softened by the many tragedies of her life, which had, fortunately, not hardened her heart, but expanded it.

"It has always been on such a day that something terrible has happened. Always, too, I have rejoiced in the day, have felt as though something wonderful and new were about to happen. Then -- but I should not dwell on the past. I have left all behind. You, my dearest brother, are the only person left alive about whom I care, from whom another crisis could arise." She stopped and looked at him. "You have no awful news for me, do you?"

Fortunatus was amazed at her quick perception. He avoided her glance, evaded her question. "There must have been many such days as this when nothing happened."

"Never the combination -- the feeling inside, the weather that" -- she frowned -- "directly contradicted the reality around me."

"Perhaps the day did not lie."

"I do not understand," she said.

"Sometimes we think an event is one way," he said, shrugging, "when, in fact, it is otherwise."

"That is surely true in many instances, but not of what I speak." She stopped and faced Fortunatus. "You know that."

"Do you remember the dream you told me the day I was leaving Athies?"

Deirdre frowned. "I could not well forget it. It returns sometimes, but I don't wish to speak of it. Look, over there. Is that not a doe?"

There was a flash of brown, the white flick of a tail. Deirdre laughed. They began walking again. "Oh, I wish I felt very, very sure of myself. Did you see how she ran, knew exactly what to do? For me, it is never so easy."

Fortunatus said nothing, and Deirdre looked at him suspiciously. "Are you well, Fortunatus?" she asked.

He did not seem to hear her. She pulled at his sleeve. "Are you well, Fortunatus?" she repeated.

"Forgive me," he said. "I did not sleep well last night, and my mind wanders."

"Nay. Let us no longer pretend. Indeed you have put me off already several times. I have allowed you to do so, out of my own putting off the bad news I sense is coming. Let us sit here." She sat on a fallen log. "Now, do tell me, Fortunatus. It's ruining our time together anyway."

"All right. But tell me something first." he settled on a stone across from her. "And do not be angry with me. You say I am the only one alive who could, once again, bring you pain. Is that true?"

Deirdre thought. "Perhaps Catherine now...."

"Do you never think of Clotaire?" He scanned her face and said quietly. "Please do not be angry."

The color rose in Deirdre's face. "What reason do you have in asking me?"

Fortunatus frowned. "My own reason. Trust me, Deirdre. Only answer."

"I never think of him, but with pain." She looked down the slope to where the doe had disappeared. It was that kind of day, so still, that when a leaf broke free from a tree, it fell to the ground, fluttering as if through layers of air.

"But don't you sometimes wish...?"

She looked hard at him. "What? That he were not so? Nay. He is so, and though that be difficult, now, for me, the most difficult is in the hating. I would that would go away."

He watched her face. "But, if it were reversed, if you suddenly discovered that he was not as you thought him...."

Deirdre rose abruptly. "I grow impatient, Fortunatus! What is this nonsense you speak? If! If! There is no if. I see no point in our continuing. If you have something to say, then say it. Is he dead? Good! Perhaps my hate will die with him." She had walked some yards away in her agitation. Fortunatus watched her until she came back to stand in front of him. "Tell me!" she cried, stamping her foot.

"Methinks we hate only whom we love, nay?"

"I know not. But if it be true, then indeed I love him dearly. Why do you look so strange?"

"How do I look, dear sister?"

"So sad you make me want to weep. What is the source of such a look?"

Fortunatus sat, looking at his hands, trying to find what it was he truly wanted to say.

"It was the woman," Deirdre said so quietly he almost did not hear her. He saw the pain in her eyes. "The woman last night."

"Ai. She knew the king."

"I remembered her. Is he dead then?" Fortunatus could not read her face, though any other would have seen her fear.

348

"No, he is not dead." He had decided. Catherine was right, and he would spare Deirdre the complication of his own love. He told her what Felice had said almost as if the words were indelibly imprinted in his mind. She asked no questions, only sat and listened. When he finished she remained as still as the weather.

The smoke in the hall twists silently like a caterpillar attempting to become a butterfly before its time.... Later, she looks back from atop the hill, leans around her uncle's broad chest, peeking under his arm, and understands what the one seashell she has seen means. The gutted building behind her cannot be her home -- it is a seashell whose inhabitants have deserted.... There were three of them: one, tall and broad, is flowing with blood. This is her father. *The other the woman who raises one thin arm to ward off the blow of the other.* And this is her mother. *It is then. That sound as the third lets fall his axe. Bone. A deep echo that will resound forever within the shadows and caves of her flesh. This is Gunther. She feels herself picked up, feels her whole body bouncing against a man's bony chest as he races with her down the stairs.* This is the same chest she later peeks around, her own uncle's.

Deirdre's head whirled. Dimly she was aware that Fortunatus watched her, that something was expected of her. She sank again into her own past.

In the turmoil, no one had heard the king approach on Deirdre's horse.... "Why have you killed the good nurse?" The good nurse, he had said. This was Clotaire. *"Dear girl, I will not harm you. I am here to help you!....Your uncle was a cruel man, milady....Therefore I killed him...."* She noticed a figure beyond the curtains standing on the balcony beyond the windows. Trancelike, a great anticipation filling her, she walked toward one of the windows. A curtain wrapped itself around her, its touch arousing a sensual response. She closed her eyes to better experience the sensations on her skin. When she opened them again, she was looking into the eyes of another....They were the strangest and most beautiful she had ever seen.... All of her being* *was aglow in a kind of ecstasy.* And yes, this too, was Clotaire.

She covered her face with her hands. The cry that came from her throat resembled a crow's, or something wild and lost, or in pain. Back in the village, the dim howl of a dog echoed hers, then was carried off on a sudden breeze.

"Dear God!" she cried. "Dear God, am I never done?" But she could not speak. The past filled her whole being. Snatches of conversations, hints at other meanings, all tumbled with images of Clotaire.

"I cannot take it," she said. "God has tested me much, has taken all away, all! It's all turned around! Lothar who knew and never once spoke a word. Gunther, Lady Sigrid, with their false smiles, a pair I loved as my own parents! Oh! Cold-blooded and cruel!"

"Deirdre, wait! How is it different except you know it now?"

"Fortunatus, all this time I have loved those who were most cruel, hated him who was most kind. How can that have been? How could all my life be so? All the gods -- pagan and Christian -- have made a toy of me!"

"But you are fortunate in one way, if you but think!"

"How?"

"Now you know the truth, however hard it is."

"Of what use be it to me?"

"In order not to hate."

"Ai!" She threw up her hands. "I learn to hate anew! I learn to lose all hope! What do I trust, dear brother, if I cannot trust those so close, not one of them!

"It takes time, dear girl. Be patient. Time will make it all right."

"Time!" She could not stay still, but paced up and down. "Time does nothing."

350

"Ah, Dierdre. Think on it, truly. You can return to Soissons. You can have back what was. You have not lost all. In truth, you have gained one. All the others are gone; they need no longer either your love or your hate."

She stood still. "Return to Soissons?"

"Would that be impossible?"

She watched a bee, late for the season, buzz aimlessly among the branches of a yellowing tree. Its drone bespoke the afternoon, which had become quite still again.

"Would it?" Fortunatus insisted.

"I...I don't know. Perhaps...." Again, she got caught up in the bee's insistent drone as if her consciousness needed something as simple and straightforward as its sound.

"I am sorry to put you in such a state. I fear you cannot think now and should rest on it until something comes clear."

Deirdre's face was tight.

"Do you think he would want me?" she asked in a small voice.

Fortunatus saw in that moment all of her fear and her hope. He bowed his head. "I had not thought so far."

"Surely it's not your concern. Ai, I would return now. I had begun -- in spite of all that I supposed he had done -- to...to care for him. But I fear he has made another life quite without me. And when last I saw him, he was most angry." She was lost a moment in the return of that last interview in the bishop's study. "But why did he never tell me himself?"

Fortunatus shrugged listlessly. "I know not. Pride perhaps."

"Ai, that he has a serving of!" She laughed briefly. "You are right. I must think on it and pray."

As she spoke, her hope overcame her fear. Fortunatus watched her whole body lighten with it, shedding the earlier weight of his news. He smiled forlornly. Catherine was right again. He felt descend upon him the weight he had borne all the

351

night and day before. *Methinks you have only picked it up*, she had said.

"Oh, dear brother!"Deirdre cried suddenly and embraced him affectionately as of old. "Your bad news was bad and good both. Be not distraught. I love you so." Like the girl he had known at Athies, she turned and fled, her robes and veil flapping around her like large wings as she ran.

CHAPTER 38

After spending the remainder of the afternoon in prayer, and in a conference of some length with Mother Briandor, Deirdre's decision was made. Now she could scarcely keep from smiling as she went about assisting Sister Melinda in preparing dinner.

Catherine had cleaned the refectory as Mother had ordered, so this evening's meal was stark in comparison to the one preceding. Deirdre placed the heavy tray on the table.

"You look tired, dear sister," she said to Catherine.

"Ai. Briandor has had me scour all the fields beyond, all for her roses. I drop with weariness." Catherine sat down heavily. "Methinks my knees are raw. Oh, I'd give myself away to a village man this day, if one but asked me," she said.

Deirdre laughed. Catherine looked up at her sharply. "You don't usually take lightly such a remark of mine."

"You are certainly filled with anger tonight," Deirdre answered softly.

"So would you be if you had worked as I have today. The plow horse has a greater ease in a full day's plowing than I have had this one."

Fortunatus entered, murmured a greeting. His face was drawn with fatigue. Catherine looked at him with sympathy.

"So," she said.

Fortunatus glanced from Catherine to Deirdre. "Catherine knows the tale of Clotaire," he said simply.

"And has not spoken a word?" Deirdre asked in surprise.

"I rattle like a leaf in autumn across the courtyard, but can, when asked, be quieter than a snake hidden in the grasses," Catherine answered with hauteur.

"Then I need not repeat," Deirdre said, "and will tell you my decision." She looked happily from one to the other.

Fortunatus and Catherine exchanged a glance.

"But let us begin our dinner," Deirdre said.

Fortunatus said the blessing; then Deirdre began. "I have prayed long all this day. I have also spoken with Mother Briandor." She paused. "You may laugh at me for saying so, Catherine, or think me foolish, but it has been a very difficult decision to make."

"Oh, such a preamble! Will you not just tell us?" Catherine burst out. "Both of you ramble round and round your tales. Methinks it has to do with both of you learning to read. 'Tis a loss indeed!" They laughed.

"Then I shall tell you straight out. 'Tis this: if Clotaire will have me, I shall return. If not, I shall go on to Athies and throw myself upon the mercy of Berthaire. But I know now that I cannot stay here. My heart is not here. I want to serve God in such a way that I can still be joyful. Others may find joy here; I cannot."

Catherine said quietly, "Oh, how I envy you. Forgive me, I cannot help it."

Deirdre ignored her and turned to Fortunatus. "If you, my dear friend, will be so kind as to escort me to Soissons, I should like to leave tomorrow, which was the day you wished also to depart. May I have your escort?"

"With the greatest pleasure, dear sister. I am at you service."

"I should like also to beg another favor of you." Fortunatus raised his eyebrows questioningly. "If the king will have me, I would want another ceremony, one in which I can say my vows with a pure heart." She smiled. "It would make me very happy if you could do that for me."

"Marry you?"

"Ai. Would you?"

"Again, I can only say it would be the greatest honor for me," he answered without hesitation, concealing his melancholy.

"And you, Catherine. If you will also be so kind as to do me

354

a favor?"

"Surely, I shall do what I can," Sister Catherine said. She looked puzzled. Deirdre laughed.

"If Clotaire receives me as his wife, I should like you to come to the court at Soissons as a lady of the court. I would charge you with the care of the rose gardens."

Catherine looked stunned. "Deirdre!" Her eyes filled with tears.

"That is, if you still wish to leave Poitiers, and have no positive word of your dowry. It would please me greatly to have you nearby."

Catherine frowned. "'Tis most kind of you. I thank you. But, what if...?"

"Yes. Then, for you, I have no solution. If I go to Athies, I cannot make such an invitation. But...."

"Of course. We must think it will happen and it will. 'Tis a sign of cowardice to think poorly of the future." She smiled at Fortunatus. "Isn't that so, Brother Fortunatus?"

"Yours is a light and happy spirit, Catherine," he said, appreciating the delicacy of her remark. "I, with so much less to imprison me, sink to the depths of despair, while you, caught here perhaps for the rest of your youth, are so alive and cheerful; truly, it amazes me."

When the bell rang, calling for the last prayers of the day, Deirdre rose with Catherine. "I am nun until morning," she whispered. Fortunatus watched them go, then crossed the hall to the guest room where, after a short prayer, he fell into a deep and dreamless sleep.

Deirdre lay awake a long time. A part of her was sad knowing that she was faced with yet another leaving. She would miss particularly this immensity of the night's Great Silence. But then she thought of Clotaire, causing her to catch her breath, to feel her breast suddenly fill with an awareness of her beating heart.

Dear God, she prayed silently, *let him take me back. Give me a chance to give the love that grows with every moment.*

Vaguely, she thought back on the first time she had seen him. Nurse had said, *Perhaps he shall be your husband.* From that dim past, so distant now, Deirdre recalled each detail. So Nurse had known; that explained her strange countenance and behavior that day. Puzzles Deirdre had not known existed, let alone thought about, suddenly appeared, to be solved: the odd glances she had had from the woman Felice who had also loved Clotaire; Clotaire's insistent impatience with herself; the total silence about her parents while at Gunther's; all of these came back to her, and now she understood. The one part of the puzzle she could not yet face was the part involving Lothar. She shied away from it, allowed herself only a feeling of gratitude that, in fact, Clotaire had not killed him. She did not want to look at Lothar hard, nor to attempt to understand his role in relation to Clotaire.

Sleeping only fitfully, she longed for the next few days to pass in order to see Clotaire; to hear him say, *Yes I want you back*; to lie close again and hear his whispering lips, feel his hands upon her. The night was a torture, until, at last, the sky that showed in the space of her tiny window began to lighten. Deirdre rose, put on her nun's robes for want of any other clothing, and waited for the bell to matins. She would depart after that. Until the second bell rang, she would remain a nun in spirit as well as practice.

The morning chant was poignant. She listened to the bell-like voice of Melinda; the deep, off-key tone of Charitas; the tenseness of Briandor; Catherine's voice with its edge of anger, a brittle sound; and Felicity's high-pitched timidity. She recalled Mother Corita's voice, deep and resonant. By the end of the chanting, her face streamed with tears. Even to herself, she would never be able to explain these tears, why or whence they came. Her heart was filled with the future; she was already on her way, yet she cried now for what would pass forever into memory. She rose after matins and tiptoed out of the chapel. Catherine peeked up and threw her a smile. Deirdre saw that her cheeks were also wet. She gathered her few possessions: a small prayer book the bishop had given her, dog-eared and yellowing, an extra veil, a cape, no more, and walked in the silent fashion that she had learned here, to the front gate where Fortunatus awaited her.

CHAPTER 39

Mother Briandor managed to borrow a villager's ass for Deirdre to ride as far as Tours. There, it would be used to carry back a load of fabric. Fortunatus walked alongside. In all his travels alone, he had never given thought to brigands and highwaymen, but on this journey, he had misgivings. Unknown to Deirdre, he had fastened a small mace beneath his robes. It gave him unease to carry the weapon, but it gave him more unease to think of being attacked with Deirdre unprotected. But the day passed uneventfully. They talked of old matters, new manuscripts Fortunatus had seen and read, his travels. Together, they invented a song, and Fortunatus would sing the completed verses each time they stopped for water or rest. By evening, they had the song completed. Deirdre helped gather the firewood, and when the fire was going well, Fortunatus pulled out his instrument and sang it for her.

"'Tis nonsense, truly," Deirdre laughed when he had finished. Tired though she was, she felt lighter and gayer each mile closer to Tours. "You don't suppose the bishop will be angry and refuse me, do you?" she asked, looking up like a chastised child. "I worked so hard to get him to agree; now I am wanting to leave."

Fortunatus laughed. His mood, too, had lightened. He was pleased to see Deirdre's happiness, even though it meant that that side of life was lost to him.

And, though he was sad, he was no sadder than he had always been, having loved Deirdre for years, the difference now being that he recognized what had lived inside him all along and deeply realized it could not be.

They slept like children beside each other by the fire and, in the morning, rose with the first sunlight, sang their song once more after a meal and prayer, and laughed at its lack of form.

"'Tis our form!" Deirdre cried. "We invent as others before

358

us have invented. Oh, Fortunatus, you must stay long at Soissons! It will be so perfect. You and Catherine and me and Clotaire! All of us together."

Fortunatus grew silent, but Deirdre did not notice.

By midday, they arrived in Tours, at the same marketplace whence Deirdre had left months before. How different this journey was, she thought. The bishop released her gladly, saying he had never been much convinced that the convent life was the right path for her.

Fortunatus and Deirdre stayed two days, then began the journey to Soissons, both of them mounted on two of the bishop's horses.

With each day's passing, Deirdre became quieter, less gay. Finally, the last day out, she confided to Fortunatus.

"I fear he will reject me. He will say no."

Fortunatus looked at her tenderly. "I shall throw off my robes and marry you myself!" Deirdre laughed. "Oh you are so wonderful, so gallant!" He was both piqued and relieved that she did not take him seriously.

Near sunset, they saw the mass of the castle at Soissons rising up against the horizon.

"Perhaps an hour more," he said.

"Oh, my heart stops," she said. "Fortunatus, I am afraid."

Fortunatus stopped his horse and looked at her. "Truly, Deirdre, you need have no fear. He cannot but love you."

"How can you know that?" she challenged.

"I only know," he answered. He clucked to the animal, which moved on.

The sky was aflame behind the castle when they finally arrived in the valley just below the gate. It was Deirdre who stopped her horse this time. She got down.

"Dear brother, perhaps we should camp outside here."

Fortunatus looked stern. "You would only put off what you desire until morning."

"Ai," Deirdre confessed simply. "All right. I will face him now. But" -- she looked at Fortunatus with pleading -- "will you wait here? If I am not back this night, then all is well and you will come in the morning." She hesitated. "It's...I would not have you there if he says no."

"He will not, I can promise you."

"If he does, I shall return, and then I would go on to Athies this night."

Fortunatus dismounted. "I shall wait until morning. But if you come not back this night, I beg your leave to let me travel on."

Deirdre looked at him. "Then, you would not marry us?" Fortunatus was looking at his hands; she could not see his face.

"Nay," he said finally, quietly. "I beg your pardon, Lady Dierdre I would move on."

Deirdre took in his words. She wanted to question, to protest or argue, but something stopped her; it was perhaps the way he turned his hands from one side to the other; the way he would not look at her; or the quietness and firmness of his request. She understood finally what he meant. She had just this moment to take it in, only this small space in which to decide irrevocably, because, once she walked toward the gate, for her, the decision would be made; she would never give Fortunatus less than her whole heart. She hesitated. Her mouth went dry. The castle was like a fist against the sky; it could crush her, but she had to know that first.

"Farewell then, my dearest friend," she said. "I love thee and always shall."

Fortunatus faced her; his eyes were dry, his face calm.

"So be it," he said. "My dearest sister, farewell. May happiness be yours, and God's blessings and mine." He bowed and kissed her hand.

She wanted to detain him, but she stopped herself, knowing she could no longer ask him for anything since she could not give him what he desired. "Farewell," she whispered again. She knew he watched her all the way to the castle gate, but she did not hesitate or turn back. She entered the castle walls.

"Who be ye?" the gate guard challenged.

"The lady Deirdre, Clotaire's queen," she answered. She would have rejection from no one but the king himself. The guard looked at her, amazed. "Ai," he said, and bowed. "The king entertains in court."

Deirdre understood he meant the central court. Indeed, already several dozen torches were lit in the quickly falling darkness on the path. In the distance, there was the sound of music, of laughter. She walked close to the walls, her heart beating furiously.

At the entrance to the courtyard in front of the huge hall, Deirdre took off her veil and unbound her hair. In the instant that her hair fell down her back, she felt both immensely free and terribly naked. She dropped the veil on the ground, then quickly crossed the courtyard. Almost fainting, she made herself climb the low stairs and entered the hall. All of the court was in attendance: ladies and gentlemen, and some traveling actors and musicians. Clotaire lounged near the front of the hall on a dais, several women surrounding him.

No one noticed Deirdre until she was halfway across the hall; then an actor dressed in a jester's costume bowed ironically in front of her and said in a loud voice, "Ah, dear sister, be ye tired of the dried-up life ye be leading? Do ye wish for pleasure?" He blocked her way; as she started around him on one side, he would leap in front. This caused attention to turn toward her. In moments, she was surrounded by laughing faces, some kind, some not.

"What is it?" The crowd separated at Clotaire's voice and

361

the sharp clap of his hands. Deirdre looked up. His face registered a quick series of emotions. Deirdre was frozen to the spot.

"What is this?" Clotaire asked with a tinge of irony in his voice.

Deirdre could not move.

"Come," he said. "Come closer." There was nothing in his voice to indicate welcome or rejection. Deirdre hesitated, then slowly moved forward. He waited until she was directly below him. Those present, after the initial wave of surprise and quick whispers and rolling of eyes, stood perfectly silent. Deirdre burned with shame, but she had promised herself that, this once, she would bite back her pride. She owed him that, this man whom she had so wronged.

"Why have you come?" he asked. Still he gave no sign in his voice or face.

Deirdre knelt and bowed low. "I would return to thee, my king," she said. There was a long silence.

"Would you?" he sneered.

She felt his words like a blow. She dropped her eyes, bowed again. "I have wronged thee, sire, with my anger and with my accusations. I beg you to forgive me and take me back as your wife."

"Do you hear her, gentlemen? The lady wishes now to return. And what are husbands if I take her back? Eh?" Clotaire laughed bitterly. "Nay! Begone! I would not have you again. Methinks I do better without you than before!" There was a titter among the ladies on the dais.

Deirdre burned. She bowed low once more. "Sire I beg you," she said with the deepest humility.

"Crawl all over the floor if you will. I would not have such a wife!"

Deirdre's head shot up. Then she was on her feet. A sudden rage replaced the shame and humility.

362

"I would not crawl for you, scum!" she cried out. "I shall gladly leave. Forgive me only for being stupid in thinking you are more than the beast you are!" She turned on her heel.

"Lady!"

She swung around. He was standing, legs akimbo, hands on his narrow hips.

"No wench speaks so to me!" he shouted.

"No wench am I!" she yelled back.

"You shall apologize here in front of the court!"

"Never!" she screamed, stamping her foot.

Clotaire leaped down onto the floor.

"You stamped your foot," he said. There was a warning in his voice and a look in his eye that she recognized immediately.

"Keep back from me," she warned.

He was walking purposefully toward her. He laughed. "Ah, 'tis the fiery Deirdre after all."

She was close to tears. "I hate you! You are an abomination!"

She turned and walked as quickly as possible without running. But suddenly she was spun around, swooped up against his chest, and moving so quickly, she had no time to react until almost to the door.

"Let me go," she said through her teeth. He only laughed.

One arm was pinned against his body, the other free enough. She raked at his face. He dropped her, caught both her arms, and scooped her up again, this time throwing her over his shoulder like a sack of root vegetables.

He carried her bouncing against him like that up to her former rooms, dropped her on the bed. He stood over her.

"You shall apologize," he commanded.

Deirdre scooted over on the bed, away from him.

"You humiliated me," she said. "I shall never apologize to you."

"I! After you ran away, became a nun!"

"I thought you had killed my brother!"

"What makes you believe differently now? Or do you come back like a bitch in heat, all this time without a man?" he sneered.

She leaped at him. "I hate you!"

He fought her off, held her down, but not before acquiring two long scratches on his cheek. "What makes you believe differently?" he insisted.

"Your woman, Felice!" she spit out at him.

"What of her?" he demanded. He squeezed hard on her arms. Deirdre cried out in pain.

"She died in Poitiers."

Clotaire loosened his grip. "You saw her?" he asked.

"Nay, not I. Fortunatus confessed her. She told of Lothar's deed and her killing of him." Deirdre was crying now. She could no longer hold back the anger and humiliation. "She also told of Gunther." She twisted away from him. "How cruel you are!"

"Cruel? I?"

"You never told me! You never said the truth!" she accused.

He pulled her to him. His face was angry. "And would you have believed me? Would you?"

"I...."

"The morning of Lothar's death, that day you fled while I lay wounded, had I called you in and told you I had not done the deed, would you have believed me?"

Deirdre bit her lip and looked away.

"And would you have believed the cold and bloody tale of your own uncle had I told you?"

"Nay," she said through her tears.

"So. You see!" he said triumphantly. "Your own brother knew all along, yet he did not believe, though others also told him."

Deirdre cried out anew. "But if others knew, why did you not have them say so? I could not have helped but believe if Berthaire, for example, had told me."

"Ai. That is how you are. You would have me grovel, would you not? Believe not me, but another, ai! I forbade all and one to utter a word. I would win you in spite of it. And did!" He released her and rose.

Deirdre looked at him in disbelief. "Such stupid pride! You would win me? Nay, you never did!"

Clotaire laughed. "Then, why did you crawl back, humiliate yourself and me in front of my whole court if I never did. Stupid, indeed!"

She got up and righted her robes. "I shall leave now," she said with dignity. She started toward the door, then was in his arms again.

"Nay," he whispered. "Do not leave."

"Let me go," she said, but knew her heart was not behind the words, and knew he heard it so.

"Apologize," he said in her ear, and pulled her closer. She felt her body go limp with wanting him. He lifted her and gently lowered her on the bed. "You stamped your foot, milady. I told you once never to do that." She was kissing him back; her arms were around him; she felt his breath warm on her neck."

"I shall not love you until you apologize," he insisted.

Deirdre moaned. "I am sorry," she finally managed.

"And I too, sweet Deirdre," he whispered to her amazement. "Let us take off these nun's robes. I would not commit that sin. Oh, how I have longed for you," he said hoarsely.

"And I for you."

365

"Never, ever, crawl like that in front of me," he said. "It pleases me not. You are a queen! Don't forget that. Ever!"

"Ai, my king, *your* queen."

But he did not hear her; the words got crushed against his shoulder in their embrace.

The End